PRAISE FOR

Chocolat

Blackberry Wine

a novel

Joanne Harris

Perennial

An Imprint of HarperCollinsPublishers

A hardcover edition of this book was published in 2000 by William
Morrow, an imprint of HarperCollins Publishers.

HarperCollins books may be purchased for educational, business, or
sales promotional use. For information please write: Special Markets
Department, HarperCollins Publishers Inc., 10 East 53rd Street,
New York, NY 10022.

First Perennial edition published 2001.

Designed by Sherrie L. Hoffman

Library of Congress Cataloging-in-Publication Data is available.

ISBN 0-380-81592-3

01 02 03 04 05 JT/RRD 10 9 8 7 6 5 4 3 2

To my Grandfather, Edwin Short;
gardener, winemaker, and poet at heart

Blackberry Wine

One

Wine talks; ask anyone. The oracle at the street corner; the uninvited guest at the wedding feast; the holy fool. It ventriloquizes. It has a million voices. It unleashes the tongue, teasing out secrets you never meant to tell, secrets you never even knew. It shouts, rants, whispers. It speaks of great plans, tragic loves and terrible betrayals. It screams with laughter. It chuckles softly to itself. It weeps in front of its own reflection. It revives summers long past and memories best forgotten. Every bottle a whiff of other times, other places, every one—from the commonest Liebfraumilch to the imperious Veuve Clicquot—a humble miracle. Everyday magic, Joe had called it. The transformation of base matter into the stuff of dreams. Layman's alchemy.

Take these six in Jay's cellar, for instance. The Specials. Not wines really meant for keeping, but he kept them all the same. For nostalgia's sake. For a special, yet-to-be-imagined occasion. Six bottles, each with its own small handwritten label and sealed with candle wax. Each had a cord of a different color knotted around its neck; raspberry red, elderflower green, blackberry blue, rose hip yellow, damson black. The last bottle was tied with a brown cord. *Specials '75*, said the label, the familiar writing faded to the color of old tea.

But inside was a hive of secrets. There was no escaping them: their whisperings, their catcalls, their laughter. Jay had hidden them behind a crate of more sober vintages the day he'd brought them back from Pog Hill Lane. Five weeks later he could almost persuade himself they were forgotten. Even so he sometimes imagined he heard them, without really knowing what it was he heard.

Jay Mackintosh was thirty-seven. Unremarkable but for his eyes, which were Pinot Noir indigo, he had the awkward, slightly dazed look of a man who has lost his way. Five years ago Kerry had found this appealing. By now she had lost her taste for it. There was something deeply annoying about his passivity and the core of stubbornness beneath. She knew there were depths to Jay, but for some reason he remained sealed off to her, neatly deflecting any attempt at intimacy. Her only point of entry to that secret place was through his books. Through his *book*.

Fourteen years ago Jay had written a novel called *Jackapple Joe*. It won the Prix Goncourt in France, translated into twenty languages. Three crates of vintage Veuve Clicquot celebrated its publication—the '76, drunk too young to do it justice. Jay was like that then, rushing at life as if it might never run dry, as if what was bottled inside him would last forever in a celebration without end.

But then something happened. Perhaps it was the unexpected success of *Jackapple Joe* which paralyzed him. Perhaps the weight of expectation, of affection from a public hungry for more. Television interviews, newspaper articles, reviews succeeded each other into silence. Hollywood made a film adaptation with Corey Feldman, set in the American Midwest. Nine years passed. Jay wrote part of a manuscript entitled *Stout Cortez* and sold eight short stories to *Playboy* magazine, which were later reprinted as a collection by Penguin Books. The literary world waited for Jay Mackintosh's new novel, eagerly at first, then restless, curious, then finally, fatally, indifferent.

Of course he still wrote. There had been seven novels to date, with titles like *The G-sus Gene* and *Psy-Wrens of Mars* and *A Date with d'Eath*, all written under the pseudonym of Jonathan Winesap, nice earners which kept him in reasonable comfort. Every month the post brought him a sizable packet of fan mail, all addressed to Jonathan Winesap, mostly from America. Sometimes the letters contained blurry photographs of UFOs or accounts of out-of-body experiences or magical amulets or newspaper clippings dealing with unexplained phenomena. These he explored, debunked and filed away in the neat drawers of a large cabinet next to his desk. He was a great advocate of keeping fiction in its place. Sometimes he attended fantasy conventions and made impassioned speeches about what he called the *Conspiracy of the Unexplained*, in which he argued that the public's appetite for strange phenomena was being deliberately nurtured by the media to divert attention from a world crisis spinning ever more wildly out of control. He bought a Toshiba laptop which he balanced on his knees like the TV dinners he made for himself on the nights—increasingly frequent now—that Kerry worked late. Occasionally he lectured at writers' groups, held creative-

writing seminars at the university. More often he wasted hours
surfing the Internet and drinking too much.

Kerry watched him with growing disapproval. Kerry
O'Neill (born Katherine Marsden), twenty-five, cropped red
hair and startling green eyes, a journalist made good into television by way of *Forum!*, a late-night talk show where popular
authors and B-list celebrities discussed contemporary social
problems against a background of avant-garde jazz. Five years
ago she might have been more tolerant. But then, five years ago
there was no *Forum!*, Kerry was writing a women's column
for the *Independent* and she was working on a lighthearted
book entitled *Chocolate—A Feminist Outlook*. The world was
filled with possibilities.

Her book came out two years later on a wave of media
interest. Kerry was photogenic, marketable and mainstream.
As a result she appeared on a number of lightweight talk
shows. She was photographed for *Marie Claire*, *Tatler* and *Me!*
but was quick to reassure herself that it hadn't gone to her
head. She had a house in Chelsea, a *pied-à-terre* in New York
and was considering liposuction on her thighs. If she sometimes wondered what had happened to the impetuous girl
who had read *Jackapple Joe* and fallen wildly in love with the
author, she seldom spoke of it. She had grown up. Moved on.

But for Jay, nothing had moved on. Five years ago he had
seemed the embodiment of the temperamental artist, drinking
half a bottle of Smirnoff a day, a doomed, damaged figure of
romance.Young as she was, he brought out her maternal instincts. Jonathan Winesap—*my evil twin*, as Jay called him—
was of no interest to her. It was the writer of *Jackapple Joe*
who fascinated her. When she finally met him at a literary
lunch in Oxford, she had told him so, with such a mixture
of arrogance and ingenuousness that in spite of himself he was
charmed. *Jackapple Joe* was only the beginning, she told him.

The first part of a long journey. A man who could write the way he did could never give up. One day, she said, something would happen to illuminate him again, and he would write a wonderful book, a book which would touch lives. . . .

"If that's what you think," he told her, grinning over his glass of wine, "then you'll be disappointed. I don't want to touch lives, or be touched by them. I've had my chance at that."

She looked at him appraisingly.

"I don't think anyone really runs out of chances. They just close their minds to them. Isn't that what you've been doing all this time?"

He was still grinning, but it was a hard expression, not entirely pleasant. She realized that he was drunk, far more so than she had first suspected. He carried it well. A less observant person than Kerry might not even have noticed. Jay made a precarious sweeping gesture with his glass.

"How is it that everyone who's read *Jackapple Joe* assumes that there's going to be a sequel? Maybe I just ran out of ideas, did anyone think of that? Maybe I got bored with the subject. Maybe I'm happy doing what I do now. You all want me to be like some old fisherman in a pub, always banging on about the one that got away. That kind of story gets old pretty quickly. I should know."

He drained what was left in the glass and poured himself another. There was a stubborn crease between his eyes. The amusement in them was gone.

Don't push this any further, his expression said. *You have reached the outer limits of the Jay Mackintosh Territorial Waters. Here be Serpents.*

Kerry gave him a mischievous look. "I don't think so, Jay," she said, not unkindly. "I think maybe you're just chicken."

He looked up sharply from his drink. For a moment she

thought she saw something in him which made her heart flip over. Possibilities still to be enacted, struggling between anger and surprise and—what?

Then he touched her hair—long in those days, before she cut it off to spite him. His eyes were filled with troubling lights. Then he smiled, quite a different expression compared to the hard grin of before.

"You know, Kerry, you remind me of someone."

"Who?"

"A fighter."

———

But that was five years ago. For all her efforts, trashy sci-fi was still what paid the rent, paperbacks with lurid covers. She had only read one of them, the first, with growing dismay. It was terrible. Worse than that, perhaps, because reading between the lines she could see the ghost of the writer he had once been. The maturity, the puckish wisdom of *Jackapple Joe* had never been duplicated, or even attempted. The style was a parody, like Jay himself, brash and flippant, all surface glitter but nothing underneath. For all its ersatz magic, his work remained staunchly, safely fictional. It might have helped if he had shown some awareness of what he had lost. Bitterness, perhaps, or a hint of the vulnerability she had glimpsed at their first meeting. But Jay had no temperament to speak of. He seemed comfortable with what he did. He actually enjoyed it. He had never given in to an impulse. He never really showed anger, never lost control. Even his drinking—his one remaining excess—seemed ridiculous now, like a man who insists upon wearing the outmoded fashions of his youth. He spent his time playing computer games, listening to old singles, surfing the Net and watching old movies on video, locked in his adolescence like a record into a groove.

Or so it seemed to her. Jay would have disagreed, if he'd

known what she was thinking. He drank, Jay told himself, for the same reason he watched movies or wrote second-rate science fiction. Cynical though he was about all aspects of the supernatural, he did it to *believe*, or at least to get in touch with the part of himself which still believed. To open up the past and to find himself there again, like the stone in a fruit. This was a lesson Joe had tried to teach him: that some things can be both real and imaginary at the same time, that some lies can also be true, that broken faith may be restored. He opened each bottle, began each story with the secret conviction that *here* was the magic draught which would restore him. Some talismans worked, or had worked once, in the days before he was so divided. Perhaps there was still a way to make them work again. Perhaps there was someone out there who was not a charlatan. But magic, like wine, needs the right conditions in order to work. Joe could have told him that. Otherwise the chemistry doesn't happen. The bouquet is spoiled.

Even so, it might have worked if Kerry had played along. But by then she had realized who it was that she reminded him of so strongly, and the knowledge made her first resentful, then aloof. Jay treated her like a little sister, with careless affection. He mocked her earnestness. Their conversations were scattered with in-jokes, flippancies, verbal sleights-of-hand designed to deflect contact. He wanted to love her, she understood. But whatever—whomever—he needed to fill the hole in himself was nothing she could provide.

Maybe she had been mistaken, thought Kerry at last. He didn't want to grow up. He didn't want to be saved. He was her first failure, and the only reason she stayed was that leaving would be much like an admission of defeat. He'd been right about that, at least. She was a fighter.

Two

London, Spring 1999

*I*t was March. Jay had been working upstairs—working in his way, with a bottle at his elbow and the television turned to a drone. Kerry was at a party—the launch of a new award for female authors under twenty-five—and the house was silent. Jay used a manual typewriter for what he thought of as his "real" work, the laptop for the Winesap paperbacks. *Another affectation,* Kerry said. *Creative schizophrenia,* countered Jay. *The PC runs on the wrong kind of goblins . . . The serious goblins live in the typewriter. They're the ones who write the good stuff.* He lowered his voice conspiratorially and leaned forward to whisper in her ear. *But you've got to feed them BLOOD—*

Kerry's mouth tightened. That was exactly the kind of talk she hated. She left him to it in secret relief.

It was ten before Jay came downstairs. He switched on the radio to an oldies station and padded aimlessly about in the kitchen. There was a drinks cabinet next to the fridge. He opened it, hesitated, closed it again. The fridge door opened. Kerry's taste dominated here, as everywhere. Wheat grass juice, couscous salad, baby spinach leaves, yogurts. What he really craved, Jay thought, was a huge bacon-and-fried-egg sandwich with ketchup and onion, and a mug of strong tea. The craving, he knew, had something to do with Joe and Pog Hill Lane. An association, that was all, which often came on when he was trying to write. But all that was finished, a phantom. He knew he wasn't really hungry. Instead he lit a cigarette and inhaled greedily. From the radio's scratchy speaker came the voice of Steve Harley singing "Make Me Smile"—another song from that distant, inescapable summer of '75—and for a moment he raised his voice to sing along—*come up and see me, make me smi-iiile*—forlornly in the echoing kitchen.

At the back of the dark cellar the six Specials were restless. Perhaps it was the music—or perhaps something in the air of this mild spring evening seemed suddenly charged with possibility—for they were effervescent with activity, seething in their bottles, rattling against each other, jumping at shadows, bursting to talk, to open, to release their essence into the air. . . . Perhaps this was why he came down, his steps heavy on the rough unpolished stairs. Jay liked the cellar; it was cool, secret. He often went down there, sometimes just to touch the bottles, to run his fingers along the dust-furred walls. For some reason he could not identify, he felt at home there.

It was dark in the cellar, the only illumination a dim light bulb hanging from the ceiling. Rows of bottles in the racks on the wall; others in crates on the flagstones. Jay touched the bottles fleetingly as he passed, bringing his face very close, as if to catch the scent of those imprisoned summers. Two or three times he pulled out a bottle and turned it in his hands before replacing it in the rack. He moved aimlessly, liking the dampness of the air and the silence. Even the sound of the London traffic was stilled here, and for a moment he was tempted simply to lie down on the smooth, cool floor and go to sleep, perhaps forever. No one would look for him here. But instead he felt very wide awake, very alert, as if the silence had cleared his head. There was a charged atmosphere in spite of the stillness, like something waiting to happen.

The new bottles were in a box at the back of the cellar. A broken ladder had been laid across the top of it, and he moved this aside, dragging the box out with an effort across the flagstones. He lifted out a bottle at random, held it up to the light to try to decipher the label. Its contents looked inky red, with a deep layer of sediment at the base. For a moment he imagined he saw something else inside there, a shape, but it was only sediment. Somewhere above him in the kitchen the nostalgia station was still tuned to 1975—Christmas now, "Bohemian Rhapsody," faint but audible through the floor, and he shivered.

Back in the kitchen, he examined the bottle with some curiosity. He had barely glanced at it since he brought it back five weeks before—the wax seal at the neck, the brown cord, the handwritten label, *Specials '75*—the glass still grimed with the dust of Joe's root cellar. He wondered why he had brought it back from the wreckage. Nostalgia, maybe, though his feelings for Joe were still too mixed for that luxury.

Old man. How I wish you were here.

He wondered what the wine would taste like. Spoiled, perhaps, after all these years? Or magically preserved, with olfactory ghosts coiling out of the bottle like a nest of genies? He had to try. If only to prove to himself that nothing remained.

———

Sometimes it happens by accident. After years of waiting— for a correct planetary alignment, a chance meeting, a sudden inspiration—the right circumstances sometimes happen of their own accord, slyly, without fanfare, without warning. Layman's alchemy, Joe would have called it. The magic of everyday things. Inside the bottle something leaped and ca- pered. The bottles in the cellar rattled and danced in reply.

Jay Mackintosh reached for a knife to cut the seal.

Three

*I*t had withstood the years. His knife sliced it open and the cork was still intact beneath. For a moment the scent was so immediately pungent that all he could do was endure it, teeth clenched, as it worked its will on him. It smelled earthy and a little sour, like the canal in midsummer, with a sharpness which reminded him of the vegetable cutter and the gleeful tang of freshly dug potatoes. For a second the illusion was so strong that he was actually *there* in that vanished place with Joe leaning on his spade and the radio wedged in a fork in a tree.

A sudden overwhelming excitement took hold of him and he poured a small quantity of the wine into a glass, trying not to spill the liquid in his eagerness. It was dusky pink, like papaya juice, and it seemed to climb the sides of the glass in a frenzy of anticipation, as if something inside it were alive and anxious to work its magic on his flesh. He looked at it in mingled distrust and longing. A part of him wanted to drink it—had waited for years for just this moment—but all the same he hesitated. The liquid in the glass was murky and flecked with flakes of brownish matter like rust. He suddenly imagined himself drinking, choking, writhing on the tiles in agony. The glass halted halfway to his mouth. He looked at the liquid again. The movement he thought he saw had ceased. The scent was faintly sweetish, medicinal, like cough mixture. Once again he wondered why he had brought the bottle with him. There was something in the glass, his mind insisted. Something special.

His concentration was such that he did not hear Kerry come in behind him.

"Jay?" Her voice was clear, with a fashionable touch of Irish. "I thought you were working."

Jay looked back at her, the wineglass still in his hand.

"I didn't feel like it. I stopped."

"I see." Kerry crossed the room, her heels tapping coolly against the tiles, and poured herself a glass of Stolichnaya.

"You should have come to the party with me," she said. "You might even have liked it. Salman Rushdie was there."

"I'd rather stick lit cocktail sticks up my nose."

Kerry shrugged. "Now you're being childish as well as antisocial. If you actually made the effort once in a while—"

"I do make an effort. It's just that the company of literary people always inflames my hemorrhoidal condition. I can't help it. It's a medical problem." He grinned and tipped the wineglass at her. In the cellar the remaining bottles rattled boisterously, as if in anticipation.

"You know, Jay, if you just tried to grow up—" Kerry stopped, listened. "Did you hear something?"

He shook his head. "I don't think so."

She came closer, looked at the glass in his hand and the bottle still standing on the table.

"What is that stuff, anyway? Some kind of cocktail? It smells disgusting."

"It's Joe's wine. One of the six." He turned the bottle around to see the label. "Jackapple '75. A classic vintage."

There was something going on in the cellar, after all. He could almost hear it, like the sounds of a distant party. Beneath his feet the bottles were in gleeful ferment. He could hear them whispering to him, singing, calling, capering. Their laughter was infectious, reckless, a call to arms. He felt a sudden burst of raucous anticipation, a knowledge that something was on the way. . . .

"Ugh. God! Don't drink it. It's bound to be off," said Kerry in distaste. "Besides, it's revolting. It's probably got all kinds of bacteria in it by now. Or worse."

"The wine was Joe's. I don't expect you to understand." His voice was flat. That warning crease was back between his eyes.

"I'd like to understand, Jay. You know I would." She was standing behind him so that he could not see her expression. For a second he caught the scent of lily-of-the-valley from her skin. Her hand came to rest on his shoulder.

"I know." He stared, fascinated, at the glass in his hand. He knew he should put it down. But the liquid inside seemed to be moving, crawling, effervescing. He couldn't take his eyes off it. Behind him he could hear Kerry's breathing. But the wine was breathing too, gustily and cheerily. It amazed him that Kerry couldn't hear it. He wondered whether he was going crazy.

"Why don't I get us both a real drink?" suggested Kerry in a gentler tone. "I'm shattered. Sometimes these social occasions are a bit much, even for me."

It was an invitation. Perhaps a truce, or more.

Jay hesitated. He lifted the glass slowly to his face. The scent hit him again, the dim cidery scent of Joe's house with the incense burning and the tomato plants ripening in the kitchen window. For a moment he thought he heard something, a clatter and glitzy confusion of glass like a chandelier falling onto a laid table.

"Hey, Kerry. You want to try some?"

It was so close, he told himself. That summer with Joe, so close he could almost taste it. Suddenly he wanted to make her taste it, to take her there, to make her *know*—

"I don't think so. Thanks." Her voice was chilly again, remote.

Jay shrugged. "All right."

He took a mouthful.

It tasted as dreadful as it had when he was a boy. There was no grape in this brew, simply a sweetish ferment of flavors like a whiff of garbage. It smelled like the canal in summer and the derelict railway sidings. It had an acrid taste like smoke and burning rubber, and yet it was evocative, catching at his throat and his memory, drawing out images he thought were lost forever. He clenched his fists as the images assailed him, feeling suddenly light-headed.

"Are you okay?" It was Kerry's voice, resonant as if in a dream. She sounded irritated, though there was an anxious edge to her voice. "Jay, I told you not to drink that stuff. Are you all right?"

He swallowed with an effort. "I'm fine. Actually, it's rather pleasant. Pert. Tart. Lovely body. Bit like you, Kes." He broke off, coughing but laughing a little at the same time.

Kerry looked at him, unamused. "Whatever turns you on. I think I'll wait for you upstairs. I've got a bit of a headache."

"I won't be long. I just want to . . ."

He left the sentence unfinished. He wasn't really sure what he wanted. The taste of Joe's wine was in him now, bringing with it a ragged cavalcade of sounds, scents, memories. It was a taste of licorice, a sour reek from the canal, it was a glass of Ben Shaw's Yellow Lemonade, it was coal dust, newsprint, overripe raspberries dripping from the bush, it was blood, tobacco, broken glass, train oil, flowers.

"It's everything I remember. It's Joe. As if he were here in this room. It's Pog Hill Lane exactly as I remember it. Try it. You'll see what I . . ."

Turning back, he realized Kerry had already left. For a moment he wanted to call her back. He was being selfish, he knew. If he went after her he might be able to salvage something. They could talk, perhaps for the first time, about what had happened and why it had affected him so deeply. But the wine had awakened something in him, something extraordinary, and he wanted to explore it further.

He took another drink and found his palate was becoming accustomed to the wine's strange flavors. He could taste old fruit now, burned to hard black sugar, he could smell the juice from the vegetable cutter and hear Joe singing along to his old radio at the back of the allotment. Impatiently he drained the glass, tasting now the zesty heart of the wine, feeling his heart beating with renewed energy, pounding as if he had run a race. Belowstairs the five remaining bottles rattled and shook in a frenzy of exuberance. Now his head felt clear, his stomach level. He tried for a moment to identify the sensation he felt and eventually recognized it as joy.

Four

Pog Hill, Summer 1975

Jackapple Joe. He introduced himself as Joe Cox—with a slanted smile, as if to challenge disbelief—but even in those days it might have been anything, changing with the seasons and his changing address.

"We could be cousins, you and me," he said on that first day as Jay watched him in wary fascination from the top of the wall. The vegetable cutter whirred and clattered, throwing out pieces of sour-sweet fruit or vegetables into the bucket at his feet. "Cox and Mackintosh. Both apples, aren't we? That must make us nearly family, I reckon." His accent was exotic, bewildering, and Jay stared at him without comprehension.

Joe shook his head, grinning. "Didn't know you was called after an apple, did you? It's a goodun, an American red apple.

Plenty of taste. Got a young tree meself, back there"—he
jerked his head toward the back of the house—"but it's not
taken that well. I reckon it needs a sight more time to get
comfortable."

The boy watched the rotating blades of the vegetable cutter
with fascination. The funnel-shaped machine bucked and roared
between Joe's hands, spitting out chunks of white and pink
and blue and yellow flesh.

"What are you doing?"

"What's it look like?" The old man jerked his chin at a
cardboard box lying by the wall which separated them. "Pass
us them jacks over there, will you?"

"Jacks?"

A slight gesture of impatience toward the box:
"Jackapples."

Jay glanced down. The drop was easy, five feet at the most,
but the garden was enclosed, with only the scrub of waste
ground and the railway line at his back, and his city upbring-
ing had taught him wariness of strangers.

Joe grinned. "I'll not bite, lad," he said mildly.

Annoyed, Jay dropped down into the garden.

The jackapples were long and red and oddly pointed at one
end. One or two had been cut open as Joe dug them up,
showing flesh which looked tropically pink in the sun. The
boy staggered a little under the weight of the box.

"Watch your step," called Joe. "Don't drop 'em. They'll
bruise."

"But these are just potatoes."

"Aye," said Joe, without taking his eyes from the vegetable cutter.

"I thought you said they were apples, or something."

"Jacks. Spuds. Taters. Jackapples. *Poms de Tair.*"

"Don't look like much to me," said Jay.

Joe shook his head and began to feed the roots into the vegetable cutter. Their scent was sweetish, like papaya.

"I brought seeds for these home from South America after the war," he said. "Grew 'em right here in my back garden. Took me five years just to get the soil right. If you want roasters, you grow King Edwards. If you want salads, it's your Charlottes or your Jerseys. If it's chippers you're after, then it's your Maris Piper. But these . . ." He reached down to pick one up, rubbing the blackened ball of his thumb lovingly across the pinkish skin. "Older than New York, so old it doesn't even have an English name. Seed more precious than powdered gold. These aren't just potatoes, lad." He shook his head again, his eyes brimful of laughter under the thick gray brows. "These are me Specials."

Jay watched him cautiously. "So what *are* you making?" he asked at last.

Joe tossed the last jackapple into the cutter and grinned. "Wine, lad. *Wine*."

That was the summer of '75. Jay was nearly thirteen. Eyes narrow, mouth tight, face a white-knuckle fist closing over something too secret to be examined. Lately a resident of the Moorlands School in Leeds, now with eight weeks of holidays stretching out strange and empty till the next term. He hated it here already. This place with its bleak and hazy skyline, its blue-black hills crawling with yellow bulldozers, its slums and pit houses and its people, with their sharp faces and flat northern voices. It would be all right, his mother told him. He would like Kirby Monckton. He would enjoy the change. Everything would be sorted out. But Jay knew better. The gulf of his parents' divorce opened up beneath him and he hated them, hated the place to which they had sent him, hated the gleaming new five-speed Raleigh bike delivered that morning for his birthday—bribery as contemptible as the message which accompanied it: *With love from Mum and Dad.* So falsely normal, as if the world weren't coming softly apart around him. His rage was cold, glassy, cutting him from the rest of the world so that sounds became muffled and people were walking trees. Rage was inside him, seething, waiting desperately for something to happen.

They were never a close family. Until that summer he had only seen his grandparents half a dozen times at Christmases or birthdays, and they treated him with dutiful, distant affection. His grandmother was frail and elegant like the china she loved and which adorned every available surface. His grandfather was bluff and soldierly and shot grouse without a license on the nearby moors. Both deplored the trade unions, the rise of the working class, rock music, men with long hair and the admission of women into Oxford. Jay soon understood that if he washed his hands before meals and seemed to listen to everything they said, he could enjoy unlimited freedom. That was how he met Joe.

Kirby Monckton was a small northern town similar to many others. Built on coal mining, it was in decline even then, with two out of the four pits shut and the remaining two struggling. Where the pits had closed, the villages built to supply them with labor died too, leaving rows of pit houses staggering toward dereliction, half of them empty, windows boarded up, gardens piled with refuse and weeds. The center was little better: a row of shops, a few pubs, a minimarket, a police station with a grille across its window. To one side, the river, the railway, the old canal. To the other, a ridge of hills reaching toward the feet of the Pennines. This was Upper Kirby, where Jay's grandparents lived.

Looking toward the hills over fields and woodland, it was almost possible to imagine that there had never been any mines. This was the acceptable face of Kirby Monckton, where terraces are referred to as "mews cottages." From its highest point you could see the town itself a few miles away, a smear of yellowish smoke across an uneven horizon with pylons marching across the fields toward the slaty scar of the open-pit mine, but the Hollow was relentlessly charming, shielded by the ridge. The houses were for the most part larger, more elaborate here, deep Victorian terraces of mellow Yorkshire stone with leaded panes and mock-Gothic doorways and huge secluded gardens with fruit trees *en espalier* and smooth, well-tended lawns.

Jay was impervious to these charms. To his London-accustomed eyes, Upper Kirby looked precarious, balanced on the stony edge of the moor. The spaces—the distances between buildings—dizzied him. The scarred mess of Lower Monckton and Nether Edge looked deserted in its smoke, like something during the war. He missed London's cinemas and theaters, the record shops, the galleries, the museums. He missed the people. He missed the familiar accents of London, the sound of traffic and the smells. He rode his bike for miles along the unfamiliar deserted roads, hating everything he saw.

His grandparents never interfered. They approved of outdoor pastimes, never noticing that he returned home trembling and exhausted with rage every afternoon. The boy was always polite, always well groomed. He listened intelligently and with interest to what they said. He cultivated a boyish cheeriness. He was the cleanest-cut comic-book schoolboy hero imaginable, and reveled sourly in his deception.

Joe lived on Pog Hill Lane, one of a row of uneven terraces backing onto the railway half a mile from the station. Jay had already been there twice before, leaving his bike in a stand of bushes and climbing up the banking to reach the railway bridge. On the far side there were fields reaching down to the river, and beyond that lay the open-pit mine, the sound of its machinery a distant drone on the wind. For a couple of miles an old canal ran almost parallel to the railway, and there the stagnant air was green with flies and hot with the scent of ash and greenery. A bridle path ran between the canal and the railway, overhung with tree branches. Nether Edge to the townspeople, it was almost always deserted. That was why it first attracted him.

He bought a packet of cigarettes and a copy of the *Eagle* from the station newspaper stand and cycled down toward the canal. Then, leaving his bike safely concealed in the undergrowth, he walked along the canal path, pushing his way through great drifts of ripe willow herb and sending clouds of white seeds into the air. When he reached the old lock he sat down on the stones and smoked as he watched the railway, occasionally counting the coal cars as they passed or making faces at the passenger trains as they clattered to their distant, envied destinations. He threw stones into the clotted canal. A few times he walked all the way to the river and made dams with turf and the accumulated garbage it had brought with it; car tires, branches, railway sleepers and once a whole mattress with springs poking out of the ticking.

That was really how it began. Perhaps because it was a secret place, an old, somehow forbidden place. Jay began to explore—there were mysterious raised concrete-and-metal cylinders which Joe later identified as capped pit heads and which gave out strange resonant breathing sounds if you came close. A flooded mine shaft, an abandoned coal car, the remains of a barge. It was an ugly—perhaps a dangerous—place, but it was a place of great sadness too, and it attracted him in a way he could neither combat nor understand. His parents would have been horrified at his going there, and that too contributed to its appeal. So he explored; here an ash pit filled with ancient shards of crockery, there a spill of exotic, dis-

carded treasures. Bundles of comics and magazines, as yet unspoiled by rain, scrap metal, the hulk of a car—an old Ford
Galaxie—a small elder tree growing out of its roof like a nov-
elty antenna, a dead television. Living alongside a railway, Joe
once told him, is like living on a beach; the tide brings new
jetsam every day. At first Jay hated it. He couldn't imagine
why he went there at all. He would set out with the intention
of taking a quite different route and still find himself in Nether
Edge, between the railway and the canal, the sound of distant
machinery droning in his ears and the whitish summer sky
pushing down on the top of his head like a hot cap.

Five

London, Spring 1999

He woke up late the next day to find Kerry already gone, leaving a short note through which disapproval showed like a watermark. He read it, trying to remember what had happened the night before.

> J—
> Don't forget the reception at Spy's tonight—it's very important for you to be there!
> K.

His head ached, and he made strong coffee and listened to the radio as he drank it. He didn't remember very much—so much of his life seemed to be like this now, a blur of days without anything to define them from each other, like epi-

sodes of a soap he watched out of habit even though none of
the characters interested him. The day stretched out in front
of him like an empty road in the desert. He had a writing class
to teach that evening, but was already considering skipping it.
It was all right; he'd missed the classes before. It was almost
expected of him now. Artistic temperament. He grinned
briefly at the thought.

The bottle of Joe's wine was standing where he left it on
the table. He was surprised to see it still over half-full. Such
a small quantity seemed too little to account for his pounding
hangover and the dreams which had finally chased him into
sleep as dawn bled into the sky. The scent from the empty
glass was faint but discernible, a sweetly medicinal scent,
soothing. He poured a glassful.

"Hair of the dog," he muttered.

This morning it was only vaguely unpleasant, almost taste-
less. A memory stirred at the back of his mind, but it was too
distant to identify.

The door rattled suddenly and he turned around, feeling
obscurely guilty, as if caught out. But it was only the mail,
half-pushed through the letter box and spilling onto the mat.
Through the glass door a square of sunlight illuminated the
top envelope, as if marking it for his special attention. Probably junk mail, he told himself. Nowadays he rarely ever re-
ceived anything else. And yet by a trick of the light the
envelope seemed to glow, giving the single word stenciled
across a new, brilliant significance: ESCAPE. As if a door could
be opened from the London dawn into another world where
every possibility remained to be played out. He stooped to
pick up the bright rectangle, opened it.

His first thought was that it was indeed junk mail. A
cheaply produced brochure entitled HOLIDAY HIDEAWAYS,
GREAT ESCAPES, blurry snapshots of farmhouses and *gîtes* inter-

spersed with blocks of text. *This charming cottage only five miles from Avignon . . . This large converted farmhouse in its own grounds . . . This sixteenth-century barn in the heart of the Dordogne . . .* The pictures were all the same: rustic cottages under Disney-colored skies, women in head scarves and white coifs, men in berets herding goats onto impossibly green mountainsides. He dropped the brochure onto the table with an odd sense of disappointment, feeling cheated. Then he caught sight of the picture. The brochure had fallen open at the center page, a double-page spread of a house which looked curiously familiar. A large squarely built house with pinkish, faded walls and a red-tiled roof. Beneath it, the words, *Château Foudouin, Lot-et-Garonne.* The surprise at seeing it there, so unexpectedly, made his heart lurch.

It was not exactly Joe's *château*, he decided after some scrutiny. The lines of the building looked slightly different, the roof more sloping, the windows narrower and set deeper into the stone. And it was not in Bordeaux but in the next county altogether, a few miles from Agen, on a small offshoot of the River Garonne, the Tannes. Still, it was close. Very close.

It couldn't be a coincidence.

Belowstairs the five new bottles had subsided into eerie, expectant silence. Not a whisper, not a rattle or a hiss escaped them.

Six

Pog Hill, July 1975

That summer most of Jay's life went on undercover, like a secret war. On rainy days he sat in his room and read the *Dandy* or the *Eagle* and listened to the radio with the volume turned down, or wrote blisteringly intense short stories with titles like "Flesh-Eating Warriors of the Forbidden City" or "The Man Who Chased the Lightning." He was never short of money. On Sundays he earned twenty pence washing his grandfather's green Austin, the same for mowing the lawn. His parents' brief infrequent letters were invariably accompanied by a postal order, and he spent this unaccustomed wealth with gleeful, gloating defiance. Comics, bubble gum, cigarettes if he could get them; anything which might have incurred the disapproval of his parents attracted him.

He kept his treasures in a biscuit tin by the canal, telling his grandparents he put his money in the bank. This was technically not a lie. A loose stone by the remains of the old lock, worked carefully free, left a space maybe fifteen inches square into which the tin could be slotted. A square of turf, cut from the bank with a penknife, concealed the entrance.

For the first fortnight of the holiday he went there almost every day, basking on the flat stones of the jetty and smoking, reading, writing stories in one of an endless series of close-scripted notebooks or playing his radio at full volume into the bright sooty air. His memories of that summer were brightly illumined in sound: Pete Wingfield singing "Eighteen with a Bullet," or Tammy Wynette and "D.I.V.O.R.C.E." He sang along much of the time, or played air guitar and made faces at an invisible audience.

It was only later that he realized how reckless he had been. The dump was easily within earshot of the canal, and Zeth and his gang might have come upon him at any time during those two weeks. They might have found him snoozing on the bank or cornered in the ashpit—or worse, with the Treasure Box left carelessly open. Jay had never considered that there might be other boys in his territory. Never imagined that this might *already* be someone's territory, someone tougher and older and altogether more streetwise than himself.

He had never been in a fight. The Moorlands School discouraged such marks of poor breeding, though his background was less refined than that of his classmates. His mother was an actress whose career had dead-ended in a TV sitcom called *Oooh! Mother!* about a widower caring for his three teenage children. Jay's mother played the part of the interfering landlady Mrs. Dykes, and much of his adolescence was made hideous by people stopping them in the street and yelling her

screen catchphrase, "*Ooo, am I interruptin' somethin'?*" Jay's
father, a self-made businessman, had never quite made enough
money to make up for his lack of pedigree, hiding his insecurity behind a facade of bluff, cigar-smoking cheer. He too
embarrassed Jay, with his East End vowels and his shiny suits.
Jay had always seen himself as a different species, as something hardier, nearer to the raw.

He couldn't have been more wrong.

There were three of them. Taller than Jay and older, fourteen, maybe fifteen, with a peculiar swing to their walk as
they strolled along the canal towpath, a cocky strut which
marked the territory as their own. Instinctively Jay snapped
off his radio and crouched in the shadows, resentful of the
proprietary air with which they lolled on the jetty, one
crouching to poke with a stick at something in the water,
another popping a match against his jeans to light up a cigarette. He watched them warily from the shadow of a tree,
hackles pricking. They looked dangerous, clannish in their
jeans and zip-up boots and cutoff T-shirts, members of a tribe
to which Jay could never belong. One of them—a tall, lanky
boy—was carrying an air rifle slung carelessly into the crook
of his arm. His face was broad and angry. His eyes were ball
bearings. One of the others had his back half turned, so that
Jay could see the roll of his paunch poking out from beneath
his T-shirt, and the broad band of his underpants showed
above his low-slung jeans. The underpants had little airplanes
on them, which made Jay laugh, silently at first into his curled
fist, then with a high helpless squawk of mirth.

Airplanes turned around at once, his face slack with surprise. For a second the two boys faced each other. Then he
shot out his hand and grabbed Jay by the shirt.

"What the fuck *thar* doin' 'ere?" The other two were
watching with hostile curiosity. The third boy—a spidery

youth with extravagant sideburns—took a step forward and poked Jay hard in the chest with an extended knuckle.

"Ast thee a question, dinty?" Their language sounded alien, almost incomprehensible, a cartoonish babble of vowels, and Jay found himself smiling again, close to laughter, unable to help himself.

"Atha deaf as well as daft?" demanded Sideburns.

"I'm sorry," said Jay, trying to pull free. "You just came out of nowhere. I didn't mean to scare you."

The three looked at him with even greater intensity. Their eyes looked the same no-color as the sky, a peculiar shifting gray. The tall boy stroked the butt of his rifle in a suggestive gesture. His expression was curious, almost amused. Jay noticed he had tattooed letters on the back of his hand, one letter pricked out across each of his knuckles to form a name or nickname: ZETH. This was no professional job, he understood. The boy had written it himself, using the sharp point of a compass and a bottle of ink. Jay had a sudden, startling vision of him doing it, with a dogged grimace of satisfaction, one sunny afternoon at the back of a math or English class, with the teacher pretending not to see, even though Zeth wasn't bothering to hide.

"Scare *us?*" The bright ball-bearing eyes rolled in counterfeit humor.

Sideburns snickered.

"Astha gotta fag, mate?" Zeth's voice was still light, but Jay noticed Airplanes had not yet released his shirt.

"A cigarette?" He began to fumble in his pocket, clumsy with the need to get away, and pulled out a packet of Players. "Sure. Have one."

Zeth took two and passed the packet to Sideburns, then to Airplanes.

"Hey, keep the pack," said Jay, beginning to feel light-headed. "Matches?" He pulled the box out of his jeans and held it out. "Keep them too."

Airplanes winked as he lit up, a somehow greasy, appraising look. The other two drew a little closer.

"Astha got any spice, anall?" asked Zeth pleasantly. Airplanes began to finger nimbly through Jay's pockets.

It was already too late to struggle. A minute earlier and he might have had the advantage of surprise, might have been able to duck between them toward the jetty and up onto the railway. Now it was too late. They had scented fear. Eager hands searched Jay's pockets with greedy, delicate fingers. Chewing gum, a couple of wrapped sweets, coins, all the contents of his pockets rolled into the cupped hands.

"Hey, get off there! Those things are mine!"

But his voice was trembling. He could let them have the stuff—most of it was worthless, anyway—but that didn't stop the bleak, hateful feeling of helplessness. Then Zeth picked up the radio. "Nice," he commented.

For a moment Jay had forgotten all about it; lying in the long grass under the shade of the trees, it was almost invisible. A trick of the light, maybe, a freak reflection on the chrome or just plain bad luck, but Zeth saw it, bent and picked it up.

"That's mine," said Jay, almost inaudibly, his mouth filled with needles.

Zeth looked at him and grinned.

"Mine," Jay whispered.

"Course it is, mate," said Zeth amicably, and held it out.

Their eyes met above the radio. Jay put out his hand, almost pleadingly. Zeth withdrew the radio, just a little—then drop-kicked it with incredible speed and accuracy over their heads in a wide arc into the air. For a second it gleamed there like a miniature spaceship, then it crashed on the stone lip of the jetty opposite and shattered into a hundred plastic and chrome fragments.

"And it's a goo-aal!" shrieked Sideburns, beginning to dance and caper among the wreckage. Airplanes chuckled sweatily. But Zeth just looked at Jay with the same curious expression, one hand just resting on the butt of his air rifle, his eyes cool and oddly sympathetic, as if to say, *What now, mate? What now? What now?*

Jay could feel his eyes getting hotter and hotter, as if the tears gathering there were made of molten lead, and he struggled to stop them from spilling over onto his cheeks. He glanced at the pieces of the radio twinkling on the stones and tried to tell himself it didn't matter. It was just an old radio, nothing worth getting beaten up for, but the rage inside him wouldn't listen. He took a step toward the lock, then turned back without even thinking and swung as hard as he could toward Zeth's patient, amused face.

Airplanes and Sideburns were on Jay at once, punching and kicking, but not before he had launched a good solid kick into the pit of Zeth's stomach, which connected as his first awkward punch had not. Zeth gave a wheezing scream and curled up onto the ground. Airplanes tried to grab Jay again, but he was slippery with sweat and managed to duck under the other boy's arm. Skidding on the remains of his broken radio, he made for the path, dodged Sideburns, slid down the banking and across the bridle path toward the railway bridge. Someone was shouting after him, but distance and the thick local dialect made the words indistinguishable, though the threat was clear. When he reached the top of the bank, Jay kissed his middle finger at the three distant figures, dug his bike out of the undergrowth where he had hidden it and in a minute was riding back toward Mockton Town. His nose was bleeding and his hands were torn from his dive through the bushes, but he was singing inside with triumph. Even his dismay over the loss of the radio was temporarily forgotten.

Perhaps it was that wild, almost magical feeling that drew him to Joe's house that day. He told himself later that it was simply chance, that there was nothing in his mind at all but the desire to ride into the wind, but he thought later that it might have been some kind of crazy predestination which pulled him there, a kind of call. He felt it too, a wordless voice of exceptional clarity and tone, and for a moment he saw the street sign—POG HILL LANE—light up briefly in the glow of the reddening sun, as if somehow *marked* for his attention, so that instead of cycling past the narrow mouth of the street, as he had done so many times before, he stopped and wheeled his bike slowly back to stare over the brick wall where an old man was cutting jackapples to make wine.

Seven

London, March 1999

*J*he agent must have scented his eagerness. There was already a bid on the house, he said. A little below the asking price. The contracts had already been drawn up. But if Jay was interested, there were other properties available. This information—true or false—made Jay reckless. It had to be this house, he insisted. This house. Now. In cash, if they liked.

A discreet phone call. Then another. Rapid French into the mouthpiece. Someone brought Jay coffee and Italian pastries from across the road as they waited. Jay suggested another price, somewhat higher than the existing offer. He heard the voice on the other end of the line rise by half an octave. He toasted them in *café-latté*. It was so easy, buying a house. A few hours' wait, a little paperwork and it was his. He reread the short paragraph under the picture, trying to translate the words into stone and mortar. Château Foudouin. It looked unreal, a postcard from the past. He tried to imagine standing outside the door, touching the pink stone, looking over the vineyard toward the lake. Joe's dream, he told himself dimly, their dream fulfilled at last. It had to be fate. It had to be.

An interior voice—perhaps it was Jonathan Winesap, that cynical advocate of Fiction In Its Rightful Place—told him that all this was happening too fast. Perhaps in fear of the inertia which had cradled him for so long, he was rushing at this headlong, without thinking of the consequences. Such expectations could only lead to bitter disappointment, the inner voice warned. Enticing though Joe's elixir might be, the dregs were always sour.

Surprisingly, Jay found the voice of his other self very easy to ignore. For the first time here was a talisman in which he could almost believe—not a *thing*, but a *place*—which might be able to mend the division inside him. As if the worlds for which he reached through his books might have a real counterpart, a place where magic and chemistry, fiction and flesh could be brought together, as once they were at Pog Hill Lane. Like the seeds in Joe's old chest, dead-looking but ready to spring into life given the right conditions.

The thought was so powerful that he could almost imagine he was fourteen again, gloating over his picture, touching it, folding and unfolding the thin paper. He wanted to show other people. He wanted to be there *now*, to take possession even though the paperwork was only half-completed. His bank, his accountant, his solicitors could deal with the formalities. The signing of the papers was merely an afterthought. The essentials were already in motion.

A few phone calls and it could all be arranged. A flight to Paris. A train to Marseille. By tomorrow he could be there.

Eight

Pog Hill, July 1975

Joe's house was a dark, crooked terrace like many of the houses which lined the railway. The front looked out onto the street, with only a low wall and a window box between the front door and the pavement. The backyards of the houses in the row were all crowded little yards hung with washing, a shantytown of homemade rabbit hutches and henhouses and pigeon lofts. This side looked over the railway, a steep bank sheared away to form a cutting through which the trains passed. The road went over a bridge at that point, and from the back of Joe's garden you could see the red light of the railway signal like a beacon in the distance. You could see Nether Edge too and the dim gray flanks of the slag heap beyond the fields. Staggering unevenly down the steep little lane, those few houses overlooked the whole of Jay's territory.

Someone was singing in a nearby garden, an old lady by the sound of it, in a sweetly quavering voice. Somebody else was hammering wood, a comforting, primitive sound.

"D'you want a drink?" Joe nodded easily in the direction of the house. "You look as if you wouldn't turn one down."

Jay glanced toward the house, suddenly aware of his torn jeans and the dried blood on his nose and upper lip. His mouth was dry.

"Okay."

It was cool inside the house. Jay followed the old man through to the kitchen, a large bare room with clean wooden floorboards and a large pine table, scarred with the marks of many knives. There were no curtains at the window, but the entire window ledge was filled with leggy green plants which formed a lush screen for the sunlight. The plants had a pleasant, earthy smell which filled the room.

"These are me toms," remarked Joe, opening the larder, and Jay saw that there were indeed tomatoes growing among the warm leaves, small yellow ones, large misshapen red or striped orange and green ones like croaker marbles. There were more plants in pots on the floor, lining the walls and growing against the doorpost. To the side of the room a number of wooden crates contained fruit and vegetables, all placed carefully to avoid bruising.

"Nice plants," he said, not really meaning it.

Joe shot him a satirical look.

"You've got to talk to 'em if you want 'em to grow. And tickle 'em," he added, indicating a long cane propped up against the bare wall. There was a rabbit's tail tied to its extremity. "This is me ticklin' stick, see? Very ticklish, toms."

Jay looked at him blankly.

"Looks like you ran into some trouble back there," said Joe, opening a door at the far side of the room to reveal a big larder. "Bin in a fight, or summat."

Guardedly, Jay spoke. When he got to the part where Zeth broke the radio, he felt his voice jump into a higher register, sounding childish and close to tears. He stopped, flushing furiously.

Joe didn't seem to notice. He reached into the larder, picking out a bottle of dark red liquid and a couple of glasses.

"You get some of this down yer," said Joe, pouring some out. It smelled fruity but unfamiliar, yeasty like beer but with a deceptive sweetness. Jay looked at it with suspicion.

"Is it wine?" he asked doubtfully.

Joe nodded. "Blackbry," he said, drinking his with obvious relish.

"I don't think I'm supposed to—" began Jay, but Joe pushed the glass at him with an impatient gesture.

"Try it, lad," he urged. "Put some 'art in yer."

He tried it.

Joe clapped him on the back until he had stopped coughing, carefully removing the glass from the boy's hand before he spilled it.

"It's *disgusting*!" managed Jay between coughing jags. It certainly tasted like no wine he had ever tasted before. He was no stranger to wine—his parents often gave him wine with meals, and he had developed quite a taste for some of the sweeter German whites, but this was a completely new experience. It tasted like earth and swamp water and fruit gone sour with age. Tannin furred his tongue. His throat burned. His eyes watered.

Joe looked rather hurt. Then he laughed.

"Bit strong for yer, is it?"

Jay nodded, still coughing.

"Aye, I shoulda known," said Joe cheerily, turning back to the pantry. "Takes a bit o' gettin used to, I reckon. But it's got '*art*,'" he added fondly, replacing the bottle with care on the shelf. "And that's what matters."

He turned around, this time with a bottle of Ben Shaw's Yellow Lemonade in one hand. "Reckon this'll do yer better for now," he said, pouring a glassful. "And as for the other stuff, you'll grow into it soon enough."

He returned the wine bottle to the larder, hesitated, turned. "I think I might be able to give you somethin' for that other problem, if you'd like, though," he said. "Come with me."

Jay was not sure what he expected the old man to give him. Kung fu lessons, perhaps? Or a bazooka left over from some war, grenades, a Zulu spear from his travels, a special invincible drop-kick learned from a master in Tibet, guaranteed never to fail? Instead Joe led him to the side of the house, where a small red-flannel bag dangled from a nail protruding from the stone. He unhooked the bag, sniffed briefly at the contents and handed it over.

"Take it," he urged. "It'll last a while yet. I'll make some fresh for us later."

Jay stared at him. "What is it?" he said at last.

"Just carry it with you," said Joe. "In yer pocket, if you like, or on a bitta string. You'll see. It'll help."

"What's in it?" He was staring now as if the old man were crazy. His suspicions, allayed for a moment, flared anew.

"Oh, this an' that. Sandalwood. Lavender. Bit o' High John the Conqueror. Trick I learned off of a lady in Haiti, years back. Works every time."

That was it, decided Jay. The old boy was definitely crazy.

Harmless—he hoped—but crazy. He glanced uneasily at the blind expanse of garden at his back and wondered if he could make it to the wall if the old man turned violent.

Joe just smiled.

"Try it," he urged. "Just carry it in yer pocket. Happen you'll even forget it's there."

Jay decided to humor him. "Okay. What's it supposed to do, then?"

Joe smiled again. "P'raps nothin'," he said.

"Well, how will I know if it's worked?" insisted Jay.

"You'll know," said Joe easily. "Next time you go down Nether Edge."

"There's no way I'm going down there again," said Jay sharply. "Not with those boys—"

"You goin' to leave yer treasure chest for 'em to find, then?"

Joe had a point. Jay had almost forgotten about the Treasure Box, still hidden in its secret place beneath the loose stone. His sudden dismay almost overshadowed the certainty that he had never mentioned the Treasure Box to Joe.

"Used to go down there when I were a lad," said the old man blandly. "There were a loose stone at the corner of the lock. Still there, is it?"

Jay stared at him. "How did you know?" he whispered.

"Know what?" asked Joe with exaggerated innocence. "What's tha' mean? I'm only a miner's lad. I don't know owt."

Jay didn't go back to the canal that day. He was too confused by everything, his mind racing with fights and broken radios and Haitian witchcraft and Joe's bright, laughing eyes. Instead he took his bike and rode slowly past the railway bridge three or four times, heart pounding, trying to find the courage to climb the bank. Eventually he rode home, depressed and dissatisfied, all his triumph evaporated. He imagined Zeth and his friends going through his treasures, rocking with dirty laughter, scattering comics and books, stuffing sweets into their mouths, pocketing the money. Worse still, there were his notebooks in there, the stories he'd written, the poems. Finally he rode home, jaw aching with rage, watched *Saturday Night at the Movies* and went to bed to a late, unsatisfying sleep through which he ran ceaselessly from an unseen enemy while Joe's laughter rang in his ears.

The next day he decided to stay at home. The red flannel bag sat on his bedside table like a mute challenge. Jay ignored it and tried to read, but all his best comics were still in the Treasure Box. The absence of the radio filled the air with a hostile silence. Outside the sun shone and there was just enough breeze to stop the air from scorching. It was going to be the most beautiful day of the summer.

He arrived at the railway bridge in a kind of daze. He never meant to go there; even as he pedaled toward town something inside him knew he was going to turn round, take a different route, leave the canal to Zeth and his gang, their territory now. Perhaps he would go to Joe's house—he hadn't asked him to come back, but he hadn't asked him to keep away either, as if Jay's presence was a matter of indifference to him. Or maybe he'd drop by at the newspaper stand and buy some smokes. Either way, he certainly wasn't going to go back to the canal. As he hid his bike in the familiar stand of willow herb, as he climbed the bank he repeated it to himself. Only an idiot would risk that again. Joe's red flannel bag was in his jeans pocket. He could feel it, a soft ball no bigger than a rolled-up hanky.

He wondered how a bag full of herbs was supposed to help him. He had opened it the previous night, laying the contents out on his bedside table. A few pieces of stick, some brownish

powder and some bits of green-gray aromatic stuff filled the
bag. A part of him had expected shrunken heads. It was a
joke, Jay told himself fiercely. Just an old man having his fun.
And yet the stubborn part of him which wanted desperately
to believe just wouldn't leave the thing alone. What if there
was magic in the bag, after all? Jay imagined himself holding
out the charm, incanting a magical spell in a ringing voice,
Zeth and his mates cowering . . . The bag pressed comfortingly
against his hip like a steadying hand. With a lurch of the
heart, he began to make his way down the bank toward the
canal. He probably wouldn't meet anyone, anyway.

Wrong again. He crept along the bridle path, keeping to
the shade of the trees, his sneakers silent against the baked
yellow earth. He was shaking with adrenaline, ready to run at
the slightest sound. A bird flapped noisily out of its reed bed
as he passed and he froze, certain that an alarm had been
given for miles around. Nothing. Jay was almost at the lock
now, he could see the place in the bank where the Treasure
Box was hidden. Pieces of broken plastic still littered the
stones. He knelt down, removed the piece of turf which concealed the stone and began to work it out.

He'd been imagining them for so long that for a second he
was sure the sounds were in his head. But now he could see
their dim shapes coming over from the ashpit side of the
canal, shielded now by bushes. There was no time to run.
Half a minute at most, before they broke cover. The bridle
path was wide open from here, too far from the railway bridge
to be a sure bet. In seconds he would be an open target.

He realized there was only one place to hide: the canal
itself. It was mostly dry except in patches, choked with reeds
and litter and a hundred years' worth of silt. The little jetty
stood about four feet above it, and he might be hidden, at
least for a while. Of course as soon as they stepped out onto

the jetty, or joined the path, or bent down to examine something at the surface of the greasy water . . .

But there was no time to think of that now. Jay slid down from his kneeling position into the canal, pushing the Treasure Box back into place as he did so. For a moment he felt his feet slide into the mud without resistance, then he touched bottom, ankle-deep in the slime. It slid into his sneakers and oozed between his toes. Ignoring it, he crouched low, reeds tickling his face, determined to present as small a target as possible. Instinctively he looked for weapons, for stones, cans, things to throw. If they saw him, surprise would be his only advantage.

He'd forgotten about Joe's charm in his jeans pocket. It got pulled out somehow as he crouched in the mud and he picked it up automatically, feeling suddenly scornful at himself.

They were close now; ten feet away, he guessed. He could hear the sounds of their boots. Someone threw a bottle or a jar hard against the stones; it exploded and he flinched as glass showered his head and shoulders. The decision to hide beneath their feet seemed ridiculous now; suicidal. All they had to do was look down and he was at their mercy. He should have run, he told himself bitterly, run when he had the chance. The footsteps came closer. Nine feet. Eight. Seven. Jay flattened his cheek against the wall's dank stones, trying to *be* the wall. Joe's charm was moist with sweat. Six feet. Five feet. Four.

Voices—Sideburns and Airplanes—sounding agonizingly close:

"Tha dun't reckon he'll be back, then?"

"Will he heckers, like. He's a fuckin' dead man if he does."

That's me, thought Jay dreamily. *They're talking about me.*
Three feet. Two feet.

Zeth's voice, almost indifferent in its cool menace: "I can wait."

Two feet. One. A shadow fell over him, pinning him to the ground. Jay felt his hackles rising. They were looking down, looking over the canal, and he didn't dare raise his head, though the need to know was like a terrible itch, like nettle rash of the mind. He could *feel* their eyes on the nape of his neck, hear the sound of Zeth's smoker's breathing. In a moment he wouldn't be able to bear it. He'd have to look up, *have* to look—

A stone dropped into a greasy puddle not two feet away. Jay could see it from the corner of his eye. Another stone. *Plap.*

They had to be teasing him, he thought desperately. They had seen him and they were prolonging the moment, stifling mean laughter, silently picking up stones and missiles to throw. Or maybe Zeth had lifted his rifle, his eyes pensive . . .

But none of that happened. Just as he was about to look up, Jay heard the sound of their boots moving away. Another stone hit the mud and skidded toward him, making him flinch. Then their voices, already receding lazily toward the ashpit, someone saying something about looking for bottles for target practice. . . .

He waited, oddly reluctant to move. It was a ruse, he said to himself, a trick to make him break cover, there was no way they could have missed him—but the voices continued to recede. Beyond the jetty, growing fainter as they took the overgrown path back toward the ashpit. The distant crack of the rifle. Laughter from behind the trees. It was impossible. They *had* to have seen him. But somehow . . .

Carefully Jay pulled out the Treasure Box. The charm was black with the sweat from his hands.

Nine

London, March 1999

Stopping at the house only long enough to pick up a few things, he saw the red light on the answering machine blinking furiously, but did not play the message. The bottles in the duffel bag were absolutely still. Now *he* was the one in ferment, jittering and rocking, exhilarated one moment, close to tears the next, rummaging through his own possessions like a thief, afraid that if he was still for even a second he would lose his momentum and collapse listlessly back into his old life again. He turned on the radio and it was the oldies station again, playing Rod Stewart and "Sailing," one of Joe's favorites—*allus reminds me of them times I were on me travels, lad*—and he listened as he stuffed clothes into the bag on top of the silent bottles. Amazing, how much he could bear to leave behind. He packed his typewriter. The unfinished manuscript of *Stout Cortez*. Some favorite books. The radio itself. And of course Joe's Specials. Another impulse, he told himself. The wine was valueless, almost undrinkable. And yet he could not shake the feeling that there was something in those bottles he needed.

He knew he wasn't drunk. He had finished the bottle hours ago, and even then he had barely felt dizzy. After that day's strange business, he had at first decided not to attend the weekly writing class he taught. But then he made up his mind to go after all, suddenly appalled at the thought of staying in the house, to face the silent disapproval of the things he and Kerry had bought together. He felt a cold impatience to be gone. Going to teach the evening class was a way of killing time until he could leave.

———

"In a novel or short story, even the dullest and coldest of characters," he told his writing class, "may be humanized by giving him someone to care for. A child, a lover—even in a pinch, a dog."

He was perched on his desk next to his bulging duffel bag, resisting the urge to touch it, to open it. The students looked at him with awed expressions. Some took notes. *Even*—writing laboriously, straining so as not to miss a single word—*even . . . a pinch . . . dog.* He taught them on Kerry's insistence, vaguely disliking their slavish obedience to his instruction. For a moment he wondered who—or what—was going to humanize *him*. There were fifteen of the students, dressed almost uniformly in black; earnest young men and intense young women with cropped haircuts and eyebrow rings and clipped, public-school vowels. One of the women was reading aloud a short story she had written, an exercise in characterization about a black single mother in a flat in Sheffield. Jay touched the ESCAPE brochure in his pocket and tried to listen, but the girl's voice was a drone, a slightly unpleasant, waspish buzz of interference. From time to time he nodded, as if he were interested. Since last night the world seemed to have shifted slightly, moving closer into focus. As if something he had been staring at for years without seeing it had suddenly come clear.

The girl's voice droned on. She scowled as she read and kicked one foot compulsively against the table leg. Jay stifled a yawn. She was so intense, he told himself. Intense and rather disgusting in her self-absorption, like an adolescent looking for blackheads. She used the word "fuck" in every sentence.

Joe's wine really should have worn off, but still he felt oddly exhilarated. As if the normal running of things had been suspended for a day, like an unexpected holiday. It must be something in the air, he thought. A whiff of happy gas, a scent of the outlands. The droning girl stopped reading—or maybe she had finished—and stared at him in accusation. She looked so hurt and indignant that he couldn't help laughing.

"I bought a house today," he said suddenly.

They stared at him without reaction. One young man in a Byron shirt wrote it down. *Bought . . . house today.*

Jay pulled out the brochure from his pocket and looked at it again. It was crumpled and grimy from so much handling, but at the sight of the picture his heart leaped.

"Not a house exactly," he corrected himself. "A *chatto.*" He laughed again. "That's what Joe used to call it. His *chatto* in Bordo."

He opened the brochure and read it aloud. The students listened obediently. Byron Shirt made notes.

Château Foudouin, Lot-et-Garonne. Lansquenet-sous-Tannes.
This authentic 18th-century château in the heart of France's most popular wine-growing region includes vineyard, orchard, lake

and extensive informal grounds plus garage block, working distill-
ery, five bedrooms, reception and living room, original oak roof
beaming. Suitable for conversion.

"Of course, it was a bit more than five thousand quid.
Prices have gone up since 1975." For a moment Jay wondered
how many of those students had even been born in 1975.
They stared at him in silence, trying to understand.

"Excuse me, Dr. Mackintosh." It was the girl, still standing,
now looking slightly belligerent. "Can you explain what this
has to do with my assignment?" Jay laughed again. Suddenly
everything seemed amusing to him, unreal. He felt capable of
doing anything, saying anything. Normality had been suspended. He told himself that this was what drunkenness was
supposed to feel like. For all these years, he had been doing
it wrong.

"Why are you here?" he demanded suddenly. "What are
you expecting to get from these lessons?"

He tried not to laugh at their appalled faces, at their polite
blankness. He felt younger than any of them, a delinquent
pupil addressing a stuffy and pedantic roomful of teachers.

"You're young. You're imaginative.Why the hell are you
all writing about black single mothers and Glaswegian dope
addicts?"

"Well, sir, *you* set the assignment." He had not won over
the belligerent girl. She glared at him, clutching the despised
assignment in her thin hand.

"Stuff the assignment!" he shouted. To emphasize his
words, he slapped at the heavy duffel bag standing on his
desk, producing the unmistakable sound of bottles clinking
together. Some of the students looked at each other. Jay
turned back to the class, feeling almost delirious.

"Where's the magic?" he asked. "That's what I want to

know. Where are the magic carpets and Haitian voodoo and lone gunslingers and naked ladies tied to railway lines? Where are the Indian trackers and the four-armed goddesses and the pirates and the giant apes? *Where are the fucking space aliens?*"

There was a long silence. The students stared. The girl clutched her assignment so hard that the pages crumpled in her fist. Her face was white.

"I don't believe this," she said.

Jay picked up his bag and hefted it onto his shoulder. "Believe what you like," he said. He gave a sudden, huge grin. "*I'll sithee.*"

Inside the bag, their work done, the Specials whispered their secrets.

Ten

Pog Hill, July 1975

He went to see Joe many more times after that, though he never really got to like his wine. Joe showed no surprise when he arrived, but simply went to fetch the lemonade bottle. Jay asked him about the charm a few times, with the skepticism of one who secretly longs to be convinced, but the old man was evasive.

"Magic," said Joe, winking to prove it was a joke. "Learned it off of a lady in Puerto Cruz."

"I thought you said Haiti," interjected Jay.

Joe shrugged. "Same difference," he said blandly.

Jay fixed him with a look.

Joe sighed and went on. "Some plants have properties, don't they?" he said.

Jay nodded.

"Aspirin. Digitalis. Quinine. What woulda been called magic in the old days."

"Medicines."

"If you like. But a few hundred years ago there were no difference between magic and medicine. People just believed things. Like chewin' cloves to cure toothache, or pennyroyal for a sore throat, or rowan twigs to keep away evil spirits." He glanced at the boy, as if to check for any sign of mockery. "Plants have properties," he repeated. "You can learn a lot if you travel enough, an' you keep an open mind."

Jay was never certain later whether Joe was a true believer or was just entertained by his gullibility. Certainly the old man liked a joke. Jay's total ignorance of anything to do with gardening amused him, and for weeks he had the boy believing that a harmless stand of lemongrass was really a spaghetti tree (showing him the pale soft shoots of "spaghetti" between the papery leaves), or that giant hogweeds could pull out their roots and walk, like triffids, or that you really could catch mice with valerian.

But in some things the old man was genuine. Maybe he had finally come to believe in his own fiction after years of persuading others. His life was dominated by small rituals and superstitions, many taken from the battered copy of *Culpeper's Herbal* he kept by his bedside. He tickled tomatoes to make them grow. He played the radio constantly, claiming that the plants grew stronger with music. They preferred Radio 1 (he claimed leeks grew up to two inches bigger after *Ed Stewart's Junior Choice*), and Joe would be there, singing along to "Disco Queen" or "Stand by Your Man" as he worked, his old crooner's voice rising solemnly above the red currant bushes as he picked and pruned. He always planted at a new moon and picked when the moon was full. He had a lunar chart in his greenhouse, each day marked in a dozen different inks; brown for potatoes, yellow for parsnips, orange for carrots. Watering too was done to an astrological schedule, as was the pruning and positioning of trees. And the garden thrived on this eccentric treatment, growing strong, luxuriant rows of cabbages and turnips, carrots which were sweet and succulent and mysteriously free of slugs, trees whose branches fairly touched the ground under the weight of apples, pears, plums, cherries. Brightly colored Oriental-looking signs taped to tree branches supposedly kept the birds from eating the fruit. Astrological symbols—painstakingly constructed from pieces of broken pottery and colored glass set into the gravel path—lined the garden beds.

With Joe, Chinese medicine rubbed shoulders companionably with English folklore, chemistry with mysticism. For all Jay knew, Joe may have believed it all. Certainly Jay believed him. But in spite of his beliefs (maybe even because of them) there was something deeply restful about Joe, an inner calm which encircled him and which filled the boy with curiosity and a kind of envy. He seemed so tranquil, alone in his little house surrounded by plants, and yet he had a remarkable sense of wonder and a gleeful fascination with the world. He was almost without education, having left school at twelve to go down the mines, but he was an endless source of information, anecdotes and folklore.

As the summer passed, Jay found himself going to see Joe more and more often. He never asked questions, but allowed Jay to talk to him as he worked in his garden or his unofficial allotment on the railway bank, occasionally nodding to show that he'd heard, that he was listening. They snacked on slabs of fruitcake and thick bacon and egg sandwiches and drank mugs of strong, sweet tea. From time to time Jay brought cigarettes and sweets or magazines, gifts Joe accepted without special gratitude and without surprise, as he did the boy's presence. As his shyness abated, Jay even read Joe some of his stories, to which he listened in solemn—and, he thought, appreciative—silence. Occasionally Joe would talk about himself, about his work in the mines and how he went to France during the war and was stationed in Dieppe for six months before a grenade blew off two fingers of his hand—here he wiggled the reduced limb like an agile starfish—then how, being unfit for service, it was the mines again for six years before he took off for America on a freighter.

" 'Cause you don't get to see much of the world from underground, lad, and I allus wanted to see what else there was. Have you done much travelin'?" Jay told him he had been to Florida twice with his parents, to the south of France, to Tenerife and the Algarve for holidays.

Joe dismissed these with a sniff. "I mean proper *travelin'*, lad. Not all that tourist-brochure rubbish but the real thing. The Pont-Neuf in the early morning when there's no one up but the tramps coming out from under the bridges and out of the Metro, and the sun shinin' on the water. New York—Central Park in spring. Rome. Ascension Island. Crossin' the Italian Alps by donkey. The vegetable *caique* from Crete. Himalayas on foot. Eatin' rice off of leaves in the Temple of Ganesh. Caught in a squall off the coast of New Guinea. Spring in Moscow and a whole winter of dog shit comin' out under the meltin' snow."

His eyes were gleaming. "I've seen all of those things, lad," he said softly. "And more besides. I promised mesself I'd see *everything*."

Joe had his maps on the walls, carefully annotated in his crabby handwriting and marked with colored pins to show the places where he had been. He told stories of brothels in Tokyo and shrines in Thailand, birds-of-paradise and banyan trees and standing stones at the end of the world. In the big converted spice cupboard next to his bed there were millions of seeds, painstakingly wrapped in squares of newspaper and labeled in that small careful script: *Tuberosa rubra maritima*, *Tuberosa panax odarata*, thousands and thousands of potatoes in their small compartments, and with them carrots, squash, tomatoes, artichokes, leeks—over three hundred species of onion alone—sages, thymes, sweet bergamots and a bewildering treasure store of medicinal herbs and vegetables collected on his travels, every one named and packaged and ready for planting. Of the millions of varieties of fruit and vegetables once grown, only a few dozen were still commonly used. Some of these seeds would grow plants which were already extinct in the wild, Joe said, their properties forgotten by everyone but a handful of experts.

"It's your intensive farming does it," he would say, leaning on his spade for long enough to take a mouthful of tea from his mug. "Too much specialization kills off variety. 'Sides, people don't want variety. They want everythin' to look the same. Round red tomatoes, and never mind there's a long yeller un that'd taste a mile better if they gave it a try. Red uns look better on shelves." He waved an arm vaguely over the allotment, indicating the neat rows of vegetables rising up the railway embankment, the homemade cold frames in the derelict signal box, the fruit trees pegged out against the wall. "There's things growin' here that you wouldn't find anywhere else in the whole of England," he said in a low voice, "and there's seeds in that chest of mine that you might not find anywhere else in the whole world."

Jay listened to him in awe. He'd never been interested in plants before. He could hardly tell the difference between a Granny Smith and a Red Delicious. He knew potatoes, of course, but Joe's talk of blue jackapples and pink fir-apples was beyond any experience of his. The thought that there were secrets—that arcane, forgotten things might be growing right there on the railway embankment with only an old man as their custodian—fired Jay with an enthusiasm he'd never felt before. Part of it was Joe, of course, the energy of the man himself. He began to see in Joe something he had never seen in anyone else. A vocation. A sense of purpose.

"Why did you come back, Joe?" he asked him one day. "After all that traveling, why come back here?"

Joe peered out gravely from under the bill of his miner's cap. "It's part of me plan, lad," he said. "I'll not be here forever. Someday I'll be off again. Someday soon."

"Where?"

"I'll show you." He reached into his workshirt and pulled out a battered leather wallet. Opening it, he unfolded a photograph clipped from a color magazine, taking great care not to tear the whitened creases. It was a picture of a house.

"What's that?" Jay squinted at the picture. It looked ordinary enough, a big house built of faded pinkish stone, a long strip of land in front with some kind of vegetation growing in ordered rows. Joe smoothed out the paper.

"That's me *chatto*, lad," he said. "In Bordo it is, in France, me *chatto* with the vineyard and me hundred-year-old orchard with peaches and almonds and apples and pears." His eyes gleamed. "When I've got me brass together I'll buy it—five grand would do it—and I'll make the best bloody wine in the South. Chatto Cox, 1975. How's that sound?"

Jay watched him doubtfully.

"Sun shines all year 'round down in Bordo," said Joe cheerily. "Oranges in January. Peaches like cricket balls. Olives. Kiwi fruit. Almonds. Melons. And space. Miles and miles of orchards and vineyards, land cheap as dirt. Soil like fruitcake. Pretty girls treadin' out the grapes with their bare feet. Paradise."

"Five thousand pounds is a lot of money," said Jay.

Joe tapped the side of his nose with his forefinger. "I'll get there," he said mysteriously. "You want somethin' badly enough, you allus get there in the end."

"But you don't even speak French."

Joe's only response was a stream of sudden, incomprehensible gibberish, like no language Jay had ever heard before.

"Joe, I do French at school," he told him. "That's not anything like—"

Joe looked at him indulgently. "It's dialect, lad," he said. "Learned it off of a band of gypsies in Marseille. Believe me, I'll fit right in there." He folded the picture carefully away again and replaced it in his wallet.

"You'll see what I mean one day, lad," he said. "Jus you wait."

"Can I come with you?" Jay asked. "Will you take me with you?"

Joe considered it seriously, head to one side. "I might, lad, if you want to come. I might anall."

"Promise?"

"All right." He grinned. "It's a promise. Cox and Mackintosh, best bloody wine makers in Bordo. That do yer?"

They toasted his dreams in warm Blackberry '73.

Eleven

London, Spring 1999

Spy's was like many other London clubs. The names and decor change, but the places stay the same: sleek and loud and soulless. By midnight most of the guests would have abandoned any pretensions to intellectualism, settling down to the serious business of getting drunk, making advances, or insulting their rivals. Getting out of the taxi with his duffel bag slung across his shoulder and his single case in his hand, Jay realized that he had forgotten his invitation.

After some altercation with the doorman, however, he managed to get a message to Kerry, who emerged a few minutes later wearing her Ghost dress and a look of one goaded to the limits of her patience.

"It's all right," she flung at the doorman. "He's just useless, that's all." Her green eyes flicked at Jay, taking in the jeans, the raincoat, the duffel bag stuffed with belongings.

"What's this?" she said softly.

The euphoria was finally gone, leaving only a kind of dim hangover in its wake, but Jay was surprised to find his resolve unchanged. Touching the duffel bag seemed to help somehow, and he did so, as if to test its reality. Under the canvas the bottles clinked quietly together.

"I bought a house," said Jay quickly, holding out the crumpled brochure. "Look. It's Joe's *château*, Kerry. I bought it this morning. I recognized it." Beneath that flat green stare he felt absurdly childish. Why had he expected her to understand? He barely understood his impulse himself. "It's called Château Foudouin," he said.

She looked at him without comprehension. "You bought a house."

He nodded.

"Just like that, you bought it?" she asked in disbelief. "You bought it today?" He nodded again. There were so many things he wanted to say. It was destiny, he would have told her, it was the magic he had searched for twenty years to recapture. He wanted to explain about the brochure and the square of sunlight and how the picture had leaped out at him from the page. He wanted to explain about the sudden certainty of it, the feeling that it was the house that chose him, and not the other way around. More than this, the conviction that he'd played out the scenario before, that somehow he'd been given a second chance—

"You can't have bought a house." Kerry was still struggling with the idea. "God, Jay, you dither for hours over buying a *shirt*."

"This was different. It was like . . ." He struggled to articulate what it had been like. It was an uncanny sensation—that overriding feeling of *must have*. He hadn't felt this way since his teens. The knowledge that life could not be complete without this one infinitely desirable, magical, talismanic object—a pair of X-ray spectacles, a set of Hell's Angels tattoos, a cinema ticket, the latest band's latest single. The certainty that its possession would change everything, its presence in the pocket to be checked, tested, retested. . . . It wasn't an adult feeling. It was more primitive, more visceral than that. With a jolt of surprise, he realized he had not really wanted anything for twenty years.

"It was like . . . being . . . back at Pog Hill again," he said, knowing she wouldn't understand. "It was as if the last twenty years hadn't happened."

Kerry still looked blank. "I can't believe you impulse-bought a house," she said. "A car, yes. A motorbike, okay. It's the kind of thing you would do, come to think of it. Big toys to play with. But a *house*?" She shook her head, mystified. "What are you going to do with it?"

"Live in it," said Jay simply. "Work in it."

"But it's in France." Bewilderment sharpened her voice. "Jay, I can't afford to spend weeks in France. I'm due to start the new series next month. I've got too many commitments— I mean, how close is the nearest airport?" She broke off, her eyes moving again to the duffel bag, taking it in, as if for the first time, the bag, the traveling clothes. There was a crease between her arched brows.

"Look, Kerry—"

She seemed to reach a decision. "Look," she said. "We can't discuss this here. Go home, Jay, relax, and we'll talk it all through when I get back. Okay?"

Jay shook his head. "I'm not going back," he said. "I need to get away for a while. All I wanted to do was say goodbye."

Even now Kerry showed no surprise. Irritation, yes. Almost

anger. But mostly bewilderment, as if this wasn't how it was supposed to happen. He had a sudden memory of a red-haired girl sitting by the canal at Nether Edge, studiously not looking at him, poking a stick into the water. The memory raked at his heart.

"Listen, Jay," said Kerry finally. "You haven't thought any of this through. You come to me with this crazy idea about a second home, and when I'm not *instantly* taken by it—"

"It isn't going to be a second home."

The tone of his voice surprised both of them. For a moment he sounded almost harsh.

"And what's that supposed to mean?" Her voice was low and dangerous.

"It means you're not listening to me. I don't think you've ever actually *listened* to me." He paused. "You're always telling me to grow up, to think for myself, to let go. But you're happy to keep me a permanent lodger in your house, to keep me dependent on you for everything. I don't have anything of my own. Contacts, friends—they're all yours, not mine. You even choose my clothes. I've got money, Kerry, I've got my books, I'm not exactly starving in a garret anymore—"

"So *this* is what it's all about? A declaration of independence?" She sounded almost relieved. "Okay. I understand you don't want to go to the party, and I'm sorry I didn't realize that this morning, okay?" She put her hand on his shoulder and smiled.

"Please. Listen." Was this what Joe had felt? he wondered. So much easier to leave without a word, to escape the recriminations, the disbelief. To escape the guilt. But somehow he just couldn't do that to Kerry. Perhaps because he knew how it had felt.

"Try to understand. This place"—his gesture included the club, the neon-lit street, the low sky, the whole of London heaving dark and menacing below it—"I don't belong here anymore. I can't think straight when I'm here. I spend all my time waiting for something to happen—some kind of sign—"

"Oh, for Christ's sake, Jay grow up!" She was suddenly furious, her voice rising like an angry bird's.

"But I am," he interrupted her. "I'm taking charge. I'm doing what you've always told me to do."

"Not by running away to France!" The note in her voice was almost panic now. "Not just like that! You can't solve your problems by running away!" She shot a glance at the doorman, who was listening to the conversation with covert interest, and lowered her voice.

"Look, I'll come home with you right now. We'll talk. We'll try to make sense of all this. And if you still feel the same way in the morning—or by the end of the week—"

Jay shook his head. "I can't, Kes."

"Why not?" She looked flushed, suddenly very young in spite of her smart hair and fashionable dress. Jay felt something twist inside him as she said, "Why do you make me fight you all the time? What's *wrong* with you?"

"I'm sorry." In that moment he realized he meant it. Whatever he'd thought, she wasn't Gilly, nor had she ever pretended to be. That was another role he'd imposed upon her.

"I'd like to go home with you. But if I did . . ." He struggled with the words. "We could talk. I could try to explain things. You might even talk me into changing my mind—God knows, you can be persuasive enough . . ."

Impossible to put into words what he felt; that feeling of chemistry, of never-to-be-repeated circumstance. A week—even a single night—might be enough to put everything out of alignment. Sanity would be reasserted. The strong, sweet certainty of it all would be lost. Château Foudouin would remain unoccupied for months—maybe years—until it was sold at last, maybe converted into a guest house or an old people's home, an embarrassing reminder of an uncharacteristic impulse.

"It's like inspiration," he said at last. "Sometimes you can't even wait until morning. Sometimes you have to drop everything—or you lose it before you even know what it is."

Kerry took a step forward, her eyes bright. "Is that it? Is it another book?" She sounded hungry now, her delicate hands outspread. "If that's what it is, you *have* to tell me, Jay. You owe me that. After all this time . . ."

Jay looked at her. It would be so easy to say yes, he told himself. To give her something she would understand, maybe forgive. "I don't know," he said at last. "I don't think so."

"Then *what?*"

A taxi was going past, its light on. Jay lifted his hand to flag it down.

"I don't know," he said again. "Maybe I'll find out when I get there."

"Well, at least leave me the address!" She was pale now, her eyes enormous. "Give me some way of getting in touch with you, a phone number, a mobile—" The taxi drew up beside the curb. Jay shouldered his bag again.

"This is crazy," whispered Kerry. "You'll be completely lost, your French is terrible, you don't know anyone—"

But at that moment, Jay thought she sounded lost. Her voice, trying for authority, wavered.

"Have you thought at all about *any* of this?"

Jay opened the door of the taxi and pushed his heavy bag inside. "Joe always said I thought too much," he said. "Kerry, I've got to go."

For a second her face looked raw, unprotected. Then she

recovered. Broken glass twinkled behind her eyes. She gave him a bright, hard smile.

She was still smiling as the taxi pulled away smoothly from the curb. For a moment he saw her standing there, looking ghostly in the neon light from the club. Exhausted, Jay closed his eyes and settled back against his duffel bag. Its contents made small contented clicking sounds all the way to the airport.

Twelve

Pog Hill, Summer 1975

Summer steered its course and Jay came more often to Pog Hill Lane. Joe seemed pleased to see him when he came by, but never commented when he did not, and the boy spent days lurking by the canal or by the railway, watching over his uncertain territory, ever on the lookout for Zeth and his two friends. His hideout at the lock was no longer secure, so he moved the Treasure Box from its place in the bank and cast about for a safer place. At last he found one in the derelict Ford Galaxie on the dumping ground and taped the box to the underside of the rotten fuel tank.

Jay liked that old car. He spent hours lounging in the one remaining seat, smelling the musty scent of ancient leather, hidden from sight by the rampant greenery. Once or twice he heard the voices of Zeth and his mates close by, but crouching in the low belly of the car—Joe's charm held tightly in his hand—he was safe from any but the closest investigation. He watched and listened, intoxictated with the delight of spying on his enemies. At such times he believed in the charm implicitly.

He realized as summer drew inevitably to its close that he had grown fond of Kirby Monckton. In spite of his resistance he had found something here that he'd never had elsewhere. July and August sailed by like cool white schooners. He went to Pog Hill Lane almost every day. Sometimes he and Joe were alone, but too often there were visitors, neighbors, friends, though Joe seemed to have no family. Jay was sometimes jealous, resentful of time given to other people, but Joe always welcomed everyone, giving out boxes of fruit from his allotment, a bunch of carrots or a bottle of blackberry wine to one, a recipe for tooth powder to another. He dealt in philters, teas, sachets. People came openly for fruit and vegetables but stayed in secret, talking to Joe in low voices, sometimes leaving with a little packet of tissue paper or a scrap of flannel tucked into hands and pockets. He never asked for payment. Sometimes people gave him things in exchange: a loaf or two, a homemade pie, cigarettes. Jay wondered where he got his money, and where the five thousand pounds to pay for his dream *château* would come from. But when he mentioned such things the old man just laughed.

As September loomed closer, every day seemed to gain a special, poignant significance, a mythical quality. Jay walked the canalside in a haze of nostalgia. He took notes of the things Joe said to him in their long conversations over the red currant bushes, replaying them in his mind as he lay in bed. He cycled for hours over deserted, now-familiar roads and breathed the sooty warm air. He climbed Upper Kirby Hill and looked out over the purple-black expanse of the Pennines and wished he could stay forever.

Joe himself remained the same as ever, picking his early fruit and laying it out in crates, making jam from windfalls, pointing out wild herbs and picking them when the moon was full, collecting bilberries from the moors and blackberries from the railway banking, preparing chutney from his tomatoes, piccalilli from his cauliflowers, lavender bags for sleeplessness, wintergreen for rapid healing, hot peppers and rosemary in oil and pickled onions for the winter. And, of course, there was the wine. Throughout all that summer Jay smelled wine brewing, fermenting, aging. All kinds of wine: beet root, pea pod, raspberry, elderflower, rose hip, jackapple, plum, parsnip, ginger, blackberry. The house was a distillery, with pans of fruit boiling on the stove, demijohns of wine waiting on the kitchen floor to be decanted into bottles, muslins drying on the clothesline for straining the fruit, sieves, buckets, bottles, funnels, laid out in neat rows ready for use.

Joe kept the still in his cellar. It was a big copper piece like a giant kettle, old but burnished and cared-for. He used it to make his "spirits," the raw, eye-watering clear alcohol he used to preserve the summer fruit which sat on shelves in the cellar in gleaming rows. *Potato vodka*, he called it, *jackapple juice*. Seventy percent proof. In it he placed equal quantities of fruit and sugar to make his liqueurs. Cherries, plums, red currants, bilberries. The fruit stained the liquor purple and red and black in the dim cellar light. Each jar carefully labeled and dated. More than one man could ever hope to eat. Apart from Joe's wine and a few licks of strawberry jam with his morning toast, Jay never saw him touch any of those extravagant preserves and spirits.

Jay went back to school in September. The Moorlands School was as he remembered it, smelling of dust and disinfectant and polish and the bland inescapable smell of ancient cooking. His parents' divorce had gone through smoothly. Surprisingly, he felt nothing. During the summer his rage had sloughed away into indifference. Anger seemed childish to him somehow. He wrote to Joe every month or so, though the old man never wrote back as regularly. He was not much of a writer, he said, and managed only a card at Christmas and a couple of lines near the end of term. His silence did not trouble Jay; it was enough to know that he was there.

The following summer, Jay went back to Kirby Monckton. Part of this was on his own insistence, but he could tell his parents were secretly relieved. His mother was filming in Ireland at the time, and his father was spending the summer on his yacht—in the company, rumor had it, of a young fashion model called Candide.

Jay escaped to Pog Hill Lane without a backward glance.

Thirteen

Paris, March 1999

Jay's plane landed late, and he spent the night at the airport. He even slept a little on one of Charles de Gaulle's contoured orange chairs, though he was still too jumpy to relax. His energy seemed inexhaustible, a ball of electricity punching against his ribs. His senses felt eerily enhanced. Smells—cleaning fluid, sweat, cigarette smoke, perfume, early morning coffee—rolled at him in waves. At five o'clock he abandoned the idea of sleep and went to the cafeteria, where he bought an espresso, a couple of croissants and a sugar fix of Poulain chocolate. The first Corail to Toulouse was at six-ten. From there, a slower train would take him to Agen, where he could get a taxi to—where was it? The map attached to the brochure was only a sketchy diagram, but he hoped to find clearer directions when he reached Agen. Besides, there was something pleasing about this journey, this blurring of speed to a place which was nothing yet but a cross on a map. As if by drinking Joe's wine he could suddenly *become* Joe, marking his passage by scratching signs on a map, changing his identity to suit his whim. And at the same time he felt lighter, freed of the hurt and anger he had carried for so long, such useless ballast, for so many years.

Travel far enough, Joe used to say, *and all rules are suspended*.

Now Jay began to understand what he had meant. Truth, loyalty, identity. The things which bind us to the places and faces of home no longer applied. He could be anyone. Going anywhere—at airports, railway stations, bus stations—no one asks questions. People reach a state of near-invisibility. He was just another passenger here, one of thousands. No one would recognize him. No one had even heard of him.

He managed to sleep for a few hours on the train, and dreamed—a dream of astonishing vividness—of himself running along the canal bank at Nether Edge, trying vainly to catch up with a departing coal train. With exceptional clarity he could see the somehow prehistoric metal of the train's undercarriage. He could smell coal dust and old grease from the cars' axles. And on the last one he could see Joe, sitting on top of the coal in his orange miner's overalls and a British Railways engineer's cap, waving goodbye, with a bottle of home-brewed wine in one hand and a map of the world in the other, calling, in a voice made tinny by distance, words Jay could not quite hear.

He awoke, needing a drink, twenty miles from Marseille, with the countryside a long bright blur at the window. He went to the minibar for a vodka and tonic and drank it slowly, then lit a cigarette. It still felt like a forbidden pleasure—guilt laced with exhilaration, like playing truant from school.

He pulled the brochure out of his pocket once more. Decidedly crumpled now, the cheap paper beginning to tear at the folds. For a moment he almost expected to feel differently, to find that the sense of *must have* was gone. But it was still there. In the duffel bag at his side, the Specials lolled and gurgled with the train's movement, and inside, the sediment of past summers stirred like crimson slurry.

Fourteen

Pog Hill, Summer 1976

Joe was waiting on the allotment. The radio was playing, tied with a piece of string to the branch of a tree, and Jay could hear him singing along—Thin Lizzy and "The Boys Are Back in Town"—in his extravagant music-hall voice. He had his back turned, leaning over a patch of loganberries with pruning shears in one hand, and he greeted Jay without turning around, casually, as if he had never been away. Jay's first thought was that Joe had aged; the hair beneath the greasy cap was thinner, and he could see the sharp, vulnerable ridge of his spine through his old T-shirt, but when the old man turned around he could see that it was the same Joe, jay-blue eyes above a smile more suited to a fourteen-year-old than a man of sixty-five. He was wearing one of his red flannel sachets around his neck.

Looking more carefully around the allotment, Jay saw that a similar charm adorned every tree, every bush, even the corners of the greenhouse and the homemade cold frame. Small seedlings protected under jars and bisected lemonade bottles each bore a twist of red thread or a sign crayoned in the same color. It might have been another of Joe's elaborate jokes, like the earwig traps or the sherbert plant, but this time there was a somber, besieged look to the old man's amusement. Jay asked him about the charms, expecting the usual joke or wink, but Joe's expression remained serious.

"Protection, lad," he said quietly. "Protection."

———

Summer began like a walk along a dusty road. Jay called by Pog Hill Lane almost every day, and when he felt in need of solitude he went over to Nether Edge and the canal. Nothing much had changed. New glories on the dump—abandoned fridges, rag bags, a clock with a cracked casing, a cardboard box of tattered paperback books. The railway too delivered riches: papers, magazines, broken records, crockery, cans, returnable glass. Every morning he combed the rails, picking up what looked interesting or valuable, and brought his finds to Joe back at the house. Joe wasted nothing. Old newspapers went into the compost. Pieces of carpet kept the weeds down in the vegetable patch. Plastic bags covered the branches of his fruit trees and protected them from the birds. He demonstrated how to make cloches for young seedlings from the round end of a plastic lemonade bottle, and potato planters from discarded car tires. They spent a whole afternoon dragging an abandoned box freezer up the railway banking to make a cold frame. Scrap metal and old clothes were piled into cardboard boxes and sold to the rag-and-bone man.

Empty paint cans and plastic buckets were converted into plant pots.

In return, Joe taught Jay more about the garden. Slowly the boy learned to tell lavender from rosemary from hyssop from sage. He learned to taste soil—a pinch between the finger and thumb slipped under the tongue, like a man testing fine tobacco—to determine its acidity. He learned how to calm a headache with crushed lavender, or a stomachache with peppermint. He learned to prepare skullcap tea and chamomile to aid sleep. He learned to plant marigolds in the potato patch to discourage parasites and to pick nettles from the top to make ale and to fork the sign against the evil eye if ever a magpie flew past. There were times, of course, when the old man couldn't resist a little joke. Like giving him daffodil bulbs to fry instead of onions or planting whole ripe strawberries in the border to see if they'd grow. But most of the time he was serious—or so Jay thought—finding real pleasure in his new role as a teacher.

Perhaps Joe knew it was coming to an end even then, though Jay never suspected it, but it was that year that he was happiest, sitting in the allotment with the radio playing, or sorting through boxes of junk or holding the vegetable cutter for Joe as they selected the fruit for the next batch of wine. They discussed the merits of "Good Vibrations" (Jay's choice) versus "Brand New Combine Harvester" (Joe's). He felt safe, *protected*, as if all this were a little pocket of eternity. At the same time something was changing. Perhaps it was in Joe; a new restlessness, the wary look he had, the diminishing number of visitors—sometimes only one or two in a whole week—or the new, eerie quiet in Pog Hill Lane. No more hammering, no singing in the yards, less washing hanging out to dry on clotheslines.

Often Joe would walk to the outer edge of his allotment

and look over the railway in silence. There were fewer trains too, a couple of passenger trains a day on the fast line, the rest shunters and coal cars ambling slowly north to the yard. The rails, so shiny and bright the last year, were beginning to show rust.

"Looks like they're plannin' to close the line," Joe remarked on one of these occasions. "Goin' to knock down Kirby Central next month." Kirby Central was the main signal box down by the station. "Pog Hill, anall, if I'm not mistaken."

"But that's your greenhouse," protested Jay. Since he had known Joe, the old man had used the derelict signal box fifty yards from the back garden as an unofficial greenhouse, and it was filled with delicate plants, tomatoes, two peach trees, a couple of vines branching out into the eaves, escaping onto the white roof in a spill of broad bright leaves.

Joe shrugged. "They usually knock 'em flat first off," he remarked. "I've bin lucky so far." His eyes moved to the red charm bags nailed to the back wall and he reached out to pinch one between finger and thumb.

"Thing is, we've bin careful," he continued. "Not drawn attention to usselves. But if they shut that line, there'll be men taking up the track all down Pog Hill and towards Nether Edge. They might be here for months. And this here—it's private property. Belongs to British Railways. You an me, lad—we're trespassers." Jay followed his gaze across the railway cutting, taking in as if for the first time the breadth of the allotment, the neat straight rows of vegetables, the cold frames, the hundreds of plastic planters, dozens of fruit trees, thick stands of raspberries, black currants, rhubarb. Funny, he'd never thought of it as trespassing before.

"Oh. D'you think they'd want to take it back?"

Joe didn't look at him. Of course they would take it back.

He could see that in the old man's profile, in the calculating look on his face—how long to replant, how long to rebuild? Not because they wanted it, but because it was theirs to take, their territory, wasteland or not, theirs. Jay had a sudden, vivid memory of Zeth booting the radio into the air. There would be the same expressions as they pulled up the railway, broke up the greenhouse, tore up plants and bushes, bull-dozed through the sweet drifts of lavender and the half-ripened pears, unearthed potatoes and carrots and parsnips and all the arcane exotica of a lifetime's collection. . . . Jay felt a sudden brimming rage on behalf of the old man and his fists clenched painfully against the bricks.

"They can't do that!" Jay said fiercely.

Joe shrugged. Of course they could.

Fifteen

The train reached Toulouse around noon. It was warm but cloudy, and Jay carried his coat over his arm as he moved through the aimless crowds. He bought a couple of sandwiches at a stand by the platform but was still too nervous, too energized to eat. The train to Agen was almost an hour late, and slow; the trip almost as long as the journey from Paris. Energy drained away into exhaustion. He slept uncomfortably as they nudged from one small station to another, feeling hot and thirsty and slightly hungover. He kept taking out the leaflet again, just to be sure he wasn't imagining it all. He tried to get the radio to work, but all he could get was white noise.

It was late afternoon when he finally reached Agen. He

was beginning to feel more alert again, more aware of his surroundings. He could see fields and farms from the carriage, orchards and plowed chocolate-colored earth. Everything looked very green. Many of the trees were already in flower, unusually early for March, he thought, though his only experience of gardening was with Joe, a thousand miles farther north. He took a taxi to the real estate agent's—the address was on the leaflet—hoping to get permission to view the house, but the place was already shut.

Damn.

In the excitement of his escape Jay had never considered what he would do if this happened. Find a hotel in Agen? Not without seeing his house. *His house.* The thought lifted the hairs on his forearms. Tomorrow was Sunday. Chances were that the agency would be closed again. He would have to wait until Monday morning.

He stood, hesitating, in front of the locked door as the taxi driver behind him grew impatient. How far exactly was Lansquenet-sous-Tannes? Surely there would be something— even something basic like a Campanile or an Ibis, failing that a *chambre-d'hôte* where he could stay? It was half-past five. He would have time to see the house—even if it was only from the outside—before the light failed.

The urge was too strong. Turning back to the bored taxi driver with unaccustomed decisiveness, Jay showed him the map. *"Vous pouvez m'y conduire tout de suite?"*

The man considered with the air of slow reflection typical of that part of the country. Jay pulled out a clip of bank notes from the pocket of his jeans and showed them to him. The driver shrugged incuriously and jerked his head toward the cab again. Jay noticed he didn't offer to help with the luggage.

The drive took half an hour. Jay dozed again in the leather-and-tobacco-scented rear of the cab while the driver smoked

Gauloises and grunted to himself in satisfaction as he blared
without signaling through files of motorway traffic, then sped
down narrow small lanes, honking his horn imperiously at
corners, occasionally sending flurries of chickens squawking
into the air. Jay was beginning to feel hungry and in need of
a drink. He had assumed he would find a place to eat when
they reached Lansquenet. But now, looking at the dirt lane
down which the taxi jolted and revved, he was beginning to
have serious doubts.

He tapped the driver on the shoulder. *"C'est encore loin?"*

The driver shrugged, pointing ahead, and slowed the car
to a rumbling halt. *"Là."*

Sure enough there it was, just behind a little copse of trees.
The red slanting light of a modest sunset lit the tiled roof and
the whitewashed walls with almost eerie brightness. Jay could
see the gleam of water somewhere to the side, and the orchard—green in the photograph—was now a froth of pale
blossoms. It was beautiful. He paid the driver too much of
his remaining French money and pulled his case out onto
the road.

"Attendez-moi ici. Je reviens tout de suite."

The driver made a vague gesture which Jay took to be
agreement, and leaving him to wait by the deserted roadside,
Jay began to walk quickly toward the trees. As he reached
the copse he found he could see more clearly down toward
the house and across the vineyard. The photograph in the
brochure had given little sense of the scale of the property.
Being a city boy, Jay had no idea of the acreage, but it looked
huge, bordered on one side by road and river, and on the
other by a long hedge which reached beyond the back of the
house onto more fields. On the far side of the river he could
see another farmhouse, small and low-roofed, and beyond that
the village: a church spire, a road winding up from the river,

houses. The path to the house led past the vineyard—already green and leggy with growth among drifts of weeds—and past an abandoned vegetable plot, where last year's asparagus, artichokes and cabbages reared hairy heads above the dandelions.

It took about ten minutes to reach the house. As he came closer, Jay noticed that, like the vineyard and the vegetable plot, it was in need of some repair. The pale pinkish paint was peeling away in places, revealing cracked gray plaster beneath. Tiles from the roof had fallen and smashed onto the overgrown path. The ground-floor windows were shuttered or boarded up, and some of the upstairs glass was broken, showing toothy gaps. The front door was nailed shut. The whole impression was of a building which had been derelict for years. And yet the vegetable plot showed signs of recent—or fairly recent—attention. Jay walked around the building once, noting the extent of the damage, and told himself that most of it looked superficial, the work of neglect and the elements. Inside might be different. He found a place where a broken shutter had come away from the plaster to leave a gap large enough to look through, and put his face to the hole. It was dark inside, and he could hear a distant sound of water dripping.

Suddenly something moved inside the building. Rats, he thought at first. Then it moved again, softly, stealthily, scraping across the floor with a sound like metal-capped boots on cellar concrete. Definitely not rats, then.

He called out—absurdly, in English—"*Hey!*" The sound stopped.

Squinting through the gap in the shutter, Jay thought he could see something move, a dim shadow just in his line of vision, something which might almost have been a figure in a big coat and a cap pulled down over the eyes—

But it was an illusion. Of course it wasn't Joe, it was just

that he'd been thinking of him so often in the past few days
that he had begun to imagine him everywhere. When he
looked again, the figure—if there ever had been a figure—was
gone. The house was silent. Jay knew a fleeting moment of
disappointment, of something almost like grief. Jay's mind
crept remorselessly to the recently abandoned vegetable
plot—there must have been *someone* to plant those seeds—
with a mad kind of logic. Someone had been there.

He looked at his watch and was startled to see that he had
been at the house for almost twenty minutes. He had asked
the taxi driver to wait at the roadside, and he didn't want to
spend the night in Lansquenet—from what he had seen of
the place, it was unlikely that he would be able to find a
decent place to stay, and he was beginning to feel very hungry.
He broke into a run as he passed the orchard, goose grass
clinging to the laces of his boots as he passed, and he was
sweating when at last he rounded the curve out of the copse
and back onto the track.

There was no sign of the taxi.

Jay swore. His case and duffel bag were lined up, incongruous, by the roadside.

Sixteen

Pog Hill, Summer 1976

irby Central went in late August. Jay was there when they closed it, hiding in a tall clump of seedy willow herb, and when they had left—taking with them the levers, light signals and anything which might otherwise be stolen— he crept up the steps and peered in through the window. Train registers and route diagrams had been left in the box, though the lever frame gaped emptily, and it looked strangely *inhabited*, as if the signalman had just stepped out and might return at any moment. Jay reckoned there was plenty of us- able glass left, if Joe and he came to fetch it.

"Don't bother, lad," Joe said when he reported this. "I'll already have me hands full this autumn."

Jay needed no explanation for his words. Since the begin-

ning of August Joe had become more and more concerned
about the fate of his allotment. He rarely spoke about it
openly, but he would sometimes stop working and gaze at his
trees, as if measuring the time they still had left. Sometimes
he lingered to touch the smooth bark of an apple or a plum
tree and spoke—to Jay, to himself—in a low voice. He always
referred to them by name, as if they were people.

"*Mirabelle*. Doin' well, int she? That's a French plum, a
yeller gage, a goodun for jam or wine or just for eatin'. She
likes it here on the bank, it's nicely drained and sunny." He
paused. "Too late to move t'old girl, though," he said regret-
fully. "She'd never survive. Yer sink yer roots deep, thinkin'
yer goin' to stay forever, and this is what happens. The
buggers."

It was the closest he had come in weeks to mentioning the
allotment problem.

"Tryin' to knock down Pog Hill Lane now, anall." Joe's
voice was louder now, and Jay realized that this was the first
time he had ever seen him close to anger. "Pog Hill Lane,
that's bin standin' for a hundred year-a-more, that were built
when there were still a pit down Nether Edge, and navvies
workin' down at canalside."

Jay stared at him. "Knock down Pog Hill Lane?" he asked.
"You mean the *houses*?"

Joe nodded. "Got a letter in't post t'other day," he told
him shortly. "Buggers reckon we're not safe anymore. Goin'
to condemn 'em all. All t'row." His face was grim in its
amusement. "Condemned. After all this time. Thirty-nine
years I've bin here since Nether Edge and Upper Kirby shut
down. Bought me own pit house offat Council anall—didn't
trust 'em, even then—" He broke off, holding up his reduced
left hand in a mocking three-fingered salute. "How much
more do they want, eh? I left me fingers down that pit. I near

as buggery left me *life*. You'd think that'd be worth somethin'. You'd think they'd *remember* summat like that!"

Jay gaped at him. This was a Joe he had never seen before. Awe—and a kind of fear—kept him silent. Then Joe stopped ranting as abruptly as he had begun, bending solicitously over a newly grafted branch to examine the healing joint.

"I thought it was during the war," said Jay at last.

"What?"

Gaudy red cotton joined the new graft to the branch. On it Joe had smeared some kind of resin which gave out a pungent sappy scent. He nodded to himself, as if satisfied with the tree's progress.

"You told me you'd lost your fingers in Dieppe," insisted Jay. "During the war."

"Aye. Well." Joe was unembarrassed. "It were a kind of war down there anyroad. Lost 'em when I were sixteen, crushed between two coal trucks back in 1931. Wouldn't take me in the army after that, so I signed up as a Bevan boy. We had three cave-ins that year. Seven men trapped underground when a tunnel collapsed. Not even grown men, some of 'em— boys my age and younger, you could go underground at four- teen on a man's wage. Worked double shifts for a week tryin' to get 'em out. We could hear 'em behind the cave-in yellin' and cryin', but every time we tried to get to 'em another bit of the tunnel came down on us. We were workin' in darkness because of the gas, knee-deep in slurry. We were soaked an' half-suffocated, an' we all knew the roof could fall in again any minute, but we never stopped tryin'. Not till at last the bosses came and closed down the shaft altogether." He looked at Jay with unexpected vehemence, his eyes dark with ancient rage. "So don't go tellin' me I never went to war, lad," he snapped. "I know as much about war—what war *means*—than any o' them lads in France."

Jay stared at him, unsure of what to say. Joe looked off into the middle distance, hearing the cries and pleading of young men long dead from the quiet scar of Nether Edge.

Jay shivered. "So what will you do now?"

Joe looked at him closely, as if checking for any sign of condemnation. Then he relaxed and gave his old, rueful smile, at the same time digging in his pocket to produce a grubby packet of Jelly Babies. He chose one for himself, then held out the packet to Jay.

"I'll do what I've allus done, lad," he declared. "I'll bloody well fight for what's mine. I'll not let 'em get away with it. Pog Hill's mine, an' I'll not be moved onto some poxy estate by them or anyone." He bit off the head of his Jelly Baby with relish and chose another from the packet

"But what can you do?" protested Jay. "There'll be eviction orders. They'll cut off your gas and electricity. Can't you—"

Joe looked at him. "There's allus *somethin'* you can do, lad," he said softly. "I reckon maybe it's time to find out what really works. Time to bring out sandbags and batten down hatches. Time to fatten up t'black cockerel, like they do in Haiti." He winked hugely. Jay glanced around at the allotment. He looked at the charms nailed to the wall and tied onto the tree branches, the signs laid out in broken glass on the ground and chalked onto flower pots, and he felt a sudden, terrible hopelessness. It all looked so touchingly fragile, so doomed. He saw the houses then, those blackened, mean little terraces with their crooked pointing and outside toilets and windows sheeted over with plastic. Wash hanging on a single line five or six houses down. A couple of kids playing in the gutter in front. And Joe—with his travels and his *chatto* and his millions of seeds and his cellar full of bottles.

"Don't take on, lad," urged Joe. "We'll be reight, you'll

see. There's more than one trick up me sleeve, as them bug-gers from Council'll find out.''

But his words sounded hollow. For all his talk, it was really just bravado; there was nothing he could do. Of course Jay pretended, for his sake, to believe him. He gathered herbs on the railway embankment. He sewed dried leaves into red sa-chets. He repeated Joe's strange words and ritual gestures.

They had to *seal the perimeter*, as Joe called it, twice a day. This involved walking around the property—up the railway embankment and around the allotment past Pog Hill box, which Joe counted as his, then into Pog Hill Lane and through the ginnel which linked Joe's house to his neighbor's, past the front door and back over the wall to the other side—carrying a red candle and burning bay leaves steeped in scented oil while they solemnly incanted a string of incomprehensible phrases which Joe claimed were Latin. From what Joe said, this ritual was supposed to shield the house and its grounds from unwanted influences, deliver protection and affirm his ownership of the territory. As the holidays came to an end, it increased daily in length and complexity, growing from a three-minute dash around the garden to a solemn procession lasting fifteen minutes or more.

Under other circumstances, Jay might have enjoyed it. But whereas last year there had been an element of mockery in everything Joe said, now the old man had less time for jokes. Jay guessed that behind this screen of unconcern his anxiety was growing. He spoke increasingly about his travels, re-counted past adventures and planned future expeditions, an-nounced his immediate decision to leave Pog Hill Lane for his *château* in France, then in the same breath swore he'd never leave his old home unless they carried him out feet first. He worked frantically in the garden—autumn came early that year and there was fruit to be harvested, jams, wine, preserves, pickles to be made, potatoes and turnips to be dug and stored. The demands of maintaining Joe's magical barrier increased as well; it now took thirty minutes to complete and involved much gesticulating and scattering of powders as well as preparation of scented oils and herbal mixtures. There was a haunted look to Joe, a *stretched* look to his features, a glittery brightness in his eyes which came of sleeplessness—or drink. For he was drinking far more now than he ever had, not just wine or nettle beer but spirits too, the potato vodka from the still in the cellar, last year's liqueurs from his downstairs store. Jay wondered whether, at this pace, Joe would survive the winter at all.

"I'll be reight," Joe told him when he voiced his concern. "It just needs a bit more work, that's all. Come winter I'll be reight again, I promise." He stood up, hands in the small of his back, and stretched. "That's better." He grinned then, and for a moment he was almost the old Joe, eyes brimming with laughter under his greasy pit cap. "I've looked after myself for a few years before you came along, lad. It'd take a sight more than a few Council monkeys to get the better of me." And he immediately launched into a long, absurd story from his traveling days about a man trying to sell cheap trinkets to a tribe of Amazonian Indians.

"And the chief of the tribe—Chief Mungawomba, his name were—handed back the stuff and said (I'd been teachin' him English in me free time): *Tha can keep thi beads, mate, but I'd be really grateful if tha could fix me toaster.*"

Seventeen

Lansquenet, March 1999

He stood beside the roadside for a moment, dismayed and disoriented. By then it was almost dark; the sky had reached that luminous shade of deep blue which just precedes full night, and the horizon beyond the house was striated with pale lemon and green and pink. The beauty of it—*his* property, he told himself again, with that breathless unreal feeling inside—left him feeling a little shaken. In spite of his predicament he could not shrug off a sensation of excitement, as if this too were somehow meant to happen.

No one—*no one*, he told himself—knew where he was.

The wine bottles rattled against each other as he picked up the duffel bag from the side of the road. A scent—of summer, of wild spinach or shale dust and stagnant water—rose briefly from the damp ground. Something fluttering from the branch of a flowering hawthorn tree caught his eye and he picked at it automatically, bringing it closer to his eyes.

It was a piece of red flannel.

In the bag the bottles began to rattle and froth. Their voices rose in a whispering, crackling, sighing, chuckling of hidden consonants and secret vowels. Jay felt a sudden breeze tug at his clothing, a murmur of something, a throbbing deep in the soft air, like a heart. *Home is where the heart is.* One of Joe's favorite sayings.

Where the 'art is.

Jay looked back at the road. It was not really so late. Not too late, in any case, to find somewhere to stay the night and to buy a meal. The village—a few lights now, winking on over the river, the distant sound of music from across the fields— must be less than half an hour's walk away. He could leave his suitcase here, safely hidden in the roadside bushes, and take only his bag. For some reason—inside the bottles jolted and chuckled—he felt reluctant to leave the bag. But the house drew him.

Ridiculous, he told himself. He had already seen that the house was uninhabitable, at least for the moment. *Looked un-inhabitable*, he amended, recalling Pog Hill Lane, the derelict gardens and boarded-up windows and the secret, gleeful life behind. What if—maybe—just behind the door . . .

Funny, how his mind kept returning to that thought. There was no logic in it and yet it was slyly persuasive. That abandoned vegetable patch, the scrap of red flannel, that feeling— that certainty—that there really was someone *inside* the house. . . .

Inside the duffel bag the carnival had begun again. Catcalls, laughter, distant fanfare.

Eighteen

Pog Hill, Summer 1977

September came. Jay went back to school with a sense of finality, a feeling that something at Pog Hill had changed. If it had, then Joe's short, infrequent letters gave no sign. There was a card at Christmas—two lines, carefully inscribed with the round printing of the barely literate—then another at Easter. The term crawled to an end. Jay's fifteenth birthday came and went (a cricket bat from his father and Candide, theater tickets from his mother). After that came exams, dorm parties, secrets told and promises broken, a couple of hot-weather fights and a school play—*A Midsummer Night's Dream*, with all the parts played by boys, as in Shakespeare's time. Jay played Puck, much to the chagrin of his father, but all the time he was thinking of Joe and Pog Hill, and as the

end of the summer term approached he grew jumpy and irri-
table and impatient. This year his mother had decided to join
him in Kirby Monckton for a few weeks, ostensibly to spend
more time with her son, but in reality to escape the media
attention following her most recent amorous breakup. Jay
wasn't looking forward to being the focus of her sudden maternal interest, and said so clearly enough to provoke an out-
burst of outraged histrionics. He was in disgrace before the
holidays even started.

They arrived in late June, by taxi, in the rain. Jay's mother
was doing her *Mater Dolorosa* act and he was trying to listen
to the radio as she passed between long, soulful silences to
girlish exclamations on seeing forgotten landmarks.

"Jay, darling, look! That little church—isn't it just the
sweetest?" He put it down to her being in so many sitcoms,
but maybe she had always talked like that. Jay turned the
radio up a fraction. The Eagles were playing "Hotel Califor-
nia." She gave him one of her pained looks and thinned her
mouth. Jay ignored her.

The rain came down nonstop for the first week of the holiday. Jay stayed in the house and watched it and listened to
the radio, trying to tell himself it couldn't last forever. The
sky was white and portentous. When he peered up into the
clouds, the falling raindrops looked like soot. His grandparents
fussed over both of them, treating his mother like the little
girl she had been, cooking all her favorite meals. For five days
they lived on fried fish and hash browns, apple pie, ice cream.
On the sixth day Jay took his bike down to Pog Hill in spite
of the weather, but Joe's door was locked and there was no
answer to his knocking. Jay left his bike at the back wall
and climbed over into the garden, hoping to look in through
the windows.

The windows were boarded up.

Panic washed over him. He hammered on one of the sealed windows with his fist. "Hey, Joe? *Joe?*"

There was no answer. He hammered again, calling Joe's name. A piece of red flannel, bleached by the elements, was nailed to the window frame, but it looked old, finished, last year's magic. Behind the house a screen of tall weeds—hemlock and wormwood and rosebay willow herb—hid the abandoned allotment.

Jay sat down on the wall, regardless of the rain which glued his T-shirt to his skin and dripped from his hair into his eyes. He felt completely numb. How could Joe have gone? he asked himself stupidly. Why hadn't he said something? Written a note, even? How could Joe have gone without him?

"Don't take on, lad," called a voice behind him. "It's not as bad as it looks."

Jay whipped around so fast he almost fell off the wall. Joe was standing some twenty feet behind him, almost hidden from sight behind the tall weeds. He was wearing a yellow sou'wester on top of his pit cap. He had a spade on one hand.

"*Joe?*"

The old man grinned. "Aye. What d'you think, then?"

Jay was beyond words.

It's me permanent solution," explained Joe, looking pleased. "They've cut off me 'lectrics, but I've wired meself up to bypass the meter, so I can still use 'em. I've bin diggin' a well 'round back so I can do waterin'. Come over, and tell me what you think."

As always, Joe behaved as if no time had passed, as if Jay had never been away. He parted the weeds which separated them and motioned the boy to follow him through. Beyond, the allotment was as ordered as it had always been, with lemonade bottles sheltering small plants, old windows arranged to make cold frames, and tires stacked up for potato planters.

From a distance the whole thing might just have been the accumulated detritus of years, but come a little closer and everything was there just as before. On the railway bank, fruit trees (some shielded with sheets of plastic) dripped rain. It was the best camouflage job Jay had ever seen.

"It's amazing," he said at last. "I really thought you'd gone."

Joe looked pleased. "You're not the only one that thinks that, lad," he said mysteriously. "Look down there."

Jay looked down into the railway. The signal box which had been Joe's greenhouse was still standing, though in a state of dereliction; vines grew out of the punctured roof and tumbled down the peeling sides. The lines had been taken up and the sleepers dug out—all but the fifty-yard stretch between the box and Joe's house, as if overlooked by some accident— between the rust-red tracks, weeds were sprouting.

"Come next year no one'll even remember there were a railway down Pog Hill. P'raps people'll let us alone then."

Jay nodded slowly, still speechless with amazement and relief.

Nineteen

Lansquenet, March 1999

The air smelled of nightfall, bitter-smoky like Lapsang tea, mild enough to sleep outside. The vineyard on the left was filled with noises: birds, frogs, insects. Jay could still see the path at his feet, faintly silvered with the last of the sunset, but the sun had left the face of the house and it was lightless, almost forbidding. He began to wonder whether he should have postponed his visit till the morning.

The thought of the walk to the village dissuaded him. He was wearing boots, which had seemed like a good enough idea when he left London, but which now, after so many hours of traveling, had grown tight and uncomfortable. If he could only get into the house—from what he'd seen of security, that

wouldn't be difficult—he could sleep there and make his way
to the village in daylight.

It wasn't as if he were trespassing, really. After all, the
house was almost his. He reached the vegetable patch. Something on the side of the house—a shutter, perhaps—was flapping rhythmically against the plaster, making a nagging,
mournful sound. On the far side of the house shadows moved
under the trees, creating the illusion of a man standing there,
a bent figure in cap and overcoat. Something whipped across
his path with a snapping noise: a prickly artichoke stem, still
topped with last year's flower, now desiccated almost to nothing. Beyond it the overgrown remnants of the vegetable patch
swayed briskly in the freshening wind. Halfway across the
abandoned garden something fluttered as if snagged on a stiff
piece of briar. A scrap of cloth. From where Jay was standing
he could see nothing more, but he knew immediately what it
was. Flannel. Red. Dropping his bag by the side of the path,
he strode into the drift of weeds which had been the vegetable
garden, pushing aside the long stems as he passed.

Just as he stepped forward to take hold of the piece of
flannel, something crunched briefly under his left foot and
gave way with an angry clatter of metal, punching through
the soft leather of his boot and into his ankle. Jay's feet gave
way, tipping him backward into the greenery, and the pain,
bad enough at first, bloomed sickeningly. Swearing, he
grabbed at the object in the dim light, and his fingers encoun-
tered something jagged and metallic attached to his foot.

A trap, he thought, bewildered. Some sort of trap.

It hurt to think straight, and for precious seconds Jay
yanked mindlessly at the object as it bit deeper through his
boot. His fingers felt slick on the metal, and he realized he
was bleeding. He began to panic.

With an effort he forced himself to stop moving. If it was

a trap, then it would have to be forced open. Paranoid to imagine someone had set it deliberately. It must have been someone trying to catch rabbits, perhaps, or foxes, or something . . .

Jay fumbled with the trap. It felt ancient, primitive. It was a clamshell design, fixed into the ground by a metal peg. There was a catch at the side. Jay cursed and struggled with the mechanism, feeling the teeth of the trap crunching deeper into his ankle with every move he made. Finally he managed the catch, but it took several tries to push open the metal jaws and pull himself clear, awkwardly, into the light, where he tried to assess the damage. His foot had already swollen tight against the leather, so that the boot would be difficult or impossible to remove in the normal way. Trying not to think about infection, he pushed himself upright and managed to hop clumsily back to the path, where he sat down on the stones to try to remove his boot. It took him nearly ten minutes. By the time he had finished, he was sweating. It was too dark to see very much, but even so he could tell that it would be some time before he dared to try walking.

Twenty

Pog Hill, Summer 1977

Joe's new defenses were not the only change at Pog Hill that year; Nether Edge had visitors. Jay still went to the Edge every couple of days, and it must have attracted the gypsies too, because one day there they were, a shabby foursome of caravans squared together like pioneers' wagons against the enemy. The caravans were gray and rusting, axles sagging under the weight of accumulated baggage, doors hanging by a string, windows whitening with age. The inhabitants themselves were equally disappointing. Six adults and as many children, clad in jeans or overalls or cheap bright polyester, they gave off an air of distant grubbiness, a visual extension of the smells which floated from their camp, the permanent

odor of frying grease and dirty laundry and gasoline and
garbage.

Jay had never seen gypsies before, but this drab, prosaic
group was not what his reading had prepared him to expect.
He had imagined horse-drawn wagons with outlandishly decorated sides, dark-haired dangerous girls with daggers in their
belts, blind crones with the gift of far seeing. Certainly Joe's
tales of his experiences with gypsies seemed to confirm this,
and as Jay watched the caravans from his vantage point above
the lock, he felt annoyed at the intrusion of these ordinary
people. Until Joe confirmed their exotic heritage, Jay was in-
clined to think they were nothing but tourists, campers from
the south walking the moors.

"No, lad," Joe said as he pointed out the distant camp, a
pale string of smoke rising from a tin chimney into the sky of
Nether Edge. "They're not trippers. They're gypsies, all right,
mebbe not proper Romanies but gyppos, you might call 'em.
Travelers. Like I was once." He squinted curiously through
cigarette smoke at the camp. "Reckon they'll stay the winter,"
he said. "Move on when spring comes. No one'll bother 'em
downt Edge. No one ever goes there anymore."

Not strictly true, of course. Jay considered Nether Edge his
territory, and for a few days he watched the gypsies with all
the resentment he had felt against Zeth and his gang that first
year. He rarely saw much movement from the caravans,
though sometimes there was washing strung out on nearby
trees. A dog tethered to the nearest of the vehicles yapped
shrilly, intermittently. Once or twice he saw a woman carry
water in large canisters to her vehicle. The water came from
two spigots set into squares of concrete at opposite ends of
the camp.

"Set it up a few years back," explained Joe. "Gypsy camp,

with water and 'lectricity laid on. There's a pay meter down there that they use, an' a septic tank. Even rubbish gets collected once a week. You'd think more people'd use it, but they don't. Funny folk, gypsies."

The last time Joe remembered gypsies on the waste ground was about ten years previously.

"Romanies, they were," he said. "You don't get many proper Romanies nowadays. Used to buy their fruit and veg from me. There wasn't many that'd sell to 'em in them days. Said they were no better than beggars." He grinned. "Well, I'm not sayin' everythin' they did was dead-straight honest, but you've got to get by when you're on the road. They worked a way to beat the meter. It took fifty pences, see? Well, they used water and 'lectricity all summer, but when they'd gone and Council came 'round to empty the meter, all there was at bottom was a pool of water. They never did find out how they'd done it. Lock hadn't been touched. Nothin' seemed to have bin interfered with at all."

Jay looked at Joe with interest. "So how did they do it?" he inquired curiously.

Joe grinned again and tapped the side of his nose. "*Alchemy*," he whispered, to Jay's annoyance, and would say no more on the subject.

Joe's tales had renewed his interest in the gypsies. Jay watched the camp for several days after that, but saw no evidence of secret goings-on. Eventually he abandoned his lookout post at the lock to hunt more interesting game, searching for comics and magazines from the dump, combing the railway for its everyday leavings. He worked out a good way of getting free coal for Joe's kitchen stove. There were two coal trains a day, rumbling slowly along the line from Kirby Main. Twenty-four cars on each, with a man sitting on the last one to make sure no one tried to climb onto the cars. There had been accidents in the past, Joe said; kids who'd dared each other to jump onto the trains.

"They might look slow," he said darkly, "but every one of them cars is a forty-tonner. Never try to get up on one, lad."

Jay never did. Instead he found a better way, and Joe's stove lived on it all through that summer into autumn, when they finally closed down the line altogether.

Every day, twice a day just before the arrival of the train, Jay would line up a row of old tin cans on the side of the railway bridge. He arranged them in pyramids, like coconuts at a carnival game, for maximum appeal. The bored workman on the last truck could never resist the challenge they presented. Every time the train passed by, he would lob chunks of coal at the cans, trying to knock them off the bridge, and Jay could always count on at least half a dozen good-sized pieces of coal each time. He stored these in an empty three-gallon paint can hidden in the bushes, and every few days when this was full, he delivered the coal to Joe's house. It was on one of these occasions, when he was fooling about by the railway bridge, that he heard the sound of gunfire from Nether Edge and froze, the coal can dropping from his hand.

Twenty-One

Lansquenet, March 1999

*J*ay pulled a handkerchief out of his duffel bag and used it to stanch the blood, beginning to feel cold now and wishing he'd brought his Burberry. He also took out one of the sandwiches he had bought at the station earlier that day and forced himself to eat. It tasted foul, but the sickness receded a little and he thought he felt a little warmer. It was almost night. A sliver of moon was rising, just enough to cast shadows, and in spite of the pain in his foot, he looked around curiously. He glanced at his watch, almost expecting to see the luminous dial of the Seiko he'd gotten for Christmas when he was fourteen, the one Zeth had broken during that last, most dreadful week of August. But the Rolex was not luminous.

In the shadows at the corner of the building, something moved. He called out—*"Hey!"*—hoisting himself up onto his good leg and limping toward the house.—*"Hey! Please! Wait! Is anyone there?"*

Something smacked against the side of the building with the same flat sound he'd heard before. A shutter, perhaps. He thought he saw it outlined against the purple-black sky, flapping loosely in the breeze. He shivered. No one there after all. If only he could get into the house, out of the cold . . .

The window was about three feet from the ground. There was a deep ledge inside, half-blocked with debris, but he found that he could clear enough space to push through. The air smelled of paint. He moved carefully, feeling for broken glass, swinging his leg over the ledge and into the room, pulling the duffel bag in behind him. His eyes had become accustomed to the dark and he could see that the room was mostly clear, except for a table and a chair in the center and a pile of something—sacks, maybe—in one corner. Using the chair for support, Jay moved over to the pile and found a sleeping bag and a pillow, rolled snugly against the wall, along with a cardboard box which contained paint cans and, strangely enough, a bundle of wax candles.

He reached in his jeans pocket for his lighter. It was only a cheap Bic, and almost out of fuel, but he managed to strike a flame. The candles were dry. The wick spluttered, then flared. The room was mellowly illumined.

He could sleep here. The room was sheltered, the night mild. There were blankets and bedclothes and the remains of that lunchtime's sandwiches. For a moment the pain in his foot was forgotten, and he grinned at the thought that this was home.

It deserved a celebration.

Rummaging through the duffel bag, he pulled out one of

Joe's bottles and cut open the seal and the green cord with the tip of his penknife. The clear scent of elderflower filled the air. He drank a little, tasting that familiar, cloying taste, like fruit left to rot in the dark. Definitely a vintage year, he told himself, and despite everything he began to laugh shakily. He drank a little more. In spite of the taste, the wine was warming, musky; he sat down on the rolled-up bedding, took another mouthful and began to feel a little better.

He reached into his bag again and took out the radio. He turned it on, half-expecting the white noise he had heard on the train all the way from Marseille, but surprisingly the signal was clear. Some kind of local French radio, a low warble of music, something he didn't recognize. Jay laughed again, feeling light-headed. Suddenly inside the duffel bag he could almost imagine that the remaining Specials were beginning their chorus again, a ferment of yahoos and catcalls and war cries redoubling in frenzy until the pitch was wild, feverish, a gleeful champagne of sounds and impressions and voices and memories all shaken into a delirious cocktail of triumph. It pulled him along with it, so that for a moment he could imagine an entire cauldron of spices frothing and seething inside those harmless old bottles. Something was getting ready to happen, the chorus assured him.

Then, suddenly, silence.

Jay looked around curiously. For a moment he shivered, as if a sudden breeze had touched him, a breeze from other places. The paint on the wall was fresh, he noticed; beside the box containing paint cans was a tray with paintbrushes, washed and neatly aligned. The brushes were not yet dry. The breeze was sharper now, smelling of smoke and the circus, hot sugar and apples and midsummer's eve.

The radio crackled softly.

"Well, lad," said a voice from the shadows. "*You* took yer time."

Jay started. It occurred to him almost at once that he must have dozed off as he rested on the rolled-up bedding. He was dreaming.

"Steady on," said Joe kindly.

He had not changed. He was wearing his old cap and a Thin Lizzy T-shirt over his work trousers and pit boots. In one hand he held two wineglasses. In front of him, on the table, stood the bottle of Elderflower '76.

"I allus said you'd get used to it one day," he remarked with satisfaction. "Elderflower champagne. Gotta bittova kick, though, annit?"

Jay felt a flare of joy go through him, so strong that it made the bottles shake. It all made sense now, he thought deliriously; it was all coming together. The signs, the memories—all for this—all finally making sense . . . He looked at the old man in the candlelight, his bright eyes and the laugh wrinkles beneath them, and for the first time he noticed that everything about him was somehow *gilded*—even to the toes of his pit boots—with an eerie glow like nostalgia.

"You're not real, are you?" he said.

Joe shrugged. "What's real?" he asked carelessly. "No such thing, lad."

"Real, as in the sense of really *here*."

Joe watched him patiently, like a teacher with a slow pupil.

Jay's voice rose almost angrily. "Real, as in corporeally present. As in *not* a figment of my deluded wine-soaked imagination, or an early symptom of infection in my foot."

Joe looked at him mildly. "So, you grew up to be a writer, then," he remarked. "Allus said you were a clever lad. Write any gooduns, did yer? Make any brass?"

"Plenty of brass, but only one good one. Too long ago. Shit, I can't believe I'm actually sitting here talking to myself."

"Only one, eh?"

Jay shivered again. The cold night wind sliced thinly
through the half-open shutter, bringing with it that feverish
draught of other places.

"I must really be sick," said Jay softly to himself. "Toxic
shock or something, from that trap. I'm delirious."

Joe shook his head. "Tha'll be reight, lad." Joe always used
to slip into broad Yorkshire when he was being satirical. "It
were only a bit of a fox trap. Old feller used to live here kept
hens. Foxes were allus in an' out at night. He even used to
mark where traps were with a bit o' rag." Jay looked at the
piece of flannel in his hand.

"I thought—"

Joe's eyes were bright with amusement. "You were allus
the same, jumpin' in half-cocked before you knew what were
goin' on. Allus askin' questions. Allus needin' to know summat an' nowt." He held out one of the wineglasses, now filled
with the yellow elderflower wine. "Get this down thi," he
suggested kindly. "Do yer good. I'd tell yer to go out back
an' get yersen some bishop's leaves, but the planets are all
wrong for pickin'. You've got to have Mercury risin', an that
in't till next month." Jay looked at him. For a hallucination,
he seemed very real. There was garden dirt under his fingernails and in the cracks in his palms.

"I'm sick," whispered Jay softly. "You left that summer.
Never even said goodbye. You're not here now. I know that."

Joe shook his head. "Aye," he said kindly. "We'll talk
about that another time, when you're feelin' more yerself."

"When I'm feeling more myself, you won't be there."

Joe laughed and lit a cigarette. The scent was pungent in
the cold air. Jay noticed—with no surprise—that it came from
an old packet of Players Number 6.

"Want one?" asked Joe, handing him the packet.

For a moment the cigarette felt almost real in Jay's hand. He took a drag, but the smoke smelled of the canal and bonfires burning. He flicked the butt against the concrete floor and watched the sparks fly. He felt slightly dizzy.

"Why don't you lie down for a while?" suggested Joe. "There's a sleeping bag and some blankets—pretty clean anall. You look all-out knackered."

Jay looked doubtfully at the pile of blankets. He felt exhausted. His head ached and his foot hurt and he was beyond confusion. He knew he should be worried. But for the moment he seemed to have lost the ability to question. He lay down painfully on the makeshift bed and pulled the sleeping bag over him. It was warm, clean, comforting. He wondered fleetingly whether this might be a hallucination brought on by hypothermia—some sick adult version of "The Little Match Girl"—and laughed softly to himself. *The Jackapple Man. Pretty funny, hey?* They'd find him in the morning with a red rag in one hand and an empty bottle of wine in the other, frozen and smiling.

"Tha's not goin' to *dee*," said Joe in amused tones.

"Old writers never do," muttered Jay. "They just lose their faculties." He laughed again, rather wildly. The candle guttered and went out—though Jay's mind still insisted he saw the old man *blow* it out. Without it the room was very dark. A single bar of moonlight touched the stone floor. Outside the window, a bird loosed a brief, heartrending warble of music. In the distance, something—cat, owl—screamed. He lay in the dark, listening, for a while. The night was full of noises. Then came a sound from outside the window, like footsteps, and he froze.

"Joe?"

But the old man—or the man conjured up by his imagination—was gone. The sound came again, softly, furtively. *It must be an animal*, Jay told himself. *A dog, maybe, or a fox.* He got up and moved toward the shuttered window.

A figure—a very real, solid figure—was standing behind the shutter.

"*Jesus!*" He took a step backward and his injured ankle gave way, almost spilling him onto the floor. The figure was tall, its bulk exaggerated by the heavy overcoat and cap. He had a brief glimpse of small features beneath the cap's peak, of hair spilling out over the collar, of angry eyes in a pale face. A flash of almost-recognition. Then the moment passed and the woman looking at him from outside the shutter was a complete stranger.

"What the hell are you doing here?" He spoke English automatically, not expecting her to understand. After that night's events he wasn't even certain she was real at all. "And who are you, anyway?"

The woman looked at him. The old shotgun in her hand was not quite pointing at him, but with a tiny movement could be made to do so.

"You are trespassing." Her English was strongly accented but good. "This house is not abandoned. It is private property."

"I know. I . . ." This woman must be some kind of care-taker, Jay told himself. Perhaps she was paid to ensure no damage was done to the buildings. Her presence explained the mysterious sounds, the candles, the sleeping bag, the smell of fresh paint. The rest—the unexpected appearance of Joe, for instance—had been his imagination. He smiled at the woman in relief.

"I'm sorry I shouted at you. I didn't understand. I'm Jay Mackintosh. The agency may have mentioned me."

She looked at him blankly. Her eyes flicked momentarily

behind him, taking in the typewriter, the bottles, the luggage.

"Agency?"

"Yes. I'm the man who bought the house. Over the phone. The day before yesterday." He gave a short, nervous laugh. "On an impulse. The first I've ever had. I couldn't wait for the paperwork. I wanted to see it right away." He laughed again, but there was no returning smile in her eyes.

"You say you *bought* the house?"

He nodded. "I wanted to come over and see it. I couldn't get the keys. Somehow I managed to get stranded here. I hurt my ankle—"

"That is impossible." Her voice was flat. "I would have been told if there had been another buyer."

"I don't think they were expecting me so soon. Look, it's perfectly simple, really. I'm sorry if I startled you. I'm actually very glad you're looking after the building."

The woman looked at him oddly but said nothing.

"I can see they've been fixing the place up a little. I noticed the paint. Did you do it yourself?"

She nodded, her eyes lightless. Behind her the sky was hazy, troubled. Jay found her silence disconcerting. Clearly his story hadn't convinced her.

"Do you—I mean, is there a lot of that kind of work hereabouts? Caretaking, I mean. Renovating old properties."

She shrugged. The gesture might mean anything. Jay had no idea what it was supposed to convey.

"Jay Mackintosh." He smiled again. "I'm a writer."

That look again. Her eyes flicked over him in contempt or curiosity. "Marise d'Api. I work the vineyard across the fields."

"Pleased to meet you." Either shaking hands wasn't a local custom, or her refusal was a deliberate insult.

Not a caretaker, then, Jay told himself. He should have known it at once. That arrogance in her face proved it. This was a woman who tended her own farm, her vines.

"I suppose we'll be neighbors."

Again, no answer. Her face was a blind. No way to tell whether beneath it lay amusement, anger or simple indifference. She turned away. For a second her face turning toward the moonlight was silvered with light and he saw that she was young—no older than twenty-eight or -nine—her features sharp and elfin beneath the big hat. Then she was gone, curiously graceful in spite of her bulky overclothes, her boots kicking a swath through the damp weeds.

"Hey! Wait!" Too late Jay realized that this woman could help him. She would have food, hot water, antiseptic perhaps, for his injured ankle. "Wait a minute! Madame d'Api! Perhaps you could help me!"

If she heard him, she did not reply. For a moment he thought he saw her, outlined briefly against the sky. The sound in the undergrowth might have been that of her passage, or something else altogether.

When he realized she was not coming back, Jay returned to his makeshift bed in the corner of the room and lit a candle. The almost-empty bottle of Joe's wine was standing by the bedside, though Jay was certain he had left it on the table. He must have moved it himself, he thought, during his fugue. By the light of the candle he peeled away his sock to examine the damage to his ankle. It was an ugly slash, the flesh around bruised and swelling. Bishop's leaves, the old man had said, and in spite of himself Jay smiled. Bishop's leaves—the Yorkshire name for water betony—had been a common ingredient for Joe's protection sachets.

But for now the only available antiseptic was the wine.

Jay tilted the bottle and poured a thin stream of yellow

liquid onto the gash. It stung for a minute, releasing its scent of summer and spice, and though he knew it was absurd, such was the power of that scent that Jay felt a little better.

The radio gave a sudden crackle of music and fell silent.

A breeze of other places—a scent of apples, a lullaby of passing trains and distant machinery and the radio playing.

Jay slept, a piece of red flannel still curled tightly into his palm.

But the wine—raspberry red, blackberry blue, rose hip yellow, damson black—stayed awake. Talking.

Twenty-Two

Nether Edge, Summer 1977

A gunshot had announced Zeth's reappearance. Jay would have recognized him instantly even without the rifle crooked into his arm, though in a year he seemed to have grown much taller, his long hair tied back now in a thin ponytail. He was wearing a denim jacket with GRATEFUL DEAD written across the back in pen, and engineer boots. From his hiding place above the canal Jay could not tell if Zeth was alone.

As Jay watched, Zeth raised his rifle and took aim at something just beyond the towpath. Some ducks which had been sitting by the water sprayed upwards. Zeth yelled and fired again. The ducks went crazy. Jay stayed where he was. If Zeth wanted to shoot ducks, he thought, that was his business; he wasn't going to interfere. But as he watched he began to have his doubts. Zeth seemed to be firing, not at the canal, but somewhere beyond. Past the trees and toward the river, though the terrain there was far too open for birds. Rabbits, maybe, thought Jay, though with the noise he was making, surely any animal would have already fled. He narrowed his eyes against the lowering sun, trying to make out what Zeth was doing. The bigger boy fired again, twice, reloaded again. Jay realized that Zeth was standing in almost exactly the same place he himself usually hid to watch—

The gypsies.

Zeth must have been firing at the clothesline strung between the nearest of the caravans, for one end already trailed limply into the grass like a bird's broken wing, flapping half-heartedly in the wind. The dog, tethered in its usual place, set up a strident barking. Jay thought he caught sight of something moving at the window of one of the caravans; a curtain pulled aside briefly, revealing a face—pale, blurry, eyes wide in anger or dismay—before the curtain was yanked back in place. There was no further movement from the caravans, and Zeth laughed again and began to reload. Now Jay could hear what he was shouting.

"Gypp-o-oh! Gypp-o-oh!"

Well, Jay told himself, there was nothing he could do. Even Zeth wouldn't be crazy enough to actually hurt anyone. Firing at a clothesline; that was his style. Trying to frighten people. Making a fair job of it too, he imagined. He thought of himself that first summer, crouching under the lock, and felt heat creep into his face.

Dammit, there was nothing he could do.

The gypsies were safe enough in their caravan. They'd wait it out until Zeth got tired or ran out of ammunition. He'd have to go home sometime. Besides, it was only an air rifle.

You couldn't do any *real* damage with an air rifle, not really. Even if you hit a person.

I mean, what was he supposed to *do*, anyway?

Jay turned to go and let out a yelp of surprise. There was a girl crouching in the bushes not five feet behind him. He had been so absorbed watching Zeth that he hadn't heard her approach at all. She looked about twelve. Under a bramble of red curls her face was small and blotchy, as if her freckles had been stretched out of shape as part of some attempt to save on skin. She was wearing jeans under a white T-shirt so large that the sleeves flapped around her thin arms. In one hand she was carrying a grubby red bandanna which looked to be filled with stones.

Quickly and silently the girl was on her feet. Jay barely had time to react to her presence before she sent a stone whizzing through the air with incredible speed and accuracy to strike against his kneecap with an audible, agonizing crack. He gave another yell and fell over, clutching at his knee. The girl looked at him, a second stone ready in her hand.

"Hey," protested Jay.

"Sorry," said the girl, without putting down the stone.

Jay rolled up the leg of his jeans to inspect the injured knee. A bruise was already rising. He glared at the girl, who returned his gaze with a flat unrepentant look.

"You shouldn't have turned 'round like that," said the girl. "You took me by surprise."

"Took *you*—!" Jay struggled for speech.

The girl shrugged. "I thought you was with him," she said, jerking her small chin fiercely in the direction of the lock. "Using our caravan and poor old Toffee as target practice." Jay rolled his trousers leg back down.

"*Him!* He's no friend of mine," he said indignantly. "He's crazy."

"Oh. Okay." The girl picked up her stone and returned it to the bandanna. Another two rifle shots sounded, followed by that ululating war cry: *"Gypp-o-oh!"* The girl peered down warily through the bushes, then lifted a branch and prepared to slide underneath and down the bank.

"Hey, wait a minute," said Jay.

"What?" The girl barely glanced back. In the shadow of the bush, her eyes were golden, like an owl's.

"What are you doing?"

"What do you think?"

"But I told you already." Jay's anger at her unprovoked attack had been replaced by alarm. "He's crazy. You don't want to have anything to do with him. He'll get tired soon enough and leave you alone."

The girl stared at him with undisguised contempt. " 'Spect that's what *you'd* do?" she demanded.

"Well . . . yes."

She made a sound which might have been amusement or scorn and passed effortlessly under the branch, steadying herself with her free hand as she slid down the bank, braking with her heels when she reached the scree. Jay could see where she was heading. Fifty yards down the slope there was a cutaway which opened out right over the lock. Red shale and loose stones smattered the bank where the hill had been opened. A screen of thin bushes provided cover. A tricky place to reach—if approached fast or carelessly you could ride the scree right off the edge onto the stones below—but it would provide her with a good place to launch her attack. If that was what she was planning. It was hard to believe that she was. Jay peered down the bank again and caught sight of her, much farther down now, barely visible in the undergrowth except for her hair. Let her do it if she wanted, he told himself. It wasn't as if he hadn't warned her.

Sighing, he picked up the coal can with its three-day load and began to scramble down the rocky path behind the girl.

He took the other path to the ashpit—shielded from view most of the way by bushes. In any case, he thought, Zeth wasn't looking. He was too busy shooting and yelling. Easy enough, then, to get across the open expanse of the ashpit and under the concealed lip beyond. It wasn't as good a hiding place as the girl's, but it would have to do, and with two of them against one, even Zeth might have to concede defeat. If it *was* two against one. Jay tried not to think about any friends Zeth might have in the area, maybe just within shouting distance.

He put down the can of coal chunks and settled himself close to the edge of the ashpit. Zeth sounded very close now; Jay could hear his breathing and the *snick*ing sound of his rifle as he broke it to reload. Glancing swiftly over the edge of the ashpit he could see him, the back of his head and a slice of profile, his neck glaring with acne, his flag of greasy hair. Above the lock there was no sign of the girl, and he wondered, in sudden anxiety, whether she had left. Then he saw a flicker of something red above the cutting and a stone zipped out of the bushes, hitting Zeth on the arm. Jay knew a moment's amazement at the accuracy of the girl's aim before Zeth swung around with a roar of pain and surprise. Another stone hit him in the solar plexus, and as he whipped around toward the cutting, Jay threw two chunks of coal at his back. One hit, the other missed, but Jay felt a hot rush of exhilaration as he ducked down again.

"Kill you, you fucker!" Zeth's voice sounded both very close and horrifyingly adult, a teenage troll in disguise. Then the girl fired again, hitting him on the ankle, missing once, then scoring a direct hit on the side of the head with a sound like a pool cue potting the ball.

"You leave us alone, then!" yelled the girl from her aerie above the lock. *"Bloody well leave us alone, you bastard!"*

Now Zeth had seen her. Jay saw him move a little closer to the railway cutting, his rifle in his hand. He could see what Zeth was doing. He would try to move *under* the overhang and out of sight, reload, then jump out firing. He'd be firing blind, but all the same . . .

Jay looked over the edge of the ashpit and took aim. He hit Zeth between the shoulder blades as hard as he could.

"Get lost!" he shouted deliriously, firing another coal chunk over the lip of the pit. "Go pick on someone else!"

But it had been a mistake to show himself so openly. Jay saw Zeth's eyes widen in recognition.

Zeth had changed after all. He'd broadened out, his shoulders fulfilling the promise of his height. He looked fully adult to Jay now, fully grown and ferocious. He smiled and began to move closer to the ashpit, rifle leveled. He kept under the overhang now, so that the girl could not target him. He was grinning. Jay threw another two pieces of coal, but his aim was off target and Zeth kept on coming.

"Get away!"

"Or what?" Zeth was close enough to see clearly into the ashpit now, with one eye on the overhang which shielded him from the girl's attack. His grin looked like a bone sickle. He leveled his rifle with a quizzical, almost a gentle smile. "Or *what*, eh? Or *what*?" Desperately Jay lobbed the remaining chunks of coal at him, but his aim was gone. They bounced off the bigger boy's shoulders like bullets off a tank. Jay looked into the barrel of Zeth's rifle. *It's only an air rifle*, his mind repeated, *only an air rifle, only a sissy pellet gun, it's not as if it were a Colt or a Luger or anything, and anyway he wouldn't dare shoot—*

Zeth's finger tightened on the trigger. There was a click. At this range the gun didn't look prissy at all. It looked deadly.

Suddenly there was a sound from behind him and a flurry of small rocks slid from the bank, scattering down onto Zeth's head and shoulders. He must have stepped out of the shelter of the overhang, Jay realized, into The girl's sights again. Funny, that leap into proper-noun status. He moved back toward the edge of the pit, never taking his eyes off Zeth. His assumption that it was The girl throwing stones from her bandanna had to be wrong; these were not isolated flung stones, but dozens—make that hundreds—of pebbles, shards, gravel chunks, small rocks and the occasional larger one falling down the bank in a cloud of ocher dust. Something had dislodged a part of the overhang and scree was shooting off the edge in gathering rockslide. Above the scar he could see her moving, an oversized T-shirt, no longer very white, topped by a carroty tangle of hair. She was on her hands and knees on the bank, rabbit-kicking at the scree for all she was worth, dislodging chunks of rock and soil and dust which fragmented onto the stones below, pelting Zeth with earth and stones and acrid orange powder. Behind the sound of falling rubble Jay could just hear her fierce voice screaming triumphantly: *"Eat shit, you bastard!"*

Zeth was taken completely off balance by the attack. Dropping his rifle, his first instinct was to take shelter under the bank, but although the overhang protected him from thrown missiles, it did nothing against the rockfall, and he stumbled, choking, right into the thick of the falling scree. He swore, holding his arms protectively above his head, as chunks of rock came suddenly down on top of him. A piece the size of a brick caught him on the bony part of the elbow, and at that, Zeth abruptly lost all interest in the fight. Coughing, choking and blinded by dust, clasping his injured arm to his stomach, he stumbled out from under the overhang. There came a triumphant war cry from above, followed by another avalanche of small rocks, but the battle was already won. Zeth flung a single murderous glance over his shoulder and fled. He ran up the side path until he reached the top, and only then did he stop to howl his defiance.

"Thar fuckin' *dead*, atha listenin'?" His voice rolled off the stones at the canalside. "If I ever see thee again, thar fuckin' *dead*!"

The girl gave a mocking yell from the trees.

Twenty-Three

Lansquenet, March 1999

Jay awoke to a spill of sunshine on his face. There was a strange yellowish quality to the light, something strained and winy, unlike dawn's clear pallor, a giveaway that it was late, but he was still amazed when, looking at his watch, he realized he had slept more than fourteen hours. He recalled being feverish—even delusional—that night, and he anxiously inspected his injured foot for signs of infection, but none were apparent. The swelling had subsided as he slept, and though there was some gaudy bruising as well as an ugly cut on his ankle, there seemed to be less damage than he remembered. The long sleep must have done him good.

He managed to replace the boot. With it on, his foot was sore, but not as much as he had feared. After eating his remaining sandwich (very stale now, but he was ravenous), he picked up his things and picked his way slowly back toward the road. He left his bag and suitcase in the bushes and began the long walk into the village.

It took almost an hour, with many rest stops, to reach Lansquenet. He came up from the river, having found a place to cross where the water ran shallow over some stones, and so he came to the café first. A bright red and white awning shielded a small window, and a couple of metal tables were set out on the pavement. A sign above the door read CAFÉ DES MARAUDS.

Looking up the hill, he could see that the village was not much more than a single main street and a few side roads, a square with a few shops and a church between two rows of linden trees.

Jay went into the café and ordered a *blonde*. The *proprié-taire* behind the bar looked at him curiously, and he realized how he must look to her: unwashed and unshaven, with a grubby T-shirt and smelling of cheap wine. He gave her a smile, but she stared back at him doubtfully.

"My name is Jay Mackintosh," he explained to her. "I'm English."

"Ah, English." The woman smiled and nodded, as if that explained everything. Her face was round and pink and shiny, like a doll's. Jay took a long drink of his beer.

"Joséphine," said the *proprietaire*. "Are you—a tourist?" She sounded as if the prospect amused her.

He shook his head. "Not exactly. I had a few problems getting here last night. I . . . got lost. I had to sleep rough," he explained briefly.

Joséphine looked at him with wary sympathy. Clearly she couldn't imagine getting lost in such a small place as Lansquenet.

"Do you have rooms? For the night?"

She shook her head.

"Is there a hotel, then? Or a *chambre d'hôte?*"

Again, that look of amusement. Jay began to understand
that tourists were not in plentiful supply. Oh, well. It would
have to be Agen.

"Could I use your telephone, then? For a taxi?"

"Taxi?" She laughed aloud at that. "A taxi, on a Sunday
evening?"

Jay pointed out that it was barely six o'clock, but Joséphine
shook her head and laughed again. All the taxis would be on
their way home, she explained. No one would come this far
for a pickup. Village boys often made hoax calls, she explained with a smile. Taxis, takeout pizzas . . . they thought
it was funny.

"Oh." There was the house, of course. His house. He had
already slept there one night, and with the sleeping bag and
the candles he could surely manage another. He could buy
food from the café. He would be able to collect wood and
light a fire in the grate. There were clothes in his suitcase. In
the morning he would change and go to Agen to sign the
papers and get the keys.

"There was a woman, back there where I slept. Madame
d'Api. I think she thought I was trespassing."

Joséphine gave him a quick look. "I suppose she did. But
if the house is yours now . . ."

"I thought she was the caretaker. She was standing guard."
Jay grinned. "To tell the truth, she wasn't very friendly."

Joséphine shook her head. "No. I suppose she wasn't."

"Do you know her?"

"Not really." Mention of Marise d'Api seemed to have
made Joséphine wary. The doubtful look was back on her

face, and she was rubbing at a spot on the countertop with a preoccupied air.

"At least I know she's real now," remarked Jay cheerfully. "At midnight last night I thought I'd seen a ghost. I suppose she does come out in the daytime?"

Joséphine nodded silently, still rubbing the countertop.

Jay was puzzled at her reticence, but was too hungry to pursue the matter.

The bar menu was not extensive, but the *plat du jour*—a generous omelette with salad and fried potatoes—was good. He bought a packet of Gauloises and a spare lighter, then Joséphine gave him a cheese baguette to take back with him, wrapped in waxed paper, along with another three bottles of beer and a bag of apples. He left while it was still light, carrying his purchases in a net bag, and made good time.

He was feeling tired by now, and his abused ankle was beginning to protest, but he dragged the suitcase into the house before he allowed himself to rest. The sun was gone, the sky still pale but beginning to darken, and he gathered some wood from the pile at the back of the house and stacked it into the gaping fireplace. The wood looked freshly cut and had been stored beneath a tarpaper cover to keep it from the rain. Another mystery. He supposed Marise might have cut the wood, but could not see why she might have done so. Certainly she hardly seemed the neighborly type.

He found the empty bottle of elderflower wine in a bin at the back of the house. He didn't remember putting it there, but in the state he'd been in last night he hadn't been thinking rationally, he told himself. The hallucination of Joe—so real he had almost believed it at the time—was proof enough of his state of mind. The single cigarette butt he discovered in the room where he'd spent the night looked old. It might have been there for ten years. He shredded it to the wind and closed the shutters from the inside.

He lit some candles, then made a fire in the grate, using old newspapers he found in a box upstairs to light the wood. Several times the paper flared furiously, then went out, but finally the split logs caught. Jay fed the fire carefully, with a slight feeling of surprise at the pleasure it gave him. There was something primitive in this simple act, something which reminded him of the westerns he'd liked so much as a boy.

He opened his case and put his typewriter on the table next to the bottles of wine, pleased with the effect. He almost felt he might be able to write something tonight, something new. No science fiction—Jonanathan Winesap was on vacation.

He sat at the typewriter. It was a clumsy thing, springy-actioned, hard on the fingers.

He'd kept it out of affectation at first, though it had been years since he had used it regularly. Now the keys felt good beneath his hands and he typed a few lines experimentally, across the ribbon.

It sounded good too. But without paper . . .

The unfinished manuscript he'd brought with him was in an envelope at the bottom of his case. He took it out and reversed the first page to its blank side as he slipped it into the slot. The machine in front of him felt like a car, a tank, a rocket. Around him the room buzzed and fizzled like dark champagne. Beneath his fingers the typewriter keys jumped and snapped. He lost track of time. Of everything.

Twenty-Four

Pog Hill, Summer 1977

The girl's name was Gilly. Jay saw her quite often after that, down at Nether Edge, and they sometimes played together by the canal collecting rubbish and treasures and picking wild spinach or dandelions for the family pot. They weren't really gypsies, Gilly told him scornfully, but *travelers*, people who couldn't stay in one place for long and who despised the capitalist property market. Her mother, Maggie, had lived in a tepee in Wales until Gilly was born, then had decided it was time for a more stable environment for the child. Hence the trailer, an old fish van renovated and refurbished to accommodate two people and a dog.

Gilly had no father. Maggie didn't like men, she explained, because they were the instigators of the Judeo-Christian patriarchal society, hell-bent on the subjugation of women. This kind of talk made Jay a little nervous, and he was always careful to be especially polite to Maggie. But although she sometimes sighed over his gender (rather in the same way one might over a handicapped infant), she never held it against him.

Gilly got on immediately with Joe. Jay introduced them the week after the rock fight, and knew a tiny stab of jealousy at their rapport. Joe knew many of the region's itinerants and had already begun to trade with Maggie, swapping vegetables and preserves for the afghan blankets she knitted from thrift-shop bargains and which Joe used to cover his tender perennials (this said with a chuckle which made Maggie squawk with laughter) on cold nights. She knew a great deal about plants, and both she and Gilly accepted Joe's talismans and perimeter-protection rituals with perfect serenity, as if such things were quite natural to them. As Joe worked in the allotment, Jay and Gilly would help him with his other tasks and he would talk to them or sing along to the radio as they collected seeds into jars or sewed charms into red-flannel bags or fetched old crates from the railway bank in which to store that season's ripening fruit. It was as if Gilly's presence had mellowed Joe somehow. There was something different in the way he spoke to her, something which excluded Jay, not unkindly, but palpably nevertheless. Perhaps because she too was a traveler. Perhaps simply because she was a girl.

Not that Gilly conformed in any way to Jay's expectations. She was fiercely independent, always taking the lead in spite of his seniority, physically reckless, cheerily foul-mouthed to a degree which secretly shocked him, filled with bizarre beliefs and ideologies culled from her mother's diverse store. Space aliens, feminist politics, alternative religions, pendulum power, numerology, environmental issues, all had their place in Maggie's philosophy, and Gilly in turn accepted them all. From her Jay learned about the ozone layer and bread loaves mysteriously shaped like Jesus, or what she called the "New Killer Threat," or shamanism or saving the whales. In her turn she was the ideal audience for his stories. They spent days together, sometimes helping Joe but often simply loafing around by the canal, talking or exploring.

They saw Zeth once more after the rock fight, some distance away by the dump, and were careful to avoid him. Surprisingly enough, Gilly wasn't in the least afraid of him, but Jay was. He hadn't forgotten what Zeth had shouted the day they routed him from the lock, and he would have been perfectly happy never to set eyes on him again.

Obviously, he wasn't going to be that lucky.

Twenty-Five

Lansquenet, March 1999

*E*arly the following morning Jay went to Agen. He had learned from Joséphine that there were only two buses a day, and after a quick coffee and a couple of croissants at the Café des Marauds he had left, eager to collect his paperwork from the agency. It took longer than Jay had expected. Legal completion had taken place the previous day, but electricity and gas had not yet been restored to the house, and the agency was reluctant to hand over the keys without all the documentation from England. And, the woman at the agency told him, there were additional complications. His offer on the farm had been made at a time when another offer was under consideration—had in fact been accepted by the owner, although nothing had yet been made official. Jay's offer—superior to this earlier one by about five thousand pounds—had effectively scratched the previous arrangement, but the person to whom the farm had been promised had called earlier that morning, making trouble, making threats.

"You see, Monsieur Mackintosh," said the agent apologetically, "these small communities—a promise of land—they don't understand that a casual word cannot be said to be legally binding." Jay nodded. "Besides," continued the agent, "the vendor, who lives in Toulouse, is a young man with a family to support. He inherited the farm from his great-uncle. He'd had no real contact with the old man for some time, and has no responsibility for what his great-uncle might have promised before his death."

Jay understood. He left them to sort it out and went shopping for supplies. Then he waited in the café across the road while papers were faxed from London. Frantic phone calls were exchanged. Bank. Solicitor. Agent. Bank.

"And you're sure this person—this previous offer—has no legal right to the property?" he asked as at last the agent handed over the keys. "I mean, I had no idea that anyone else—"

She shook her head. "No, monsieur. The arrangement with Madame d'Api may be of long standing, but she has absolutely no legal right. In fact we only have her word that the old man accepted her offer in the first place."

"D'Api?"

"Yes, Madame Marise d'Api. A neighbor of yours, in fact, with property adjacent to your own. A local businesswoman, by all accounts."

That explained a lot. Her hostility, her surprise at being told that he'd bought the house. Even the fresh paint on the ground floor. She had assumed the house would be hers. She had done what he himself had done: moved in a little early, before completion of the deal. No wonder she had looked so angry! Jay resolved to see her as soon as he could. To explain. To reimburse her, if necessary, for the work she had done on the house. After all, if they were going to be neighbors . . .

It was nearing late afternoon by the time the business was finished. Jay was tired. Hasty negotiations meant that the gas supply had been restored to the house, though he would have to wait another five days for electricity. The agency woman suggested a hotel while the house was made habitable, but he refused. The romance of his derelict, lonely farmhouse was now too much to resist. Besides, there was the question of the new manuscript, the twenty pages written that night on the reverse of the old . . . To leave it for the sterile comfort of a hotel room might kill the idea before it had even begun. Even now as he taxied back to Lansquenet with a cabful of purchases and a head ringing with fatigue, he could feel the drag of those written pages, the urge to continue, to feel the keys of the old typewriter beneath his fingers and to follow the story where it led.

When he got back, the sleeping bag was gone. The candles too, and the box of painting things. Nothing else had been touched. He guessed that Marise must have removed all remaining traces of her illicit occupancy. It was too late to stop by her house tonight, but Jay promised himself he would do so the next day. There was no point being on bad terms with his only close neighbor.

He kindled a fire in the grate and lit the oil lamp—one of the day's purchases—and placed it on the table. He had bought a sleeping bag of his own, and some pillows, as well as a folding camp bed, and with these he managed to make a comfortable enough sleeping area in the inglenook by the fire. As it was still light, he ventured as far as the kitchen. There was a gas stove there, old but functional, and a fire-

place. Above it a blackened cast-iron pot hung, furry with
cobwebs. An ancient enameled range covered half the space
from wall to wall, but the oven was choked with leavings,
coal and half-burned wood and generations of dead insects.
Jay decided not to use it until he could clean it out.

The fire was another matter, though. It lit easily enough
and he managed to heat enough water for a wash and a cup
of coffee, which he took with him on his tour of the house.
This, he found, was even larger than his earlier search had
revealed. Living rooms, dining room, pantries, cupboards as
large as storerooms, storerooms like caverns. Three cellars,
though the darkness down there was too thick for him to
risk the broken steps, stairs leading up into bedrooms, lofts,
granaries. There was furniture there too, much of it spoiled
by rain and neglect, but some of it usable. A long table of
some age-blackened wood, scarred and warped by many years
of use. A dresser of the same rough make, chairs, a footstool.
Polished and restored, he told himself, they would be beautiful, exactly the type of furniture Kerry sighed over in elegant
Kensington antiques shops. Other things had been stored in
boxes in corners all over the house: tableware in an attic, tools
and gardening equipment at the back of a woodshed, a whole
case of linen, miraculously unspoiled, under a box of broken
crockery. He pulled out stiff starched sheets, yellowed at the
creases, each sheet embroidered with an elaborate medallion
in which the letters D.F. twined above a garland of roses; some
woman's trousseau from a hundred—two hundred—years
back. There were other treasures too: sandalwood boxes of
handkerchiefs, copper saucepans dulled with verdigris, an old
radio from before the war, he guessed, its casing cracked to
reveal tubes as big as doorknobs. Best of all was a huge old
spice chest of rough black oak, some of its drawers still labeled
in faded brown ink: *Cannelle, Poivre Rouge, Lavande, Menthe*

Verte. The long-empty compartments were still fragrant with the scents of those spices, some dusted with a residue which colored his fingertips with cinnamon and ginger and paprika and turmeric. It was a lovely thing, fascinating. It deserved better than abandonment. Jay promised himself that when he could, he would have it brought downstairs and cleaned.

Joe would have loved it.

Night fell; reluctantly Jay abandoned his explorations. Before retiring to his camp bed, he inspected his ankle again, surprised and pleased at the speed of his recovery. He barely needed the antiseptic he'd bought. The room was warm, the fire's embers casting hot reflections onto the whitewashed walls. It was still early—no later than eight—but his fatigue had begun to catch up with him and he lay on his camp bed watching the fire and thinking over the next day's plans. Behind the closed shutters he could hear the wind in the orchard, but there was nothing sinister about the sound tonight. Instead it sounded eerily familiar, the wind, the sound of distant water, the night creatures calling and bickering, and beyond that the church clock carrying distantly across the marshes . . . A sudden surge of nostalgia came over him, for Gilly, for Joe, for Nether Edge and that last day on the railway below Pog Hill Lane, for all the things he had never written about in *Jackapple Joe* because they were too mired in disillusion to put into words.

He gave a sleepy, sour croak of laughter. *Jackapple Joe* never even came close to what really happened. It was a fabrication, a dream of what things should have been like, a naïve reenactment of those magical, terrible summers. It gave a meaning to what had remained meaningless. In his book Joe was the bluff, friendly old man who steered him toward adulthood. Jay was the generic apple-pie boy, rosily, artfully ingenuous. His childhood was gilded, his adolescence charmed.

Forgotten, all those times when the old man bored him, troubled him, filled him with rage. Forgotten, the times Jay was sure he was crazy. His disappearance, his betrayal, his lies . . . papered over, tempered with nostalgia. No wonder everyone loved that book. It was the very triumph of deceit, of whimsy over reality, the childhood we all secretly *believe* we had, but which none of us ever did. *Jackapple Joe* was the book Joe himself might have written, the worst kind of lie; half-true, but lying in what really matters. Lying in the heart.

"Tha should 'ave gone back, tha knows," said Joe matter-of-factly. He was sitting on the table next to the typewriter, a mug of tea in one hand. He'd changed the Thin Lizzy T-shirt for one from Pink Floyd's *Animals* tour. "She waited for you, and you never came. She deserved better than that, lad. Even at fifteen, you should have known that."

Jay stared at him. He looked very real. Jay touched his forehead with the back of one hand, but the skin was cool. Jay knew what it was, of course. All that thinking about Joe, his subconscious desire to find him there.

"You never did find out where they went, did you?" asked Joe.

"No, I never did."

Joe seemed to listen, head cocked slightly to one side, the mug held loosely between his fingers. Even though he knew it was a hallucination Jay felt the old, familiar anger lock into place again. Jay could barely remember a time when he was not angry at someone. His parents. His school. Himself. And most of all, there was Joe; Joe, who had vanished one day without warning or reason, leaving only the packet of seeds like something out of a mad fairy tale. A bad vintage, that anger. It had left a part of him forever cold, aloof from the real world, escaping into fictions which grew ever more ambitious in an attempt to compensate for their lack of substance.

_____

It was a division which had grown progressively deeper, the cut-off part of him growing harder and colder and more remote as the years passed. Now he felt as if something had cut right to the heart of that hard place, and the pain was as sharp and astonishing as that of the fox trap he'd stumbled on in the vegetable patch. His voice wavered, sounding suddenly high and furious.

"*You* were the one left *me*, remember? After everything you promised. You left me. You never even said goodbye. You've got no right to judge anyone!"

Joe shrugged, unruffled. "People move on," he said calmly. "People go to find themselves, or lose themselves, whatever. Pick your own *clee-shay*. Anyroad, isn't that what you're doing now?"

"I don't know what I'm doing now," said Jay.

"That Kerry . . ." Joe continued as if he hadn't heard. "She were another one left waitin' for you. You could 'ave had something with her, if only you'd let her be herself. Never were much good at fightin' yer own battles, were you, lad?"

Jay shook his head, as if to shoo away a stinging insect. "This is ridiculous," he muttered. "You're not even here."

"Here? Here?" Joe turned toward him, pushing his cap back from his face in the characteristic gesture Jay remembered. He was grinning, the way he always did when he was about to say something outrageous. "Who's to say where here is, anyroad? Who's to say *you're* here?"

Jay closed his eyes. The old man's afterimage danced briefly on his retina like a moth at a window.

"I always hated it when you talked like that," said Jay slowly.

"Like what?"

"All that mystical stuff."

Joe chuckled. "Philosophy of the Orient, lad. Learned it off of monks in Tibet, that time when I were on the road."

"You never were on the road," Jay muttered. "Nowhere farther than the M1, anyhow."

He fell asleep to the sound of Joe's laughter.

Twenty-Six

Pog Hill, Summer 1977

Joe was in splendid form for the beginning of that last summer. He seemed more youthful than Jay had ever seen him, filled with ideas and projects. He worked on his allotment most days, though with more caution than of old, and they took their tea breaks in the kitchen surrounded by tomato plants. Gilly came over every couple of days, and they would go down into the railway cutting and collect treasures in the usual way, which they would then bring up the bank to Joe's house.

She and her mother had moved away from Monckton Town in May, Gilly explained, when a group of local kids had begun causing trouble at their previous camp.

"Bastards," she said casually, dragging on the cigarette they were sharing. "First it was name-calling. Big fucking deal. Then they kept banging at the doors at night, *then* it was stones at the windows, *then* fireworks under the van. Then they poisoned our old dog, and Maggie said enough was enough."

Gilly had been going to the local school that year. She got along with most people, she said, but with these kids it was different. She was casual enough about the problem, but Jay guessed it must have gotten pretty bad for Maggie to move the trailer so far away.

"The worst of them—the ringleader—was a girl called Glenda," she told him. "She's in the year above me at school. I fought her a couple of times. No one else dares do anything to her because of her brother."

Jay shifted uneasily.

"You know him," said Gilly, taking another drag from the cigarette. "That big bastard with the tattoos."

"Zeth."

"Aye. At least *he's* left school now. I don't see him much, except down by the Edge sometimes, shooting birds." She gave a shrug. "I don't go there often," she added with a touch of defensiveness. "Not really often, anyway. I don't like to."

Nether Edge belonged to this new gang now, Jay gathered. A gang of six or seven, aged twelve to fifteen and led by Zeth's sister. On weekends they would go into the town and dare each other to shoplift small items—usually sweets and cigarettes—from the mini-market, then down to the Edge to hang out or to set off fireworks. Passersby tended to avoid them, fearing abuse or harassment. Even the usual dog walkers avoided the place now.

The news left Jay feeling bereft. After the rock fight he had remained wary of the Edge, always carrying Joe's talisman in his pocket, always on the lookout for trouble. He avoided the canal, the ashpit and the lock, which seemed too risky now. He wasn't going to run into Zeth if he could help it.

But then he realized that *Gilly* wasn't afraid. Not of Zeth, or of Glenda. Her caution was for him, not for herself.

Jay felt a surge of indignation.

"Well, *I'm* not going to stay away," he said hotly. "I'm not afraid of a bunch of little girls. Are you?"

"Of course not!" Her denial confirmed his suspicions. Jay felt a sudden impulse to prove to her that he could hold his own as well as she could—ever since the rock fight in the ashpit he had felt that for natural aggression, she had him at a disadvantage.

"We could go tomorrow," he suggested. "Go to the ashpit and dig up some bottles."

Gilly grinned. In the sunlight her hair glowed almost as brightly as the end of her cigarette. There was a pink stripe of sunburn over her nose. Jay felt a wave of emotion wash over him, so strong that he felt slightly sick. As if something had shifted inside, tuning in to a frequency hitherto unknown and unguessed-at. He felt a sudden, incomprehensible urge to touch her hair.

Gilly looked at him derisively. "You sure you're up for it?" she asked. "You're not *chicken*, are you, Jay?" She pumped her arms and squawked—"*Bwrakka-bwraaak!* Not even a teeny-tiny bit?"

The feeling—that moment of mysterious revelation—had passed. Gilly flicked her cigarette butt into the bushes, still grinning. Jay grabbed at her and mussed her hair to hide his confusion, until she screamed and kicked him in the shin. Normality—at least what passed for normal between them—was resumed.

That night he slept badly, lying awake in the dark thinking of Gilly's hair—that wonderful, gaudy shade between maple leaf and carrot—and the red shale of the scree above the ash-pit, and Zeth's voice whispering *I can wait* and *You're dead*, until at last he had to get up and take out Joe's old red flannel talisman from its usual place in his satchel. He gripped it—worn and shiny with three years of handling—in the palm of his hand, and immediately felt better.

Twenty-Seven

Lansquenet, March 1999

That night was a continuous slide from one dream into another. Maybe it was the air of the place, or the small, disquieting sounds of the old building as it shifted and ticked around him, but it seemed to Jay that he had never dreamed so much, or so vividly. Several times he half-awoke with the certainty that there was someone else in the room with him, and saw Joe sitting by his bedside, smoking and reading his *Culpeper*, before turning over into another dream in which he was standing at the top of Pog Hill cutting, the packet of seeds in his hand. They drifted down into the darkness beneath him, and he was suddenly, sickly certain that it was *Joe* he'd thrown away, that somehow Joe was *in* the seeds, waiting for the right conditions for his return, now lost forever in the rubbish and dereliction of the railbed. Then he was running after the coal train again, with Joe perched on the last truck and throwing out seeds in double handfuls, while the train picked up speed relentlessly toward the place where the track had been taken up. Then he was back at the university, trying to explain to a group of identical students that the only way to humanize a dull character was to give him something to care for, holding out a handful of seeds toward them and saying in Joe's voice, *"They look dead, don't they? Never believe it,"* over and over again, before sliding at last into a dark, uneasy sleep.

When Jay awoke in the morning, Joe was still there. Sitting at the table with his mug of tea, elbows propped up, his cap at an angle, his little half-moon reading glasses perched on the end of his nose. Dusty sunlight came through a knothole in the shutters and gilded one shoulder into almost-invisibility. He was made of the same airy fabric that filled his bottles; Jay could see right through him where the light hit him full on, though he looked solid enough in the shade.

"Morning," said the old man.

"I see what this is," whispered Jay hoarsely. "I'm going crazy."

Joe grinned. "You allus were a bit daft," he said. "Fancy throwin' 'em seeds out over the railway. You were supposed to keep 'em. *Use* 'em. If you 'ad of done, like you were meant to, then none of this would ever 'ave 'appened."

"What do you mean?"

Joe ignored the question. "You know, there's still a good old crop of *Tuberosa rosifea* growin' under that old railway bridge. Probly the only place in the world with such a good crop. You ought to go and see it sometime. Make yerself some wine. See what comes of it."

"Right. Why didn't I see that from the start?" said Jay with sarcasm. "A few bottles of potato wine would have solved all my problems."

Joe shook his head in exasperation. "Them jackapples were *Specials*, I told you. I even wrote it on the packet. I tell you, lad, I put a couple of them *Rosifeas* in every single bottle of wine I ever made. Every bottle I ever made, since I brought 'em back from South America. Took me five years just to get the soil right. I tell you—"

"Don't bother." Jay's voice was harsh. "You never went to South America. I'd be surprised if you ever even made it out of South Yorkshire."

Joe laughed and brought out a packet of Players from his coat pocket.

"Mebbe not, lad," he admitted, lighting one. "But I saw it all the same. Saw all of them places I told you about."

"Course you did."

Joe shook his head sorrowfully. "*Astral* travel, lad. Astral bloody travel, how the bloody else d'you think I'd be able to do it if I was underground half me bloody life?"

He sounded almost angry. Jay eyed the cigarette in his hand with longing. It smelled like burning paper and Bonfire Night.

"I don't believe in astral travel."

"Then how'd you bloody think I got *here*?"

Bonfire Night, licorice, frying grease, smoke and Abba singing "Name of the Game" at Number One all that month. Himself sitting in the empty dorm smoking—not out of pleasure but just because it was against the rules. Not a letter. Not a card. Not even a forwarding address.

"You're *not* here. I don't want to have this conversation."

Joe shrugged. "You allus were a stubborn beggar. Never happy just to take things as they were."

Silence. Jay began to lace his boots.

"Remember them Romanies? That beat the meter at Nether Edge that time?

Jay looked up for a moment. "Yes. I remember."

"D'you ever figure out how they did it?"

Jay shook his head slowly. "Alchemy, you said."

Joe grinned. "*Layman's* alchemy." He lit a Players, looking smug. "Made 'emselves some molds shaped like fifty pences, see? Made 'em out of ice. Lad from t' Council thought them fifties had melted into thin air." He laughed hugely. "But nothin' really disappears, does it?"

Twenty-Eight

Lansquenet, March 1999

The next thing Jay did in Lansquenet was to find a builder's yard. The house needed extensive repairs, and although he could probably manage some of the work himself, most of it would have to be done by professionals. Jay was lucky to find them nearby. He imagined it would have cost a great deal more to have them come over from Agen. The yard was large and sprawling. Wood had been stacked in towers at the back. Window frames and doors propped up the walls. The main warehouse was a converted farm, low-roofed, with a sign above the door which read:

CLAIRMONT—MENUISERIE-PANNEAUX-CONSTRUCTION

Unfinished furniture, fencing, concrete blocks, tiles and slates were piled messily by the door. The builder's name was

Georges Clairmont. He was a short, squat man with a mournful mustache and a white shirt grayed with perspiration. He spoke with the thick accent of the region, but slowly, reflectively, and this allowed Jay to understand his words.

Somehow everyone here knew about Jay already. He supposed Joséphine had spread word. Clairmont's laborers—four men in paint-smattered overalls and caps turned down against the sun—watched with wary curiosity as Jay passed. He caught the word *"Angliche"* in a rapid mutter of patois. Work—money—was limited in the village. Everyone wanted a share in Château Foudouin's renovation. Clairmont flapped his hand in annoyance as four pairs of eyes followed them into the lumberyard.

"Back to work, *hé*, back to *work*!"

Jay caught the eye of one of the laborers—a man with red hair tied back with a bandanna—and grinned. The redhead grinned back, one hand across his face to hide his expression from Clairmont. Jay followed the manager into the building.

The room was large and cool, like a hangar. A small table near the door served as a desk, with papers, files and a telephone-fax machine. Next to the telephone, a bottle of wine and two small glasses. Clairmont poured out two shots and handed one to Jay.

"Thanks." The wine was red-black and rich. It was good, and he said so.

"It should be," said Clairmont. "It was made on your land. The old proprietor—Foudouin—was well-known here once. A good wine maker. Good grapes. Good land." He sipped his wine appreciatively.

"I suppose you'll have to send someone out to see the house," Jay told him.

Clairmont shrugged. "I know the house. Went to see it again last month. Even drew up some estimates." He saw

Jay's surprise and grinned. "She's been working on it since December," he said. "Painting this, plastering that. She was so sure of her agreement with the old man."

"Marise d'Api?"

"Who else, *hé*? But he'd already made a deal with his nephew. A steady income—a hundred thousand francs a year until his death—in exchange for the house and the farm. He was too old to work. Too stubborn to leave the place. No one else wanted it but her. There's no money in farming nowadays, and as for the house itself—*hé*!" Clairmont shrugged expressively. "But with her it's different. She's stubborn. Been eyeing the land for years. Waiting. Fencing it off bit by bit. Serve her right, *hé*!" Clairmont gave his short, percussive laugh. "She'd never give me any work, she said. Rather get a builder in from town than owe money to someone from the village. Do it herself, more likely." He rubbed his fingers together in a speaking gesture. "Close with her savings," he explained shortly, finishing the rest of his wine. "Close with *everything*."

"I expect I'll have to offer her some kind of compensation," said Jay.

"Why?" Clairmont looked amused.

"Well, if she's spent money—"

Clairmont gave a raucous laugh. "Money! More likely to have been robbing the place. Look at your fences. Your hedges. Look how they've been moved. A dozen meters here, half a dozen there. Nibbling at the land like a greedy rat. She was at it for years when she thought the old man wasn't watching. Then, when he died . . ." Clairmont shrugged expressively. "*Hé!* She's poison, Monsieur Mackintosh, a viper. I knew her poor husband, and though he never complained, I couldn't help hearing things. . . ."

That shrug again, both philosophical and businesslike.

"Give her nothing, Monsieur Macintosh. Come to my house this evening and meet my wife. Have dinner. We can discuss your plans for the Foudouin place. It will make a wonderful holiday home, monsieur. With investment anything is possible. The garden can be replanted and landscaped. The orchard restored. A swimming pool, maybe. Paving, like the villas in Juan-les-Pins. Fountains." His eyes gleamed.

Cautiously, Jay spoke. "Well, I hadn't really thought beyond immediate repairs—"

"No, no, but there will be time, *hé?*" He slapped Jay's arm companionably. "My house is off the main square. Rue des Francs Bourgeois. Number four. My wife is longing to meet our new celebrity. It would make her very happy." His grin, part humble, part acquisitive, was oddly infectious. "Take dinner with us. Try my wife's *gésiers farcis*. Caro knows everything there is to know in the village. Get to know Lansquenet."

Jay expected a simple meal. Potluck with the builder and his wife, who would be small and drab in an apron and head scarf, or sweet-faced and rosy like Joséphine at the café, with bright bird's eyes. They would perhaps be shy at first, speaking little, the wife pouring soup into the earthenware bowls, blushing with pleasure at his compliments. There would be homemade terrines and red wine and olives and pimentos in their spiced oils. Later they would tell their neighbors that the new Englishman was *un mec sympathique, pas du tout prétentieux*, and he would be quickly accepted as a member of the community.

The reality was quite different.

The door was opened by a plump, elegant lady, twin-setted and stillettoed in powder blue, who exclaimed as she saw him. Her husband, looking more mournful than ever in a dark suit and tie, waved to him over his wife's shoulder. From inside Jay could hear music and voices, and glimpse an interior of such relentless chintziness that he blinked. In his black jeans and T-shirt under a simple black jacket he felt uncomfortably underdressed.

There were three other guests apart from the Clairmonts. Caroline Clairmont introduced them as she distributed drinks—"our friends Toinette and Lucien Merle, and Jessica Mornay, who owns a fashion shop in Agen,"—simultaneously pressing one cheek against Jay's and a champagne cocktail into his free hand.

"We've been *so* looking forward to meeting you, Monsieur Mackintosh—or may I call you Jay?"

He began to nod, but was swept away into an armchair.

"And of course you *must* call me Caro. It's so wonderful to have someone new in the village—someone with *culture*— I do think culture is so *important*, don't you?"

"Oh, yes," breathed Jessica Mornay, clutching at his arm with red nails. "I mean, Lansquenet is wonderfully unspoilt, but sometimes an educated person simply longs for something *more*. . . . You must tell us about yourself, you're a writer, Georges tells us?"

Jay disengaged his arm and resigned himself to the inevitable. He answered innumerable questions. Was he married? No? But there was someone, surely? Jessica flashed her teeth and drew closer. To distract her, he feigned interest in banalities. The Merles—small and dapper in matching cashmere— were from the north. He was a wine buyer, working for a firm of German importers. Toinette was in some kind of local journalism. Jessica was a pillar of the village drama group— "her Antigone was *exquisite*"—and did Jay write for the theater?

He outlined *Jackapple Joe*—which everyone had heard of

but no one had read—and provoked excited squeals from Caro when he revealed that he had begun a new book. Caro's cooking, like her house, was ornate; he did justice to the *soufflé au champagne* and the *vol-au-vents*, the *gésiers farcis* and the *boeuf en croûte* (secretly longing for the homemade terrine and the olives of his fantasy). He gently discouraged the ever more eager advances of Jessica Mornay. He was moderately witty. He accepted many undeserved compliments on his *français superbe*. After dinner he developed a headache, which he attempted—without success—to dull with alcohol. He found it difficult to concentrate on the increasingly rapid French. Whole segments of conversation passed by like clouds. Fortunately his hostess was garrulous—and self-centered—enough to take his silence for rapt attention.

By the time the meal was over, it was almost midnight. Over coffee and petits fours the headache subsided and Jay was able to grasp the thread of the conversation once more.

Clairmont, his tie pulled away from the collar, his face mottled and sweaty: "Well, all I can say is it's high time *something* happened to put Lansquenet on the map, *hé*? We've got as much going for us as Le Pinot down the road—if we could only get everybody organized."

Caro nodded agreement. Jay could understand her French better than her husband's, whose accent had thickened as his wineglass emptied. She was sitting opposite him on the arm of a chair, legs crossed and cigarette in hand.

"I'm sure that now Jay has joined our little community"— she bared her teeth through her smoke—"I'm *sure* things will begin to progress. The *tone* changes. People begin to develop. God knows I've worked hard enough—for the church, for the theater group. For the literary society. I'm sure Jay would agree to address our little writers' group one day soon?"

He bared his own teeth noncommittally.

"Of *course* you would!" Caro beamed as if Jay had answered aloud. "You're exactly what a village like Lansquenet needs most. A breath of fresh air. You wouldn't want people to think we were keeping you all to *ourselves*, would you?" She laughed, and Jessica exclaimed hungrily. The Merles nudged each other in glee. Jay had the strangest feeling that the lavish dinner had been peripheral, that in spite of the champagne cocktails and iced Sauternes and *foie gras* he was the real main course.

"But why Lansquenet?" It was Jessica, leaning forward, her long blue eyes half-shut against a sheet of cigarette smoke. "Surely you would have been happier in a bigger place—Agen, maybe, or farther south toward Toulouse?"

Jay shook his head. "I'm tired of cities," he said. "I bought this place on impulse—"

"Ah," exclaimed Caro rapturously. "Artistic temperament!"

"—because I wanted somewhere quiet, away from the city." Clairmont shook his head. "*Hé*, it's quiet enough," he said. "Too quiet for us. Property prices rock-bottom, while in Le Pinot only forty kilometers away—"

His wife interrupted to explain that Le Pinot was a village on the Garonne much beloved by foreign tourists. "Georges does a lot of work there, don't you, Georges? He put in a swimming pool for that lovely English couple, and he helped renovate that old house by the church. If only we could generate the same kind of interest in *our* village." Tourists. Swimming pools. Gift shops. Burger bars. Jay's enthusiasm must have shown in his face, because Caro nudged him archly.

"I can see that our Monsieur Mackintosh is a romantic, Jessica! He loves the quaint little roads and the vineyards and the lonely farmhouses. So very English!"

Jay smiled and nodded and agreed that his eccentricity was *tout à fait anglais*.

"But a community like ours, *hé*, it needs to grow." Clairmont was drunk and earnest, his voice thickening so that Jay could hardly follow his words. "We need *investment*. Money. There's no money left in farming. Our farmers make barely enough to keep alive as it is. The work is all in the cities. The young move away. Only the old people and the riffraff stay. The itinerants, the *pieds-noirs*. That's what people don't want to understand. We have to progress or die, *hé*, progress or die."

Caro nodded. "But there are too many people here who can't see the way ahead." She frowned. "They refuse to sell their land for development, even when it's clear they can't win. When the plans were suggested to build the new Inter-marché up the road, they protested for so long that the Inter-marché went to Le Pinot instead. Le Pinot was just like Lansquenet twenty years ago. Now look at it."

Le Pinot was the local success story. A village of three hundred souls put itself on the map thanks to an enterprising couple from Paris who had bought and refurbished a number of old properties to sell as holiday homes. Thanks to a strong pound—and several excellent contacts in London—these were sold or rented to wealthy English tourists, and little by little a tradition had been established. The villagers soon saw the potential in this. Business expanded to serve the new tourist trade. Several cafés opened, soon followed by a couple of bed and breakfasts. Then came a scatter of specialty shops selling luxury goods, a restaurant with a Michelin star, and a small but luxurious hotel with a gym and a swimming pool. Local history was dredged for items of interest, and the wholly unre-markable church was revealed—by a combination of folklore and wishful thinking—to be a site of historical significance. A television adaptation of *Clochemerle* was filmed there, and after that there was no end to the new developments. An Intermarché within easy distance. A riding club. A whole row of holiday chalets along the river. And now, as if that wasn't enough, there were plans for an Aquadome and health spa only five kilometers away, which would bring trade all the way from Agen and beyond.

Caro seemed to take Le Pinot's success as a personal insult. "It could just as easily have been Lansquenet," she complained, taking a petit four. "Our village is at least as good as theirs. Our church is genuine fourteenth-century. We have the ruins of a Roman aqueduct down in Les Marauds. It could have been us. Instead the only visitors we get are the summer farm hands and the gypsies down the river." She bit petulantly at her petit four.

Jessica nodded. "It's the people here," she told him. "They don't have any ambition. They think they can live exactly as their grandfathers did."

Le Pinot, Jay understood, had been so successful that the production of its local vintage, after which the village was named, had ceased altogether.

"Your neighbor is one of those people." Caro's mouth thinned beneath the pink lipstick. "Works half the land between here and Les Marauds, and still barely makes enough from wine making to keep body and soul together. Lives holed up all year 'round in that old house of hers with never a word to anyone. And that poor child holed up with her . . ."

Toinette and Jessica nodded, and Clairmont poured more coffee.

"Child?" Nothing in Jay's brief glimpse of Marise d'Api had led him to imagine her as a mother.

"Yes, a girl. No one ever sees her. She doesn't go to school.

We never see them in church. We tried to suggest that they might''—Caro made a face—''but the torrent of abuse from the mother was quite disgusting.''

The other women made sounds of agreement. Jessica moved a little closer, and Jay could smell perfume.

''She'd be better off with the grandmother,'' said Toinette emphatically. ''At least she'd get the affection she needs. Mireille was absolutely devoted to Tony.'' Tony, explained Caro, had been Marise's husband.

''But she'd never let her have the child,'' said Jessica. ''I think she only keeps her because she knows it galls Mireille. And, of course, we're too far out for anyone to take much notice of what an old woman says.''

''It was *supposed* to have been an accident,'' continued Caro darkly. ''I mean, they *had* to say that, didn't they? Even Mireille played along, because of the funeral. Said his gun exploded when a cartridge got stuck in the chamber. But everyone knows *that woman* drove him to it. Did everything but pull the trigger. I'd believe anything of her. Anything at all.''

The conversation was beginning to make Jay feel uncomfortable. His headache had returned. This was not what he'd expected, he told himself, this genteel spite, this gleeful hint of cruelty behind the prettiness. He hadn't come to Lansquenet for this. His book—if there was ever going to be a book—didn't need this. The ease with which he'd written the first twenty pages on the reverse of the old manuscript proved it. He wanted apple-faced women picking herbs in their gardens. He wanted a French idyll, a *Cider with Rosette*, a lighthearted antidote to Joe.

And yet there was something curiously pervasive about the story itself, about the three women's faces drawn close in identical expressions of vulpine enjoyment, eyes squinched down, mouths lipsticked wide over white well-tended teeth.

It was an old story—not even an original story—and yet it drew him. The feeling—that sense of being yanked forward by an invisible hand in his gut—was not entirely unpleasant.

"Go on," he said.

"She was always at him." Jessica took over the narrative. "Even when they were first married. He was such an easygoing, sweet man. A big man, but I'll swear he was frightened of her. He let her get away with anything. And when the baby was born she just got worse. Never a smile. Never made friends with anyone. And the arguments with Mireille! I'm sure you could hear them right across the village."

"That's what drove him to it in the end."

"Poor Tony."

"She found him in the barn, what was left of him. His head half-blown away by the shot. She put the baby in the crib and rode off to the village on her moped, cool as you like, to fetch help. And at the funeral—when everyone was mourning . . ." Caro shook her head.

"Cold as ice. Not a word or a tear. Wouldn't pay for anything more than the plainest, cheapest funeral. And when Mireille offered to pay for something better—Lord! The fight that caused!"

Mireille, Jay understood, was Marise's mother-in-law. Almost six years later, Mireille, who was seventy-one and suffered from chronic arthritis, had never spoken to her granddaughter or even seen her except from a distance. And Marise reverted to her maiden name after her husband's death. She apparently hated everyone in the village so much that she employed only itinerant labor—and that on the condition that they ate and slept at the farm for the duration of their employment. Inevitably, there were rumors.

"I don't suppose you'll see much of her, anyway," finished

Toinette. "She doesn't talk to anyone. She even rides over into La Percherie to buy her weekly shopping. I imagine she'll leave you well alone."

Jay walked home, despite offers from Jessica and Caro to drive him back. It was almost two, and the night was fresh and quiet. His head felt peculiarly light, and although there was no moon, there was a skyful of stars. As he skirted the main square and moved downhill toward Les Marauds, he became aware, with some surprise, of how dark it really was. The last street lamp stood in front of the Café des Marauds, and at the bottom of the hill the river, the marshes, the little derelict houses teetering haphazardly into the water dipped into shadow so deep that it was almost blindness. But by the time he reached the river, his eyes had adapted to the night. He crossed in the shallows, listening to the *hisssh* of the water against the banks. He found the path across the fields and followed it to the road, where a long avenue of trees stood black against the purple sky. He could hear sounds all around him, night creatures, a distant owl, mostly the sounds of wind and foliage from which vision distracts us.

The cool air had cleared his head of smoke and alcohol and he felt alert and awake. As he walked he found himself going over the last part of the evening's conversation with increasing persistence. There was something about that story, ugly as it was, which attracted him. It was primitive. Visceral. The woman living alone with her secrets, the man dead in the barn, the dark triangle of mother, grandmother, daughter . . . And all around this sweet, harsh land, these vines, orchards, rivers, these whitewashed houses, widows in black head scarves, men in overalls and drooping nicotine-stained mustaches . . .

The smell of thyme was pungent in the air. It grew wild

by the roadside. *Thyme improves the memory*, Joe used to say. He used to make a syrup out of it, keeping it in a bottle in the pantry. Two tablespoonsful every morning before breakfast. That clear greenish liquid smelled exactly like the night air over Lansquenet, crisp and earthy and nostalgic, like a summer day's weeding in the herb garden, and the radio on . . .

Suddenly Jay wanted to be home. His fingers itched. He wanted to feel the typewriter keys under them, to hear the clack-clacking of the old machine in the starry silence. More than anything he wanted to catch that story.

He found Joe waiting for him, stretched out on the camp bed, hands laced behind his head. He had left his boots by the foot of the bed, but he was wearing his old pit helmet cocked at a jaunty angle on his head. A yellow sticker on the front read:

PEOPLE WILL ALWAYS NEED COAL

Jay felt no surprise at seeing him. His anger had disappeared, and instead he felt a kind of comfort. Almost as if he were expecting to see him, the ghostly apparition becoming familiar as he began to anticipate it, becoming . . .

Everyday.

He sat down at the typewriter. The story had him in its hold now and he typed rapidly, his fingers jabbing at the keys. He typed solidly for more than two hours, feeding sheet after sheet of the old, abandoned manuscript into the machine, translating it, reversing it with his own layman's alchemy. This was always how he'd fought back in the old days; his own version of Joe's maps and traveling. He was amazed at how good it felt. Words pranced across the page almost too fast for him to keep pace. From time to time he paused, vaguely conscious of Joe's presence on the bed beside him, though the old man said nothing while he worked. At one point he smelled smoke. Joe had lit a cigarette. At about five in the morning he made coffee in the kitchen, and when he returned to his typewriter he noticed—with a curious feeling of disappointment—that the old man had gone.

Twenty-Nine

Nether Edge, Summer 1977

Jay and Gilly visited the Edge with increasing boldness, but mostly when they were fairly certain no one would be there. There were a couple of clashes with Glenda and her mates, once at the dump, over ownership of an old deep freeze (they won that encounter) and once at the river crossing (one-up to Gilly and Jay). Nothing serious ensued. Name-calling, a few flung stones. Threats and gibes. Gilly and Jay knew Nether Edge better than the others in spite of their out-of-town status. They knew the best hiding places, the shortcuts.

And they had imagination. Glenda and her mates had little but spite and swagger to sustain them. Gilly liked to lay traps. A bent sapling with a taut wire across the base, designed to fly in the face of anyone who tripped it. A paint can of dirty canal water balanced on the precarious door of Glenda's den, which they found easily and raided again and again until it was finally abandoned. They left their signature everywhere. On disused ovens in the dump. On trees. On the walls and doors of a series of dens. Gilly made a slingshot and practiced shooting at discarded cans and jam jars. She was a natural. She never missed. She could break a jar at fifty feet without even trying.

Of course there were a few narrow escapes. Once Glenda and her gang almost cornered Jay near the place where he hid his bike close to the railway bridge. It was getting dark and Gilly had already gone home, but he'd found a stash of last year's coal—maybe as much as a couple of sacks full—in a patch of weeds, and he wanted to move it before anyone else came across it by accident. He was too busy bagging coal chunks to notice the four girls coming out from the other side of the railway, and Glenda was almost on him before he knew it.

Glenda was his own age, but big for a girl, Zeth's narrow features overlaid with a meatiness which squeezed her eyes into crescents and her mouth to a pouty bud. Her slabby cheeks were already covered with acne. It was the first time Jay had seen her so close, and her resemblance to her brother was almost paralyzing. Her friends eyed him warily, fanning out behind Glenda as if to cut off his escape. The bike was ten feet away, hidden in the long grass. Jay began to edge toward it.

"Iz on iz own today," remarked one of the other girls, a skinny blonde with a cigarette butt clamped between her teeth. "Wheer's tha girlfriend?"

Jay moved closer to the bike. Glenda moved with him, skidding down the shingle of the bank toward the road. Pieces of gravel shot out from under her sneakers. She was wearing a cutoff T-shirt and her arms were red with sunburn. With those big fishwife arms she looked troublingly adult. Jay feigned indifference. He would have liked to say something clever, something biting, but the words which would have come so easily in a story refused to cooperate. Instead he scrambled down the bank to where he had hidden the bike and pulled it out of the long grass onto the road.

Glenda gave a crow of rage and began to slide toward him, paddling the shingle with large, spatulate hands. Dust flew.

"I'll fuckin' ave thee, tha bastard," she said, sounding alarmingly like her brother, but she was too busy watching Jay to control her slide, and she overshot the bank with comical suddenness, tipping into the dry ditch at the bottom, where a stand of nettles was just coming into flower. Glenda screamed with rage and chagrin. Jay grinned and straddled his bike. In the ditch Glenda thrashed and struggled, her face in the nettles.

He rode off while Glenda's three friends were hauling her out, but as he reached the top of the street, he stopped and turned. He could see Glenda half-out of the ditch now. Her face was a dark blur of fury. He gave a small, insolent wave.

"I'll ave thee!" Her voice reached him thinly across the space which separated them. *"Mi fuckin' brother'll ave thi anall!"*

Jay waved again and did a wheelie as he turned down the lane and out of sight. He was laughing giddily, his jaw aching with laughter, his ribs tight. The talisman tied to the loop of his jeans fluttered from his hip like a banner. He whoop-whooped all the way down the hill to the village, and his voice whipped past his face, stolen by the wind. He was exhilarated. He felt invulnerable.

But August was drawing to an end, and September loomed.

Thirty

Lansquenet, March 1999

During the week that followed, Jay wrote every night. On Friday the electricity was finally restored, but by then he'd become accustomed to working by the light of the oil lamp. It was friendlier somehow, more atmospheric. The pages of his manuscript formed a tight wedge on the tabletop. He had almost a hundred now.

On Monday, Clairmont arrived with four workmen to make a start on the repairs to the house. They began with the roof, which was missing a great number of tiles. The plumbing too needed attention. In Agen he managed to find a car rental company and rented a five-year-old green Citroën to carry his purchases and to speed up his visits to Lansquenet. He also bought three reams of typing paper and some typewriter ribbons. He worked after dark, when Clairmont and his men had gone home, and the stack of typed pages mounted steadily.

He did not reread the new pages. Fear, perhaps, that the block which afflicted him for so many years might still be waiting. But somehow he didn't think so. Part of it was this place. Its air. The feeling of familiarity in spite of the fact that he was a stranger here. Its closeness to the past. As if Pog Hill Lane had been rebuilt among these orchards and the vines.

On fine mornings he walked into Lansquenet to buy bread. His ankle had healed quickly and completely, leaving only the faintest of scars, and he began to enjoy the walk and to recognize some of the faces he saw along the way. Joséphine told him their names, and sometimes more; as the owner of the village's only café, she was in an excellent position to know everything that happened. For example, the dry-looking old man in the blue beret was Narcisse, a market gardener who supplied the local grocer and the florist's. In spite of his reserve there was wry, hidden humor in his face. Jay knew from Joséphine that he was a friend of the gypsies who came downriver every summer, trading with them and offering them seasonal work in his fields. For years he and a succession of local *curés* battled over his tolerance of the gypsies, but Narcisse was stubborn, and the gypsies stayed. The red-haired man from Clairmont's yard was Michel Roux, from Marseille, a traveler from the river who had stopped for a fortnight five years ago and never left. The woman with the red scarf was Denise Poitou, the baker's wife. The pansy-faced, plump woman in the red sweater was Popotte, the postmistress. The wan-looking fat woman in black, her eyes shaded from the sun by a wide-brimmed hat, was Mireille Faizande, Marise's mother-in-law. Jay tried to catch her eye as she passed the café *terrasse*, but she did not seem to see him.

There were stories behind all of these faces. Joséphine, leaning over the counter with her cup of coffee in one hand, appeared more than willing to tell them. Her early shyness had vanished, and she greeted him with pleasure. Sometimes, when there were not too many customers, they talked. Jay knew very few of the people she mentioned. But this did not seem to discourage Joséphine.

"Do you mean I never told you about old Albert? Or his daughter?" She sounded amazed at his ignorance. "They used to live next door to the bakery—well, what used to be the bakery before it became the *chocolaterie*. Opposite the florist's." At first Jay simply allowed her to talk. He paid little attention, letting names, anecdotes, descriptions wash past him as he sipped his coffee and watched the people go by.

"Didn't I ever tell you about Arnauld and the truffle pig? Or the time when Armande dressed up as the Immaculate Conception and laid in wait for him in the churchyard? Listen . . ."

There were many stories also of her best friend Vianne, who had moved away some years go, and of people long dead whose names meant nothing to him. But Joséphine was persistent. Perhaps she too was lonely. The morning habitués of the café were a silent lot for the most part, many of them old men. Perhaps she welcomed a younger audience. Little by little the ongoing soap opera of Lansquenet-sous-Tannes drew him in.

Jay was aware he was still an oddity here. Some people stared at him in frank curiosity. Some smiled. Most were reserved, politely dour, a nod in greeting and a sidelong glance as he walked past. Most days he called at the Café des Marauds for a blonde or a *café-cassis* on the way back from Poitou's. The walled *terrasse* was small, no more than a wide piece of pavement on the narrow road, but it was a good

place to sit and watch as the village came to life. Just off the
main square, it was a vantage point from which everything
was visible; the long hill leading down toward the marshes,
the screen of trees above the Rue des Francs Bourgeois, the
church tower whose carillon rang out across the fields at seven
every morning, the square pink schoolhouse at the road's fork.
At the bottom of the hill the Tannes was hazed and dimly
gleaming, the fields beyond barely visible. The early sunlight
was very bright, almost crude in comparison, cutting out the
white fronts of the houses against their brown shadow. On
the river a boat was moored, close to the huddle of derelict
houses which overhung the river on their precarious wooden
stilts. From the boat's chimney he could see a scrawl of smoke
and smell frying fish. Between seven and eight o'clock several
people—mostly women—passed by carrying loaves or paper
bags of croissants from Poitou's bakery.

At eight the bells rang for Mass. Jay always recognized the
churchgoers. There was a look of solemn reluctance to their
good spring coats, their polished shoes, their hats and berets,
which defined them. Caro Clairmont was always there with
her husband, he awkward in his tight shoes, she elegant in a
series of silk scarves. She always greeted Jay as she passed,
with an extravagant wave and a cry of, "How's the book?"
Her husband nodded briefly and hurried by, hunched, humble. While Mass was in progress, a number of old men parked
themselves with tired defiance at the *terrasse* of the Café des
Marauds to drink *café-crème* and play chess or talk among
themselves. Jay recognized Narcisse, the market gardener, always in the same place by the door. He carried a tattered
seed catalogue in his coat pocket, which he read in silence, a
cup of coffee at his elbow.

On Sundays Joséphine bought *pains au chocolat* and the

old man always took two, his big brown hands oddly delicate as he lifted the pastry to his mouth. He rarely spoke, contenting himself with a brief nod in the direction of the other customers before settling in his usual place. At eight-thirty the schoolchildren began to pass, incongruous in their anoraks and fleeces, a procession of logos against purple, scarlet, yellow, turquoise, lime-green. They looked at Jay with open curiosity. Some of them laughed and called out their mocking name for Englishmen in cheery derision—*"Rosbif! Rosbif!"*—as they dashed by. There must have been about twenty children of primary-school age in Lansquenet, divided into two classes—the older ones had to take the school bus into Agen, its windows smudged with curious noses and thick with finger graffiti.

During the day Clairmont had been overseeing the repairs to the house. Already the ground floor looked better and the roof was almost completed, though Jay could tell Clairmont was disappointed at his lack of ambition. Clairmont dreamed of conservatories and indoor swimming pools, Jacuzzis and piazzas and landscaped lawns, though he was philosophical enough when Jay told him that he had no ambition to live in a St. Tropez villa.

"Bof, ce que vous aimez, à ce que je comprends, c'est le rustique," he told Jay with a shrug. There was a new kind of speculative look in his eyes, and Jay realized that if he didn't take a hard line with the man he would almost certainly be deluged with unwanted "rustic" objects—broken crockery, milking stools, bad reproduction furniture, walking sticks, cracked tiles and chopping boards and ancient farming utensils—all the unloved and abandoned detritus of loft and cellar—with which he would then be expected to decorate his home. He should have deflated Clairmont on the spot. But

there was something rather touching about the humble and
absurdly hopeful look in the ratty black eyes gleaming above
the drooping mustache which made it impossible.

Sighing, Jay resigned himself to the inevitable.

On Thursday he caught sight of Marise for the first time
since their first brief meeting.

He was coming home after his morning walk, a loaf tucked
under his arm. At the point at which his field backed onto
hers there was a blackthorn hedge, along which a path ran
parallel to the boundary. The hedge was young, three or four
years at the most, the new March growth barely sufficient to
form a screen. Behind it he could see the broken line where
the old hedge had been, an uneven row of stumps and tus-
socks imperfectly hidden by a new furrow. Mentally Jay calcu-
lated the distance. Clairmont had been right. She had moved
the boundary by about fifty feet, probably when the old man
first fell ill.

He looked more closely through the hedge, faintly curious.
The contrast between her side and his was striking. On the
Foudouin side the vines were sprawled and untrimmed, their
new growth barely showing except for a few hard brown buds
on the ends of the tendrils. Hers had been cut back hard,
twelve inches from the ground, in readiness for the summer.
There were no weeds on Marise's side of the hedge, the fur-
rows neat and clean-edged, a path running along each row
wide enough to allow easy passage for the tractor. On Jay's
side the rows had run into each other, the uncut vines clinging
lasciviously to one another across the paths. Gleeful spikes of
ragwort and mint and arnica poked through the tangle. Looking back toward Marise's land, he found that he could just
see the gable end of her farmhouse at the edge of the field,
screened from full view by a stand of poplars. There were
fruit trees there too—the white of apple blossom against bare

branches—and what might be a vegetable garden. A woodpile, a tractor, something else which could only be the barn.

She must have heard the shot from the house. She had put the baby in the crib. Gone out. Taken her time. The image was so vivid that Jay could almost see her doing it, pulling on her boots over thick socks, the oversized jacket around her shoulders—it was winter—the frosty soil crunching under her feet. Her face was impassive, as it had been when they'd met that first morning.

The image haunted him. In this guise Marise had already walked more than once across the pages of his new book; he felt as if he knew her, and yet they had barely spoken. There was something in her which drew him, an irresistible air of secrecy. She was like a woman under siege, hanging on to her land and her life in spite of the disapproval of her neighbors. Perhaps it was that fighting quality that somehow made him think of Joe. Certainly there was no resemblance to Joe in her features. Joe could never have had that bleak, empty face.

It was then that he saw her. Half-turning to go, Jay caught sight of something, a figure moving quickly along the other side of the hedge a few hundred yards from where he was standing. Shielded as he was by the thin screen of bushes, he saw her before she caught sight of him. It was a warm morning and she had shed her bulky outer clothes in favor of jeans and a striped fisherman's sweater. The change of clothing revealed a boyishly slender shape. Her hair had been cut off inexpertly at jaw level—Jay guessed she'd probably done it herself. In that unguarded moment her face was vivid, eager. For a moment Jay barely recognized her. Then her eyes flicked toward him and it was as if a blind had been slammed down, so fast that he was left wondering if he had only imagined her before.

"*Madame . . .*"

For a second she halted, looked at him with a blankness which was almost insolent. Her eyes were green, a curiously light verdigris color. In his book he'd colored them black. Jay smiled and reached out his hand over the hedge in greeting.

"Madame d'Api. I'm sorry if I startled you. I'm—"

But before he could say anything else she had left, turning sharply into the rows of vines without a backward glance.

"Madame d'Api!" he called after her. "Madame!"

She must have heard. And yet she ignored his call. He watched her for a few minutes more as she moved farther and farther away; then, shrugging, he turned toward the house. He told himself that his disappointment was absurd. There was no reason why she should want to talk to him. He was allowing his imagination too much freedom. In the bland light of day she was nothing like the dark woman of his story.

When Jay got home, Clairmont was waiting for him with a truckload of junk. He winked as Jay turned into the drive, pushing his blue beret back from his eyes.

"*Holà*, Monsieur Jay," he called from the cab of his truck. "I've found you some things for your new house!"

Jay sighed. His instincts had been right, and now every few weeks he would be badgered to take off Clairmont's hands a quantity of overpriced *brocante* masquerading as country chic. From what he could see of the truck's contents—broken chairs, sweeping brushes, half-stripped doors, a really hideous papier-mâché dragon head left over from some carnival or other—his suspicions hardly began to cover the dreadful reality.

"Well, I don't know. . . ." he began.

Clairmont grinned. "You'll see. You'll love this," he announced, jumping down from his cab. As he did, Jay saw he was carrying a bottle of wine. "Something to put you in the mood, *hé*? Then we can talk business."

There was no escaping the man's persistence. Jay wanted a bath and silence. Instead there would be an hour's haggling in the kitchen, wine he didn't want to drink, then the problem of how to dispose of Clairmont's objets d'art without hurting his feelings. He resigned himself.

"To business," said Clairmont, pouring two glasses of wine. "Mine and yours." He grinned. "I'm going into antiques, *hé*? There's good money in antiques in Le Pinot and Montauban. Buy cheap now, clean up when the tourists come."

Jay tried the wine, which was good.

"You could build twenty holiday chalets on that vineyard of yours," continued Clairmont cheerily. "Or a hotel. How'd you like the idea of your own hotel, *hé*?"

Jay shook his head. "I like it the way it is," he said.

Clairmont sighed. "You and La Païenne d'Api," he sighed. "Got no vision, either of you. That land's worth a fortune in the right hands. Crazy to keep it as it is, when just a few chalets could—"

Jay struggled with the word and his accent. "La Païenne? 'The godless woman'?" he translated hesitantly.

Clairmont jerked his head in the direction of the other farm.

"Marise Faizande. We used to call her La Parisienne. But the other suits her better, *hé*? Never goes to church. Never had the baby christened. Never talks. Never smiles. Hangs on to that land out of sheer stubborn spite, when anyone else . . ." He shrugged. "*Bof*. It's none of my business, *hé*? But I'd keep the doors locked if I were you, Monsieur Jay. She's crazy. She's had her eye on this land for years. She'd do you an injury if she could."

Jay frowned, remembering the fox traps around the house.

"Nearly broke Mireille's nose once," continued Clairmont. "Just because she went near the little girl. Never came into

the village again after that. Goes into La Percherie on her
motorbike. Seen her going into Agen too."

"Who looks after the daughter?" inquired Jay.

Clairmont shrugged. "No one. I expect she just leaves her."

"I'm surprised the social services haven't—"

"*Bof.* In Lansquenet? They'd have to come all the way over
from Agen or Montauban, maybe even Toulouse. Who'd
bother? Mireille tried. More than once. But she's clever. Put
them off the scent. Mireille would have adopted the child if
she'd been allowed. She's got the money. The family would
have stood by her. But at her age, and with a deaf child on
top of that, I suppose they thought—"

Jay stared at him with increasing interest. "A deaf child?"

Clairmont looked surprised. "Oh, yes. Didn't you know?
Ever since she was tiny. *She's* supposed to know how to look
after her." He shook his head. "That's what keeps her here,
hé? She can't go back to Paris."

"Why?" asked Jay curiously.

"Money," said Clairmont shortly, draining his glass.

"But the farm must be worth something."

"Oh, it is," said Clairmont. "But she doesn't own it. Why
do you think she was so anxious to get the Foudouin place?
It's on a lease. She'll be out the day it expires—unless she
can get it renewed. And there isn't much chance of that after
what's happened."

"Why? Who owns the lease?"

Clairmont drained his glass and licked his lips with satisfaction. "Pierre-Emile Foudouin. The man who sold you your
house. Mireille's great-nephew."

They went out onto the drive then, to inspect Clairmont's
offerings. They were as bad as Jay had feared. But his mind
was on other things. He was intrigued by this new information
about Marise and her daughter, his conviction growing that

there was something more than reserve—or even hostility—behind her silence. His picture of her as a woman under siege intensified, and in spite of her rudeness toward him—even in spite of the fact that she'd pointed a shotgun at him that first night in the house—he felt a sympathy for her, a grudging admiration. Under pressure from all sides, but still she refused to run away. She held fast.

In desperation to get rid of Clairmont, Jay offered him five hundred francs for the whole truckload.

The builder's eyes widened briefly, but he was quickly persuaded. Winking slyly: "An eye for a good bargain, *hé*?" The note disappeared into his rusty palm like a card trick. "And don't worry, *hé*. I can find you plenty more!" He drove off, his exhaust blatting out pink dust from the drive. Jay was left to sort through the wreckage.

Joe's training still held good: Jay still found it hard to throw away what might conceivably be useful. Even as he determined to use the entire truckload for firewood, he found himself looking speculatively over this and that. A glass-paneled door, cracked down the middle, might make a reasonable cold frame. These jars, each turned upside down on a small seedling, would give good protection from late frost. Little by little the oddments Clairmont had brought began to spread themselves around the garden and the field. He even found a place for the carnival head. He carried it carefully to the boundary between his own vineyard and Marise's and set it on top of a fence post, facing toward her farm. Through the dragon's open mouth a long crêpe tongue lolled redly, and its yellow eyes gleamed. Sympathetic magic, Joe would have called it, like putting gargoyles onto a church roof. Jay wondered what La Païenne would make of it.

Thirty-One

Pog Hill, Summer 1977

Jay's memories of that late summer were blurry in a way the previous ones were not. Several factors were to blame. The pale and troubling sky, for one thing, which made him squint and gave him headaches. Joe seemed a little distant, and with Gilly present, they did not have the long discussions they'd had the year before.

And Gilly herself . . . it seemed that as summer drew to a close, Gilly was always at the back of his mind. Jay found himself dwelling upon her more and more. His pleasure at her company was colored by insecurity, jealousy and other feelings he found it difficult to identify. He was in a state of perpetual confusion. He was often close to anger without knowing why. He argued constantly with his mother, who seemed to get more deeply under his skin that summer than ever before—*everything* got under his skin that year—he felt raw, as if every nerve were constantly exposed. Writing was one of the few things which calmed him. The closely written pages—not quite a diary, which were, years later, to grow into *Jackapple Joe*—multiplied almost daily. He liked to think this was his own talisman, his escape from himself, the inner war he waged against the outside world. Joe had his *chatto*; Jay his stories. He wrote furiously until late into the night, sometimes reading the results out loud to Gilly the next day.

Often he and Gilly helped Joe in the allotment, and occasionally Joe would talk to them about his travels and his time in Africa with the Masai or his journeys through the Andes. But to Jay it seemed perfunctory, an afterthought, as if Joe's mind were already on something else. The perimeter ritual too seemed abbreviated, a minute or two at most with a stick of incense and a sachet of herbs. It did not occur to him to question it then, but afterward he realized why.

One day the old man took him into his back room and showed him the seed chest again. It had been over a year since he had last done so, pointing out the thousands of seeds packaged and wrapped and labeled for planting, and in the semidarkness—the windows were still boarded up—the chest looked dusty, abandoned, the paper packages crisp with age, the labels faded.

"It dun't look like owt, does it?" said Joe, drawing his finger through the dust on top of the chest. "I reckon you think it looks dead."

Jay nodded. The room smelled airless and damp, like a place where tomatoes had been grown.

Joe grinned, a little sadly. "Never believe it, lad. Every one of them seeds is a goodun. You could plant 'em right now an they'd go up champion. Like rockets. Every one of 'em." He put his hand on the boy's shoulder. "Just you remember, it's not what things look like that matters. It's what's *inside*. The *'art* of it. Nothing ever really disappears."

But Jay wasn't really listening. He never really listened that summer, too preoccupied by his own thoughts, too sure that what he had would be there forever. He took this wistful little aside of Joe's as just another adult homily; nodding vaguely, feeling hot and bored and choked in the airless dark, wanting to get away.

Thirty-Two

Lansquenet, March 1999

Joe was waiting when he reached the house, looking critically out of the window at the abandoned vegetable plot. "You want to do something with that, lad," he told Jay as he opened the door. "Else it'll be no good this summer. You want to get it dug over and weeded while you've still got time. And them apple trees, anall. You want to check 'em for mistletoe. Bloody kill 'em if you let it."

During the past week Jay had almost become used to the old man's sudden appearances. He had even begun in a strange way to look forward to them, telling himself they were harmless, finding ingenious post-Jungian reasons to explain their persistence. A part of it was loneliness, he told himself. Another was the book—that stranger growing on the reverse of the old manuscript. The process of writing is a little like madness, a kind of possession not altogether benign. Back in the days of *Jackapple Joe* he had talked to himself all the time, striding back and forth in the little Soho bedsit with a glass in one hand, arguing fiercely with himself, with Joe, with Gilly, with Zeth and Glenda, almost expecting to see them there as he looked up from the typewriter, his eyes grainy with exhaustion, his head pounding, the radio playing full blast. It had taken him years to begin writing it, though the story had been clear in his mind since that last year at Pog Hill Lane. When he had finally found the courage to write it down—some of it, at least—for a whole summer he had gone a little insane.

But this book would be different. Easier, in a way. The characters were all around him. They marched effortlessly across the pages: Clairmont the builder, Joséphine the café owner, Michel from Marseille with the red hair and the easy smile. Caro in an Hermès head scarf. Marise. Joe. Marise.

There was no real plot. There were instead a multitude of anecdotes loosely knitted together—some remembered from Joe and relocated to Lansquenet, some recalled by Joséphine over the counter of the Café des Marauds, some put together from scraps. In a way it was very like the story—not quite a diary—he had begun that year at Pog Hill, the story which had finally become *Jackapple Joe*. He liked to think he had caught something of the air, of the light of Lansquenet. Perhaps some of Joséphine's bright, untrained narrative style. Her gossip was never tainted by malice. Her anecdotes were always warm, often amusing. He began to look forward to his visits, enough to feel a dim sense of disappointment on the days Joséphine was too busy to talk. He found himself going to the café every day, even when he had no other excuse to be in the village. He made mental notes.

When he had been in the village for a little under three weeks, he went into Agen and sent the first hundred and fifty pages of the untitled manuscript to Nick Horneli, his agent in London. Nick handled the Jonathan Winesap books as well as the royalties for *Jackapple Joe*, and Jay had always liked him, a wryly humorous man who had the habit of sending little clippings from newspapers and magazines in the hope of generating new inspiration. Jay sent no contact address, but a general delivery number in Agen, and waited for a reply.

To his disappointment, he found that Joséphine would not speak to him about Marise. In the same way there were people she rarely mentioned: the Clairmonts, Mireille Faizande, the Merles. Herself. Whenever he tried to encourage her to talk about these people, she would find work to do in the kitchen. He felt more and more strongly that there were things—secret things—she was reluctant to discuss.

"What about my neighbor? Does she ever come to the café?"

Joséphine picked up a cloth and began to polish the gleaming surface of the bar. "I don't see her. I don't know her very well."

"I've heard she doesn't get along with people from the village."

A shrug. *"Bof."*

"Caro Clairmont seems to know a lot about her."

Again the shrug. "Caro makes it her business to know everything."

"I'm curious."

Flatly: "I'm sorry. I have to go." She faced him for a second, her cheeks flushing. Her arms were folded tightly against her body, the thumbs digging into her ribs in a defensive gesture.

"Monsieur Jay. Some people like to pry into other peoples'

business. God knows there was enough gossip about me once. Some people think they can judge." He was taken aback by her sudden fierceness. Suddenly she was someone else, her face tight and narrowed. It occurred to him that she might be afraid.

———

Later that night, back at the house, he went over their conversation. Joe was sitting in his usual spot on the bed, hands laced behind his neck. The radio was playing quietly. The typewriter keys felt cold and dead under his fingertips. The bright thread of his narrative had finally run out.

"It's no good." He sighed and poured coffee into his half-empty cup. Joe watched him lazily, his cap over his eyes.

"I can't write this book. I'm blocked. It doesn't make sense. It isn't going anywhere." The story, so clear in his mind a few nights before, had receded into almost nothing. His head was swimming with wakefulness.

"You should get to know her," advised Joe. "Forget listening to other people's talk and find out for yourself. Get to know what she's really like."

Jay made an impatient gesture. "How can I do that? She obviously doesn't want to have anything to do with me. Or anyone else, for that matter."

Joe shrugged. "Please yourself. You never did learn how to put yourself out much, did yer?"

"That isn't true! I tried—"

"You could live next door to each other for ten years and neither of you'd make the first move. Too bloody stuck-up, both of yer."

Jay thought about this. Surely Joe was being unfair, he thought. He liked to think of himself as friendly, approachable.

"I'm not the one who's stuck-up," he protested. "I gave her a chance. It isn't my fault if she wouldn't take it."

Joe got up and wandered to the radio. For a moment he fiddled with the dial before finding a clear signal. Somehow Joe had the knack of locating the oldies station wherever he happened to be. Rod Stewart was singing "Tonight's the Night."

"There you go again," observed Joe mildly. "How many chances have people given *you*, eh? How many of 'em do you think you deserved?"

"I don't know what you mean, Joe."

Joe shook his head. "I was allus givin' you chances. You never took 'em, either. Look at what happened with them seeds. You never even gave 'em a try."

"Maybe I didn't want to."

"Happen you didn't."

Joe's voice was growing fainter, his outline fading so that Jay could see the newly whitewashed wall behind him. At the same time the radio crackled harshly, the signal breaking up. A burr of white noise replaced the music.

"Joe?"

The old man's voice was almost too faint to hear. *"I'll sithee, then."*

Thirty-Three

Pog Hill, Summer 1977

*I*t really started with Elvis. Mid-August, that was, and Jay's mother grieved with a vehemence which was almost genuine. Perhaps because they were the same age, he and she. Jay felt it too, even though he'd never been a special fan. That overcast sense of doom, the feeling that things were coming apart at the center, unraveling like a ball of string. There was death in the air that August, a dark edge to the sky, an unidentifiable taste. There were more wasps that summer than he ever remembered before, long, curly, brown wasps which seemed to scent the end coming and turned spiteful early. Jay was stung twelve times—once in the mouth as he swigged a bottle of Coke—and together Gilly and he started a crusade against the wasps that summer.

On hot, moist afternoons when the insects were sleepy and more docile, the two of them went wasping. They would find the nests, stuff the hole with shredded newspaper and matches and flame the whole thing. As the fire took and smoke poured into the nest, the wasps would come flying out, some buzzing and burning like German aircraft in old black and white war movies, darkening the air and *sighing*, an eerie, chill sound as they spread, bewildered and enraged, over the war zone. Gilly and Jay lay quiet in a hollow nearby, far enough away from the danger spot but as close as they dared, watching. Needless to say, this tactic was Gilly's idea. She would squat, eyes wide and bright, as close as she could. No wasp ever stung her. She seemed as immune to them as a honey badger to bees, and as naturally lethal. Jay had been secretly terrified, crouching in the hollows with his head down and pounding with black exhilaration, but the fear was addictive and they sought it time and again, clinging to each other and laughing in terror and excitement.

Once, urged by Gilly, Jay put two Black Cat firecrackers into a nest under a stone wall and lit the fuses. The nest blew apart, but smokelessly, scattering stunned and angry wasps everywhere. One managed to get into the T-shirt he was wearing and stung him again and again. It felt like being shot, and Jay screamed and rolled on the ground. But the wasp was indestructible, twitching and stinging even as he crushed it beneath his frantic body. They killed it at last by tearing off the shirt and dousing it in lighter fluid. Later Jay counted nine separate stings.

Autumn loomed close, smelling of fire.

Thirty-Four

Lansquenet, April 1999

He saw her again the next day. As April ripened, the vines had grown taller and Jay occasionally watched her at work among the plants, dusting with fungicides, inspecting the shoots, the soil. She would not speak to him. She seemed enclosed in a capsule of isolation, profile turned toward the earth. He saw her in a succession of overalls, bulky jumpers, men's shirts, jeans, boots, her hair pulled severely back under her beret. Difficult to even make out her shape beneath them. Even her hands were cartoonish in overlarge gloves. Jay tried to talk to her several times with no success. Once he even stopped by her farm, but there was no answer to his knock, though he was sure he could hear someone behind the door.

"I'd have nothing to do with her," said Caro Clairmont when he mentioned this. "She never talks to anyone in the village. She knows what we all think of her."

They were at the *terrasse* of the Café des Marauds. Caro had taken to joining him there after church while her husband collected cakes from Poitou's. In spite of her exaggerated friendliness there was something unpleasant about Caro, perhaps the willingness to speak ill of others. When Caro was there, Joséphine kept her distance and Narcisse scrutinized his seed catalogue with studied indifference. But she remained one of the few people from the village who seemed happy to answer questions. And she knew all the gossip.

"You should talk to Mireille," she advised, sugaring her coffee extravagantly. One of my dearest friends. Another generation, of course. The things she's had to bear from that woman. You can't imagine." She blotted her lipstick carefully on a napkin before taking the first sip. "I'll have to introduce you one day," she said.

As it happened, no introduction was necessary. Mireille Faizande sought him out by herself a few days later, taking him completely by surprise. It was warm: Jay had begun work on his vegetable garden some days earlier, and now that the major repairs to the house were completed, he was spending a few hours a day in the garden. He hoped somehow that physical exertion might give him the insights he needed to finish his book. The radio was hanging from a nail sticking out of the side of the house, and the oldies station was playing. He had brought out a couple bottles of beer from the kitchen, which he had left in a bucket of water to cool. Stripped to the waist, with an old straw hat he had found in the house to keep the sun from his eyes, he hadn't anticipated visitors. He was hacking at a stubborn root when he noticed her standing there. She must have been waiting for him to look up.

"Oh. I'm sorry." Jay straightened up, surprised. "I didn't see you." She was a large shapeless woman who should have looked motherly, but did not. Huge breasts, hips like boulders, she looked curiously *solid*, the comfortable wadding of fat petrified into something more dense than flesh. Beneath the brim of her straw hat, her mouth turned downward as if in perpetual grief.

"It's a long way out," she said. "I'd forgotten how long." Her local accent was very pronounced, and for a moment Jay barely understood what she was saying. Behind him the radio was playing "Here Comes the Sun" and he could see Joe's shadow just behind her, the light gleaming off the bald patch at his crown.

"Madame Faizande—"

"Let's not be formal, please. Call me Mireille. I'm not disturbing you, *hé?*"

"No. Of course not. I was just about to call it a day, anyhow."

"Oh." Her eyes flicked briefly over the half-finished vegetable patch. "I didn't realize you were a gardener."

Jay laughed. "I'm not. Just an enthusiastic amateur."

"You're not planning on maintaining the vineyard, *hé?*" Her voice was sharp.

He shook his head. "I'm afraid that's probably beyond me."

"Selling it, then?"

"I don't think so."

Mireille nodded. "*Hé*, I thought you might have come to some agreement," she said. "With her." The words were almost toneless. Against the dark fabric of her skirt, her arthritic hands twisted.

"With your daughter-in-law?"

Mireille nodded. "She's always had her eye on this land," she said. "It's higher above the marshes than her place. It's better-drained. It never floods in winter or dries up in summer. It's good land."

Jay looked at her uncertainly. "I know there was a . . . misunderstanding," he said carefully. "I know Marise expected . . . Perhaps if she spoke to me we could arrange—"

"I will top any price she offers you for the land," said Mireille abruptly. "It's bad enough that she has my son's farm, *hé*, without having my father's land too. My father's farm," she repeated in a louder voice, "that should have been my son's, where he should have raised his children. If it hadn't been for her."

Jay switched the radio off and reached for his shirt. "I'm sorry," he said. "I didn't realize there was a family connection."

Mireille's eyes went almost tenderly to the facade of the house. "Don't apologize," she said. "It looks better now than it has in years. New paint, new windows, new shutters. After my mother died, my father let it all go to ruin. Everything but the land. The wine. And when my poor Tony—" She broke off abruptly, her hands twisting. "She wouldn't live in the family house, *hé*, no. Madame wanted her own house, down by the river. Tony converted one of the barns for her. Madame wanted her flower garden, her patio, her sewing room. Every time it seemed as if the house was finished, Madame would think of something else. As if she were stalling for time. And then, at last, he brought her home." Mireille's face twisted. "Home to me."

"She's not from Lansquenet?" That would explain the physical differences. The light eyes, small features, exotic coloring. And her accented but accurate English.

"She was from Paris." Mireille's tone conveyed all her mistrust and resentment of the capital. "Tony met her there on holiday. He was nineteen."

She must not have been more than a few years older, thought Jay. Twenty-three, maybe twenty-four. Why had she married him? This farmer's boy from the country?

Mireille must have read the question in his face. "He looked older than that, Monsieur Jay. And he was handsome, *hé oui*, too much for his own good. An only son. He could have had the farm, the land, everything. His father never refused him a thing. Any girl from the village would have thought herself lucky. But my Tony wanted better. *Deserved* better." She broke off with a shake of the head.

"Enough, *hé*. I didn't come here to talk about Tony. I wanted to know if you were planning to sell the land."

"I'm not," he told her. "I like owning the land, even if I don't have any serious plans for the vineyard. For a start, I enjoy the privacy."

Mireille seemed satisfied. "You would tell me if you changed your mind, *hé*?"

"Of course. Look, you must be hot." Now that she was here, Jay didn't want her to go without asking more about Tony and Marise. "I have some wine in the cellar. Perhaps you'd like to take a glass with me?"

Mireille looked at him for a moment and nodded. "Perhaps a small glass," she said. "If only to be back in my father's house again."

"I hope you'll approve," said Jay, leading her through the doorway.

———

There was nothing of which to disapprove. Jay had left the house much as it was, substituting modern plumbing for the ancient waterworks but keeping the porcelain sinks, the woodstove, the pine cupboards, the scarred old kitchen table as they were. He liked the feeling of age in these things, the way each mark and scar told a story. He liked the worn-shiny flagstones on the floor, which he swept but did not attempt to cover with rugs, and though he cleaned and oiled the wood, he made no attempt to sand away the damage of years. Mireille looked at everything with a critical eye.

"Well?" asked Jay, smiling.

"*Hé*," replied Mireille. "It could have been worse. I expected plastic cupboards and a dishwasher."

"I'll get the wine."

The cellar was dark. The new fixtures had not yet been fitted, and the only lighting was a dim bulb on the end of a frayed cord. Jay reached for a bottle from the short rack by the stairs.

The Specials moved imperceptibly, shifting, snugging, rubbing up against each other like sleeping cats, purring. Rose Hip '74 began to rattle. A rich golden scent of hot sugar and syrup reached his nostrils. Jay mistook it for the last lovely yellow Sauternes from the other side of the river, the perfect wine to loosen an old woman's tongue, and picked up the bottle with a small sound of satisfaction. "I *knew* I had one left."

The label was smeared, and in the dimness he did not try to read it. He carried it up the stairs and into the kitchen, opened, poured. A tiny chuckle emerged from the bottle's throat as the wine filled the glass.

Thirty-Five

"My father used to make the best wine in the region," said Mireille. "When he died, his brother Emile took over the land. After that it should have been Tony's."

"I know. I'm sorry."

She shrugged. "At least when he died it passed back to the male line," she said. "I would have hated to think it went to her, *hé*?"

Jay smiled, embarrassed. There seemed to be something in her which went far beyond grief. Her eyes were flaming with it. Her face was stone. He tried to imagine what it must be like to lose an only son.

"I'm surprised she stayed," he told her. "Afterwards."

Mireille gave a short laugh. "Of course she stayed," she

said harshly. "You don't know her, *hé*? Stayed out of sheer
spite and stubbornness. Knew it was only a matter of time till
my uncle died, then she'd have the estate to herself, just as
she'd always wanted it. But he knew what he was doing, *hé*.
Kept her hanging on, the old dog. Made her think she could
have it cheap." She laughed again.

"But why should she want it? Why not leave the farm and
move back to Paris?"

Mireille shrugged. "Who knows, *hé*? Maybe to spite me."
She sipped curiously at her wine. "What is this?"

"Sauternes. Oh. Damn." Jay couldn't understand how he
had mistaken it. The smudgy handwritten label. The yellow
cord tied around the neck. Rose Hip '74.

"Oh, damn. I'm sorry. I must have picked up the wrong
bottle." He tried his own glass. The taste was incredibly
sweet, the texture syrupy and flecked with particles of
sediment.

He turned to Mireille in dismay. "I'll open another. I do
apologize. I never meant to give you this. I don't know how
I could have mistaken the bottles—"

"It's quite all right." Mireille held on to her glass. "I like
it. It reminds me of something. I'm not sure what. A medicine
Tony took as a child, perhaps." She drank again, and he
caught the honeyed scent of the wine from her glass.

"Please, *madame*. I really—"

Firmly: "I *like* it."

Behind her through the window he could still see Joe under
the apple trees, the sun bright on his orange overalls. Joe
waved as he saw him watching and gave him the thumbs up.
Jay corked the bottle of rose hip wine again and took another
mouthful from his own glass, reluctant somehow to throw it
away. It still tasted terrible, but the scent was pungent and
wonderful, waxy red berries bursting with seeds, splitting their

sides with juice into the pan by the bucketful. He could almost see Joe making the wine in his kitchen with the radio playing full volume—"Kung Fu Fighting" at Number One all that month—pausing occasionally to demonstrate some specious *atemi* learned on his travels through the Orient, and the October sunlight dazzling through the cracked panes. . . .

The wine seemed to have a similar effect on Mireille, though her palate was clearly more receptive to the wine's peculiar flavor. She took the drink in small, curious sips, each time pausing to savor the taste.

Dreamily: "*Hé*, it tastes like . . . rosewater. No, roses. Red roses."

So he was not the only one to experience the special effect of Joe's home-brewed wine. Jay watched the old woman closely as she finished the glass, anxiously scanning her expression for possible ill effects. There were none. On the contrary her face seemed to lose some of its habitual fixed look, and she smiled.

"*Hé*, fancy that. Roses. I had my own rose garden once, you know. Down there by the apple orchard. Don't know what happened to it. Everything went to ruin when my father died. Red roses, they were, with a scent—*hé*! I left when I married Hugues, but I used to go there and pick my roses every Sunday while they were in bloom. Then Hugues and my father died in the same year—but that was the year my Tony was born. A terrible year. But for my dear Tony. The best summer for roses I ever remember. The house was filled with them. Right to the eaves. *Hé*, but this is strong wine. Makes me feel quite dizzy."

Jay looked at her, concerned. "I'll drive you home. You mustn't walk back all that way. Not in this sun."

Mireille shook her head. "I want to walk. I'm not so old that I'm afraid of a few kilometers of road. Besides"—she jerked her head in the direction of the other farm—"I like to see my son's house across the river. If I'm lucky I might catch sight of his daughter. From a distance."

Of course. Jay had almost forgotten there was a child. Certainly he had never seen her, either in the fields or on the way to school.

"My little Rosa. Seven years old. Haven't been close to her since my son died. Not once." Her mouth was beginning to regain its customary sour tuck. Against her skirt her big misshapen hands moved furiously. "*She* knows what that's done to me. She knows. I'd have done anything for my son's child. I could have bought back the farm, *hé*, I could have given them money—God knows I've no one else to give it to." She struggled to stand up, using her hands on the tabletop to hoist her bulk upward.

"But she knows that then she'd have to let me see the child," continued Mireille. "I'd find out what's happening. If they knew how she treated my Rosa—if I could only prove what she's doing . . ."

"Please." Jay steadied her with a hand under her elbow. "Don't upset yourself. I'm sure Marise looks after Rosa as well as she can."

Mireille snapped him a contemptuous look. "What do you know about it, *hé*? Were you there? Were you perhaps hiding behind the barn door when my son died?" Her voice was brittle. Her arm felt like hot brick beneath his fingers.

"I'm sorry. I was only—"

Mireille shook her head with effort. "No, it is I who should apologize. The sun and the strong wine, *hé*? It makes my tongue run wild. And when I think of her my blood boils—*hé*!" She smiled suddenly, and Jay caught an unexpected glimpse of the charm and intelligence beneath the rough exterior. "Forget what I said, Monsieur Jay. And let me invite you

next time. Anyone can point you to my house." Her tone
allowed no refusal.

"I'd be pleased to. You can't imagine how happy I am to
find someone who can bear my dreadful French."

Mireille looked at him closely for a second, then smiled.
"You may be a foreigner, but you have the heart of a French-
man. My father's house is in good hands."

Jay watched her go, picking her way stiffly along the overgrown path toward the boundary until she finally vanished
behind the screen of trees at the end of the orchard. He wondered whether her roses still grew there.

He poured his glass of wine back into the bottle and stop-
pered it once more. He washed the glasses and put away the
gardening tools in the shed. It was only then that he realized
that after days of inactivity, struggling to put together the
fugitive pieces of his unfinished novel, he could see it again.
Bright as ever, like a lost coin shining in the dust.

"I reckon you could start 'em again if you wanted," said Joe,
eyeing the tangled rose hedge. "It's been a while since they
were cut back, and some of 'em have run to wild, but you
could do it, with a bit of work."

Joe had always pretended indifference to flowers. He
preferred fruit trees, herbs and vegetables, things to be
picked and harvested, stored, dried, pickled, bottled, pulped,
made into wine. But there were always flowers in his garden
all the same. Planted as if on an afterthought: dahlias, pop-
pies, lavender, hollyhocks. Roses twined among the tomatoes. Sweet peas among the bean poles. Part of it was
camouflage, of course. Part of it a lure for bees. But the
truth was that Joe liked flowers, and was reluctant even to
pull weeds.

Jay would not have seen the rose garden if he had not

known where to look. The wall against which the roses had once been trained had been partly knocked down, leaving an irregular section of brick about fifteen feet long. Greenery had shot up it, almost reaching the top, creating a dense thicket in which he hardly recognized the roses themselves. With the sheers he clipped a few briars free and revealed a single large red rose almost touching the ground.

"Old rose," remarked Joe, peering closer. "Best kind for cookin'. You should try makin' some rose petal jam. Champion."

Jay wielded the shears again, pulling the clinging tendrils away from the bush. He could see more rosebuds now, tight and green away from the sun. The scent from the open flower was light and earthy.

He had been writing half the night. Mireille's visit the day before had brought enough of the story for ten pages, and it fit easily with the rest, as if it needed only this to carry on. Without this central tale, his book was no more than a collection of anecdotes. With Marise's story to bind them together, it might become a rich, absorbing novel. If only he knew where it was leading.

In London he had gone to the gym to think. Here he made for the garden; garden work cleared his mind. He remembered those summers at Pog Hill Lane, cutting and pruning under Joe's careful supervision, mixing resin for graftings, preparing herbs for the sachets with Joe's big old mortar. It felt right to do that here too; red ribbons on the fruit trees to frighten the birds, sachets of pungent herbs for parasites.

"They'll need feeding, anall," remarked Joe, leaning over the roses. You want to get some of that rose hip wine onto the roots. Do 'em no end of good. Then you'll want summat for them aphids."

Sure enough the plants were infested, the stems sticky with insect life.

Jay grinned at the persistence of Joe's guiding presence. "Perhaps I'll just use a chemical spray," he suggested.

"You bloody won't, though," exclaimed Joe. "Buggerin' everything up with chemicals. That's not what you came here for, is it, anyroad?"

"So what did I come here for?"

Joe winked. "What—or who?" His gaze went to the boundary between the two vineyards.

Jay scrutinized the roses carefully. "I've got my story now," he said. "I'm not making a fool of myself, thank you. If she wants to be a recluse—"

Joe made a disgusted sound. "Tha knows nowt," he said. " 'Asn't tha learnt anythin'?"

"Enough not to be caught out again," Jay told him. "You and your chances. Your talismans. Your travels in the Orient. You really had me going, didn't you? You must have been splitting yourself laughing all the time."

Joe looked at him sternly over his half-moon glasses. "I never laughed," he said. "And if you'd had any sense to look farther than the end o yer nose—"

"Really?" Jay was getting annoyed now, tugging at the loose brambles around the rose bed with unnecessary violence. "Then what did you leave for? Without even saying goodbye? Why did I have to come back to Pog Hill and find the house empty?"

"Oh. Back to that again, are we?"

Joe settled against the apple tree and lit a Players. The radio lying in the long grass began to play "I Feel Love," that August's Number One.

"Cut that out," Jay told him crossly.

Joe shrugged. The radio whined briefly and went off. "If only you'd planted them *Rosifeas*, like I meant you to," said Joe.

"I needed a bit more than a few stupid seeds," retorted Jay.

"You allus was hard work." Joe flipped his cigarette butt neatly over the hedge. "I couldn't tell you I was going because I didn't know myself. I needed to get on the move again, breathe a bit of sea air, see a bit of road. And besides, I thought I'd left you provided for. I thought I'd left *us* provided for. I telled yer, if only you'd planted them seeds—"

Jay had had enough. He turned to face him. For a hallucination Joe was very real, even to the grime under his fingernails. For some reason that enraged him all the more.

"I never asked you to come!" He was shouting. He felt fifteen again, alone in Joe's abandoned cellar with broken bottles and jars all around. "I never asked for your help! I never wanted you here! Why *are* you here, anyway? I don't need *you*, or *her*, or anyone! Why don't you just leave me alone?"

Joe waited patiently for him to finish. " 'Ave you done?" he said when Jay fell silent. " 'Ave you bloody done?"

Jay began to cut away at the rosebushes again, not looking at him. "Get lost, Joe," he said almost inaudibly.

"I bloody might, anall," said Joe. "Think I've not got better things to be doing? Better places to travel to? Think I've got all't time in t'bloody world, do yer?" His accent was thickening, as it always did on the rare occasions Jay saw him annoyed. "There was allus summat missin' with you, lad, back in t'old days, and it dun't look like things 'ave changed much neither. No bloody 'art, that's your problem. Allus 'as been."

Jay turned his back.

"*Reight.*" There was a heavy finality in Joe's voice which made Jay want to turn back, but he did not. "Please thyssen. I'll sithee."

Jay forced himself to work at the bushes for several minutes. He could hear nothing behind him but the singing of birds and the *shlush* of the freshening wind across the fields.

Thirty-Six

Going into Agen the next morning, Jay found a note from his literary agent. In it Nick sounded plaintive and excited, the words underscored heavily to emphasize their importance. *Get in touch with me. It's important.* Jay phoned him from Joséphine's café. There was no phone at the farm, and he had no plans to install one. Nick sounded very faint, like a distant radio station. In the foreground Jay could hear café sounds, the chinking of glasses, shuffle of checkers pieces, laughter, raised voices.

"Jay! Jay, I'm so glad to hear you. The new book's great— I've sent it to half a dozen publishers. It's going crazy here. It's—"

"It isn't finished," Jay pointed out.

"That doesn't matter. It's going to be terrific. Obviously the foreign climate is doing you good. Now what I urgently need is a—"

"Wait." Jay was beginning to feel disoriented. "I'm not ready."

Nick must have heard something in his voice, because he slowed down then. "Hey, take it easy. No one's going to pressure you. No one even knows where you are."

"That's fine by me," Jay told him. "I need some more time on my own. I'm happy here, pottering around the garden, thinking about my book."

He could hear Nick's mind clicking over the possibilities. "Okay. If that's what you want, I'll keep people away. I'll slow things down. What do I tell Kerry? She's been on the phone to me every other day, demanding to know what—"

"You *definitely* don't tell Kerry," Jay told him urgently. "She's the last person I want over here."

"O-ho," said Nick.

"What do you mean?"

"Been doing a bit of *cherchez la femme*, have you?" He sounded amused. "Checking out the talent?"

"No."

"You sure?"

"Positive."

It was true, he thought. He had hardly thought about Marise in weeks. Besides, the woman who first strode out across the pages of his book was a far cry from the recluse across the fields. And it was her story he was interested in.

At Nick's insistence, he gave him Joséphine's number in case he needed to pass an urgent message. Again, Nick asked when he would be able to see the rest of the manuscript. Jay couldn't tell him. He didn't even want to think about it. He already felt uncomfortable that Nick had shown it unfinished without his permission, even though he was only doing his job. He put down the phone to find that Joséphine had already brought over a fresh pot of coffee to his table. Roux and Poitou were sitting there with Popotte. Jay knew a moment's complete disorientation. London had never seemed so far away before.

He came home as usual, across the fields. It had rained during the night and the path was slippery, the hedges dripping. He skirted the road and followed the river to the border of Marise's land, enjoying the silence and the rain-heavy trees. There was no sign of Marise in the vineyard. Jay could see a small blur of smoke above the chimney of the other farm, but that was the only movement. Even the birds were silent. He was planning to cross the river at its narrowest, shallowest point, where Marise's land joined his. On either side there was a swell of banking topped by trees; a screen of fruit trees on her side and a messy tangle of hawthorn and elder on his. He noticed as he passed that the red ribbons he had tied to the branches were gone—blown away by the wind most likely. He would have to find a better way of securing them. The river flattened and shallowed out at that point, and when it rained the water spread out, making islands of the clumps of reeds and digging the red soil of the riverbank to make extravagant shapes, which the sun baked hard as clay when it returned. There were stepping-stones at this crossing place, worn shiny by the river and the passage of many feet, though only he passed here now. At least, so he thought.

But when he reached the crossing place there was a girl squatting precariously by the riverbank, poking a stick at the silent water. At her side a small brown goat stared placidly. The movement he made alerted the child, and she stiffened. Eyes as bright and curious as the goat's fixed on him.

For a moment they stared at each other, she frozen to the

spot, eyes wide, Jay transfixed with an overwhelming sense of déjà vu.

It was Gilly.

She was wearing an orange pullover and green trousers rolled up to her knees. Her discarded shoes lay a short distance away in the grass. A short distance away lay a red rucksack, its mouth gaping. The necklace of knotted red ribbons around her neck solved the mystery of what had been happening to Jay's talismans.

Looking at her more closely, he could see that the curly hair was more chestnut than red, and she was young, surely no more than eight or nine, but all the same the resemblance to Gilly was more than striking. She had the same vivid, freckled face, wide mouth, suspicious green eyes. She had the same way of looking, the same knee cocked out at an angle. Not Gilly, no, but so like her that it caught at the heart. Jay understood that this must be Rosa.

She fixed him with a long unsmiling stare, then grabbed for her shoes and fled. The goat shied nervously and danced across toward Jay, stopping briefly to chew at the straps of the abandoned rucksack. The girl moved as quickly as the goat, using her hands to pull herself up the slippery banking toward the fence.

"Wait!" Jay called after her. She ignored him. Quick as a weasel she was up the bank, only turning then to poke out her tongue at him in mute challenge.

"Wait!" Jay held out his hands to show her he meant no harm. "It's all right."

The girl stared at him—whether in curiosity or hostility, he could not tell—her head slightly to one side as if concentrating. There was no way of knowing whether she had understood.

"Hello, Rosa," said Jay.

The child just stared.

"I'm Jay. I live over there." He pointed to the farm, just visible behind the trees.

She was not looking directly at him, he noticed, but at something slightly to the left and down from where he was standing. Her posture was tense, ready to pounce. Jay felt in his pocket for something to give her—a sweet, perhaps, or a biscuit—but all he could find was his lighter. It was a Bic, made of cheap colored plastic, and it shone in the sun.

"You can have it if you like," he suggested, holding it out across the water. The child did not react. Maybe she couldn't lip-read, he told himself.

The goat bleated and butted gently against his legs. Rosa glanced at him, then at the goat, with a mixture of scorn and anxiety. He noticed her eyes kept moving back to the discarded rucksack, abandoned by the side of the river. He bent down and picked it up. The goat transferred its interest from the sack to the sleeve of Jay's shirt with unnerving rapidity. He held out the rucksack.

"Is this yours?"

On the far bank the girl took a step forward.

"It's all right." Jay spoke slowly, in case she couldn't lip-read, and smiled. "Look. I'll bring it over." He made for the stepping-stones, holding the heavy rucksack in his arms. The goat watched him with a cynical expression. Hampered as he was with the rucksack, his approach was clumsy. He looked up to smile at the girl, lost his footing on a rain-slippery stone, skidded and almost fell. The goat, which was following him curiously across the stones, nudged past unexpectedly, and Jay took a blind step forward, and stepped squarely into the swollen river.

Rosa and the goat watched in silence. Both seemed to be grinning.

"Damn." Jay tried wading back to the bank. There was more current than he had expected, and he moved drunkenly across the river stones, his boots skidding in the mud. The rucksack seemed to be the only dry thing on his person.

Rosa grinned again.

The expression transformed her. It was a curiously sunny, sudden grin, her teeth very white in her dappled face. She laughed almost soundlessly, stamping her bare feet on the grass in a pantomime of mirth. Then she was off again, picking up her shoes and clambering up the incline toward the orchard. The goat followed her, nibbling affectionately at a dangling shoelace. As they reached the top, Rosa turned and waved, though whether this was a gesture of defiance or affection, Jay could not tell.

When she had left he realized he still held her rucksack. On opening it he found inside a number of items only a child could treasure: a jar of snails, some pieces of wood, river stones, string and more of the red talismans, carefully tied together with their ribbons to form a bright garland. Jay replaced all the treasures inside the bag. Then he hung the rucksack up on a gatepost close to the hedge, next to the dragon's head. He was sure Rosa would find it.

―――

"I haven't seen her for months," said Joséphine later in the café. "Marise doesn't send her to school anymore. It's a pity. A little girl like that needs friends."

Jay nodded.

"She used to go to the village play group," remembered Joséphine. "She must have been three, maybe a little younger. She could still talk a little then, but I don't think she could hear anything."

"Oh?" Jay was curious. "I thought she was born deaf."

Joséphine shook her head.

"No. It was some kind of infection. It was the year Tony died. A bad winter. The river flooded again, and half of Marise's fields were underwater for three months. Plus there was that business with the police. . . ."

Jay looked at her inquiringly.

"Oh, yes. Ever since Tony died, Mireille had been trying to pin the blame on Marise. There'd been some kind of a quarrel, she said. Tony would never have killed himself. Tried to make out there was another man or something, that together they'd conspired to murder Tony." She shook her head, frowning. "Mireille was half out of her mind," she said. "I think she would have said anything. Of course, it never came to that. The police came around, asked some questions, went away. I think they had the measure of Mireille by then. But she spent the next three or four years writing letters, campaigning, petitioning. Someone came 'round once or twice, but nothing came of it. Mireille's been spreading rumors that Marise keeps the child locked up in a back room or something."

"I don't think that's true." The vivid, sun-dappled child Jay had seen gave no such impression.

Joséphine shrugged. "No, I don't think so either," she said. "But by that time the damage was done. Gangs of people gathering at the gate of the farm and across the river. Just nosy people, for the most part, harmless enough, but Marise wasn't to know that, holed up in her house with torches burning outside and people letting off firecrackers and throwing stones at the shutters." She shook her head. "By the time things settled down, it was too late," she explained. "She was already convinced everyone was against her. And then when Rosa disappeared . . ."

Joséphine poured a measure of cognac into her coffee.

"I suppose she thought we were all in on it. You can't hide

much in a village, and everybody knew that Mireille had Rosa staying with her. The child was three then, and we all thought they must have come to an agreement and Rosa was there for a visit. Of course, Caro Clairmont knew otherwise, and so did a few others, Joline Drou, who was her best friend at the time, and Cussonnet, the doctor. But the rest of us . . . well. No one asked. People reckoned after what had happened, perhaps they ought to mind their own business. And no one really knew Marise, of course."

"She doesn't make it easy," observed Jay.

"Rosa was missing for about three days. Mireille only tried taking her out of the house once. The first day. That didn't last long. You could hear her screaming right down to Les Marauds. Whatever else was wrong with her, she had a good pair of lungs. Nothing would make her be quiet, not sweets, or presents, or fussing, or shouting. They all tried: Caro, Joline, Toinette. But still the child wouldn't stop screaming. Finally Mireille got worried and called the doctor. They put their heads together and took her to a specialist in Agen. It just wasn't normal for a child that age to scream all the time. They thought she was disturbed, that perhaps she'd been mistreated in some way." She frowned. "Then Marise found out that the doctor and Mireille had taken her to Agen. I've never seen *anyone* so angry. She followed them on her moped, but all she could find out was that Mireille had taken Rosa to some kind of hospital. For tests, she said. I don't know what they were trying to prove."

She shrugged again.

"If she'd been anyone else, she could have counted on help from the village," she said. "But Marise—never says a word unless she has to, never smiles—I suppose people just minded their own business. That's all it was, really, there was no malice in it. She wanted to be left alone, and that's what people

did. Not that anyone really knew where Mireille had taken
Rosa—except maybe Caro Clairmont. Oh, we heard all kinds
of stories. But that was afterward. How Marise stamped into
Cussonnet's surgery with a shotgun and marched him out to
the car. Hear people talking, half of Lansquenet saw that. It's
always the same, *hé*! All I can say is, I wasn't there. And
though Rosa was back at home before the end of that week,
we never saw her in the village again, not in the school or
even at the fireworks display on the fourteenth of July, or
the chocolate festival at Easter." Joséphine drained her coffee
abruptly and wiped her hands on her apron.

"So that was that," she concluded with an air of finality.
"That was the last we saw of Marise and Rosa. I see them
from time to time—perhaps once a month or so—on the road
to Agen or walking to Narcisse's nursery, or in the field across
the river. But that's all. She hasn't forgiven the village for
what happened after Tony's death, or for taking sides, or for
turning a blind eye when Rosa disappeared. You can't tell her
it had nothing to do with you. She won't believe it."

Jay nodded. It was understandable.

"It must be a lonely life for them," he said. Thinking of
Maggie and Gilly, of the way they had always managed to
make friends wherever they went, trading and fixing and doing
odd jobs to make ends meet, always on the move, fielding
insults and prejudice with the same cheery defiance. How
different was this dour, suspicious woman from Joe's friends
of Nether Edge. And yet the child looked so very like Gilly.

He checked for the rucksack on his way back to the farm,
but as he expected, it had already been removed. Only the
dragon's head remained, still lolling its long crêpe tongue, now
embellished with a garland of fluttering red ribbons which sat
jauntily on the thick green mane. Coming closer Jay noticed
that the stump of a clay pipe had been carefully positioned

between the dragon's teeth, from which a dandelion gone to seed protruded. And as he passed, hiding a grin, he was almost sure he saw something move in the hedge next to him, a brief flash of orange under the new green, and heard the impudent bleating of a goat in the distance.

Thirty-Seven

Later, over his favorite *grand crème* in the Café des Marauds, he was listening with half an ear to Joséphine as she told him the story of the village's first chocolate festival and the resistance it had met from the church. The coffee was good, sprinkled with shavings of dark chocolate and with a cinnamon biscuit by the side of the cup. Narcisse was sitting opposite with his usual seed catalogue and a *café-cassis*. In the afternoons the place was busier, but Jay noticed that the clientele still consisted mainly of old men, playing chess or cards and talking in their low rapid patois. In the evening it would be full of workers back from the fields and the farms. He wondered aloud where the young people went at night.

"Not many young people stay here," Joséphine explained.

"There isn't the work, unless you want to go into farming. And most of the farms have been divided so often between all the family's sons that there isn't much of a livelihood left for anyone."

"Always the sons," said Jay. "Never the daughters?"

"There aren't many women who'd want to run a farm in Lansquenet," said Joséphine, shrugging. "And some of the growers and distributors don't like the idea of working for a woman."

Jay gave a short laugh.

Joséphine looked at him. "You don't believe that?"

He shook his head. "It's hard for me to understand," he explained. "In London—"

"This isn't London." Joséphine seemed amused. "People hold close to their traditions here. The church. The family. The land. That's why so many of the young people leave. They want what they read about in their magazines. They want the cities, cars, clubs, shops. But there are always some who stay. And some who come back."

She poured another *grand crème* and smiled. "There was a time when I would have given anything to get out of Lansquenet," she said. "Once I even set off. Packed my bags and left home."

"What happened?"

"I stopped on the way for a cup of hot chocolate." She laughed. "And then I realized I couldn't leave. I'd never really wanted to in the first place." She paused to pick up some empty glasses from a nearby table.

"When you've lived here long enough you'll understand. After a time people find it hard to leave a place like Lansquenet. It isn't just a village. The houses aren't just places to live. Everything belongs to everybody. Everyone belongs to everyone else. Even a single person can make a difference."

He nodded, remembering Pog Hill Lane. The comings and goings. The conversations over the wall. The exchange of recipes, of baskets of fruit and bottles of wine. The constant presence of other people. While Joe was still there, Pog Hill Lane stayed alive. Everything died with his departure. Suddenly he envied Joséphine her life, her friends, her view over Les Marauds. Her memories.

"What about me?" he wondered. "Will I make a difference?"

"Of course."

He hadn't realized he had spoken aloud.

"Everyone knows about you, Jay. Everyone asks me about you. It takes a little time for someone to be accepted here. People need to know if you're going to stay. They don't want to give themselves to someone who won't stay. And some of them are afraid."

"Of what?"

"Change. It may seem ridiculous to you, but most of us like the village the way it is. We don't want to be like Montauban or Le Pinot. We don't want tourists passing through, buying up the houses at high prices and leaving the place dead in the winter. Tourists are like a plague of wasps. They get everywhere. They eat everything. They'd clean us out in a year. There'd be nothing of us left but guest houses and games arcades. Lansquenet—the *real* Lansquenet—would disappear."

She shook her head. "People are watching you, Jay. They see you so friendly with Caro and Georges Clairmont, and they think perhaps you and they . . ." She hesitated. "Then they see Mireille Faizande going to visit you, and they think how perhaps you might be planning to buy the other farm, next year, when the lease expires."

"Marise's farm? Why should I want to do that?" he asked, curious.

"Whoever owns it controls all the land down to the river. The fast road to Toulouse is only a few kilometers away. Easy enough to develop. To build. It's happened before, in other places."

"Not here. Not me." Jay looked at her evenly. "I'm here to write, that's all. To finish my book. That's all I'm interested in."

Joséphine nodded, satisfied. "I know. But you were asking so many questions about her—I thought perhaps—"

"No!" exclaimed Jay.

Narcisse shot him a curious glance from behind his seed catalogue. Lowering his voice quickly, Jay said, "Look. I'm a writer. I'm interested in what goes on. I like stories. That's all."

Joséphine poured herself another coffee and sprinkled hazelnut sugar on the froth.

"It's the truth," insisted Jay. "I'm not here to make any changes. I like the place the way it is."

Joséphine looked at him for a moment, then nodded, seemingly satisfied. "All right, Monsieur Jay," she said, smiling. "I'll tell them you're okay."

They toasted her decision in hazelnut coffee.

Thirty-Eight

Since that time at the stream, Jay had seen Rosa only from a distance. A few times he thought he had caught her watching from behind the hedge, once he was sure he heard quiet footfalls from behind an angle of the house, and, of course, he had seen signs of her presence. The adornment of the dragon head, for instance. The little garlands of flowers and leaves and feathers left on gatepost and fence to replace the red ribbons she had stolen. Once or twice, a drawing (a house, a garden, stick-children playing under purple trees) tacked to a stump, the paper already curling and fading in the sunlight. There was no way of telling whether these things were offerings, toys, or some way of taunting him. She was as elusive as her mother, but curious as her goat, and their meeting must have convinced her that Jay was harmless.

Once, he saw them together. Marise was working behind the hedge. For a time Jay was able to see her face. Again he realized how far this woman differed from the heroine of his book. He had time to notice the fine arch of her brows, the thin but graceful line of her mouth, the sharp angle of cheekbone grazed with color by the sun. Given the right circumstances, she could be beautiful. Not plump and sweet-faced like Popotte, or dark and sensual like the young girls of the village. No, hers was a grave, pale, northern beauty, small-featured beneath the blunt chestnut hair. As he watched, something moved behind her. She sprang to her feet, whipping around as she did, and in that instant he had time to glimpse another transformation. She was quicker than a cat, turning defensively—not toward him, but away. Even her speed did not hide that look. . . .

It lasted less than a second. Rosa leaped at her, crowing, arms outstretched, face split in a wide, delighted grin. A new emotion crossed Marise's features. Jay had imagined the child intimidated, perhaps, by her mother's moods, hiding among the vines as he'd hid from Zeth in the old Nether Edge days, but that look held nothing but adoration. He watched as she climbed Marise like a tree, legs wrapped around her mother's waist, arms locked around her neck. For a moment Marise held her and he saw their profiles close together. Rosa's hands moved softly close to her mother's face, signing in the language of the deaf. Marise snubbed Rosa's nose gently against hers. Her face was illuminated more sweetly than he could ever have imagined. Suddenly he felt ashamed at having believed—or half-believed—Mireille's suggestion that Marise might be mistreating the child. Their love was something which

colored the air between them like sunlight. The interchange
between them was perfect in its silence.

Marise put Rosa down and signed to her. Jay had never
watched anyone signing before, and he was struck by the grace
and animation of the movements, of the facial expressions.
Rosa signed back, insistently. His feeling of intrusion was accentuated. The gestures were too quick for him to guess at
the subject of conversation. They were in their circle of privacy. Their conversation was the most intimate thing Jay had
ever witnessed.

Marise laughed silently, like her daughter. The expression
illuminated her like sunlight through glass. Rosa rubbed her
stomach as she laughed and stamped her feet. They held each
other as they communicated, as if every part of the body were
a part of their talk, as if, instead of losing a sense, they had
gained something more.

Since witnessing that moment, Jay had thought about them
both more often. It had now gone far beyond his intellectual
curiosity for their story, even further than an instinctive feeling of kinship with people who, like him, were regarded as
outsiders. He envied Marise, he realized with some astonishment. He envied the harsh simplicity of her life. Her capacity
for survival.

He realized how unconsciously arrogant he had been when
he first arrived; so quick in his assumptions, so confident in
his intellectual superiority, so ready to accept people merely
as amusing, ready-made characters in his as-yet-unfinished
book. He saw himself as Marise must have seen him: a rich
Englishman playing at farming until the next whim came
along, ignorant of the land's most basic requirements, contemptuous of its people. The thought humbled him. He remembered his arrival at Kirby Monckton that first summer,

and his early, stubborn refusal to see anything of worth there. Maybe Joe had been right, after all.

He began work at Château Foudouin in earnest, systematically restoring the plots by sections, cutting back the straggling vines, stripping mistletoe from trees. For a while his muscles ached from the unaccustomed effort, and there were blisters on his hands, but soon he found that he was actually enjoying the process of rebuilding the farm. While he worked, he watched almost without realizing it for signs of movement over the hedge, but Marise gave no sign either of acknowledgment or curiosity. Sometimes Rosa watched him from afar, though she never responded to his gestures of greeting.

Mireille Faizande was the only person he knew who would talk about Marise interminably. Jay had been to see her several times, though he could not bring himself to mention the intimate scene he witnessed between mother and daughter. When he tried to hint at a warmer relationship between them than she had portrayed, Mireille turned on him in scorn.

"What do you know about it?" she snapped. "How can you possibly know what she's like?" Her eyes went to the fresh vase of roses by the table. There was a framed photograph beside it, showing a laughing boy sitting on a motorbike. Tony.

"She doesn't want Rosa," she said in a lower voice. "Just as she didn't want my son." Her eyes were hard. "She took my son as she takes everything. To spoil. To play with. That's what my Rosa is to her now. Something to play with, to discard when she's had enough." Her hands worked. "It's her fault if the child's deaf," she said. "Tony was perfect. It couldn't have come from his side of the family. She's vicious. She spoils everything she touches."

She glanced again at the photograph by the side of the

vase. "She'd been deceiving him all the time, you know. There was another man all along. A man from the hospital."

Jay remembered someone saying something about a hospital. A nerve clinic in Paris.

"Had Marise been ill?" he inquired.

Mireille made a scornful sound. "Ill? That's what Tony said. Said she needed protecting. My Tony was a rock to her, young as he was. *Hé*, he was strong, clear. He imagined everyone was as honest as he was." She glanced again at the roses. "You've been busy," she commented without warmth. "You've brought my poor rosebushes back from the dead."

The phrase hung between them like smoke.

"I tried to feel sorry for her," went on Mireille. "For Tony's sake. But even then it wasn't easy. She'd hide out in the house, wouldn't talk to anyone, not even to family. Then, for no reason, rages. Terrible rages, screaming and throwing things. Sometimes she'd hurt herself with knives, razors, anything which came to hand. We had to hide everything which could be dangerous."

"How long were they married?"

She shrugged. "Less than a year. He courted her for longer. He was twenty-one when he died."

Her hands moved again, clenching and unclenching. "I can't stop thinking about it," she said finally. "Thinking about both of them. That other man must have followed her from the hospital. Settled somewhere close, where they could meet. *Hé*, I can't stop thinking during all that year when she was married to Tony, when she was carrying his baby, the bitch was laughing at him. Both of them laughing at my boy." She glared at me. "You think about that, *hé*, before you go talking about things you don't understand. You think about what that did to my boy."

"I'm sorry. If you'd prefer not to talk about it—"

Mireille snorted. "It's other people who'd prefer not to talk about it," she said sourly. "Prefer not to think about it, *hé*, prefer to think it's only crazy old Mireille talking, Mireille who's never been the same since her son killed himself. So much easier to mind your own business, to let Marise get on with her life, and never mind that she stole my son and ruined him just because she could, *hé*, the way she's stolen my Rosa." Her voice cracked, then smoothed again, became almost smug in satisfaction.

"But I'll show her," she went on. "Come next year, *hé*, when she needs a roof over her head. When the lease runs out. She'll have to come to me then. If she wants to stay here, *hé*? And she does want to stay." Her face was sly and glossy.

"Why should she?" It seemed that whomever he asked, it came back to this. "Why should she want to stay here? She has no friends. There's no one for her here. If she wants to get away from Lansquenet, how can anyone stop her?"

Mireille laughed, but would not answer.

When Jay visited her again, he found her guarded and un-communicative. He understood that one of them had over-stepped the mark with the other, and he tried to be more cautious in the future, wooing her with roses. She accepted the gifts cheerfully enough, but made no further move to confide in him. He had to be content with what information he had already gleaned.

What fascinated him most about Marise was the conflicting views of her throughout the village. Everyone had an opinion, though no one except Mireille seemed any more informed than the others. To Caro Clairmont, Marise was a miserly recluse. To Mireille, a faithless wife who had deliberately taken advantage of a young man's innocence. To Joséphine, a brave woman raising a child alone. To Narcisse, a shrewd businesswoman with a right to privacy. Roux, who had

worked her *vendanges* every year when he was traveling on
the river, remembered her as a quiet, polite woman who carried her baby in a sling on her back even when she was working in the fields, who brought him a cooler of beer when it
was hot, who paid cash.

"Some people are suspicious of us, *hé*," he said with a grin.
"Travelers on the river, always on the move. They imagine
all kinds of things. They lock up their valuables. They watch
their daughters. Or they try too hard. They smile too often.
They slap you on the back and call you *mon pote*. She wasn't
like that. She always called me *monsieur*. She didn't say much.
It was business between us, man to man."

He shrugged and drained his can of Stella.

Popotte remembered a morning just after the funeral when
Marise had turned up outside Mireille's house with a suitcase
and the baby in a carrier. Popotte had been delivering letters
and arrived at the house just as Marise was knocking at the
door.

"Mireille opened it and fairly dragged Marise inside," she
recalled. "The baby was asleep in the carrier, but the movement woke her and she started to scream. Mireille grabbed
the letters from my hand and slammed the door behind them,
but I could hear their voices even through the door, and the
baby screaming and screaming." She shook her head. "I think
Marise was planning to leave that morning—she looked all
ready and packed to go—but Mireille talked her out of it
somehow. I know that after that she hardly came into the
village at all. Perhaps she was afraid of what people were
saying."

The rumors began soon after. Marise had an uncanny ability to arouse curiosity, hostility, envy, rage, and everyone had
a story. Lucien Merle believed that her refusal to give up the

uncultivated marshland by the river had blocked his plans for redevelopment.

"We could have made something of that land," he repeated bitterly. "There's no future in farming anymore. The future's in tourism." He took a long drink of his *diabolo-menthe* and shook his head. "Look at le Pinot. One man was all it took to begin the change. One man with vision." He sighed. "I bet that man's a millionaire by now," he said mournfully.

Jay tried to sift through what he had heard. In some ways he felt he had gained insights into the mystery of Marise d'Api, but in others he was as ignorant as he had been from the start. None of the reports quite tallied with what he had seen. Marise had too many faces, her substance slipping away like smoke whenever he thought he had captured it. And no one had yet mentioned what he had seen. That fierce look of love for her child. And that moment of fear, the look of a wild animal which will do anything to protect itself and its young.

Thirty-Nine

Pog Hill, Summer 1977

*I*t was late August when everything soured for good. The time of the wasps' nests, Nether Edge, Elvis. Then Jay's father wrote to say that he and Candide were getting married, and for a while the papers were full of them both, snapped getting into a limo on the beachfront at Cannes, at a movie premiere, at a club in the Bahamas, on his yacht. Jay's mother collected these articles with zeal and read and reread them, insatiably scrutinizing Candide's hair, Candide's dresses. His grandparents took this badly, mothering his mother even more than before and treating Jay with cool indifference, as if his father's genes were a time bomb in him.

The gray weather grew hotter, mulchy and dull. There was often rain, but it was warm and unrefreshing. Joe worked cheerlessly in his allotment; the fruit was spoiled that year, rotting on the branches and green from lack of sunlight.

"Might as well not bother, lad," he would mutter, fingering the blackened stem of a pear or apple. "Might as well just bloody jack it in this year."

Gilly's mother did well enough, though; she'd somehow gotten hold of a whole truckload of the transparent bell-shaped umbrellas which were so popular then, and was selling them at a mighty profit on the market. Gilly reckoned they could live right until December on the takings. The thought merely accentuated Jay's sense of doom. It was only days until the end of August, and the return to school was barely a week away. Gilly would leave in the autumn—Maggie was talking about moving south to a commune she'd heard of near Abingdon, and there was no certainty she would ever come back. Jay felt prickly inside, fey one moment and the next blackly paranoid, saying the opposite of what he meant, reading mockery in everything that was said to him. He quarreled with Gilly about nothing. They made up, cautiously and incompletely, circling each other like wary animals, their intimacy broken. A sense of doom colored everything.

On the last day of August he went to Joe's house alone, but the old man seemed distant, preoccupied. Although it was raining, he did not invite Jay in, but stood with him by the door in an oddly formal manner. Jay noticed that he had piled up a number of old crates by the back wall, and his gaze kept moving toward these as if he were eager to get back to some job he had abandoned. Jay felt a sudden surge of anger. He ran from the house with his cheeks flaring. He left his bike close to Joe's—after the incident at the railway bridge, that hiding place was no longer secure—and walked down the abandoned railway track from Pog Hill, cutting down into the Edge and toward the river. He wasn't expecting to see Gilly—

they had made no plans to meet—and yet Jay was unsurprised
when he caught sight of her by the riverbank, hair scrawling
down toward the water, a long stick in one hand. She was on
her knees, poking the stick at something in the water, and he
got quite close to her before she looked up.

Her face was pinkish and mottled, as if she'd been crying.
Jay rejected the thought almost instantly. Gilly never cried.

"Oh, it's you," she said indifferently.

Jay said nothing. He dug his hands into his pockets and
tried a smile, which felt stupid on his face. Gilly didn't
smile back.

"What's that?" He nodded at the thing in the water.

"Nothing." She slung the stick into the current and it
washed away. The water was scummy, brownish. Gilly's hair
was starred with droplets which clung in her curls like burrs.

"Bloody rain."

Jay would have liked to say something then, something
which might have made it all right between them. But the
sky felt heavy over them, and the smell of smoke and doom
was overwhelming. Suddenly Jay was certain he would never
see Gilly again.

"Shall we go and have a look at the dump?" he suggested.
"I thought I saw some good new stuff there on the way down.
Magazines and stuff."

Gilly shrugged. "Nah."

"Good wasping weather." It was a last, desperate ploy. He
had never known Gilly to refuse an offer of wasping. Wasps
were sleepy in wet weather, allowing easier, safer access to
the nest. "Do you want to come and look for nests? I've seen
a place down by the bridge that might have a couple."

Again the shrug. Gilly shook her damp curls.

The silence was longer still this time, spinning out end-
lessly, unraveling.

"Maggie's moving on next week," said Gilly at last. "We're going to some bloody commune in Oxfordshire. She's got a job waiting for her there, she says."

"Oh." He had expected it, of course. This was nothing new. So why, then, did his heart wrench when she said it? Her face was turned toward the water, studiously watching something on the brown surface. Jay's fists clenched in his pockets. As they did he felt something brush against one hand. Joe's talisman. It was smooth with much handling. He had become so accustomed to carrying it with him that he had forgotten it was even there. He squatted next to her. He could smell the river, a sour, metallic smell like pennies soaked in ammonia.

"Are you coming back?" Jay asked.

"Nah." There must have been something interesting on the surface of the water. Her eyes refused to meet his. "Don't think so. Maggie says I need stability now. Don't need all this moving about."

Again that flare of hateful, irrational rage. Jay looked at the water in loathing. Suddenly he wanted to hurt someone— Gilly, himself—and he stood up abruptly.

"*Shit.*" He struggled to find a word which would make her react. His mouth felt numb. His heart too. He kicked viciously at the river's edge and a clod of earth and grass tore free and plunked into the water. Gilly didn't look at him.

He let his temper run freely then, kicking again at the bank so that earth and grass showered into the water. Some of it flew at Gilly too, spattering her jeans and her embroidered shirt.

"Stop it, for crying out loud," said Gilly flatly. "Stop being so childish." It was true, he thought. He *was* being childish, and to hear it from her enraged him. That she should accept their separation with such ease—such indifference. Something yawned blackly inside Jay's head, yawned and grimaced.

"Fuck it, then," he said. "I'm off."

Feeling slightly dizzy, he turned and walked off up the banking toward the canal towpath, sure she'd call him back. Ten paces. Twelve. He reached the towpath, not looking back, knowing she was watching. He passed the trees to a point where she couldn't see him and turned, but Gilly was still sitting where she'd been before. She hadn't looked up, just stared down into the water, hair over her face and the crazy silver scrawl of the rain fanning down from the hot summer sky.

"Fuck it, then," Jay repeated fiercely, wanting her to hear. But she never turned, and at last it was he who turned away and began to walk toward the bridge.

Forty

Lansquenet, May 1999

He had not seen Joe since the day after Mireille's visit. At first he felt relieved by his absence, then as days passed he grew uneasy. He tried to *will* the old man to appear, but Joe remained stubbornly absent, as if his appearances were not a matter of Jay's choosing. His leaving left a strangeness behind. A bereavement. At any moment Jay expected him to be there, in the garden, looking over the vegetable patch, in the kitchen, lifting the lid from a pan to find out what was cooking. He was aware of Joe's absence as he sat at his typewriter, of the Joe-shaped hole in the center of things, of the fact that try as he might he could not seem to get the radio to pick up the oldies station which Joe had found with such ease. Worse, his new book had no life without Joe. He no longer felt like writing. He wanted a drink, but drunkenness merely accentuated that feeling of loss.

Finally, he brought out the last of Joe's rose hip wine. The bottle was dusty from its time in the cellar, the cord at its neck straw-colored with age. Its contents were silent, waiting. Feeling self-conscious but at the same time oddly excited, Jay poured a glassful and raised it to his lips.

"I'm sorry, old man. Friends, okay?"

He waited for Joe to come.

He waited until dark.

In the cellar, laughter.

Forty-One

J oséphine must have spread the word about him at last. Jay found people became more friendly. Many of them greeted him as he passed, and Poitou in the bakery, who had spoken to him only with shopkeeper's politeness before, now asked about his book and gave him advice on what to buy.

"The *pain aux noix* is good today, Monsieur Jay. Try it with goat's cheese and a few olives. Leave the olives and the cheese on a sunny window ledge for an hour before you eat them to release the flavors." He kissed his fingertips. "*That's* something you won't find in London."

Poitou had been a baker in Lansquenet for twenty-five years. He had rheumatism in his fingers, but claimed that handling the dough kept them supple. Jay promised to make

him a grain pack which would help—another trick of Joe's.
Strange, how easily it all came back. With Poitou's approval
came more introductions: Guillaume the ex-schoolteacher;
Darien, who taught the infants' class; Rodolphe, the minibus
driver who took the children to school and brought them
home every day; Nénette, who was a nurse in the nearby old
peoples' home; Briançon, who kept bees at the other side of
Les Marauds. As if they had merely been waiting for the all-
clear to indulge their curiosity. Now they were all questions.
What did Jay do in London? Was he married? No, but surely
someone, *hé*? No? Astonishment. Now that suspicions had
been allayed, they were insatiably curious, broaching the most
personal of topics with the same innocent interest. What was
his last book? How much exactly did an English writer earn?
Had he been on television? Been to America? Sighs of rapture
over the reply.

This information would be eagerly disseminated across the
village over cups of coffee and bottles of *blonde*, whispered in
shops, passed from mouth to mouth and elaborated upon each
time in the telling. Gossip was currency in Lansquenet. More
questions followed, robbed of offense by their ingenuousness.
And I? Am I in your book? And I? And I?

At first Jay hesitated. People don't always respond well to
the idea that they have been observed. But here it was different. Suddenly everyone had a story to tell. *You can put it in
your book*, they told him. Some even wrote them down—on
scraps of notepaper, wrapping paper, once on the back of a
packet of seeds. Many of these people—especially the older
ones—rarely picked up a book themselves. Some, like Narcisse, had difficulty reading at all. But still the respect for
books was immense.

Joe had been the same. With his miner's background came
the belief, from an early age, that reading was a waste of time.

He'd hid his *National Geographic*s under the bed, but had been delighted by the stories Jay read to him, nodding his head as he listened, unsmiling. And though Jay never saw him read more than *Culpeper's Herbal* and the occasional magazine, he would occasionally come out with a quote or a literary reference which could only have come from extensive, if secret, study. Joe liked poetry in the same way he liked flowers, hiding his affection almost shamefacedly beneath a semblance of disinterest.

But his garden had betrayed him. Pansies staring up from the edges of cold frames. Wild roses intertwined with runner beans. Lansquenet was like Joe in this. There was a thick vein of romance running through its practicality.

Jay found that almost overnight he had become someone new to cherish, to shake heads over in bewilderment—the English writer, *dingue mais sympa, hé!*—someone who provoked laughter and awe in equal doses. Lansquenet's holy fool. For the moment he could do no wrong. There were no more cries of *"Rosbif!"* from the schoolchildren.

And the presents. He was overwhelmed with presents. A jar of comb honey from Briançon, with an anecdote about his younger sister and how she once tried to prepare a rabbit (after over an hour in the kitchen she flung it out of the doorway shouting, *Take it back! I can't pluck the damn thing!*) and a note: *You can use it in your book.* A cake from Popotte, carried carefully in her post bag with the letters and balanced in her bicycle basket for the journey. An unexpected gift of seed potatoes from Narcisse, with mumbled instructions to plant them by the sunny side of the house. Jay tried to repay this stream of small kindnesses by buying drinks in the Café des Marauds, but found he still bought fewer rounds than anyone else.

"It's all right," explained Joséphine when he mentioned

this to her. "It's how people are here. They need a little time to get used to you. Then—" She grinned. Jay was carrying a shopping bag filled with gifts which people had left for him under Joséphine's bar—cakes, biscuits, bottles of wine, a cushion cover from Denise Poitou, a terrine from Toinette Arnauld. Joséphine looked at the basket and her grin widened.

There was one main exception to this newfound welcome—Marise d'Api remained as remote as ever. It had been three weeks since he'd last tried to speak to her. He had seen her since, but only from a distance, twice on the tractor and once on foot, always at work in the field. Jay told himself that his feeling of disappointment was absurd. From what he had heard, he could hardly expect Marise to embrace him along with the others.

He had written back to Nick with another thirty pages of the new manuscript. Since then progress had been slower. Part of this had to do with Joe's disappearence. The rest had to do with the garden. There was still a great deal of work to be done there, and now that summer was in sight, the weeds had begun to take over the vineyard. Joe was right. He would need to sort it out while it was still possible. The vegetable plot was looking better now: a square of herbs about twenty feet across, with the remains of a tiny thyme hedge around it. He'd planted three rows each of potatoes, turnips, globe artichokes, carrots and celeriac. He'd seeded marigolds between the rows of potatoes to eliminate beetles, and lemon balm around the carrots for the slugs. But he still needed to consider the winter's vegetables and the summer salads. He went to Narcisse's nursery for seeds and seedlings: sprouting broccoli for September, rocket and *frisée* for July and August. In the cold frame he made from Clairmont's doors he had already seeded some baby vegetables—Little Gem lettuces and fingerling carrots and parsnips—which might be ready in a month or so.

Joe was right; the land here was good. The soil was a rich russet, at the same time moist and lighter than across the river. There were fewer stones too: the ones he found he would sling onto what would become his rock garden. He had almost finished restoring the rose garden. Pinned into place against the old wall, the roses had begun to swell and bud: a cascade of half-opened flowers dripping against the pinkish brick to release their winy scent. They were almost free of aphids now. Joe's old recipe—lavender, lemon balm and cloves stitched into red flannel sachets and tied onto the stems just above the soil—had worked its usual magic.

Every Sunday or so he would pick a bunch of the most open blooms and take them to Mireille Faizande's house in the Place Saint-Antoine after she had returned from Mass.

On the first occasion Mireille looked at the roses for a long time. Lifting them to her face, she breathed the scent. Her arthritic hands, oddly delicate in comparison with the bulky whole, touched the petals gently.

"Thank you." She gave a formal little nod. "My lovely roses. I'll put them into water. Come in, and I'll make some tea."

Her house was clean and airy, with the whitewashed walls and stone floors of the region, but its simplicity was deceptive. An Aubusson rug hung on one wall, and there was a grandfather clock in the corner of the living room for which Kerry would have sold her soul. Mireille saw him looking. "That belonged to my grandmother," she said. "It used to be in my nursery when I was a child. I remember listening to the chimes when I lay awake in bed. It plays a different carillon for the hour, the half and the quarter. Tony loved it." Her mouth tightened, and she turned away to arrange the roses in a bowl. "Tony's daughter would have loved it."

The tea was weak, like flower water. She served it in what must have been her best Limoges, with silver tongs for the sugar and lemon.

"I'm sure she would," said Jay. "If only her mother were a little less reclusive."

Mireille looked at him. Derisively: "Reclusive? *Hé!* She's antisocial, Monsieur Jay. Hates everyone. Her family more than anyone else." She sipped her tea. "I would have helped her if she'd let me. I wanted to bring them both to live with me. Give the child what she needs most. A proper home. A family. But she . . ." She put down the cup. Jay noticed that she never called Marise by name. "She insists upon maintaining the terms of the lease. She insists she will stay until next July, when it expires. Refuses to come to the village. Refuses to talk to me or to my nephew, who offers to help her. And afterwards, *hé?* She plans to buy the land from Pierre-Emile. Why? She wants to be independent, she says. She doesn't want to owe us anything." Mireille's face was a clenched fist. "*Owe* us! She owes me everything. I gave her a home. I gave her *my son!* There's nothing left of him now but the child. And she's even managed to take *her* from us. Only she can talk to her, with that sign language she uses. The girl will never know about her father and how he died. She's even fixed that. Even if I could—" The old woman broke off abruptly.

"Never mind, *hé!*" she said with an effort. "She'll come 'round eventually. She'll have to come 'round. She can't hold out forever. Not when I—" Again she broke off, her teeth snapping together with a small brittle sound.

"I don't see why she should be so hostile," said Jay at last. "The village is such a friendly place. Look how friendly everyone's been to me. If she gave people a chance, I'm sure they'd welcome her. It can't be easy, living on her own. You'd think she'd be pleased to know people were concerned—''

"You don't understand." Mireille's voice was contemptuous. "She knows what sort of welcome she'd get if she ever showed her face here. That's why she stays away. Ever since he brought her here from Paris, it's been the same. She never fit in. Never even tried. Everyone knows what she did, *hé*. I've made sure of that." Her black eyes narrowed in triumph. "Everybody knows how she murdered my son," she said.

Forty-Two

"Well, she exaggerates, you know," said Clairmont peaceably. They were in the Café des Marauds, which was filling up rapidly with its after-work crowd, he in his oil-stained overalls and blue beret, a group of his workers—Roux among them—gathered around a table behind him. The comfortable reek of Gauloises and coffee filled the air. Someone behind them was discussing a recent soccer match. Joséphine was busy microwaving pizza slices.

"Hé, José, un croque, tu veux bien?"

On the counter stood a bowl of boiled eggs and a dish of salt. Clairmont took one and began to peel it carefully.

"I mean, everyone knows she didn't actually *kill* him. But there are plenty of other ways than pulling the trigger, hé?"

"She drove him to it, you mean?"

Clairmont nodded. "He was an easygoing lad. Thought she was perfect. Did everything for her, even after they were married. Wouldn't hear a word spoken against her. Said she was highly strung and delicate. Well, maybe she was, *hé?*" He helped himself to salt from the dish. "The way he was with her, you'd have thought she was glass. She'd just come out of one of those hospitals, he said. But anyone dared say anything about her . . ." He shrugged. "Killed himself trying to please her, poor Tony. Worked himself half to death for her, then shot himself when she tried to leave him." He bit into his egg with melancholy gusto.

"Oh, yes, she was going to leave," he added, seeing Jay's surprise. "Had her bags all packed and ready. Mireille saw them. There'd been some argument," he explained, finishing the egg and gesturing to Joséphine for a second *blonde*. "There was always some kind of a fight going on in that place. But this time it really looked as if she was going to go through with it. Mireille—"

"What is it?" Joséphine was carrying a tray of microwaved pizzas, and looked flushed and tired.

"Two Stellas, José."

Joséphine handed him the bottles, which he opened using the bottle opener fixed into the bar. She gave him a narrow look before moving on with the pizzas.

"Well, anyway, that was that," finished Clairmont, pouring the beers. "They made out it was an accident, *hé*, as you would. But everyone knows that crazy wife of his was behind it." He grinned. "The funny thing was that she didn't get a penny from his will. She's at the mercy of the family. It was a seven-year lease, they can't do anything about that, but when it runs out—*hé!*" He shrugged expressively. "Then she'll be gone, and good riddance to her."

"Unless she buys the farm herself," said Jay. "Mireille said she might try."

Clairmont's face darkened for a moment. "I'd bid against her myself if I could afford it," he declared, draining his glass. "That's good building land. I could build a dozen holiday chalets on that old vineyard. Pierre-Emile's an idiot if he lets it go to her." He shook his head. "All we need is a bit of luck, and land prices in Lansquenet could rocket. Look at Le Pinot. That land could make a fortune if you developed it properly. But you'd never see her doing that. Wouldn't even give up the marshland by the river when they were thinking about widening the road. Blocked the plan out of sheer meanness." He shook his head.

"But things are on the up now, *hé?*" His good humor was already restored, his grin oddly at variance with his mournful mustache. "In a year—maybe two—we could make Le Pinot look like a Marseille *bidonville.* Now that things are beginning to change." Once again he gave his humble, eager grin. Then he tapped the rim of his glass against Jay's and winked. *"Santé!"*

Forty-Three

*I*t had been four weeks now since his last sighting of Joe, but he still felt as if the old man might reappear at any moment. The red flannel sachets were in place in the vegetable garden and at the corners of the house. The trees at the land's boundary were similarly adorned, though the wind kept stripping them. Marigolds, propagated in the homemade cold frame, were beginning to open their bright petals among Narcisse's seed potatoes. Poitou baked a special *couronne* loaf in thanks for Jay's grain pack, which, he claimed, had given him more relief than any drug. Of course, Jay knew he would have said that no matter what. But now his garden had the best collection of herbs in the village. The lavender was still green but already more pungent than Joe's ever was, and there was thyme and cologne mint and lemon balm and rosemary and great drifts of basil. He gave a whole basket of these to Popotte when she came by with the mail, and another to Rodolphe. Joe had often given out little charms (*goodwill charms*, he called them) to visitors, and Jay began to do the same: tiny bunches of lavender or mint or pineapple sage, tied with ribbons of different colors. Red for protection, white for luck, blue for healing.

Funny how it all came back. People assumed this was another English custom, the general explanation for all his eccentricities. Some took to wearing these little posies pinned to their jackets. Strangely enough, Jay found the return to Joe's familiar customs rather comforting. When he was a boy, Joe's perimeter rituals, his incense, sachets, pig-Latin incantations, sprinklings of herbs had too often irritated him. He'd found them embarrassing, like someone singing too fervently in school assembly. To his adolescent self much of Joe's everyday magic seemed rather *too* commonplace, too natural, like cooking or gardening, stripped of its mysteries. He would have preferred solemn invocations, black robes, midnight ritual. *That* he might have believed. Reared on comic books and trash fiction, that at least would have rung true. Nevertheless, Jay found he had rediscovered the peace of working with the soil. Now he understood what the old man had meant when he spoke of layman's alchemy. Jay prepared the land for his arrival like a well-raked seedbed. He planted and weeded according to the lunar cycle, as Joe would have done. But in spite of all this, Joe stayed away.

He had told himself that Joe had never been there at all, that it was in his imagination. But perversely, now that Joe was gone, he needed to believe it was otherwise. If only he could make him come back, Jay promised himself, things would be different. There were so many things left unfinished. He felt a helpless rage at himself. He'd been given a second chance, and stupidly, he'd blown it. He worked in the garden every day until dusk, still hoping Joe would come.

Forty-Four

Perhaps as a result of dwelling so constantly on the past, Jay found himself spending more and more time by the river, where the cutaway dropped sharply into the water. There he found a wasps' nest in the ground under the hedge, and watched it with relentless fascination, recalling that last summer and how he had been stung, and Gilly's laughter at Nether Edge. He lay on his stomach and watched the wasps shuttling in and out of the hole in the ground and imagined he could hear them moving just under the surface. Above them the sky was white and troubling. The remaining Specials were as silent, as troubled as the sky. Even their whispering was suspended.

It was as he lay beside the riverbank that Rosa found him.

His eyes were open, but to her, he did not seem to be looking at anything. The radio, swinging from a branch overhanging the water, was playing Elvis Presley. At his side stood an opened bottle of wine. Its label, though too far away for her to read it, said *Raspberry '75*. There was a red cord knotted around the neck of the bottle which caught her eye. As she watched, the Englishman reached for the bottle and drank from it. He made a face, as if the taste were unpleasant, but from across the river she caught the scent of what he was drinking, a sudden bright flare of ripe scarlet, wild berries gathered in secret.

She studied him for a moment from the other side of the river. In spite of what *maman* told her, he looked harmless, this man who tied the funny little red bags on the trees. She wondered why. At first her taking of them had been a defiant gesture, erasing him as much as possible from her place, but she had come to like them, their dangling shapes like small red fruit on the shaken branches. She no longer minded sharing her secret place with him.

Rosa shifted her position to squat more comfortably in the long weeds on the far side of the river. She considered crossing, but the stepping-stones had been submerged in recent showers, and she was wary of jumping to the far bank. At her side the curious brown goat nuzzled restlessly at her sleeve. She pushed the goat away with a flapping motion of her hand. *Later, Clopette, later.* She wondered whether the Englishman knew about the wasps' nest. He was, after all, less than a meter from its opening.

Jay lifted the bottle again. It was over half-empty, and already he felt dizzy, almost drunk. It was in part the sky which gave him this impression: the raindrops zigzagging down like flakes of soot onto his upturned face. This was one of the days when the memory of Joe seemed dim, out of focus. The sky went on forever. Even the writing, to which he always turned when he was in need of solace, seemed remote and lifeless. Instead Jay had worked in the orchard all morning. It was rewarding work, though it was physically demanding; every fruit tree was different, each one with its own individual shape and habit, each with its story. One had been struck by lightning. Others had suffered from infections, or had survived radical surgeries. A long-abandoned swing dangled between two low branches. Beneath some of the trees, small plaques set into the hard ground were still legible, and he could read names which Joe would have relished: *Belle d'Aquitaine, Reine-Claude, Beurre du Roi Henry, Charles d'Orléans.*

But absorbing though he found the work, today it still wasn't enough. He felt restless, edgy, bored. Something—something important—was missing.

From the bottle the scent intensified, became something which bubbled and seethed. It was a gleeful scent, a breath of high summer, of overripe fruit dripping freely from the branches, heated from below by the sun reflecting off the chalky stones of the railbed. This memory was not entirely pleasant. Perhaps because of the sky, he also associated it with the last summer at Pog Hill, of the disastrous confrontation with Zeth, and the wasps' nests. He poured the rest of the wine onto the ground and closed his eyes.

A red chuckle from the bottom of the bottle. Jay opened his eyes again, uneasy, certain that someone was watching him. The dregs were almost black in this dull daylight, black and syrupy, like molasses, and from where he was lying, there almost seemed to be movement around the neck of the bottle, as if something were trying to escape. He sat up and looked a little closer. Inside the bottle, several wasps had gathered, attracted by the scent of sugar. Two crawled stickily on the neck. Another had flown right into the belly of the bottle to investigate the residue at the bottom, crawling thickly against the glass. Its wings were clotted with syrup. He thought he could hear the insect inside the bottle, buzzing in growing frenzy, but perhaps that was the wine itself calling. Its hot bright scent distressed the air, rising like a column of red smoke, a signal, perhaps, or a warning.

Suddenly his closeness to the wasps' nest appalled him. He realized he could hear the insects beneath him under the soil's thin crust. He sat up, meaning to move away, but a reckless-ness seized him, and instead of retreating, he moved a little closer. *If Gilly were here . . .*

Nostalgia was upon him again before he could stop it. It dragged at him like a caught bramble. Perhaps it was the scent from the bottle, from the spilled wine on the ground making him feel this way, this trapped summer scent, intoxicating, overwhelming. The radio nearby gave a quick crackle of static and began to play "I Feel Love."

An idea came to him, and he shivered. Ridiculous, he told himself. He had nothing to prove. It had been twenty years since he had fired a wasps' nest. It was a reckless, lethal thing to do, the kind of thing only a child would do, oblivious of the risks. Besides . . . A voice (from the bottle, he thought, though it might still be the wine talking), cajoling, a little scornful. It sounded something like Gilly's voice, something like Joe's. It was impatient, amused beneath the irritation.

If Gilly were here you wouldn't be so chicken.

Something moved in the long grass on the other side of the river. For a second he thought he saw her, a blur of russet which might be her hair, something else which might be a stripy T-shirt or pullover.

"Rosa?"

No response. From the long grass she stared out at him, her green eyes bright with curiosity. He could see her now that he knew where to look. From a short distance away, he could hear the sound of a goat bleating.

Rosa seemed to look at him with encouragement, almost with expectation. Beneath him he could hear the wasps buzzing, a strangely *yeasty* sound, as if something below the earth were fermenting wildly. The sound, coupled with Rosa's expectant look, was too much for him. He felt a burst of exhilaration, something which stripped the years away and made him fourteen again, invulnerable.

"Watch this," he said, and began to move closer to the nest.

Rosa watched him intently. He moved awkwardly, inching toward the hole in the bank. He moved with his head down, as if this would fool the wasps into thinking him invisible. A couple of wasps settled momentarily on his back. Rosa watched as he pulled his handkerchief out of his pocket. There was a lighter in one hand, the same lighter he had offered Rosa that day by the stream. Carefully, he opened the lighter and doused the handkerchief in the fluid. Holding the object at arm's length, he moved closer to the nest. There was a larger hole under the bank, a hole which might once have housed rats. Around it, a complex of mud honeycomb. He hesitated a moment, choosing his spot, then pushed the handkerchief right into the nest, leaving a tag-end of fabric dangling down like a fuse. As Rosa watched, he looked at her and grinned. Rosa grinned back.

Banzai.

He must have been drunk. That was the only explanation he could think of later, but it hadn't felt like that at the time. At the time it felt right. Good. Exciting.

Amazing, how quickly these things came back. He only had to flip the Bic once. The flame caught instantly, flaring with sudden, incredible fierceness. There must have been plenty of oxygen down the hole. Good. Briefly Jay wished he had brought some firecrackers. For a second or two there was no response from the wasps, then half a dozen came flying out like hot cinders.

Jay felt a surge of euphoria and jumped to his feet, ready to run. That was the first mistake. Gilly always taught him to keep low, to find a hiding place under a root or behind a tree stump, as the enraged wasps came flying out. This time Jay was too busy watching Rosa. The wasps came out in a dreadful surge, and he ran for the bushes. The movement attracted them, excited them. He could smell burning lighter fluid and a vicious stink like burned carpet. Something stung him on the arm and he slapped at it. Several wasps stung him then, maddeningly, through his T-shirt and on his hands and arms, zinging by his ears like bullets, darkening the air, and Jay lost what little cool he had left. He swore and slapped at his skin. Another wasp stung him just under the left eye, driving a brilliant lance of pain into his face, and he stepped out blindly right over the edge of the cutaway and into the water. If the river had been shallower, he might have broken his neck. As it was, his fall saved him. He hit the water face-first, sank, screamed, swallowed river water, surfaced, sank again, made for the far bank and found himself a minute later several yards downriver, his T-shirt nubby with drowned wasps.

Under the nest, the fire he had lit was already out. Jay coughed up river water. He swore shakily. Fourteen had never seemed so far away. From her distant island in time, he could hear Gilly laughing. The water was shallow at this side of the river, and he waded out onto the bank and flopped on all fours into the grass. His arms and hands were already swelling from dozens of stings, and one eye was puffed shut like a boxer's.

Gradually he became aware that Rosa was still watching

from her vantage point upstream. She had wisely moved back to avoid the angry wasps, but he could see her, perched now on the top rung of the gatepost beside the dragon's head. She looked curious, but unconcerned. Beside her, the goat cropped grass.

"Never again," gasped Jay under his breath. "God, never again."

He was just beginning to consider the idea of getting up when he heard footfalls in the vineyard beyond the fence. He looked up, just in time to see Marise d'Api as she arrived breathlessly at the gate and swept Rosa in her arms. It took her a few moments to register his presence, for she and Rosa had begun a rapid interchange of signing. Jay tried to get up, slipped, smiled, made a vague gesture with one hand, as if by following the rules of country etiquette he might somehow make her overlook everything else. He felt suddenly very conscious of his swollen eye, wet clothes, muddy jeans.

"I had an accident," he explained.

Marise's eyes went to the wasps' nest in the bank. The remains of Jay's charred handkerchief still protruded from the hole, and he could smell lighter fluid across the water.

"How many times were you stung?" He thought he heard amusement in her cool voice.

Jay looked briefly at his arms and hands. "I don't know. I—I didn't know they'd come out so fast." He could see her looking at the discarded wine bottle, drawing conclusions.

"Are you allergic?"

"I don't think so." Jay tried to stand up again, slipped and fell on the wet grass. He felt sick and dizzy. Dead wasps clung to his clothes. Marise looked both dismayed and almost ready to laugh.

"Come with me," she said at last. "I have a stings kit in the house. Sometimes there can be a delayed reaction."

Carefully Jay pulled himself up the bank toward the hedge. Rosa trotted behind, closely followed by the goat. Halfway to the house, Jay felt the child's small cold hand slip into his, and, looking down, saw that she was smiling.

The house was larger than it had seemed from the road, a converted barn with low gables and high, narrow windows. Halfway up the front wall, a door stared out in midair from the loft. An old tractor was parked by one of the outbuildings. A neat kitchen garden had been planted by the side of the house. A small orchard—twenty well-kept apple trees—stood at the back. Wood was piled at the other side, stacked in readiness for the winter. Two or three more small brown goats wandered skittishly across the vineyard's small paths. Jay followed Marise along the rutted pathway between the rows of vines, and Marise put out a hand to steady him as they approached the gate, though he sensed this was less out of concern for him than for the vines, which his clumsy approach might have damaged.

"In here," she told him shortly, indicating the kitchen door. "Sit down. I'll get the kit."

Her kitchen was bright and tidy, with a shelf of stone jugs above a porcelain sink, a long oak table like the one at his own farm, and a giant black stove. Bunches of herbs hung from low beams above the chimney: rosemary, sage and pennyroyal. Rosa went to the pantry and fetched some lemonade, pouring a glassful and sitting at the table to drink it, watching Jay with curious eyes.

"*Tu as mal?*" she asked.

He looked at her. "So you can talk," he said.

Rosa smiled mischievously.

"Can I have some of that?" Jay gestured at the glass of lemonade, and she pushed it across the table toward him. *So*, he told himself, *she can lip-read as well as sign*. He wondered whether Mireille knew. Somehow he didn't think so. Rosa's voice was childish but steady, without any of the usual fluctuations of tone of the deaf. The lemonade was homemade and good.

"Thank you."

Marise flicked him a suspicious look as she came into the kitchen with the stings kit. She had a disposable syringe in one hand.

"It's adrenaline. I used to be a nurse."

After a moment's hesitation, Jay held out his arm and closed his eyes.

"There."

He felt it as a small burning sensation in the crook of his elbow. There was a second's light-headedness, then nothing. Marise was looking at him in some amusement.

"You're very squeamish, for a man who plays with wasps."

"It wasn't like that," said Jay, rubbing his arm.

"If you behave like that, you can expect to be stung. You got away lightly." He supposed that was true, but it didn't feel that way. His head was still pounding. His left eye was swollen tight. Marise went to the kitchen cupboard and brought out a shaker of white powder. She shook some out into a cup, added a little water, and stirred with a spoon. She handed him the cup.

"Baking soda," she advised. "You should put some of this onto the stings." She did not offer to help. Jay followed her advice, feeling rather foolish. This wasn't how he'd envisaged their next meeting at all.

"I must have been crazy," he said, half to himself. "I've always been terrified of wasps."

Marise shrugged and turned back to the cupboard. Jay watched as she poured pasta into a black pan, added water and salt, placed the pan carefully onto the hob.

"I have to make lunch for Rosa," she explained. "Take what time you need." In spite of her words, Jay got the distinct impression she wanted him out of her kitchen as soon as possible. He struggled with the baking soda, trying to reach the stings on his back. The brown goat poked its head around the door and bleated.

"*Clopette, non! Pas dans la cuisine!*" Rosa jumped from her place and shooed the goat away. Marise shot her a look of fierce warning, and the child put her hand over her mouth, subdued.

Jay looked at Marise, puzzled. Why should she not want her child to speak in front of him? She motioned toward the table, asking Rosa to set the plates out. Rosa took out three plates from the cupboard. Marise shook her head again. Reluctantly the child returned the plate to the cupboard.

"Thanks for the first aid," said Jay.

Marise nodded, busy chopping tomatoes for the sauce. There was fresh basil in a window box on the ledge, and she added a fistful.

"You have a lovely farm."

"Oh?" He thought he detected a defensive edge in her voice.

"Don't worry, I don't want to buy it," added Jay quickly. "I mean, it's just a nice farm. Pretty. Unspoiled."

Marise turned and looked at him. "What do you mean?" Her face was vivid with suspicion. "What do you mean, buying it? Have you been talking to someone?"

"No!" he protested. "I was just trying to make conversation. I swear—"

"Don't," she said flatly. The fleeting warmth he had glimpsed in her was gone. "Don't say it. I know you've been talking to Clairmont. I've seen his van parked outside your house. I'm sure he's been giving you all kinds of ideas."

"Ideas?"

She laughed without humor. "Oh, I know about you, Monsieur Mackintosh. Sneaking around. Asking questions. First you buy the old Château Foudouin. Then you show a great curiosity about the land down to the river. What are you planning? Holiday chalets? A sports complex, like Le Pinot?"

Jay shook his head. "You've got it wrong. I'm a writer. I came here to finish my book. That's all." She looked at him cynically. Her eyes were lasers.

"If I ask questions," he said, "it's just because I'm a writer, I'm curious." He was hardly aware of what he was saying now, eyes fixed on her fierce, vivid face. "It's different here, somehow. I've been working like crazy. I've been restoring the gardens, the orchard. Surely you must have noticed?"

She turned then, a red onion in one hand, the knife in the other.

He persisted. "I promise, I'm not here to develop anything. For Christ's sake, I'm sitting in your kitchen soaked to the skin and covered in baking soda. Do I look like an entrepreneur?"

She considered this for a moment. "Perhaps not," she said at last, with the tiniest of smiles.

"I bought the place on impulse. I didn't even know you wanted . . . I didn't think you . . . I don't usually have impulses," he finished lamely.

"I find that hard to believe," said Marise. "For a man who deliberately puts his hand into a wasps' nest, I find it very hard. What were you trying to do, smoke them out?"

She was still smiling. Jay shook his head. "It was a kind of game—years ago, anyway. A sort of test, I suppose. I never was much good at that kind of thing, even then. Joe would have said I didn't have the 'art for it."

Marise stirred the onions into the pan. "Who is Joe?"

Jay hesitated. "A friend."

Jay told her about Nether Edge, and Pog Hill Lane, and *Jackapple Joe*. Of course, he didn't mention Joe's mysterious presence and subsequent disappearence, or the six bottles. He didn't want her to think he was crazy. In turn, losing her earlier stiffness, Marise was beginning to reveal herself a little. Jay had already sensed her fierce independence, tenderness for her daughter, pride in her work, in the house, the land. Now he saw other facets of her: a way of smiling, grave-seeming, but with a kernel of sweetness. A way of listening in silence, an economy of movement which belied the quick mind, the occasional wry twist of humor beneath the practicality. In this too she reminded him strangely of Joe.

"I always wanted to live in a place like this," said Marise, tossing greens with vinaigrette. "Like Lansquenet, or like your Pog Hill. Somewhere with orchards and farms."

Marise was from Paris, had never even seen a vineyard before she moved to Lansquenet. Even though he had known she was not local, Jay found it hard to believe that she could have learned so much about wine making at such speed.

"I didn't realize . . . I assumed . . . It can't have been easy," he finished awkwardly.

Marise shrugged. "I managed. It's better than Paris, at any rate. I wouldn't have wanted Rosa to grow up the way I did, looking down at the world from the top of an apartment building. It's better here. Things are simple. There is a rhythm. An order."

It was the kind of thing Joe might have said. Jay felt an increased respect for this woman who had come to Lansquenet, like him, a stranger, who had made a life for herself and her daughter in this closed, suspicious little community.

"I'm not sure I would have had the courage to stay," he told her at last.

"It isn't courage," said Marise. "Not when you have no

other choice. I—'' Just then Rosa came in, with Clopette at her heels.

Marise spoke, looking almost relieved. ''Lunch is ready. Pasta and salad. Wash your hands first.''

Rosa signed something.

Marise glanced at Jay, hesitated. ''He can stay for lunch if he likes.''

Before the meal, she let Jay change his wet clothes for a pair of Tony's overalls, while Rosa fed Clopette. Jay found it strange that she did not refer to Tony as her husband, but as ''Rosa's father.'' Still, the rapport between them was clearly too new—too tenuous—for him to endanger it by asking questions. When—if—she wanted to discuss Tony, she would do it in her own time.

The food was good, accompanied by wine from Marise's own vineyard. Jay realized that he was very hungry. They ate in silence for a while.

''*Maman*—''

Marise gave Rosa a sharp look and signed something to her with a quick gesture. Rosa looked abashed, but only for a few moments. Soon the goat drew her attention again, and she ran to the door to feed her scraps. Jay heard her talking quietly to the animal.

''Come on, Clo—good girl. *Good* girl!''

''Her speech is really very good, isn't it?'' he observed, watching Marise.

Marise did not reply, but began to clear the plates from the table.

''Rosa, dessert.''

Without any real surprise, Jay saw that Rosa turned at her mother's voice, just as, a little earlier, she had turned when Clopette came into the kitchen.

''Apple tart and ice cream!'' crowed Rosa in delight.

"Maman, I *love* you!" She gave Marise a hug, almost spilling the dishes from the table.

Jay looked at Rosa, now bouncing impatiently on her chair. "There's nothing at all wrong with her hearing, is there?"

It was barely a question. Without looking at Jay, Marise began to cut the tart. Her movements were slow and deliberate.

"I expect it seems strange to you," she said.

Jay did not reply. He sensed that any unexpected movement or unconsidered word would end her confidences before they were properly begun.

"I expected you to find out before now," continued Marise. "The farms are too close to each other. You would have heard something eventually." Her voice was calm, almost uninflected. Jay could only guess at the level of self-control needed to keep it so.

"At first I thought it might be different with a foreigner. I thought maybe you didn't speak enough French to talk to people in the village. You would renovate the house, then sell it, or maybe use it in the summer as a holiday home. I did not expect you to want to live there."

She had been watching him, Jay realized. Behind her indifference had been a curiosity as great as his own.

"Then you spoke to me in French. I saw Clairmont's van. Then Mireille called." There was some defensiveness in her voice. "I expect she has already spoken to you about us."

Jay smiled. "A little. She's an old woman, used to her own way. She must have been difficult to live with."

Marise continued, without returning his smile. "Rosa went deaf before Tony died. It was a bad winter. She developed ear infections. There was a complication. She was completely deaf for almost a year." Rosa looked up at the mention of her name and grinned.

Marise continued. "I took her to see specialists. There was an operation, very expensive. I was told not to expect too much. I paid for lessons for her. We learned sign language together. There was another operation, even more expensive. Ninety percent of her hearing was restored. But by then things had changed," she finished.

Jay nodded. "But why the pretense? Why not simply—"

"Mireille. She's already tried to take her from me. All she has left of Tony, she says. I knew that if she once managed to get hold of Rosa, I'd never get her back. I wanted to stop her. It was the only way I could think of. If she thought she couldn't talk to Rosa—if she thought she was damaged in some way . . ." She glanced at Jay, almost shyly. "Mireille can't bear imperfection. Less than perfect doesn't interest her. That's why when Tony . . ."

Jay did not try to make her say more. His heart was pounding. He knew that a single word might be enough to tip the precarious balance between them. Thinking back to his first glimpse of her, to his previous assumptions, to the way he had listened to—and half-believed—the opinions of people like Caro Clairmont and Mireille Faizande, he felt a rush of shame. The heroine of his novel—unpredictable, dangerous, possibly mad—bore no relation to this quiet, calm woman. He had let his imagination run far ahead of the truth, and for once, the truth was what interested him most.

Forty-Five

Nether Edge, Summer 1977

fter he left Gilly, Jay sat by the bridge for a while, feeling angry and guilty and certain she would come after him. When she didn't appear, he lay in the wet grass for a while, relishing the bitter smells of earth and weeds, and looked into the sky until the falling drizzle made him dizzy. He began to feel cold, so he got up and began to make his way back to Pog Hill along the disused railbed, stopping every now and then to examine something by the side of the tracks, more out of habit than real interest. He was so lost in his brooding that he completely failed to hear—or see—the four figures which emerged silently from the trees at his back and fanned out behind him in pursuit.

By the time he saw them it was too late. Glenda was there,

and two of her friends, the skinny blonde (he thought her name was Karen) and a younger girl, Paula (or was it Patty?), who was ten or eleven, maybe, with pierced ears and a mean, sulky mouth. They were already moving across his path to cut him off, Glenda to one side, the other two to the other. Their faces shone with rain and eagerness. Glenda's eyes met his across the track and they were gleaming. For a moment she looked almost pretty. Worse still, Zeth was with her.

For a second or two, Jay froze. The girls were nothing special. He had outrun, outtalked, outbluffed them before, and there were only three of them. They were familiar, part of the Edge, like the open-pit mine or the scree above the canal lock, like the wasps, a natural hazard, something to be treated with caution but no fear. Zeth was another matter.

He was wearing a Status Quo T-shirt with the sleeves rolled up. In one sleeve was tucked a pack of Winstons. His hair was long, flapping around his thin, clever face. His acne had cleared up, but there were deep marks on his cheeks where it had been, initiation scars, channels for crocodile tears. He was grinning.

"Astha been pickin' on my sister?"

Jay was already running before he finished his sentence. It was the worst possible place to be cornered; high above the canal and its many hiding places, the straight, open railbed lay in front of him like a desert. The bushes on either side were too thick to squeeze through, too small to offer protection. A deep ditch and a screen of bushes hid him from even the closest houses. His sneakers skidded dangerously on the gravel. Glenda and her mates were in front of him. Zeth was a heartbeat behind. Jay took the best option, dodging the two girls and making straight for Glenda. She stepped out to intercept him, her meaty arms held out as if fielding a wide ball, and he pushed her with all his strength, shouldering her aside like an American football player, and hurtled free down the abandoned tracks. Behind him he heard Glenda wail. Zeth's voice pursued him, ominously close:

"Tha little bastard!"

Jay didn't look around. There was a railway bridge and a cutting about a quarter of a mile from Pog Hill, with a path leading up onto the street. There would be other paths too, leading to the cutaway and waste ground beyond. If he could only get there . . . The bridge wasn't far. He was younger than Zeth. Lighter. He could outrun him. If he could reach the bridge, there would be places to hide.

He glanced over his shoulder. The gap between them had widened. Thirty or forty yards separated them, though Glenda was back on her feet and running. In spite of her size, Jay wasn't worried. She looked out of breath already, her over-large breasts bobbing ludicrously under her straining shirt. Zeth was jogging quite slowly next to her, but as Jay looked around, Zeth put on a sudden, terrifying burst of speed, his arms pumping, gravel spraying fiercely up around his ankles.

Jay was beginning to feel dizzy now, his breath stuck in his throat like a hot stone. He could see the bridge just around the curve of the line, and the row of poplars which marked the abandoned points, manual railway switches. Five hundred yards would do it.

Joe's talisman was still in his pocket. He could feel it against his hip as he ran, and he felt dim relief it was there.

He just hoped it still worked.

He reached the bridge with the gap between them widening, and cast about for somewhere to hide. Too risky to try the steep path up toward the road. Jay was winded by now, and there were maybe fifty feet of twisting dirt path before the road and safety. He clenched his fist over Joe's talisman and took the opposite direction, the one they wouldn't expect him to take, under the bridge and behind, toward Pog Hill. There was a swath of willow herb gone to seed behind the rail arch, and he bobbed down among it, head pounding, heart tight with dark exaltation.

He was safe.

From his hideout he could hear voices. Zeth's sounded close, Glenda's more distant, thickened by distance, rebounding over the empty spaces between the bridge and the cutaway.

"Wheer the bleedinell izzy?"

Jay could hear him on the other side of the arch, imagined him checking the path, measuring distances. He made himself small under the waving white heads of the willow herb.

Glenda's voice, breathy with running: *"Thaz lost im, tha beggar!"*

" 'Ave not. He's here somewhere. He can't have gone far."

Minutes passed. Jay clung to the talisman as they went over the area. Joe's talisman. It had protected him on so many previous occasions, and he had no doubt at all that it would do so again.

He heard a sound as someone crunched over the accumulated litter in the space underneath the bridge. Footsteps across the gravel. But he was safe. He was invisible. He believed.

"Iz 'ere!"

It was the ten-year-old, Paula or Patty, standing waist-deep in the foamy weeds. *"Quick, Zeth, gettim! Gettim!"*

Jay began to back off toward the bridge, clouds of white seeds puffing away with every move he made. The talisman dangled loosely from his fingers. Glenda and Karen rounded the curve of the arch, faces sweaty. There was a deep ditch just beyond the arch, ripe with late-summer nettles. No escape that way. Then Zeth came from under the bridge, took his arm, drew Jay toward him by the shoulders in a dreadfully intimate, not-to-be-refused gesture of welcome and smiled.

"Gotcha."

The magic had finally run out.

Jay never liked to think about what happened after that. It existed in a curious silence, like some dreams. First they pulled off his T-shirt and pushed him, kicking and screaming, into the ditch where the nettles bloomed. He tried to climb out, but Zeth kept pushing him back, the leaves raising welts which would itch and burn for days. Jay put his arms up to cover his face, thinking remotely, *How come this never happens to Clint?* before someone yanked him up by the hair and Zeth's voice said, very gently, "Now it's my turn, yer bastard."

In a story he would have fought back. He would at least have shown defiance, some hint of desperado swagger. He didn't.

He began to scream before he felt the first blow. Perhaps that was how he escaped a serious beating. It could have been worse, he thought as he assessed the damage later. A bloody nose. Some bruises. Both the knees of his jeans taken out from a skid across the railbed. The only thing broken was his watch. Later he came to understand that there had been something more, something more serious, more permanent than a watch, or even a bone. It had to do with faith, he thought dimly. Something inside had been broken and could not be mended.

As Joe might have said, the *'art* was gone.

He told his mother he had fallen off his bike. It was a plausible lie—plausible enough, anyway, to explain his shredded jeans and swollen nose. She didn't fuss as much as Jay had feared—it was late, and everyone was watching a rerun of *Blue Hawaii*, part of the Elvis postmortem season.

Slowly he made himself a sandwich and took a can of Coke

from the fridge. Then he went to his room and listened to the radio. Everything seemed speciously normal, as if Gilly, Zeth and Pog Hill were already a long time in the past. The Stranglers were playing "Straighten Out." Jay and his mother left that weekend.

Forty-Six

Lansquenet, May 1999

Jay was at work in the garden when Popotte arrived with her post bag. She always left her ancient bicycle at the side of the road and brought any mail along the footpath.

"*Hé*, Monsieur Jay," she sighed, handing over a packet of letters. "If only you lived a little closer to the road! My *tournée* is always half an hour longer when there's something for you. I lose ten kilos every time I come over here. It can't go on! You must put up a post box!"

Jay grinned. "Come in and have one of Poitou's fresh *chaussons aux pommes*. I have some coffee on the stove. I was just going to have some myself."

Popotte looked as severe as her merry face would allow. "Are you trying to bribe me, *Rosbif*?"

"No, *madame*." He grinned. "Just lead you astray."

She laughed. "Maybe one. I need the calories."

Jay opened the letters as she ate her pastry. An electricity bill. A questionnaire from the Town Hall in Agen. A small flat package, wrapped in brown paper, addressed to him in small, careful, almost-familiar script.

It was postmarked Kirby Monckton. Jay's hands began to tremble.

"I hope they're not all bills," said Popotte, finishing her pastry and taking another. "Don't want to wear myself out bringing you unwanted mail."

Jay opened the packet with difficulty. He had to pause twice for his hands to stop shaking. The wrapping paper was thick and stiffened with a sheet of card. There was no note inside. Instead there was a piece of yellow paper carefully folded over a small quantity of tiny black seeds. One word was inscribed in pencil on the paper:

Specials.

"Are you all right?" Popotte seemed concerned. Jay must have looked strange, the seeds in one hand, the paper in the other, gaping.

"Just some seeds I was expecting from England," said Jay with an effort. "I—I'd forgotten."

His mind was dizzied with possibilities. He felt numbed, shut down by the enormity of that tiny packet of seeds. He took a mouthful of coffee, then laid the seeds out on the yellow paper and examined them.

"They don't look like much," observed Popotte.

"No, they don't, do they?" There were maybe a hundred of the seeds, barely enough to cover the palm of his hand.

"For God's sake, don't sneeze," said Joe behind him, and Jay nearly dropped the lot. The old man was standing against the kitchen cupboard, as casually as if he had never left, wearing madras shorts and a Springsteen *Born to Run* T-shirt with his pit boots and cap. He looked absolutely real standing there, but Popotte's gaze never flickered, even though she seemed to be staring right at him. Joe grinned and lifted a finger to his lips.

"Take your time, lad," he advised kindly. "Think I'll go and have a look at the garden while I'm waiting."

Jay watched helplessly as he sauntered out of the kitchen and into the garden, fighting back an almost uncontrollable urge to run after him.

Popotte put down her coffee mug and looked at him curiously. "Have you been making jam today, Monsieur Jay?"

He shook his head. Behind her, through the kitchen window, he could see Joe leaning over the makeshift cold frame.

"Oh." Popotte still looked doubtful, sniffing the air. "I thought I could smell something. Black currants. Burning sugar."

Pog Hill Lane had always had that scent of yeast and fruit and caramelized sugar, whether or not Joe was making wine. It was steeped into the carpets, the curtains, the wood. The scent followed him around, clinging to his clothes, even permeating the haze of cigarette smoke which so often surrounded him.

"I should really get back to work," said Jay, trying to keep his voice level. "I want to get these seeds into the ground as soon as I can."

"Oh?" She peered at the seeds again. "Something special, are they?"

Forty-Seven

Pog Hill, Autumn 1977

September was no better. Elvis was in the charts again with "Way Down." Jay studied listlessly. Normality seemed restored. But that sense of doom was still there, accentuated if anything by the humdrum continuation of things. He heard from neither Joe nor Gilly, which surprised him even though it was unsurprising—especially given he'd left Kirby Monckton without saying goodbye to either of them. His mother was snapped by *Sun* photographers on the arm of a twenty-four-year-old fitness instructor outside a Soho night-club. Marc Bolan died in a car accident—then, only a few weeks later, Ronnie Van Zant and Steve Gaines of Lynyrd Skynyrd were wiped out in a plane crash. It seemed suddenly as if everything and everyone around him was dying, coming apart. No one else seemed to notice. His friends smoked illicit cigarettes and sneaked off to the movies after hours. Jay watched them with contempt. He'd practically stopped smoking. It seemed so pointless, almost childish. The gulf between himself and his classmates broadened, and some days he felt ten years older.

Bonfire Night came. The others lit a fire and roasted potatoes in the quad. Jay stayed in the dorm and watched from a distance. The scent of the air was bitter, nostalgic. Showers of sparks puffed up from the bonfire into the smoke and into the mild sky. He could smell the hot scent of grease frying and the cigarette-paper reek of firecrackers. For the first time he realized how much he missed Joe.

In December he ran away.

He took his coat and his sleeping bag, his radio and some money, which he stuffed into his sports bag. He forged his permission papers and left school just after breakfast, to give himself plenty of time to get as far as possible. He hitched a lift from town to the motorway, then another down the M1 toward Sheffield. He knew exactly where he was going.

It took him two days to reach Kirby Monckton. He walked most of the way after leaving the motorway, cutting across fields under a sullen sky onto the higher ground of the moor. He slept in a bus shelter for a while until a police patrol car drew up and he was forced to leave. After that, he dared not stop again in case he was picked up. It was cold, though not snowing, and Jay put on all the spare clothing he had brought. He didn't feel any warmer. His feet were blistered, his boots clotted with mud, but throughout it all he clung to the memory of Pog Hill Lane, to the knowledge that Joe was waiting for him there, to Joe's house with its warm kitchen and the scent of hot jam and oven-dried apples and the radio playing on the window ledge above the tomato plants. . . .

It was late afternoon when he arrived. He pulled himself up the last few feet toward the back of Pog Hill Lane, slung his sports bag over Joe's wall and himself after it. The yard was deserted.

Beyond it the allotment looked bare, abandoned. Joe had certainly done a fine camouflage job on it. Even from the yard it looked as if no one had lived there for months. Weeds had sprouted between the flagstones and died there in the cold, silvered with frost. The windows were nailed shut. The door was locked.

"Joe!" He knocked on the door. "Joe? Open up, will you?"

Silence. The house looked blind, stolid beneath its winter sheen. Under Jay's fist the door handle rattled meaninglessly. From inside, his voice returned to him, a dim echo in a hollow chamber.

"Joe!"

"It's empty, lad." The old woman was peering over the wall, black eyes curious beneath a yellow head scarf. Jay recognized her vaguely; she had been a frequent visitor that first summer, and she would sometimes make strawberry pies which she brought to Joe in exchange for allotment produce.

"Mrs. Simmonds?"

"Aye, that's right. You'll be wantin' Mester Cox, will yer?"

Jay nodded.

"Well, iz gone. Thought id passed on, like, but our Janice sez he just upped an left one day. Upped an left," she repeated. "You'll not find 'im 'ere now." Jay stared at her.

"They're knockin' down Pog Hill Lane, you know," said Mrs. Simmonds conversationally. "Goin' to build some luxury flats. Could do with a bit of luxury after everythin' we've bin through."

Jay ignored her. "I know you're in there, Joe!" he shouted. "Come out! Bloody come out!"

"There's no call for that kind of language," said Mrs. Simmonds.

"Joe! Joe! Open up! *Joe!*"

"You watch it, lad, or I'm callin' the police."

Jay spread his hands placatingly. "Okay. Okay. I'm sorry. I'm going. I'm sorry."

He waited until she was gone. Then he crept back and made his way around the house, still certain Joe was in there somewhere, angry at him perhaps, waiting for him to give up and leave. He searched the overgrown allotment, expecting to see him checking his trees or in his greenhouse at the signal box, but there was no sign of any recent presence but his own. It was only when he realized what was missing that the truth of it came home. Not a rune, not a ribbon, not a scrawled sign on a tree trunk or a stone. The red sachets had disappeared from the sides of the greenhouse, from the wall, from the branches of the trees. The careful arrangements of pebbles on the paths had been scattered. The lunar charts tacked to the wall of the shed and the greenhouse, the arcane symbols taped to the trees—all were gone. The cold frames had been tumbled, leaving the plants inside to fend for themselves. The orchard was strewn with summer's windfalls, gray-brown and half-melted into the hard ground. Hundreds of them. Pears, apples, plums, cherries.

That was when he really knew. Those windfalls.

The back door was imperfectly closed. Jay managed to pry it open and let himself into the empty house. It smelled foul, like fruit gone to rot in a cellar. In the kitchen, tomato plants had grown monstrously leggy in the dark, reaching out pale, fragile fingerlings toward the thin edge of light at the window before dying. Apparently Joe had left everything just as it was. His kettle on the hob, his biscuit box—still with a few biscuits in it, stale but edible—his coat hanging up on the peg behind the door. The light in the cellar was burned out, but there was enough daylight from the kitchen to see the rows of bottles, jars and demijohns ranked neatly on the shelves there, gleaming like buried gems in the undersea light.

Jay searched the house. There was little enough to find; Joe's possessions had not been many, but even so he could see the old man had taken practically nothing with him. The old kit bag was missing, his *Illustrated Herbal* and his few clothes. The seed chest was still there by his bed, but when Jay opened it, he found that its contents had been removed. The seeds, roots, packages and envelopes and neatly labeled twists of crinkly brown newspaper were gone. Inside the chest, nothing but dust remained.

Wherever Joe had gone, he'd taken his seeds with him.

But where had he gone? His maps were still hanging in place on the walls, labeled and marked in Joe's small painstaking script, but there was no clue as to where he might be heading. There was no pattern to his many itineraries, the colored lines joining at a dozen different points, Brazil, Nepal, Haiti, French Guyana . . . Jay searched under his bed, but found nothing but a cardboard box filled with old magazines. He pulled them out, curious. But these magazines were old, faded but kept tidily away in the box and covered with a piece of card so that the dust would not damage them. The dates on the covers were a revelation—1947, 1949, 1951, 1964—old magazines, their covers colored the same distinctive yellow and black. Old copies of *National Geographic*.

Jay sat on the ground for a few minutes, turning pages gone crispy with age. There was something comforting about those magazines, as if by simply touching them he could bring Joe closer. Here were the places which Joe had seen, the people among whom Joe had lived—mementoes perhaps, of his long years on the road.

Here was French Guyana. Egypt. Brazil. South Africa. New Guinea. The once-bright covers lay side by side on the dusty floor. Jay saw that Joe had marked some passages in pencil, annotated others. Haiti. South America. Turkey. Antarctica. These were his travels. This the itinerary of his wandering years. Each one dated, signed, coded in many colors.

Dated and signed.

A cold finger of suspicion traced its way down his back.

Slowly at first, then turning the pages with growing, dreadful certainty, he began to understand. The maps. The anecdotes. The back copies of *National Geographic*, dating right back to the war. . . .

There had never been any years on the road. Joe Cox was a miner, had always been a miner, from the day he left school to the moment he retired. When Nether Edge pit closed down, he'd gone to his house on Pog Hill Lane on his miner's pension and dreamed of traveling. All his experiences, his anecdotes, his adventures, near-misses, his swashbucklings, his ladies in Haiti, his traveling gypsies—all taken from this pile of old magazines, all as fake as his magic, his layman's alchemy, his precious seeds, no doubt collected from growers or mail-order suppliers while he wove his dreams—his *lies*— alone . . .

Sudden, overwhelming anger shot through Jay. All the hurt and confusion of the past few months, Gilly's abandonment and Joe's betrayal, his parents, himself, his school, Zeth, Glenda and her gang, the wasps—his rage at everything coalesced for a moment into a single bolt of pain and fury. He flung the magazines across the floor, kicking and stamping the pages. He tore off the covers, treading the pictures into the mingled dust and mud. He pulled down the maps from the walls. He tipped over the empty seed chest. He ran down into the cellar and smashed everything he could see there, the bottles, the jars, the fruit and the spirits. His feet crunched on broken glass.

How could Joe have lied?

How could he?

Okay, so maybe it had been he who had run away. But he had come back, hadn't he? All he could think of was Joe's deception.

His back hurt—he must have strained it when he went crazy in the cellar—and he walked back into the kitchen feeling leaden and useless. He had cut his hand on a piece of glass. He tried to rinse it in the sink, but the water had already been turned off.

That was when he saw the envelope.

It had been propped up neatly against the draining board by the window, next to the dried-up bar of Coal Tar soap. His name was written across the top in small, shaky capitals. Jay tore the envelope clumsily, thinking perhaps this was it, Joe hadn't forgotten him after all, this had to be some kind of explanation, a sign . . .

A talisman.

There was no letter in the envelope. He looked twice, but there wasn't even a slip of paper. Instead, there was a small packet—he recognized it as one of Joe's seed packets from the chest—faintly labeled in red pencil: *Specials*.

Jay tore open a corner. There were seeds inside, tiny black-fly seeds, a hundred or more, rolling between his clumsy fingers as he tried to understand. No note. No letter.

No instructions. Just seeds.

Anger lashed him again. What was he supposed to do with them? Plant them in his garden? Grow a beanstalk to the

Land of Make-believe? He gave a furious croak of laughter. Just what exactly was he supposed to *do* with them?

The seeds rolled meaninglessly between his fingers. Tears of angry, desolate laughter poured from his eyes.

Jay went outside and climbed up onto the back wall. He tore the packet open and let the seeds float down into the cutting on the damp winter wind. He sent the shredded envelope fluttering after them, feeling sourly exultant.

Forty-Eight

Lansquenet, Summer 1999

June came in like a ship, blue sails unfurled and swelling. A good time for writing—Jay's book lengthened by another fifty pages—but even better for planting, picking out the new seedlings and setting them in their raked beds, thinning out potato plants and putting them into rows, or weeding, stripping garlands of goose grass and ground elder from the currant bushes, or picking strawberries and raspberries from their green hollows to make jam. Joe was especially pleased by this.

"There's nothin' like pickin' yer own fruit from yer own garden," he pointed out, teeth clamped around the stub of a cigarette. The strawberries were abundant this year—three rows fifty meters long, enough to sell if he had a mind to—

but Jay was uninterested in selling. Instead he gave them away to his new friends—Rosa and Clopette were especially fond of them—made jam, ate strawberries by the pound, sometimes straight from the field, with the pink soil still dusting the flesh. Joe's crow scarers—flexible canes decorated with foil streamers and the inevitable red talisman—were enough to discourage the bird population.

"You should make some wine, lad," advised Joe. "Never made any strawberry myself. Never grew enough of 'em to bother. I'd like to see what it turns out like."

Jay found he could accept Joe's presence without question now, though not because he had no questions to ask. It was simply that he could not bring himself to ask them. Better to remain as he was, to accept it as another everyday miracle. Too much investigation might open up more than he was willing to examine. Nor was his anger entirely gone. It remained a part of him, like a dormant seed, ready to sprout in the right conditions. But in the face of everything else it seemed less important now, something which belonged to another life. *Too much ballast*, Joe always said, *slows you down*.

With Marise too he exercised the same caution. Since the day she had confided in him about Rosa, she was more approachable, but still wary. She tolerated his approach in much the same way that a wild animal—a fox, maybe, or a polecat—tolerates the presence of a human who has not yet shown hostility. Jay guessed that she was waiting to see if he would reveal her secret in the village. As the days passed and he kept it to himself, he hoped she would open up a little more.

June was a busy month. The vegetable patch needed attention: new potatoes to dig and store in pallets filled with dry earth, young leeks to peg out, endives to cover with black plastic shells to protect them from the sunlight. In the evenings, when the day cooled, he worked on his book as Joe watched from the corner of the room, lying on the bed with his boots against the wall, or smoking and watching the fields with bright, lazy eyes. Like the garden and the orchard, the book needed more work than ever at this stage, but as Jay neared the ending, he began to slow, to falter.

"Tha's not written much tonight, lad," Joe commented on one unproductive evening. His accent had broadened, as it did when he was at his most satirical.

Jay shook his head. "I'm doing all right."

"Tha should get it finished," continued Joe. "Get it out of your system while you still can."

Irritably: "I can't do that."

Joe shrugged.

"I mean it, Joe. I can't."

"No such bloody word." It was another of Joe's sayings. "Does tha want to finish that bloody book or not? I'm not goin' to be here forever, tha knows."

Jay looked up sharply. "What do you mean? You've only just come back."

Again Joe gave his loose shrug. "Well . . ."

As if it were obvious. Some things did not need to be said. But Joe went on to be even more blunt.

"I wanted to get you started," he said at last. "See you in, if you like. But as for *stayin'* . . ."

"You're going away."

"Well, probably not just yet."

Probably. The word was like a stone dropping into still water.

"Again." The tone was more than accusatory.

"Not just yet."

"But soon."

Joe shrugged. Finally, "I don't know."

Anger, that old friend. Like a recurring fever. Jay could

feel it in him, a blush and prickle at the nape of his neck. Anger at himself, at this neediness never to be satisfied.

"Got to move on sometime, lad. Both of us have. You more than ever."

Jay was silent.

"I'll probly hang on for a while, though. Till autumn, at least."

It occurred to Jay that he had never seen the old man in winter, as if he were a figment of the summer air.

"Why are you here, Joe, anyway?"

Joe laughed. In the slice of moonlight needling from behind the shutters he did look ghostly, but there was nothing ghoulish in his grin. "Tha allus did ask too many questions. I telled yer first off, didn't I? *Astral* travel, lad. I travel in me sleep. Got it down to an art, anall. I can do anywhere. Egypt. Bangkok. The South Pole. Dancin' girls in Hawaii. Northern lights. I've done 'em all. That's why I do so much bloody sleepin'."

He laughed, and flicked the stub of his cigarette against the concrete floor.

"If that's true . . . where are you now?" Jay's tone was suspicious, as it always was when he thought Joe was mocking him. "I mean—where are you—really? The seed packet was marked Kirby Monckton. Are you—"

"Aye, well." Joe lit another cigarette. Its scent was eerily strong in the small room. "That dun't matter. Thing is, I'm here now."

He would say no more. Beneath them, in the cellar, the remaining Specials rubbed together in longing and anticipation. They made barely any sound, but their activity was a fast and yeasty ferment, like trouble brewing.

Soon, they seemed to whisper from their glassy cradles in the dark. *Soon. Soon. SOON.* They were never silent now. They seemed more alive, more alert than they ever were, their voices swelling to a cacophony of squeaks, grunts, laughter and shrieking which rocked the house to the foundations. Blackberry blue, damson black. Only two remained, but still the voices had grown louder. As if the spirit released from the other bottles were still active, lashing the remaining three to greater frenzies. The air sparkled with their energy. They had penetrated the soil. Even Narcisse, delivering garden supplies, seemed aware of it. He looked at the newly restored orchard garden with gruff approval.

"Not bad," he said, "for an Englishman. You might make a farmer yet." He smiled. "Still, there's not much of a living in fruit," he continued. "Everyone grows it, but there's too much and you end up feeding it to the pigs. But if you like preserves . . ." He shook his head at the eccentricity. "There's no harm in it, I suppose, *hé?*"

"I thought I might try and make some wine," admitted Jay, smiling.

Narcisse looked puzzled. "Wine from fruit?"

Jay pointed out that grapes were also a fruit, but Narcisse shook his head, bewildered. *"Bof,* if you like. C'est bien anglais, ça."

Forty-Nine

s July veered into sight, the weather grew hotter, then scorching. Jay found himself feeling grateful that he had only a few rows of vegetables and fruit to care for, for in spite of the nearby river, the earth had become dry and cracked, its russet color paling into pink and then almost-white under the sun's attack. Now he had to water everything for two hours every day, choosing the cool evenings and early mornings so that the soil's moisture would not evaporate. He used equipment he found in Foudouin's abandoned shed: a hand pump to bring water up from the river—which he installed close to the dragon's head at the boundary between his land and Marise's vineyard—and large metal watering cans to carry it from there. Rosa often sat and chatted with him as he did this, while Clopette nibbled the green tops of the carrots and the feathery shoots of asparagus gone to seed. Sometimes Marise dropped by with a gift—a cake, a batch of biscuits—in return for the strawberries, though she never stayed long. She seemed awkward, formal when she was on Jay's land, less ready to make conversation than when she was in her own territory. On her own side of the boundary she seemed more relaxed.

"She'll be doing well enough from this weather," confided Narcisse over coffee in Les Marauds. "That land of hers never dries out, even in high summer. Oh, there was some kind of drainage put in years ago, when I was a boy, pipes and tiling I think, but that was before old Foudouin even thought of buying it. Now it's fallen into disrepair, though. I doubt she ever thought of restoring the drainage." There was no rancor in his voice. "If she can't do it herself," he said bluntly, "then she won't have it done at all. It's the way she is, *hé!*"

Narcisse himself was suffering from July's intense heat. His nursery garden was at its most delicate, with gladioli and peonies and camellias just ready to be sold to the shops, with baby vegetables at their most tender, and fruit just forming on the branches of his trees. The sudden clap of heat would wither the flowers (each one needed a whole watering canful of water every day), burn the fruit from the branches, scorch the leaves.

"*Bof.*" He shrugged, philosophical. "It's been looking that way all year. No rain to speak of since February. Maybe enough to wet the soil, *hé,* but not enough to go deep, where it matters. Business will be bad again." He gestured toward the basket of vegetables beside him—a gift for Jay's table— and shook his head. "Look at that," he said. The tomatoes looked as large as cricket balls. "I feel ashamed to sell them.

I'm giving them away." He drank his coffee mournfully. "I might as well give it up now," he said.

Of course, he meant no such thing. Narcisse, once so monosyllabic, had become quite garrulous in recent weeks. There was a kindly heart beneath the dour exterior, and a gruff warmth which endeared him to people who took the time to know him. He was the only person from the village with whom Marise did business, perhaps because they used the same workers. Once every three months he delivered supplies—fertilizer, insecticide powder for the vines, seeds for planting—to her farm.

"She keeps herself to herself," was his only comment. "More women should do the same." Last year she had installed a sprinkler at the far edge of her second field, using water from the nearby river. Narcisse helped her carry it and put it together, though she installed the thing herself, digging trenches across the field to the water, then burying the pipes deep. She grew corn there, and sunflowers every third year. These crops do not withstand dryness as vines do. Narcisse had offered to help her with the installation, but she refused.

"If it's worth doing, it's worth doing yourself," she commented. This summer the sprinkler was working all night—it was useless in daytime, the water evaporating in midair before it even touched the crop. Jay could hear it from his open window, a dim whickering in the still air. In the moonlight the white spume from the pipes looked ghostly, magical.

Her main crop was grapes. She grew the corn and sunflowers for cattle feed, the vegetables and fruit for her and Rosa. There were a few goats, for cheese and milk, and these, like Clopette, roamed free around the farm. The vineyard was small, yielding only eight thousand bottles a year. It sounded a lot to Jay, and he said so.

Narcisse smiled. "Not enough," he said shortly. "Of course, it's good wine. Old Foudouin knew what he was doing when he put in those vines. You've noticed how the land tilts sharply down toward the marshes?"

Jay nodded.

"That's how she can grow those vines. Chenin grapes. She picks them very late, in October or November, sorts them, one by one, by hand on the vine. They're almost dried out by then, *hé*. But as the mist rises from the marshes every morning it dampens the vine and encourages the *pourriturre noble*, the rot which gives the wine its sweetness and its flavor." Narcisse looked thoughtful. "She must have a hundred barrels of it by now, maturing in oak, in that cellar of hers. I saw them when I made last year's delivery. Eighteen months on, that wine's worth a hundred francs a bottle, maybe more. That's how she could afford to bid for your farm."

"She must really want to stay here," commented Jay.

Narcisse looked at him. "She minds her own business," he said sharply. "That's all." Then the talk turned once again to farming.

Fifty

Summer was a door swinging open into a secret garden. Jay's book remained incomplete, but he rarely thought about it now. There were more pressing concerns. Principally, Marise. It seemed to Jay that as summer moved on, she was never far from his mind. One day furtive, the next close to expansive. Either way, she and the woman of his story grew steadily further apart. Jay did not regret this. To him Marise was more interesting than any fiction—and more in what she did not tell him than in what she said.

"These little things," she said one day, holding out one of Jay's charm bags across her hedge. "What are they? Why do you put them here?"

A little self-consciously, Jay explained about the talismans and Joe's perimeter ritual. "I don't know why I still make them," he admitted. "For luck, perhaps."

Marise brought the charm bag to her nostrils.

"Lavender," she commented. "My grandmother used it in her linen drawers." She told him that her grandmother had lived in the country. Every year until her tenth birthday Marise had spent two weeks with her, in her little cottage in Normandy.

"That was a good time," said Marise, still fingering the charm bag. "I think maybe your Joe must have been something like her."

Behind her in the orchard, Jay caught sight of the old man watching them, his pit cap cocked jauntily on the back of his head. He was wearing a T-shirt which read, CAMPAIGN FOR REAL FICTION. As Jay looked up, Joe winked.

"Did you hear that?" said Marise suddenly.

Jay shook his head.

"A car backfiring, I think. Or someone shooting at birds. And there's a funny smell, like sugar burning."

Until the end of July the heat intensified, made worse by a brisk, hot wind which dried out the corn so that its husks rattled wildly in the fields. Narcisse shook his head glumly and said he'd seen it coming. Joséphine doubled her sales of drinks. Joe consulted tidal and lunar charts, and gave Jay specific instructions on when to water in order to achieve the best effect. "It'll change soon enough, lad," he said. "You'll see."

Not that there was a great deal to lose. A few rows of vegetables. Even with the drought the orchard would yield more fruit than Jay could possibly use. In the café Lucien Merle shook his head in dark relish.

"You see what I mean," he said. "Even the farmers know it. There's no future in it anymore. People like Narcisse carry on because they don't know anything else, but the new generation—*hé*! They know there's no money in it. Every year the crop sells for less. They're living from government subsidies. All it takes is one year to be bad, and then you're taking out loans from the Crédit Mutuel so you can plant next year. And the business of the vines is no better.'' He gave a short laugh. ''Too many small vineyards, too little money. There's no living in a small farm anymore. That's what people like Narcisse don't understand.'' He lowered his voice and came closer. ''All that's going to change, though,'' he said.

''Oh?'' Jay was getting a little bored with Lucien and his great plans for developing Lansquenet. He and Georges Clairmont had put up signs on the main road and on the Toulouse road nearby which were supposed to encourage the influx of tourists.

Visitez LANSQUENET-sous-Tannes!
Visitez notre église historique
Notre viaduc romain
Goûtez nos spécialités

Most people viewed this with indulgence. If it brought business, good. Mostly they were indifferent, as Georges and Lucien were known for hatching grandiose schemes which never came to anything. Caro Clairmont tried several times to invite Jay to dinner, though so far he had managed to delay the inevitable. She also hoped that he would address her literary group in Agen. The thought appalled him.

That day it rained for the first time in weeks. A fierce rain from a hot white sky, barely refreshing. Over on the other side of the boundary, Rosa splashed around the muddy fields in her Wellingtons and sky-blue mac, while Marise herded the goats into the barn. Narcisse grumbled that, as usual, the rain came too late, that anyway it would never last long enough to wet the ground. As if to spite him, it endured late into the night, pouring out of the gutters and onto the baked ground with lively plashing sounds.

The next morning was foggy. The heavy rain had stopped, to be replaced by a dull drizzle. Jay could see from the water-logged state of the garden how heavy the downpour had been, but even without sunlight to dry it out, the standing water had already begun to dissipate, drawing the cracks in the earth together, sinking down deep.

"We needed that," remarked Joe, bending down to examine some seedlings. "Good thing you got these jackapples covered, otherwise they'd have been washed away." The Specials were in a cold frame, carefully snugged against the side of the house, and remained unharmed. Jay notoiced they were a remarkably quick-growing plant; the ones he seeded first were twelves inches tall now, their heart-shaped leaves fanning out against the glass. He had about fifty seedlings ready to be bedded out, an excellent success rate for such a demanding species.

"Aye." Joe looked at the plants with satisfaction. "Mebbe the soil here's right just as it is."

That morning also brought another letter from Nick, with news of two more offers from publishers for Jay's incomplete novel. These were not final offers, he said, though already the sums involved seemed extravagant, almost ridiculous, to Jay. His life in London, Nick, the university, even the negotiations on the novel seemed abstract here, eclipsed by even the small damage caused by an unexpected rainstorm. He worked in the garden for the rest of the morning, thinking of nothing at all.

Fifty-One

August began freakishly wet for Lansquenet. It rained every other day, and was overcast the rest of the time, with winds which lashed at crops and stripped their leaves. Joe shook his head and said he had expected it. Certainly no one else had anticipated the sudden reversal of weather patterns: the merciless rain, tearing away topsoil and washing tree roots bare. Jay went to the orchard in the rain and wrapped pieces of carpet around the bases of his trees to protect them from water and rot. It was another old trick from Pog Hill Lane, and it worked well. But without adequate sunshine, the fruit would fall unformed and unripened from the branches. Joe shrugged. There would be other years.

Jay was not so sure. He felt preternaturally sensitive to the changes in Joe, marking every change of expression, every word. He noticed that Joe spoke less than he had before, that sometimes his outline was blurry, that the radio, tuned permanently to the oldies station since May, sometimes played white noise for minutes before finding a signal. As if Joe too were a signal, gradually fading. Worse, he had the feeling that it was somehow his fault that it was happening, that something in Lansquenet was claiming him, eclipsing Joe. The rain and the falling temperature dampened the scents which were so characteristic of the old man's appearances, the scents of sugar and fruit and yeast and smoke. During the past few weeks these too had faded, so that for unbearable moments Jay felt absolutely alone, bereaved, a man sitting at a dying friend's bedside listening for the next breath.

It was mostly concern for Marise and Rosa which brought him out of this introspective mood. Now that the weather had turned so sour, Jay found himself talking to Marise more often—in Lansquenet the weather was not merely an excuse to pass the time of day, but a topic which preoccupied everyone almost to the point of obsession. The rain, which had been so welcome three weeks previously, was now a matter of serious concern to Marise.

"If it goes on like this, there won't be any fruit this autumn," she said. Peaches and apricots and other soft-skinned fruit were already done for. The rain ate through the tender flesh and they dropped, rotten, to the ground, before they had even finished developing. Tomatoes failed to ripen. Apples and pears were hardly any better. Their waxy skin might protect them to some extent, but not enough. Vines were the worst.

At this stage the grapes needed sunlight, Marise explained. Especially for the later harvests—the Chenin grapes for the noble wines—which had to be sun-dried like raisins. These grapes rely on the exceptional conditions of Lansquenet's marshland: the hot, long summers, the mists which the sun brings from across the river. This year, however, the *pourriture noble* had nothing noble about it. Rot, pure and simple, set in.

"It's like some kind of a curse," declared Narcisse gloomily from over his seed catalogue. "It's unnatural. I've never seen weather like this in Lansquenet, not in fifty years of farming."

"La Faizande has been saying it's because of La Païenne at Foudouin," remarked Briançon.

"She would," said Narcisse.

"Still, you hear stories. . . ." Briançon lowered his voice. "A suicide's always brought bad luck, in any case. And so close."

Narcisse snorted. "Bébert, aren't you getting a bit old to be listening to children's stories? Or have you got water on the brain, *hé*?"

"You said it yourself, Narcisse," said Briançon stubbornly. "It's a curse."

Marise did what she could. She ordered plastic coverings from town, which she fixed into place over the rows of vines with the help of metal hoops. This saved the vines from the worst of the rain, but did nothing to protect the roots. Any sunlight too was hampered by the presence of the sheets, and the fruit sweated inside the plastic. The earth had long since been trodden into mud soup. Like Joe, she laid pieces of carpeting and cardboard between the rows to avoid further damage to the ground. But it was a futile gesture.

"We'll manage," she assured him when Jay voiced his concern. Her voice was light, but there was a grimness in her words. "We have always managed."

"If there's anything I can do . . ." he suggested. "I could help you to dig drainage trenches, the way Joe did at Pog

Hill. Let the water flow back into the Tannes. Together we could do a decent job in a week or so."

Marise shook her head abruptly. "Thank you, no. It isn't necessary. We'll manage."

"It's no trouble," insisted Jay. "I'd *like* to help."

"*Please!*"

This was not a matter of simple reticence, Jay understood. Marise's face had been almost anguished, as if deep emotions were at war within her. There was more than mere pride at stake here. An instant later the look was gone, to be replaced by a polite remoteness which disturbed him even more. It was too close to her attitude during his early days at Château Foudouin, and Jay felt unhappily that for some reason all the progress he had made with her had been lost.

Narcisse blamed the disastrous summer on global warming. Others muttered vaguely about El Niño, the Toulouse chemical plants, the Japanese earthquake. Mireille Faizande curled her lip and talked about Last Times and the wrath of God. Briançon called in the local *curé* to bless his beehives, in case there really was a curse. Joséphine remembered the dreadful summer of '75, when the Tannes dried up and rabid foxes came running out of the marshes into the village.

Jay's own garden fared a little better than most. Farther from the marshland, raised above the water level, his land had natural drainage channels which carried excess water down to the river. Even so, the Tannes rode higher than ever, spilling out across the vineyard on Marise's side and cutting dangerously close on Jay's own, eroding the bank so sharply that great slices of earth had already fallen into the river. Rosa was under instructions not to play near it.

The barley was a disaster. Fields all around Lansquenet had already been abandoned to the rain. In one of Briançon's fields a crop circle appeared, and the more gullible of Joséphine's drinkers began to speculate about space aliens, though Roux thought that it was more likely that Clairmont's mischievous young son and his girlfriend knew more than they were telling. In spite of holy intervention, the bees were less productive this year, Briançon reported, with fewer flowers and poor-grade honey. Belts would have to be tightened throughout the winter.

"It's hard enough getting enough money from this year's crop to plant next spring," explained Narcisse. "When the crop's bad, you have to plant on credit. And with rented land becoming less and less viable—*hé!*" He poured Armagnac carefully into the hot dregs of his coffee and downed it in a single mouthful. "There's not enough money in sunflowers or corn anymore," he admitted. "Even flowers and nursery produce aren't making what they used to. We need something new."

"Rice, maybe," suggested Roux.

Clairmont was less downcast, in spite of poor business throughout the summer. Recently he had gone north with Lucien Merle for a few days, returning full of enthusiasm. It transpired that he and Lucien were planning to go into partnership on a new scheme to promote tourism in Lansquenet, though both of them seemed unusually secretive about the matter. Caro too was arch and self-satisfied, calling at the farm twice "in passing"—though it was miles out of her way—and staying for coffee. She was full of gossip, delighted with the way Jay had renovated the farm, intensely curious about the book and hinting that her influence with the regional literary societies would be certain to make it a success.

"You really should try to get yourself some French contacts," she told him naively. "Toinette Merle knows a lot of people in the media, you know. Perhaps she could arrange for you to give an interview to a local magazine?"

He explained, with an attempt not to smile, that one of the main reasons for escaping to Lansquenet had been precisely to avoid such things.

Caro simpered and said something about the artistic temperament. "Still, you really should consider it," she insisted. "I'm sure the presence of a famous writer would give us all the boost we need."

Jay barely paid attention. He was close to completing the new book, for which he'd now been offered a contract with WorldWide, a large international publisher. He'd set himself a deadline of October for finishing. He was also working on improving the old drainage channels on his land, with the aid of some concrete piping supplied by Georges. His roof too had developed a leak, and Roux had offered to help him mend it and repoint the tiles. Marise remained distant while this went on, though he sometimes caught sight of her over the hedge and thought she looked ill, or maybe just tired. He began thinking about her even more often, making unrealistic plans to help her (and to put her in his debt, he admitted secretly to himself). He walked her perimeter, hanging red sachets on the hedge, though he felt that maybe this time even Joe's remedies needed something more practical to help them along. He was certainly too preoccupied to give too much time to Caro and her plans.

Which was why the newspaper article took him completely by surprise. He would have missed it altogether if Popotte hadn't spotted it in an Agen paper and cut it out for him to read. Popotte was touchingly pleased by the whole thing, but it immediately made Jay uneasy. It was, after all, the first sign that his whereabouts were known.

The article began with a great deal of nonsense about his brilliant early career. There was some crowing about the way he had fled London and had rediscovered himself in Lansquenet. Much of it consisted of clichés and vague speculation. Worse, there was a photograph, taken in the Café des Marauds on the fourteenth of July, showing Jay, Georges, Roux, Briançon and Joséphine sitting at the bar with bottles of *blonde* in their hands. In the picure Jay was wearing a black T-shirt and madras shorts. Georges was smoking a Gauloise. Jay did not remember anyone taking a photograph. The caption read: *Jay Mackintosh and friends at the Café des Marauds, Lansquenet-sous-Tannes.*

"Well, tha couldn't have kept it quiet forever, lad," observed Joe when Jay told him. "It had to get out sometime."

He was at his typewriter in the living room, a bottle of wine at one elbow, a cup of coffee at the other. Joe was wearing a T-shirt which read, ELVIS IS ALIVE AND WELL AND LIVING IN SHEFFIELD. His outline seemed translucent at the edges, like an overdeveloped photograph.

"If I want to live here it's my own business, isn't it?" Jay said.

Joe shook his head. "Aye. Mebbe. But you're not goin' to carry on like this forever, are you?" he said. "There's papers to sort out. Permits. Practical things. Brass, anall. You'll be short of that soon." It was true that four months of living in Lansquenet had cut heavily into his savings. The repairs to the house, furniture, tools, supplies for the garden, drainage pipes, the day-to-day expenses of food and clothing—plus, of course, the purchase of the farm itself—had eroded them beyond his expectations.

"There'll be money soon enough," he replied. "I'm signing the book contract anytime now." He mentioned the sum involved, expecting Joe to be awed into silence.

Instead he shrugged. "Aye. Well. I'd rather have a quid in me hand than a check in t' post," he said dourly. "I just wanted to see you sorted, that's all. Make sure you're all right."

Fifty-Two

Still the rain continued unrelenting. Oddly, the temperature remained high, and the wind was hot and unrefreshing. At night there were often storms, with lightning dancing on stilts across the horizon and ominous red lights in the sky. A church in Montauban was hit by lightning and burned down. Briançon announced with gloomy satisfaction that it was a sign.

On September 13, the Tannes finally broke its banks and flooded the vineyard. The top end of the field suffered less, because of the sharp incline, but a foot of water covered the lower end. Other farmers suffered too, but it was Marise, with her marshy pastures, who was the worst affected. Standing pools of rainwater surrounded her house. Two goats were lost in the floodwater from the Tannes, and she had to bring the remaining goats into the barn to avoid further damage to the ground. But the fodder was wet, the roof began to leak and the stores were suffering from damp.

Marise told no one of her predicament. It was a habit with her, a matter of pride. Even Jay, who could see some of the damage, did not guess at the full extent. The house was in the hollow, below the vineyard, far from the boundary. Water from the Tannes now stood around it like a lake. The kitchen was flooded. Marise used a broom to sweep the water from the flagstones. But it always returned. The cellar was knee-deep in water. The oak barrels had to be moved, one by one, to safety. The electricity generator, which was housed in one of the small outbuildings, short-circuited and failed. The rain continued unabated.

Finally Marise contacted her builder in Agen. She ordered fifty thousand francs' worth of drainage pipes and asked for them to be delivered as soon as possible. She planned to use the existing drainage channels to install a system of piping which would channel the water away from the house and back toward the marshes, where it would drain away naturally into the Tannes. A bank of earth—like a dike—would be raised to give some protection to the farmhouse. But it would be difficult. She began the job herself, digging out channels while she waited for the delivery of pipes. It was a slow, filthy business, like digging war trenches. She told herself that it was indeed a war, herself against the rain, the land, the people. This thought cheered her a little. It was romantic.

On September 15, Marise made another decision. Until now Rosa had slept with Clopette, in her little room under the eaves of the house. But now, with no electricity and hardly any dry firewood, she had little choice. The child must leave.

The last time the Tannes had flooded, Rosa had contracted the infection which had left her temporarily deaf in both ears. She was still a baby then, and there had been no one to whom Marise could send her. They had slept together in the room under the eaves for a whole winter, with the fire gouting black smoke and rain streaming down the panes. The child had developed abscesses in both ears and screamed incessantly during the night. Nothing—not even penicillin—seemed to offer any relief.

Never again, Marise told herself. This time Rosa must go away until the rain stopped, until the generator could be fixed, until the drainage could be put into place, until the house was not so damp. This rain would not last forever. Even now, if the work could be completed, some of the crop might be salvaged.

Rosa must go away for a few days, but to whom? Marise felt her heart tighten at the thought of Mireille. Who, then? No one from the village. Mireille had spread the rumors, yes—and everyone had listened.

Well, maybe not everyone. Not Roux, or newcomers like him. Not Narcisse. But to leave Rosa with either of them would be impossible. People would find out. In the village, nothing could remain a secret for long.

She considered a *pension* in Agen, but the child was very young to be left alone. And besides, the thought of Rosa so far away was like a pain in her chest. She needed her to be close.

Only the Englishman remained. He could be trusted—to some extent, anyway. He was a foreigner, removed from the small-town politics of Lansquenet. He meant well.

Marise forced herself to think logically, suppressing a feeling of dangerous warmth at the thought of the Englishman. The location was ideal: far enough from the village for privacy, but close enough to her own farm for her to see Rosa every day. Maybe Jay could make up a room for Rosa in one of the old bedrooms—Marise remembered a blue room under the south gable which must have been Tony's, a child's bed shaped like a boat, a blue glass ball which was a lamp. It would only be for a few days, maybe a week or two. She would pay him. It would be a business arrangement, she told herself firmly, nothing more. It was the only solution.

Fifty-Three

She arrived unannounced one evening. Jay hadn't seen her for several days. In fact he hadn't really gone out, except to the village to buy bread. The café was mournful in the rain, the *terrasse* reverting back to a road as the tables and chairs were taken in, rain dripping steadily from parasols bleached colorless by the weather. In Les Marauds the Tannes had begun to stink, hot foul waves rolling off the marshes toward the village. Even the gypsies moved on, taking their houseboats to sweeter waters. Poitou was talking about calling in a weatherworker to solve the rain problem—there are still a few in this part of the country—and the idea met with less scorn than it would have a few weeks before. Narcisse scowled.

It was close to ten o'clock when Marise appeared at Jay's

door wearing a yellow slicker. Rosa was standing behind her in her sky-blue mac and red boots. Rain silvered their faces. Behind them the sky was occasionally lit by a dull orange flare of distant lightning. Wind shook the trees.

"What's wrong?" Marise's sudden appearance surprised Jay so much that at first he didn't even think to invite them in. "Has something happened?"

Marise shook her head.

"Come in, please. You must be freezing." Jay cast an automatic glance behind him. The room was tidy enough to pass muster. Only a few empty coffee cups littered the table. He caught Marise looking curiously at his bed in the corner. Even after the roof was fixed, he'd never quite got around to moving it upstairs to a bedroom.

"I'll make you a drink," he suggested. "Here, take your coats off." He hung their slickers in the kitchen to drip and put on some water to boil. "Coffee, hot chocolate? Wine?"

"Some chocolate for Rosa, thank you," said Marise. "Our electricity is down. The generator shorted."

"Jesus."

"It doesn't matter." Her voice was calm and businesslike. "I can fix it. We've had this kind of problem before. The marshland is very prone to flooding." She looked at him. "I have to ask you for help," she said.

Jay thought it was an odd way of putting it. *I have to ask you.*

"Of course," he said. "Anything."

Marise sat down stiffly at the table. She was wearing jeans and a green sweater which brought out the green in her eyes. She touched the typewriter keys tentatively. Jay saw that her nails were cut very short, and that there was dirt under them.

"You don't have to say yes," she said. "It's just an idea I had."

"Go on."

"Do you write with this?" She touched the typewriter again. "Your books, I mean?"

Jay nodded. "Can't stand computers."

She smiled. She looked tired, he noticed, her eyes strained and bruised-looking. The smile did not reach them. Her voice was crisp and resolutely businesslike.

"It's Rosa," she said at last. "I'm worried she might catch cold—fall ill—if she stays in our damp house. I wondered if you would perhaps find room for her in your farm for a few days. Only a few days," she repeated. "Until I can get the house back into shape. I'll pay you." She pulled out a bundle of notes from the pocket of her jeans and pushed them across the table. "She's a good girl. She wouldn't interfere with your work."

"I don't want money," said Jay.

"But I—"

"I'd be happy to take Rosa. You too, if you like. I have plenty of room for both of you." She looked at him with an air of bewilderment, as if in surprise—almost resentment— that he was so eager to help.

"I can imagine the problems the flooding has caused," he told her. "You're very welcome to use the farm for as long as you like. If you want to bring some clothes—"

"No," she said quickly. "I have too many things to take care of at home. But Rosa . . ." She swallowed. "I would be very grateful. If you would."

Rosa was exploring the room. Jay could see her looking at the pile of typed sheets he had arranged in a box on the end of his bed.

"Is this written in English?" Rosa inquired curiously. "Is this your book?"

Jay nodded. "See if you can find some biscuits in the

kitchen," he told her. "The chocolate will be ready soon." Rosa scampered off through the doorway.

"Can I bring Clopette with me when I come?" she called from the kitchen.

"I don't see why not," said Jay.

From the other room Rosa gave a crow of triumph. Marise looked at her hands. Her face was slightly flushed.

"Thank you." It was almost a whisper. She tightened her lips, as if afraid of what might come out. Her green-blue eyes were all summer flecked with gold. Her hair was black with the rain.

"Your hair's wet," said Jay. "I'll get you a towel."

Marise began to protest, looking anxiously toward the door. "I should go back," she said. "The generator—"

"It's all right," Jay told her, suddenly desperate to make her stay, if only for a few minutes. "At least wait until Rosa settles down. I'll open a bottle of wine."

———

As he reached for it in the rack it was already alive in his hand, black-corded Damson '76, releasing its scent as he touched it, effervescent. Jay could just see Joe, standing in the shadows beside the kitchen door, the light from the table-lamp gleaming on his bald forehead. He was wearing a T-shirt with the words ART FOR ART'S SAKE written on it in red, and holding his pit-cap in his hand. His face was little more than a blur, but Jay knew he was smiling.

"I don't know if you'll like it," said Jay, pouring the wine. "It's a special kind of home brew." The purple scent was thick, almost cloying. To Jay it had an aftertaste which reminded him of the sherbert fountains Gilly had enjoyed so much. To Marise it was more like a jar of jam which has remained sealed for too long and turned to sugar. The taste was tannic, penetrating. It warmed her.

"It's strange," she said through numbed lips. "But I think I like it." She sipped again, feeling the heat crawl down her throat and into her body. A scent like distilled sunlight filled the room. To Jay it suddenly felt right that they should drink it together. He wondered why he had never thought to share Joe's wine with her before. Strange too that the taste, though odd, should be so pleasant. Maybe at last, as Joe had predicted, he was getting used to it.

"I've found the biscuits," announced Rosa, appearing at the doorway with one in each hand. "Can I go upstairs and look at my room?"

Jay nodded. "You do that. I'll call you when the chocolate's ready."

Marise looked at him. She knew she should feel wary, but instead there was a softness working through her, smoothing all tension. She felt very young again, as if the scent of the strange wine had released something from her childhood. She remembered a party dress precisely the color of the wine, a velvet party dress cut down from an old skirt of her grandmother's, a tune played on the piano, a night sky wide with stars. His eyes were exactly the same color. She felt as if she had known him for years.

"Marise," said Jay quietly. "If there's something wrong—"

"It's made of fruit, isn't it? Black currant, is it? Or elderberry?" She was speaking too fast, she knew, trying to divert Jay from what she feared he might say. "It tastes . . . like plum jam, a little, or like the pies my grandmother used to make from her windfalls. There's something else in there, too, cinnamon, maybe, or—"

"Please. Whatever it is, you can trust me. You can talk to me."

It was as if she had been dragging a heavy plow behind her for the past seven years and had only just realized it. It

was as simple as that. *You can talk to me*. Joe's bottle was a
hive of secrets, uncoiling like busy vines in the still air, peo-
pling the shadows.

Jay touched her face, making her look at him.

"Marise. Whatever you're hiding—this secret you feel you
can't tell me—it goes further than just keeping Rosa away
from Mireille. You seem as if you're under siege. You're so
terrified someone's going to find out, whatever it is, that you
can hardly bear to accept an offer of help from me."

Marise made a gesture of protest. "That's not true. I'm
trusting you with Rosa. I've never done that before with
anyone."

"Why won't you accept more of my help, Marise? You're
killing yourself on the farm, and what for? To prove to everyone that you can manage alone?"

"No. Of course not."

"You look sick, Marise. You look scared."

She shook her head. "Please—"

"If it's a financial problem, I can help. If it's—"

"It isn't *money*!" Her voice was scornful. "You think that's
what it is? You think I get hysterical every time the rent is a
little late, or the rain spoils the harvest?" She should not trust
Jay, Marise thought to herself. The wine was drawing more
out of her than she was prepared to give. But the wine was
strong. It rocked her gently in a cradle of scents and memories.
It teased out her secrets.

Trust me. The voice from the bottle snickered and crooned.
Trust me.

She poured another glassful of wine, downed it recklessly.
Her eyes were fierce and brilliant.

"Listen," she said.

Fifty-Four

"*I* met him when I was twenty-one," she began. "I was a student nurse at a psychiatric hospital in Nantes, and he was a lecturer in the Université de Rennes. He was divorced. He was much older than me. His name was Patrice."

He had been tall and dark, like Jay. They had had lodgings in the same block of flats on the outskirts of the city. She had moved from Paris six months before and had made few friends in Nantes. She was estranged from her parents.

Marise did not look up as she spoke, but instead watched her hands climbing up and down the stem of the wineglass as if playing a glass flute.

"At twenty-one you're so eager to find love that you see

it in every stranger's face," she said softly. "Patrice was a real stranger. I slept with him once. That was enough."

He had changed almost instantly. As if a steel cage had come down over the two of them, they were trapped together. He became possessive, not in the charming, slightly insecure way which had first attracted her, but in a cold, suspicious manner which frightened her. He quarreled with her constantly. He followed her to work and harangued her on the ward. He tried to make up for his rages with lavish presents which frightened her even more. His harassment grew ingenious, escalated. A funeral wreath, delivered to her workplace. Graffiti on her door. A mountain of unwanted mail-order items in her name: fetishwear, farm equipment, orthopedic supplies, erotic literature. Little by little her courage was eroded. The police were powerless to help. Without proof of physical harm, they would have had little with which to charge him.

"Finally I moved out," she said. "I left the flat and accepted a transfer to Paris. I rented a little apartment in Rue de la Jonquière, and I found a job in a clinic in Marne-la-Vallée." It had taken him eight months to find her.

"He used my medical records," explained Marise. "He must have managed to talk someone at the hospital into giving them to him. He could be very persuasive. Very plausible."

Patrice had changed since their last meeting, she had noticed immediately. He had shaved his head and wore army surplus. His siege of her flat had all the precision of a military campaign. There were no more practical jokes, no unwanted pizzas or begging notes. Even the threats stopped. She saw him twice, sitting in a car beneath her window. Then two weeks passed and there was no further sign of him. She began to believe she had been mistaken, that it hadn't been Patrice sitting in that car.

A few days later she awoke to the smell of gas. He had bypassed the main valve somehow, and she could find no way to turn it off. She tried the door, but it was jammed shut, wedged from the outside. The windows too had been nailed shut, though her flat was on the third floor. The phone was out. She finally broke a window and screamed for help. But the police weren't willing to take Patrice into custody. And it had been too close a call.

Reluctantly she moved to Marseille. That was where she met Tony.

"He was nineteen," she remembered. "I was working on the psychiatric ward of Marseille general hospital, and he was an outpatient. From what I understood, he had been suffering from a minor bout of depression following his father's death." She smiled wryly. "I should have known better than to involve myself with a patient. But we were both vulnerable. He was so young. His attention flattered me. That was all. And I was good with him. I could make him laugh. That flattered me too."

By the time she realized how he felt, it was too late. He was infatuated with her.

"I told myself I could love him," she said. "He was funny and kind and easy. After Patrice, I thought that was all I wanted. And he kept telling me about this farm, this place. It sounded so safe, so beautiful. It was everything I'd dreamed of since my grandmother died. And Tony needed me. That already meant a lot."

She had allowed herself to be persuaded. And at first Lansquenet had seemed everything she had ever wanted. But soon there were clashes between Marise and Tony's mother.

"She hated me on sight," explained Marise. "I couldn't do anything well enough for her boy. I didn't deserve him. I was too old for him. I couldn't sew, or cook properly. She disapproved of my clothes. She disapproved of my accent. The first week I arrived in Lansquenet I caught a cold, and after that she was always telling people I was sickly."

Jay poured the last of the wine into her glass. Even the dregs were highly scented, and for a moment he thought he could distinguish all the rest of Joe's wines in that glassful, raspberry and roses and elderflower and blackberry and damson and jackappple all in one.

"The worst thing was, she was right, in a way. I *didn't* deserve Tony. I loved the farm more than him. And more than him, I loved the idea of a family. I wanted to build everything I'd never had with my own family. I had a picture in my mind of how it would be, of living in a tiny little community, of having a family and friends, of making wine and digging potatoes and everything being so simple—"

Marise stopped talking. Her hair obscured her face. Jay had the sudden feeling that he'd known her for years. Her presence at his table was as natural, as familiar as that of his old typewriter. He put his hand on hers. Her kiss would taste of roses. She looked up, and her eyes were green as his orchard.

"Mireille says I killed him, doesn't she? She says it's my fault Tony died."

Jay nodded. "But Mireille's an old woman with a grudge," he said reassuringly. "No one really believes what she says."

"But it's true," said Marise flatly. "I *am* responsible. Tony—"

"*Maman!*" Rosa's voice cut through the moment with shrill insistence. "I've found a little room upstairs! There's a round window and a blue bed shaped like a boat! It's a bit dusty, but I could clean it up, couldn't I, *Maman*? Couldn't I?"

Marise looked up abruptly. She looked confused, awoken in the middle of a dream. She pushed the half-empty wine-glass away from her.

"I should go," she said quickly. "It's getting late. I'll bring Rosa's things across. Thank you for—"

"It's all right." Jay tried to put his hand on her arm, but she pulled away. "You can both stay if you like. I have plenty of—"

"No." Suddenly she was the old Marise again, the confidences at an end. "I have to bring Rosa's sleeping things. It's time she was asleep." She hugged Rosa briefly but fiercely. "You be good," she said to her daughter. "And please"—this was to Jay—"don't mention in the village that she's staying here." She unhooked her yellow slicker from the peg behind the kitchen door and pulled it on. Outside, the rain was still falling.

"Promise?" said Marise.

"Of course."

She nodded, a curt, polite nod, as if concluding the business between them. Then she was gone into the rain.

Jay closed the door behind her and turned to Rosa.

"Well? Is the chocolate ready?" she asked.

"Let's see, shall we?"

He poured the drink into a wide-mouthed cup with flowers on the rim. Rosa curled up on his bed with the cup and watched curiously as he tidied away the cups and carried them into the kitchen.

"Who was he?" she called out. "Is he English too?"

"Who's that?" Jay said from the kitchen, washing dishes in the sink.

"The old man," said Rosa. "The old man from upstairs."

Jay turned off the tap and turned to look at her.

"You saw him? You talked to him?"

Rosa nodded. "An old man with a funny hat on," she said. "He told me to tell you something." She took a long drink of her chocolate, her lips emerging from the cup with a frothy foam mustache.

Jay felt suddenly shivery, almost afraid. "What did he say?" he whispered.

Rosa frowned. "He said to remember the Specials," she said. "That you'd know what to do."

"Anything else?" Jay's mouth was dry, his head pounding.

"Yes." She nodded energetically. "He told me to say goodbye."

Fifty-Five

Pog Hill Lane, 1999

s an adult, Jay had never felt as if he belonged anywhere. London certainly hadn't been home. The
places he lived all looked the same to him, even Kerry's Kensington house. And twenty years had passed without him ever
returning to Kirby Monckton.

But this year was different. Perhaps it was simply that for
the first time, there were greater fears to face than going back
to Pog Hill. It had been nearly fifteen years since *Jackapple
Joe*, for example. Since then, nothing.

This went beyond writer's block. He felt as if he were
stuck in time, forced to write and rewrite the fantasies of his
adolescence. *Jackapple Joe* was the first—the only—adult book
he had written. But instead of releasing him, it had trapped

him in childhood. He'd lost the art, he'd rejected magic. As
if when he dropped Joe's seeds into the cutting at Pog Hill
he was also letting go of everything he'd clung to during those
past three years: the talismans, the red ribbons, Gilly, the
dens, the wasps' nests, the treks along the railway lines and
the fights at Nether Edge. Everything blowing away into the
cutting with the litter and the ash of the railbed.

But there must have been something left. Curiosity, perhaps. An itch at the back of his mind which refused to be
scratched. Perhaps he'd mistaken the signs at Kirby Monckton.
After all, what evidence had he found that Joe was nothing
like what he'd claimed to be? A few boxes of magazines? A
map marked in colored pencils? Perhaps he jumped to a false
conclusion. Perhaps Joe was telling the truth after all.

And perhaps Joe hadn't left for good.

It was something Jay had hardly dared imagine. Joe back
at Pog Hill? In spite of himself, the idea brought his heart
into his throat. He imagined the house as it had been, overgrown perhaps, but with the allotment still well ordered behind the camouflage of Joe's solution, the trees decorated with
red ribbons, the kitchen warm with the scent of brewing
wine. . . .

He waited several weeks before he actually made the trip.
Kerry was supportive—imagining perhaps a renewed source
of inspiration, a new book which would propel him back into
the limelight. She wanted to come with him; was so persistent
that he finally agreed.

But the moment he arrived, he knew it had been a mistake
to come. Rain the color of soot leaked from the clouds. Nether
Edge had been reclaimed as a riverside building development;
bulldozers and tractors had crawled across the disused railbed,
leaving behind neat identical bungalows. Fields had become
car showrooms, supermarkets, shopping centers.

Kirby's remaining mines had been closed for years. The canal was being renovated; with the help of Millennium funding, there were ongoing plans for the development of a visitors' center, where tourists could descend an especially converted mine shaft or ride a barge on the newly cleaned canal.

But that wasn't the worst.

In spite of everything, he had expected Pog Hill to have survived. The main road was still more or less unchanged, with its graceful, if slightly blackened Edwardian houses, and its avenue of lindens. The bridge, too, was as he remembered it, the only change a new pedestrian crossing at one end. The same line of poplars marked the entrance to Pog Hill Lane, and Jay's heart played a funny little riff against his ribs as he pulled the car over to the roadside and looked up the hill.

"Is that it?" Kerry asked eagerly. "I don't see any sign or anything."

Jay said nothing and got out of the car. Kerry followed him.

"So this is where it all began," Kerry said musingly.

He ignored her and took a few steps forward up the hill.

They had changed the name of the lane. There was no Pog Hill on any map now, or Nether Edge, or any of the places around which his life had revolved for those three long-ago summers. It was called Meadowbank View now, the houses knocked down to give way to a row of brick-built two-story flats with little balconies and geraniums in plastic planters. A sign on the nearest building read MEADOWBANK QUALITY RETIREMENT FLATS. Jay went to stand where Joe's house would have been. There was nothing but a small parking area (RESIDENTS ONLY). Behind the flats, where Joe's garden had once stood, there was a bland square of lawn with a single small tree. Of Joe's orchard, of the herb garden, the rows of black currants and raspberries and gooseberries, the vines, plums, pears, the carrots, parsnips, the Specials—nothing remained.

"Nothing."

Kerry took his hand.

"Poor darling," she whispered into his ear. "You're not too *terribly* upset, are you?"

Jay shook his head. He needed to be alone here. Kerry's sympathy—well-meaning though he knew it to be—only made him feel worse. The division between them—between those times at Pog Hill Lane and his life with her in London— was too deep to be bridged by good intentions. He would never be able to make her understand.

"Wait for me in the car, okay?"

Kerry looked slightly hurt. "If you like, Jay. I just thought you might want someone with you, that's all."

Jay gave her what he hoped was a reassuring smile. "Two minutes, okay?"

Just in time, she left. He felt as if he might explode if he held it in anymore. He ran to the back of the garden and looked over the wall down into the cutting. It was filled with rubbish. Sacks of household waste covered the ground; discarded fridges, car tires, crates, pallets, tin cans, stacks of magazines tied together with twine. Jay felt a kind of laughter welling in his throat. Rubbish sprawled down the steep hill, as if flung there by passersby. A baby carriage. A shopping cart. The frame of an ancient bicycle. Pog Hill cutting had been converted into a landfill site.

With an effort Jay pulled himself up so that he could straddle the wall. The hidden railbed looked a long way down from here, a sheer drop for most of the way into a scrub of bushes and a continent of litter. On the far side of the wall graffiti artists had been at work. A scree of broken glass sparkled in the sun. One unbroken bottle lay against a protruding stump, the light gleaming on its dusty base. A red cord, grubby with age, was knotted around its neck. He knew at once it was Joe's.

How it had escaped the demolition of Joe's house, Jay couldn't imagine; how it could have remained intact since then was an even greater mystery. But it was one of Joe's bottles, all right—one of the Specials. The colored cord proved it, as did the label, the old man's painstaking handwriting still legible. As Jay made his way down toward the bridge, he thought he saw more of Joe's belongings strewn down the bank. A broken clock. A spade. Some buckets and pots in which plants had once grown. It looked exactly as if someone had stood at the top of the hill and had simply hurled the contents of Joe's house into the cutting below. Jay picked his way through the sad wreckage, trying to avoid broken glass. There were ancient copies of *National Geographic*. Here were pieces of a kitchen chair. And finally, a little farther down, he found the seed chest, its legs broken off, one door hanging. Sudden white rage pumped through him. It was a complex feeling, directed as much at himself and his foolish expectations as at Joe for letting this happen. It included rage at the person who had stood at the top of the hill and dumped an old man's life into the gully. Worse, there was fear, the dreadful knowledge that he should have come here sooner, that there had been something here for him to find, but that—as always—he had come too late.

He searched until Kerry came to find him almost an hour later. He was filthy, muddied to the knees. But he'd collected six bottles, scattered around the cutting, and miraculously unbroken.

Specials.

Fifty-Six

Lansquenet, Summer 1999

After Rosa's announcement, Jay knew at once that Joe was gone. There was a finality in that goodbye which could not be ignored. For several days he denied the certainty, but the house no longer smelled of his smoke. The oldies station had stopped broadcasting, to be replaced by a local station on the same frequency, blasting out modern hits. And there were no more glimpses of Joe just around the corner of a cold frame, or behind the shed, or in the orchard inspecting the trees. No one sat and watched Jay work at his typewriter, unless it was Rosa. And wine was just wine.

This time he felt no anger at Joe's absence. Instead there was a sense of inevitability.

A week passed. The rain began to taper off, leaving damage

in its wake. Jay and Rosa stayed mostly indoors. Rosa was easy to please. She occupied herself. She read quietly in her newly furnished room under the eaves or played Scrabble on the floor or went for splashy walks around the field with Clopette. Sometimes she listened to the radio, or played with dough in the kitchen, baking small, hard, floury biscuits. Every evening Marise joined them and made dinner, staying just long enough to eat and to talk to Rosa before returning to work. There were no more confidences, and Jay, too preoccupied with his own thoughts, did not invite any. Instead Marise and Jay made small talk about practical matters: the house, the repairs, the rain.

The generator had been restored. The drainage ditches were taking time, but would be complete in a few more days. Marise had enlisted Roux and some other workers from Clairmont's yard to help her. Even so, the vineyard remained half-flooded.

Jay had few visitors. Popotte called by twice with the mail and once with a cake from Joséphine; luckily Rosa was around the back of the house and went unnoticed. Once Clairmont came by with another load of bric-a-brac, but did not stay. Now that the worst of the weather was past, most of the others had work of their own to do.

After Joe's departure, Rosa's presence was more than welcome, for the house seemed oddly bereft. For a child of her age she was very quiet, however, and sometimes Jay could almost believe that she belonged more to Joe's world than to his. And the child missed her mother. Except for on one occasion, they had never been apart, and she greeted Marise every evening with a fierce, wordless hug.

A few days later Popotte brought a package from Nick, containing the contracts for the purchase of his novel, which Jay was supposed to sign and return. The package also included a number of newspaper clippings, dated from July to September. A brief note from Nick read: *I thought you might be interested in these.*

Jay pulled out the clippings. All related to him in some way. He read them. Three small news items from national papers speculating about his disappearance from London. A piece from *Publishers Weekly* outlining his return to writing. A retrospective from the *Sunday Times* entitled WHATEVER HAPPENED TO JACKAPPLE JOE? with pictures of Kirby Monckton. Jay turned the page. There, staring out at him with an impudent smile, was a photograph of Joe.

WAS THIS THE ORIGINAL JACKAPPLE MAN? queried the headline.

He stared at the image of Joe at fifty, maybe fifty-five. Bareheaded, a cigarette at the corner of his mouth, his small half-moon glasses perched on the end of his nose. In his hands he was holding a large pot of chrysanthemums adorned with a rosette. The caption read: *Local eccentric.*

The article continued:

Mackintosh, with his usual reticence, has never chosen to reveal the identity of the original Joe, though sources suggest that this man may have been the inspiration for the nation's favourite gardener. Joseph Cox, born in Sheffield in 1912, worked first as head gardener at a stately home, then for thirty years at Nether Edge Coalworks in Kirby Monckton before ill-health forced him to retire. A well-known local eccentric, Mr Cox lived for many years in Pog Hill Lane, but recently took up residence at the Meadowbank Retirement Home. Miss Julie Moynihan, a day nurse at the home, described him to our reporter. "He's really a lovely old gentleman, with such a wonderful store of anecdotes. I'm thrilled to think he might have been the original Joe."

Jay barely looked at the rest of the article. Conflicting emotions raked through him. Amazement that he should have come so close to seeing Joe and not known, not sensed his presence somehow. Most of all, an overwhelming sense of relief, of joy. The past could be redeemed after all.

He forced himself to read the rest of the article. He learned nothing new. There was a summary of *Jackapple Joe*, with a picture of the original cover. And at the end, the journalist's byline.

Of course. Kerry. That made sense. She had known about Pog Hill Lane, and about Joe. And of course she knew a great deal about Jay. She had access to photographs, diaries, papers. Five years of listening to his ramblings, his reminiscences. He knew a fleeting moment of anxiety. What exactly had he told her? What had he given away? He didn't suppose that after the way he'd walked out he had a right to expect any loyalty or discretion from her. He could only hope that she would stay professional and keep his private life private. He suddenly realized that he didn't feel like he knew Kerry well enough to predict what she'd do.

But at the moment none of that seemed really important. What mattered was Joe. Jay could be on a plane to London within a few hours, he told himself giddily, then catch the express north. He could be in Kirby Monckton by that evening. He could see Joe again. He could even bring him back to Lansquenet, if that's what the old man wanted. He could show him Château Foudouin.

A strip of newsprint, barely the size of a book of stamps, fluttered free of the rest and came to land on the floor; he must have missed it among the other clippings. Jay picked it up and turned it over.

A note at the top of the paper read:

Kirby Monckton Post.
Obituaries—ctd.
Joseph Edwin COX, on September 15th, 1999, quietly, after
a long illness.

> *The kiss of the sun for pardon,*
> *The song of the birds for mirth,*
> *One is nearer God's heart in a garden*
> *Than anywhere else on earth.*

Jay looked at it for a long time. The paper slipped from
between his fingers, but he could still see it, brightly illuminated in his mind's eye in spite of the dullness of the day.

Fifty-Seven

The next few days were spent inhabiting a kind of vacuum. Jay slept, ate, drank in a daze. The Joe-shaped hole in things had become something monstrous, blotting out the light. The book lay abandoned, close to completion, in a box under his bed. Even though the rain had stopped, he could not bear to look at the garden. The Specials grew leggy, unattended in their pots, awaiting transplanting. What fruit had survived the weather fell unregarded to the ground. The weeds, which had grown hungrily throughout the wet weather, were beginning to take over. In a month there would be no sign of any of his work.

The kiss of the sun for pardon . . .

The worst of it was to have been within reach of the mystery and to have lost it again, stupidly. It all seemed so pointless. He imagined Joe watching from the wings, waiting to jump out.

Jay remembered a quote he'd once heard about the past being an island surrounded by time. With Joe gone, it was as if Pog Hill never existed.

The kiss of the sun for pardon . . .

Joe had been there, he told himself. Joe had been alive at Pog Hill throughout that summer. *Astral travel*, he'd said. *Why'd you think I do so much bloody sleepin'?* Joe had come to him after all. Joe had tried to make amends. And still Joe died alone.

It was good for Jay that Rosa was still here. Marise's visits too lifted him temporarily. At least this way he had to stay sober during the daytime. Routines needed to be observed, even if they had become meaningless.

Jay realized that Marise had half-noticed a change in him, but there was already too much to think about at the farm for her to give this more than passing attention. The drainage work was almost completed, the vineyard free of standing water, the Tannes shrinking back to its banks at last. She'd had to give up a proportion of her savings to pay for the work and the new supplies, but she felt heartened. If the harvest could be salvaged, there was still hope for next year. If only she could raise enough money to buy the land. . . .

She only hoped Mireille would not interfere. After all, the old woman had no interest in seeing her leave. Quite the opposite. She and Mireille needed each other, however much the old woman loathed the thought.

Marise had no qualms about the fact that she'd lied. She had, after all, done Mireille a favor. The truth lay dormant,

like the unused capacity for mutually assured destruction between two powerful nations. Each possessed a weapon too
terrible to be used in war.

But time was running out for both of them. For Marise,
the lease's end was drawing near. For Mireille, age and illness.
With an increased sense of urgency in the air, Marise only
wondered whether the old threat would hold fast. Perhaps it
meant nothing to Mireille now. The thought of losing Rosa
once kept them both silent. But now . . . she wondered what
Rosa meant to Mireille anymore. She wondered if Mireille
still felt she had something to lose.

Fifty-Eight

Jay awoke to birdsong. He could hear Rosa moving around upstairs; straw-colored sunlight was coming through the shutters. For a fleeting moment, he experienced a sensation of well-being. Then the recollection of Joe's death hit him, a bolt of grief he was unable to field, taking him by surprise.

Every day he woke up expecting things to be different, but every morning it was the same.

He stumbled out of bed, half-dressed, and put some water on to boil. He splashed cold water on his face from the kitchen tap. He made coffee and drank it scalding. Upstairs he could hear Rosa running a bath. He put food and milk on the table for her breakfast. One bowl of *café-au-lait*, with three wrapped sugar lumps on the side. A slice of melon. Cereal. Rosa had a healthy appetite.

"Rosa! Breakfast!" His voice sounded hoarse. There were a number of cigarette butts in a saucer on the table, though he could not recall having bought or smoked any, and for a second he felt a stab of something which might have been hope. But none of the butts were Players.

There was a knock at the door. Popotte, he thought dimly, probably bringing another bill, or an anxious letter from Nick demanding to know why he hadn't signed and returned the contracts. He drank another mouthful of coffee and made for the door. Someone was standing outside, immaculate in gray slacks and cashmere cardigan and Louis Vuitton document case. She gave him a brilliant smile.

"Kerry?"

For a second he saw himself in her eyes, barefoot, unshaven.

"Is this a bad time?" she said doubtfully.

For a moment he just stared at her.

"I know you weren't expecting me, but I just couldn't resist surprising you. What a *wonderful* place!" She looked curiously behind him into the house. "It's lovely. You've kept everything so authentic."

Jay turned and pulled some dirty clothes off the back of a chair. Then he turned back and nodded to her.

"Come in. Sorry it's such a mess," he began, trying not to sound so apologetic. "How did you find me? I didn't exactly go out of my way to advertise where I was staying."

"What do you think? Nicky told me." She smiled. "Of course, I had to *persuade* him. You know everyone's been very worried about you? Running off like that. Keeping this new project to yourself. But Nicky knew you wouldn't mind if he told *me*."

"I read your article," he said. "It was very good."

Kerry smiled. "I've been writing a few pieces for the literary supplements," she said. "There's going to be a terrific amount of interest in the new book, you know. The moment I saw the manuscript—"

"You've read it?"

Kerry's face was flushed and animated.

"Of course I did, and I love it. Do you think Nick could have kept it away from me? When you left London in that extraordinary way, you practically admitted to me that you were working on something new. You could have told me, you know—I suppose you felt I'd cramp your style."

Jay sat down, feeling slightly dazed.

"Kerry, it wasn't like that—"

"Anyway, it's wonderful. I always knew you'd do it eventually—fourteen years isn't really such a long time, after all. And it's better—it's actually better than *Jackapple Joe*. The way you depict this place—you make everything so *real*—I just had to see it all for myself. Then, when I saw how well it could tie in—your book, and my program—"

Jay shook his head. It was aching, and he couldn't help thinking that he'd missed something important. "*What* program?"

Kerry glanced at the cereal and coffee and fruit laid out on the table. "Can we talk about this over breakfast? I'm absolutely *starving*." Jay watched her pour a bowlful of *café-au-lait*. "You've really gone native, haven't you? I mean, coffee in bowls and Gauloises for breakfast. Were you expecting company, or am I not supposed to ask?"

"I'm looking after a neighbor's child," Jay told her, trying not to sound defensive. "Just for a few days until the floods go down. Look, Kerry, about this program you mentioned—"

Kerry nodded. "Channel Five. *Pastures New*. It's going to be all about British people living abroad. One of those lifestyle-travelogue shows. And when Nicky mentioned this wonderful *place*—plus everything that's happening with your book—it just seemed like serendipity."

"Wait a minute." Jay put down the coffee cup. "You're not thinking of getting me involved, are you?"

"Why, of *course*," replied Kerry impatiently. "The place is ideal. I've already spoken to a few of the locals, and there's terrific interest. And *you're* ideal. I mean, just think of the publicity. When the new book comes out—"

Jay shook his head. "I'm not interested," he said. "Kerry, I know you're trying to help, but the last thing I want right now is publicity. I came here to be alone."

Jay saw that she was looking beyond him into the kitchen. He turned around. Rosa was standing behind the door in her red pajamas, eyes bright with curiosity, hair corkscrewing in all directions.

"*Salut!*" said Rosa, grinning. "*C'est qui, cette dame? C'est une Anglaise?*"

Kerry looked at her in surprise. "What a sweet little girl. Is she the neighbor's daughter? What's her name?"

Rosa stared at Kerry with cheery and frank curiosity, before sitting at table, a croissant in each hand.

"Kerry," said Jay, feeling his discomfort grow, "I'm really not interested in doing a television program."

"I'm sure you'll change your mind when you've had the chance to have a think about it," she said.

"I won't," said Jay.

Kerry raised her eyebrows. "Whyever not? It's just perfect. It could relaunch your career."

Jay shook his head.

Kerry looked at him narrowly, silent for a moment. Then

she spoke. "There's something changed about you," she said reflectively. "At first, when you opened the door, I thought it was this place. This little place with its single stop sign and its wooden houses on the river. It would have been just like you to fall in love with it. To make it another Pog Hill. But that isn't all, is it?"

He shook his head. Kerry glanced at Rosa and poured herself another coffee. A flicker of comprehension passed through her green eyes.

"I knew it would happen sometime," she said softly. "Someone would manage to light the fuse. At one point I even thought it was going to be me."

Jay said nothing.

"It's her mother, isn't it?" said Kerry. "Your neighbor. Marise." Her smile was painful. "Does she even know about your work, Jay? Does she care about what you do?"

Jay thought about it for a moment. "No," he said, with an odd smile. "I don't think she does. She cares about the land. The vines. Her daughter."

"You'll tire of a woman who is only interested in simple things," predicted Kerry without bitterness. "I know you too well. If you really cared about simple things, you wouldn't write books. You'd raise goats, or dig potatoes for a living." She stood up and kissed him lightly on the cheek. "Give it some thought," she advised. "Take your time over the decision. Trust me, Jay, *Pastures New* is exactly what your career needs right now."

As soon as Kerry had left, Jay drove into Lansquenet, leaving Rosa with strict instructions not to leave the house, and blew off some of his anger on the phone to Nick Horneli. Nick was less contrite than he'd expected.

"I thought it would be a good bit of promotion for you,"

he said blandly. "It isn't often you get a second chance in the publishing business, Jay, and I have to say I thought you'd be a bit more keen to make the most of this one."

"Oh." It wasn't what he'd expected to hear, and for a moment he was taken off balance.

"Plus, I don't like to rush you, but I'm still waiting for your signed contracts and the last part of the new manuscript. The publishers are getting edgy, wondering when you're going to finish. If I could only have a first draft—"

"No." Jay could hear the strain in his own voice. "I'm not going to be pressured, Nick. I told you—"

"Sure you told me." Nick's voice was sharp, almost impatient. "You also told me you were serious about getting back into print."

"Well, of course I'm serious!"

"Then you should behave as if you are." Nick's tone was suddenly, terrifyingly indifferent. "Remember you're an unknown quantity nowadays, Jay. A bit of a legend, sure. That's no bad thing. But you've got a reputation too."

"What reputation?"

"I don't think it's very constructive at this—"

"*What* fucking reputation?"

Nick's shrug was audible. "You're a risk, Jay. You're full of great ideas, but you haven't produced anything of real value in years. You're temperamental. You don't meet deadlines. You're always late to meetings. You're a bloody prima donna living on a reputation years out of date who doesn't understand that in this business you can't afford to be precious about publicity."

Jay tried to keep his voice level. "What are you trying to say, Nick?"

Nick sighed. "All I'm saying is be a little flexible," he said.

"Publishing has moved on since *Jackapple Joe*. In those days it was okay for you to be eccentric. It was expected. Even a little charming. But nowadays, you can't afford to let anyone down. Least of all me."

"So?"

"So I'm telling you that if you don't want to do *Pastures New*, then that's your decision. But if you don't sign the contract and finish the manuscript within a reasonable time—say a month or so—then WorldWide will pull out and I'll have blown my credibility for nothing. I have other clients, Jay. I have to think about them too."

"I see."

"Look, Jay. I'm on your side, you know."

"I know." Suddenly he wanted to get off the phone. "I've had a bad week, Nick. Too much has been happening. And when Kerry turned up on my doorstep—"

"She wants to help, Jay. She cares about you. We all do."

"Sure. I know."

He hung up feeling suddenly insecure. Something had shifted. As if with the removal of Joe's protective influence he had become vulnerable again. Jay clenched his fists.

"Monsieur Jay? Are you all right?" It was Joséphine, her face pink with concern.

He nodded.

"You'll have some coffee? A slice of my cake?"

Jay knew he ought to be getting back to check on Rosa, but the temptation to stay a while was too strong. Nick's words had left a nasty taste in his mouth, not least because they were true.

Joséphine was full of news. "Georges and Caro Clairmont have been in touch with an English lady, someone from the television. She says she might want to make a film here, something about travel. Lucien Merle is full of it too. He thinks it could be the making of Lansquenet."

Jay nodded wearily. "I know."

"You know her?"

He nodded again. The cake was good, glazed apple on almond pastry. He concentrated on eating. Joséphine explained that Kerry had been talking to people for several days, making notes with her little tape recorder, taking snapshots. There was a photographer with her too, an Englishman, *très comme il faut.*

"They're here because of me," Jay acknowledged. He explained the situation, from his hasty departure from London to Kerry's arrival.

Joséphine listened in silence. "How long will they stay, do you think?"

Jay shrugged indifferently. "As long as it takes."

"Oh." Pause. "Georges Clairmont is already talking about buying up derelict properties in Les Marauds. He thinks land prices will go up when the TV program airs."

"They probably will."

She looked at him oddly. "It is a good time to buy now, after the wet summer," she continued. "People need the money. There's been no harvest to speak of. They can't afford to keep unproductive land. Lucien Merle has already spread word in Agen."

Jay couldn't shake the feeling of reproach that he heard in her voice.

"It won't harm your business, though, will it?" he said with an attempt at lightness. "All those thirsty people hanging around the café."

She shrugged. "Not for long," she said. "Not here."

Jay paused, remembering that Le Pinot now had twenty cafés, restaurants, a McDonald's and a leisure center. Local businesses had closed down when real estate prices went up, to be replaced by more enterprising outfits from the cities. Farmers had sold their land, which now was worth more for development than for the income it produced when worked. Rents doubled, trebled. He wondered if Joséphine could handle the competition if this kind of change came to Lansquenet. On the whole, it was unlikely.

He drove back to the farm with a feeling of unease reinforced by Joséphine's lukewarm goodbye. He saw Narcisse on the road and waved, but he did not wave back.

Jay returned to Château Foudouin almost an hour after he'd left. He parked the car on the drive and went in search of Rosa, who, he supposed, must be getting hungry. The house was empty. Clopette was wandering about at the edge of the vegetable patch. He called Rosa's name, but there was no reply. Feeling slightly worried now, he went around the back of the house, then to Rosa's favorite spot by the river. Still nothing. What if she had fallen in the water? The Tannes was still dangerously swollen, its banks eroded to the point of near-collapse. What if she had wandered onto one of the old fox traps? Or fallen down the cellar steps?

He searched the house again, then the grounds. The orchard. The vineyard. The shed and the old barn. Nothing. Not even footprints. Finally he crossed Marise's field, hoping the child might have gone to see her mother. But Marise was putting the finishing touches to her newly dry and repainted kitchen, hair bound up in a red scarf, paint on the knees of her jeans.

"Jay!" She seemed pleased to see him. "Is everything all right? How's Rosa?"

He couldn't bear to tell her that he couldn't find her daughter.

"Rosa's fine. I wondered . . . if you needed anything from the village."

Marise shook her head. She seemed not to have noticed his unease.

"No, I'm all right," she said cheerfully. "I've almost finished here. Rosa can come back tomorrow morning."

Jay nodded. "Great. I mean . . ."

She flashed him one of her rare, warm smiles.

"I know," she said. "You've been very kind and patient. But you'll be pleased to have the house to yourself again."

Jay grimaced. His head was beginning to hurt again. He swallowed.

"Look, I should be getting back," he said awkwardly. "Rosa . . ."

She nodded.

"You've been very good with her," she said. "You can't imagine—"

Jay couldn't bear her gratitude. He ran all the way back to the farm.

————

He spent another hour searching for possible hiding places. He knew he should never have left her. Rosa was a mischievous child, subject to all kinds of whims and fancies. She might even now be hiding from him, as she had often hidden during his first weeks on the farm. All this might be her idea of a joke. But as time passed and Rosa was nowhere to be found, he began to consider other options. It was all too easy, for example, to imagine her climbing the banks of the Tannes and sliding in, being taken downriver for a couple of kilometers to be washed up against a mudbank, or even as far as Les Marauds. Easy too to imagine her simply wandering off down the road to Lansquenet, perhaps being picked up by some stranger in a car.

Some stranger? But there were no strangers in Lansquenet. Everyone knew everyone else. Doors were left unlocked. Unless . . . Suddenly he remembered Patrice, Marise's stalker from her Paris days. Surely not, in seven years . . . But that would explain many things. Marise's reluctance to come into the village. Her refusal to leave the place which had become a safe haven for her. Her fierce protectiveness of Rosa. Could Patrice have somehow traced them to Lansquenet? Had he been watching the farm, waiting for an opportunity to make his move? Could he be one of the villagers themselves, keeping close, biding his time?

The idea was ridiculous. Pure comic-book fiction, the kind of thing he himself might have written, aged fourteen, on a lazy afternoon by the canal. All the same, he felt his chest contract at the thought. He imagined Patrice looking a little like Zeth, grown taller and meaner with age, his tribal cheeks thinner, his eyes crazy and clever. Zeth with a real shotgun this time, waiting at the gate with that look of mean appraisal in his eyes. The conflation of Zeth and Patrice, in his mind, was at once ridiculous and somehow fitting. As if his life kept repeating the same patterns—a red-haired girl, Joe's disappearance, and on and on. The way his thoughts had slipped back relentlessly toward that last October at Pog Hill Lane.

Jay thought of taking the car to look for Rosa, but rejected the idea. Rosa might be hiding in a bush or by the roadside, too easy to miss, even driving slowly. Instead he walked along the road toward Lansquenet, stopping occasionally to call her name in a barely audible voice. He looked in ditches and behind trees. He detoured to a welcoming duck pond which might possibly have tempted an inquisitive child, then to a deserted barn. But there was no sign of her. Finally, on reaching the village, he tried his last realistic option. He made for Mireille's house.

The first thing he noticed on arrival was the car parked in front. A long gray Mercedes with a smoked-glass windshield and rental-car plates. A gangster's car, he thought, or that of a game-show host.

Heart pounding in sudden realization, Jay made for the door. Without pausing to knock, he opened it, calling harshly, "Rosa?"

She was sitting on the landing in her orange sweater and jeans, looking at an album of photographs. Her Wellingtons were parked by the door. She looked up as Jay called her name and grinned. Relief almost brought him to his knees.

"What have you been playing at? I've been looking everywhere for you. How did you get here?"

Rosa looked at him, unabashed. "But your friend came to fetch me. Your English friend."

"Where is she?" Jay could feel the relief washing away into black rage.

"Jay?" Kerry was standing in the kitchen doorway with a glass of wine in one hand. "What's wrong?" Behind her stood Mireille, monumental in her black housedress.

"I called to have another word with you, but you'd gone out," explained Kerry. "Rosa answered the door. She and *grand-maman* have been having a lovely talk, haven't we, Rosa?" This last utterance was in French, presumably to include Mireille, who stood wordlessly behind her. "I've been talking to people in the village, Jay, and I have to say I think poor Madame Faizande has every right to see her granddaughter."

Jay glanced at Mireille, who was watching, hands crossed over her enormous bosom. "Kerry," he began. "You know nothing about this situation—"

"Oh, I don't know as much as you do, of course, but I do know that this is an old lady with no family left but this little girl, and whatever quarrel your friend Marise may have had with her in the past, Rosa has nothing to do with it." Kerry looked defiant. "I told Madame Faizande her granddaughter was staying with you. She honestly didn't know you'd be out when we called. Jay, if you'd only seen the look on her face when she heard Rosa's voice."

Jay realized that the minute Kerry had suspected his feelings for Marise, Kerry would be no friend of hers.

Mireille glared at him. "You had no right to keep her from me," she said stonily. "I have a right to see my Tony's daughter." As her gaze fell on Rosa, Mireille's expression lost some of its rigidity. "*Hé!* She's so very like him," she said in a gentler tone. "So very bright. Very full of life." Then her voice changed again, making Rosa look up in surprise from her album. "She didn't even remember my Tony's face," moaned the old woman. "She didn't know her father's *face!* That's what her mother's done to me. Erased me from their lives!" Against her chest the big hands clutched fitfully.

Jay looked upstairs at Rosa. "Come here, Rosa," he said quietly. "Time to go home."

Rosa looked at Mireille with curiosity. "Are you really my grandmother?" she asked.

Mireille gave a strangled cry and turned abruptly toward the kitchen.

Kerry handed Rosa's Wellingtons to Jay. "You see? No harm done," she said, and paused. "I hear you've made a lot of friends here, by all accounts," she went on. "You'll be quite the local hero when *Pastures New* takes off. The place needs a boost."

Jay ignored her. There was already too much to think of without getting into a discussion with Kerry about publicity.

"Are we going to be on television?" queried Rosa smartly, stepping into her Wellingtons. "*Maman* and you and everyone? We've got a television at home. I like *Cocoricoboy* and *Nos Amis Les Animaux*. But *Maman* doesn't let me watch *Cinéma de Minuit*." She made a face. "Too much kissing."

Jay took her hand. "No one's going to be on television," he told her.

"Oh."

"It's all right if you don't want to appear," remarked Kerry. "I have the makings of an excellent program already, with or without you. The artist, his influences, you know the thing. Forget what Peter Mayle did for Provence. Before you know it, people will be flocking here."

"Please, Kerry—"

"Oh, for Christ's sake, Jay! Anyone would think I had a gun to your head. Anyone else would give their right arm for this kind of free publicity!"

"Not me. I don't want people rushing here," he said. "You know what that kind of media attention does to a place."

Kerry shrugged. "I don't see anyone turning business away."

She was right, of course. That was the worst of it. The momentum sweeps everyone along. He imagined Lansquenet, like Pog Hill, relegated to the growing ranks of things which only existed in the past.

Fifty-Nine

*M*arise arrived at seven as usual, carrrying a bottle of wine and a closed wicker basket. She had washed her hair, and was wearing a long red skirt with her black sweater. It made her look different, gypsylike, and there was a touch of color on her lips. Her eyes were shining.

"I feel like celebrating," she announced, putting the bottle on the table. "I've brought some cheese, and *foie gras*, and some nut bread. There's a cake too, and some almond biscuits. And some candles."

She brought out two brass candlesticks from the hamper and stood them on the table. Then she fixed a pair of candles into the openings.

"It looks nice, doesn't it?" she said. "I can't remember when we last had dinner by candlelight."

"Last year," replied Rosa pertly. "When the generator broke down."

Marise laughed. "We didn't have a choice then. That doesn't count."

That evening, she was more relaxed than Jay had ever seen her. She and Rosa laid the table with brightly painted plates and crystal wineglasses. Rosa picked flowers from the garden for a centerpiece. They had *foie gras* on nut bread with Marise's own wine, which tasted of honey and peaches and toasted almonds, then salad and warm goat's cheese, then coffee, cakes and petits fours. Throughout the little party Jay tried hard to concentrate. Rosa, under instructions not to mention their visit to Lansquenet, was cheery, insisting on her *canard*— a sugar lump dipped in wine. When that was done, she began surreptitiously feeding Clopette scraps under the table, until the goat was banished to the garden, through the half-open window. Marise was bright and talkative and lovely in the golden light.

It should have been perfect. He told himself he was waiting for the right time to tell her about Rosa's afternoon. Of course he knew there would be no right time, he was simply procrastinating. He had to tell her before she found out from someone else. Worse still, before Rosa let something slip.

But as the evening passed, it felt harder and harder to say the words. His conversation died. His head began to ache. Marise seemed not to notice. Instead she was full of details about the next phase of her drainage plan, the extension to the cellar, relief that there would still be a wine crop, though much reduced, optimism for next year. She was planning to buy the land when the lease ran out, she said. There was money in the bank, plus fifty barrels of *cuvée spéciale* in her cellar, increasing in value each year. Land was cheap in Lansquenet, especially poorly drained, problem land like hers. After the bad summer, prices might drop still more. And Pierre-Emile, who had inherited the estate, was no businessman. He would be happy to get what he could for the farm and the vineyard. The bank would make up the rest with a long-term loan.

The more she said, the worse Jay felt. Remembering what Joséphine had told him about land prices, his heart sank. Tentatively he asked what might happen if for some reason she was unable to buy the farm.

Her face hardened a little. She shrugged. "I would have to leave," she said simply. "Leave everything, go back to Paris or to Marseille. Let Mireille—" She bit off the rest of the sentence and made her expression resolutely cheerful. "But that won't happen," she said firmly. "None of that will happen. I've always dreamed of actually owning my own place," she went on, her face softening. "A farm, land of my own, trees, perhaps a little river. Somewhere private. Safe." She paused. "Perhaps when I have the land to myself and there is no lease to hang over my head, things will be different," she said unexpectedly. "Perhaps I could begin again with the people in Lansquenet. Find Rosa some friends her own age. Give people another chance." She poured another glass of the sweet golden wine. "Give myself another chance."

Jay swallowed with difficulty. "But what about Mireille? Wouldn't she cause problems for you?"

Marise shook her head. Her eyes were half-closed, catlike, sleepy. "I can handle Mireille," she said at last. "Just as long as I own the farm."

For a while the conversation turned to other things. They drank coffee and Armagnac, and Rosa fed more petits fours

to the goat through the gap in the shutters. Then Marise sent
Rosa to bed, evincing only a token complaint—it was almost
midnight and she had been up for much longer than she was
used to. Jay could hardly believe that the child had not given
him away during the course of the meal. In a way, he regret-
ted that she hadn't.

As Rosa vanished upstairs (with a biscuit in each hand
and a promise of pancakes for breakfast), he turned on the
radio, poured another glass of Armagnac and passed it to
Marise.

"Mmm. Thanks."

"Marise?"

She glanced at him lazily.

"Why does it have to be Lansquenet?" he asked. "Couldn't
you have moved somewhere else after Tony died? Avoided
all this—this bitterness with Mireille?"

She reached for the last petit four. "It has to be here," she
said at last. "It just has to be."

"But why? Why not Montauban or Nérac or one of the
villages nearby? What is there in Lansquenet which you can't
have anywhere else? Is it because Rosa has always lived up
here? Is it—is it because of Tony?"

She laughed then, not unkindly, but on a note he couldn't
quite identify. "If you like. Because of Tony."

Jay's heart tightened suddenly. "You don't talk about
him much."

"No. No, I don't." She looked into her drink in silence.

"I'm sorry. I shouldn't ask so many questions. Forget I
said it."

Marise gave him an odd look, then looked back into her
drink. Her long fingers moved nervously.

"It's all right. You've helped me. You've been kind. But

it's complicated, you know? I wanted to tell you. I've wanted to tell . . . *someone* . . . for a long time."

Jay tried to say that she was wrong, that he didn't want to know after all, that there was something else he desperately needed to tell *her*. But nothing came out.

"For a long time I had a problem with trust," said Marise slowly. "After Tony. After Patrice. I told myself I didn't need anyone else. That we would be safer on our own, Rosa and I. That no one would believe the truth if I told it anyway." She paused, tracing a complicated figure on the dark tabletop. "Truth is like that," she went on. "The more you want to tell someone, the harder it gets. The more impossible it seems."

Jay nodded. He understood that perfectly.

"But with you . . ." She smiled. "Maybe it's because you're a foreigner. I feel I've known you a long time. Trusted you. Why else should I have trusted you with Rosa?"

"Marise . . ." He swallowed again. "There's something I really . . ."

"Shhh." She was flushed now with the wine and the warmth of the room. "I need to explain. I tried before, but . . ." She shook her head. "I thought it was so complicated," she said softly. "It's really very simple. Like all tragedies. Simple and stupid." She took a breath. "I was caught up in it all before I knew it. Then I realized it was too late. Pour me some more Armagnac, please."

He did.

"I liked Tony. I never loved him. But love doesn't sustain anything for long anyway, I thought. Money does. Security—the farm, the land. That was what I needed, I told myself. Escape from Patrice. Escape from the city, and from loneliness. I fooled myself into believing it was enough, that I didn't need anything else. Worse still, I fooled myself that Tony wouldn't notice, that it wouldn't make any difference."

It had been all right for a time. Marise liked Lansquenet, and Tony was touchingly pleased with her approval. Mireille remained cool, but Tony was dismissive of Marise's fears. All mothers-in-law were difficult at first.

But as Mireille became increasingly demanding, Tony's behavior grew increasingly erratic. In Mireille's presence, he was often unusually silent and introverted, letting her cook his meals and iron his clothes and fuss over him as if he were still a boy of twelve. He spoke to his mother in a low, furious voice when Marise was out of the room, lapsing into sudden silence when she entered. He had violent swings of mood. Marise suspected a return of the depression which had first afflicted him when his father died and tried to talk to Mireille about it, but without success. As far as Mireille was concerned, there was nothing wrong with Tony.

"He's a strong, healthy boy," she would repeat stubbornly. "Stop trying to protect him, wrap him in cotton. You'll make him as neurotic as you are yourself."

From then on every peculiarity of Tony's behavior was blamed on Marise. The sullen silences, the angry outbursts. When Tony behaved like a spoiled child, Mireille humored him, even encouraging him—as long as his bad temper was turned toward Marise.

When he learned Marise was pregnant, Tony seemed to soften. Everything about the pregnancy delighted him. He waited on Marise constantly, protesting if she so much as stood up unaided. Mireille saw this as evidence of his devotion. Marise felt both touched and irritated at his boyish exuberance. Then, when she was least expecting it, the letters started coming.

"I knew it was Patrice straightaway," admitted Marise. "It

was his style. The usual abuse. But somehow, here, he didn't frighten me. We had guard dogs, guns, space. I thought Patrice knew it too. Somehow he'd found out about my pregnancy. The letters were all about it. Get rid of the baby and I'll forgive you, that kind of thing. I ignored them."

Then Tony, who had never known about Patrice, found out.

"I told him everything," she said wryly. "I thought I owed it to him. Besides, I wanted him to understand that we were safe, that it was all in the past. Even the letters weren't coming as often. It was dying down."

She sighed. "I should have known better. Tony took the letters as a personal attack. He was desperate to prove to me that he could deal with it. He stocked up on food so we only needed to go into town once a month. Tony bought an expensive security system and kept his shotgun loaded by the door every night. He was like a boy playing soldiers. I told him it wasn't necessary, but I think that excited him even more. Of course, Mireille blamed me."

Rosa was born at home. Mireille helped deliver her. She was disappointed that Rosa wasn't a boy, but said there would be plenty of time for more children. She expressed surprise that Rosa looked so small and delicate. She gave advice on feeding, changing and care. Often the advice came close to tyranny.

"Of course, Tony had already told her everything about Patrice," Marise remembered. "I should have expected it. He was incapable of hiding anything from her. In her mind I quickly became the guilty party, a woman who led men on, then expected her husband to protect her from the consequences."

A fierce cold sprang up between the two women. Mireille was always at the house, but rarely addressed Marise directly.

Whole evenings would pass with Tony and Mireille talking of events and people of which Marise knew nothing. Tony, cocooned in maternal affection, never seemed to notice that Marise was not included. Avidly Mireille fussed over the baby, pointing out the slightest touch of rash or hint of the sniffles with grim satisfaction.

Then, out of the blue, Patrice came to call.

"It was late summer," Marise recalled. "About eight in the evening. I'd just fed Rosa and was upstairs putting her to bed; Tony went to the door. It was Patrice."

He had changed again since the last time she had seen him. Now he was plaintive, almost humble. He did not demand to see Marise. Instead he told Tony how sorry he was about his behavior, that he had been ill, that only now had he been able to face up to the fact. Marise listened from upstairs. He had brought money, he explained, twenty thousand francs. Not enough to pay for the harm he had done, no. But perhaps enough to start a trust fund for the baby; he wanted to somehow make up for terrorizing Marise.

"He and Tony went out back together. They were gone a long time. When Tony returned, it was dark and he was alone. He told me it was over, that Patrice wouldn't trouble us again. He was more loving than he'd been for a long time. I began to think things were okay."

For a few weeks they were happy together. Marise looked after Rosa. Mireille was unusually absent. Tony no longer stood guard at night. Then one day, as she went to pick some herbs by the side of the house, she noticed the barn door half-open. Going to shut it, she found Patrice's car, ill-concealed behind some bales of straw.

"At first Tony denied it," she said. "Just like a boy. Refused to admit I'd seen it at all. Then he went into one of his rages. Called me a whore. Accused me of seeing Patrice behind his back. At last he admitted it—he'd taken Patrice into the barn that day and killed him with a spade.''

Marise was utterly paralyzed—it seemed completely unreal. So dramatic—like a film or a novel. It couldn't possibly be her life, it was too horrifying. Tony showed no remorse. He'd had no choice, he said. If anyone was at fault, it was Marise herself. Grinning like a guilty schoolboy, he explained how he had brought the car into the barn and hidden it, then buried Patrice somewhere on the estate.

"Where?" Marise had asked.

Tony had shaken his head. "You know I can't tell you that," he said.

Marise guessed that Mireille had been responsible for Tony's reluctance to talk. His mother had already half-persuaded him that Marise had never loved him, and that she had only married him to gain a hold on his inheritance.

"I tried to make him tell me where he'd buried the body," explained Marise. "I said he had to go to the police. I still had the letters from Patrice, and we could have proved that he'd been threatening me. But Tony wouldn't listen. He burned the letters. He was like a child, pretending it hadn't happened.''

Tony's behavior worsened rapidly. He would spend hours alone with his mother, then would lock himself in his room with the television blaring. He would not even look at Rosa.

"Finally I'd had enough. I packed my things. I said that if he didn't go to the police, I would leave him. Mireille screamed at me that it was my fault, that I'd driven him to it, that I was welcome to leave, but that they'd fight me for Rosa. Tony started shouting at Mireille, saying he didn't want me to go. Mireille was saying he'd be better off without me, that she'd look after Rosa, that everything would be back as it was. . . ."

Marise took another glass of wine. Her voice was unsteady.

"Finally one night he promised me he would go to the police the next morning. Mireille walked out in a terrible rage, accusing him of choosing me over her. I was so relieved—I really thought . . ."

At eight the next morning she had found him in the barn.

"I tried to leave then," she said in a flat voice. "I packed my bags a second time. I even booked a train ticket to Paris for myself and Rosa. But Mireille stopped me. Before Tony died, she said, he'd told her everything. He'd also told her that Patrice was buried somewhere on the Foudouin estate. Only she knew where."

"You'll have to stay here now, hé," said Mireille in triumph. "I won't let you take my Rosa away. Otherwise I'll tell the police you killed that man from Marseille, that my son told me about it before he died, that he killed himself because he couldn't stand the burden of protecting you."

"She was very persuasive," said Marise with a touch of bitterness. "Made it clear that she was keeping quiet for Rosa's sake. Keeping it in the family. It was all so unreal, like a nightmare."

After that came Mireille's campaign to isolate Marise from the rest of the village. It wasn't difficult; in the course of that year she had hardly gotten to know anyone and had spent most of her time on the farm. Mireille released all her hidden resentment. She spread rumors around the village, hinted at dark secrets. Tony had been popular in Lansquenet. Marise was only an outsider from the city. Soon the reprisals began.

"Oh, nothing too serious," said Marise. "Letting off fireworks under my windows. Letters. Comments. General harassment. I'd had a lot worse with Patrice."

But it soon became clear that Mireille's campaign was designed for more than simple spite.

"She wanted Rosa," explained Marise. "She thought that if she could drive me out of Lansquenet, she might be able to keep Rosa for herself. I'd have to let her, you see. Because of what she knew."

She shivered.

Marise had managed to keep them at bay. All of them. Holed herself up in her farm, deliberately isolating herself from everyone in Lansquenet. Isolating Rosa by using her temporary deafness to deceive Mireille. Patrice's car she dumped in the marshes, letting it sink deep under the reeds and standing water. Its presence incriminated her still further, she understood. But she needed it to be close. On her land. Where she knew where it was.

The burial site of the body remained a mystery.

"At first I looked for it," she told me. "I searched the buildings. Under the floors. Methodically. But it was no use. All the land right down to the marshes belonged to the estate. I couldn't search every meter."

Plus there was old Emile. It was always possible that Tony had gone as far as Emile's property. In fact Mireille had hinted at it already, in her sour, gleeful way, relishing her power and her hold. It was this which had made Marise so eager to bid for the Foudouin farm.

It was such a dramatic story, and such a dark one. It was hard to imagine that there *was* so much more to Marise than he'd even begun to guess. Jay tried to imagine what she must have felt, seeing him in the house, watching him dig up the beds, wandering around the orchard. Wondering every day whether maybe today . . .

Impulsively he took her hand. It was cold. He could feel a thin tremor through her fingertips, almost imperceptible. A wave of admiration for her dizzied him. For her courage.

"That was why you didn't want anyone working on your land," he said. "That was why you didn't give up the marshland for the new hypermarket. That's why you have to stay here."

She nodded.

"I couldn't let anyone find it," she said. "So long after, no one would believe I'd had nothing to do with it. And I knew Mireille wouldn't back me up. She'd never admit that her precious Tony . . ." She took a deep breath.

"So now you know," she said with an effort. "Now someone else knows."

She smelled of thyme and rain. Her hair was a fall of flowers. Jay imagined himself telling her what had happened today, imagined her face tightening, stony, forbidding.

"I've been so afraid to tell anyone," she said in a low voice. "You see, it happened because of me. Because I wanted this place, this land. Mireille is right: I should never have married Tony. Whatever *she* might have done, however responsible she feels, *I* was the one who brought Patrice here. That's why I can't let her near Rosa. What if she told Rosa about the damage I'd done?"

It was at this point that Jay should have told her about how he'd lost Rosa earlier that day. Someone else might have told her then. Someone of greater courage, greater clarity. But she was too precious to him suddenly, and he couldn't conceive of causing her pain by teaching her a lesson about one more man who couldn't be trusted.

Instead he pulled her toward him, feeling her hair against his face, her lips against his, her eager softness in his arms and her breath against his cheek. Her kiss tasted exactly how he'd imagined it: raspberries and smoky roses. They made love there, on Jay's unmade bed, with the goat looking curiously through the half-closed shutters and the sweet golden light kaleidoscoping across the dim blue walls.

Sixty

oon. Soon. They were in everything now—the Specials—
in the air, the ground, in the lovers, in him lying on his
bed staring at the ceiling, in her, asleep, her face turned into
the pillow like a child's, her bright hair a pennant against the
linen. More potent now than ever, their eager voices urged,
coaxed. *Soon*, they whispered. *It has to be soon. It has to be
now.*

Jay looked at Marise asleep beside him. She looked trusting, secure. She murmured something quiet and wordless in
her sleep. She smiled. Jay pulled the blanket closer around
her and she buried her face in it with a long sigh.

Jay watched her and thought about the morning. There

must be something he could do to prevent the terrible things his presence had set in motion. He could not abandon Lansquenet to developers. The film crew was arriving tomorrow. That gave him—what? Six hours? Seven?

To do what? What could he do in seven hours? Or seventy, for that matter? What could *anyone* do?

Tha could do somethin'. The voice was almost familiar. Cynical, hearty, a little amused.

Tha never did have much sense, lad.

This time it really was Joe's voice. For a second his heart leaped, but he realized that Joe's voice was in his mind, in his memory. Re-creating it was just a way of whistling in the dark.

Remember the Specials, I told you. Don't you remember?

"Of course I do," whispered Jay helplessly. "But—"

Why don't you bloody listen? Joe's voice was everywhere now, in the air, in the light from the dying embers, in the glow of her hair spread out across the pillow. *Where were you when I was teaching you, all those times at Pog Hill? Didn't you learn anything?*

"Sure." Jay shook his head, puzzled. "But without you none of that stuff works anymore. Like that last time at Pog Hill—"

From the walls, laughter. The air was rich with it. A phantom scent of apples and smoke seemed to rise from the coals. The night sparkled.

Put your hand often enough in a wasps' nest, said Joe's voice, *and you're going to get stung. Even magic won't stop that. Even magic doesn't go against nature. You've got to give magic a hand sometimes, lad. Give it a chance to work for itself. You've got to create the right conditions for magic to work.*

"But I had the talisman. I believed—"

Never needed any talisman, replied the voice. *You could have helped yourself. You could have fought back, couldn't you?*

Jay thought about that for a moment.

———

No one saw him leave the house. No one was watching. Nor was the deep basket of herbs which he carried in any way unusual. The broad-leaved plants which filled it might be a present for someone, a gift for a flagging garden. Even the fact that he was muttering something under his breath—something which sounded a little like Latin—would not surprise them. He was, after all, English, therefore a little crazy. *Un peu fada, monsieur Jay.*

He found he remembered Joe's perimeter ritual very well indeed. There was no time to make incense, nor to prepare any new sachets, but he did not think that mattered now. He could sense the Specials around him now, hear their whispering voices, their fairground laughter. He took the seedlings carefully from the cold frame, as many as he could carry, along with a trowel and a tiny fork. At intervals at the roadside, he planted them. He planted several at the intersection with the Toulouse road, two more at the stop sign, two more on the road to Les Marauds. Fog—Lansquenet's special fog which rolled off the marshes and into the vineyards—rose about him like a bright sail in the early sun. Jay Mackintosh hurried on his circuit, half-running in his haste, planting Joe's *Tuberosa rosifea* wherever there was a branch in the road. Road signs he turned around, or covered with greenery when he could not dig them out of the soil. Georges and Lucien's "welcome" placard he removed altogether.

By the time he had finished, there was not a single signpost for Lansquenet-sous-Tannes remaining. It took him almost four hours to complete the fourteen-mile circuit, looping around the village toward the Toulouse road, then back across Les Marauds. By the end he was exhausted. His head ached, his legs felt shaky as stilts. But he had finished. It was done.

As Joe had hidden Pog Hill Lane, Jay thought in triumph, he had hidden the village of Lansquenet-sous-Tannes.

Marise and Rosa had left by the time he got back. The sky began to lighten. The mist cleared.

Sixty-One

It was nine before Kerry arrived—crisp and cool in a white blouse and gray skirt, her document case in one hand. Jay was waiting for her.

"Good morning, Jay."

"You're back."

She looked over his shoulder into the room, noting the empty glasses and the wine bottles.

"We *should* have started earlier," she said, "but would you believe it? We got lost in the fog. Great blankets of white fog, just like what they make with dry ice at a heavy metal concert." She laughed. "Can you imagine? Half a day wasted already. And on our budget . . . I'm still waiting for the camera crew. They took some kind of a wrong turn and ended up halfway back to Agen. These roads. It's a good thing I already knew the way."

Jay looked at her. It hadn't worked, he thought bleakly. In spite of everything, in spite of his faith.

"So you're still going ahead with it?"

"Well, of course I'm going ahead," replied Kerry impatiently. "It's too good an opportunity to miss." She smiled brightly. "You're a celebrity. When the book comes out and I can show the world where you got your inspiration . . . It's such a wonderful book," she added. "It's going to be a terrific success. If anything, even more successful than *Jackapple Joe*."

Jay nodded. She was right, of course. Pog Hill and Lansquenet: two sides of the same tarnished coin. Both sacrificed, each in its own way, to the writing career of Jay Mackintosh.

"I don't know why you're looking like that," said Kerry. "After all, you've got the WorldWide contract. That's a very generous sum you're looking at—more than generous."

"You're right." A most peculiar feeling of calm, almost of drunkenness, was beginning to steal over him. His head felt as if it were filled with bubbles. The yeasty air seethed and hissed.

"They must want you very much," remarked Kerry.

"Yes," said Jay slowly. "I think they do."

That was it, he thought dazedly. So simple. So . . . simple.

"I mean, publishing has changed." Kerry was warming to her subject. "You can't go off doing your own thing all the time anymore. You can't—"

That was when Jay laughed. All at once his head was full of light. He could smell smoke and swampy water and the sweet heady scent of ripe blackberries. The air was elderflower champagne. He knew Joe was with him, that Joe had never left. Not even in '77, Joe had never left. He could almost see him standing by the door in his old pit cap and boots, grinning in that way he had when he was especially pleased with something, and though Jay knew it was in his imagination, he knew it was real too. Sometimes real and imaginary are the same thing after all.

Two paces took him to the bed where the manuscript and the WorldWide contracts were still lying in their box. He pulled it out.

Kerry turned toward him curiously. "What are you doing?"

Jay picked up the manuscript in his arms. "Do you know what this is?" he asked her. "It's the only copy I have of the book. And this—" holding out the signed contract for her to see—"is the paperwork. Look. It's all completed. Ready to be sent off."

"Jay, what are you doing?" Her voice was sharp.

Jay grinned and took a step toward the fireplace. "You told me that if I didn't need to do *this*"—he gestured at the thick typescript in his arms—"then I'd be digging potatoes, or breeding goats. Or maybe I'd be making wine."

"Jay?"

"Well, I *don't* need the words on the page." He was still grinning. "It's already here. It's all around me. It always was."

"You can't—" began Kerry.

Jay looked at her. "No such bloody word," he said.

And behind Kerry's sudden shriek, he thought he could hear the sound of an old man's chuckle.

She shrieked because she suddenly knew what he was going to do. It was crazy, ridiculous, the kind of impulse to which he had never been prone, and yet there was also a strange light in his eyes which had never been there before. As if someone had lit a fuse. His face was illuminated. He took the contracts in his hands, crumpled them and pushed them into the back of the grate. Then he began the same with the pages of the typescript. The paper began to catch, first crisping, then turning brown, then leaping into gleeful flame. The air was whirling with black butterflies.

He grinned at her, breathless with laughter.

"You're crazy," Kerry told him, her voice unsteady. "You're not going to make me believe you don't have copies of that manuscript. Plus the contracts can be replaced."

"Sure they can. But they won't. And what use to anyone is a writer who never writes? How long can you sustain public interest in that? What's it worth? What am *I* worth without it?"

Kerry looked at him. The man who had left her six months ago was unrecognizable. The old Jay was vague, sullen, directionless. This man was driven, illuminated. His eyes were shining. In spite of what he was throwing away—stupid, criminal, mad—he looked happy.

"You really are crazy," she said in a strangled tone. "Throwing everything away—and for what? Some gesture? It isn't you, Jay. I know you. You'll regret it."

Jay just looked at her, smiling a little. Patiently.

"I don't see you staying here beyond a year." Her voice was shaking. "What are you going to do? Farm? You've hardly any money. You've blown it all on this place. What will you do when the money runs out?"

"I don't know." His tone was cheery, indifferent. "Do you care?"

"Jay, it's such a *waste*!"

He shrugged. "You'd better page your film crew and tell them to meet you somewhere else," he told her quietly. "There's no story for you here. Better try Le Pinot, just across the river. I'm sure you'll get something suitably upbeat and entertaining there."

She stared at him, amazed. Just for a moment, she thought she smelled something, a strange, vivid scent of sugar and apples and blackberry jelly and smoke. It was a nostalgic scent, and for a second she could almost understand why Jay loved this place so much, with its little vineyards and its apple trees and its roaming goats on the marsh flats. For that instant she was a little girl again, with her mother in the kitchen making pies, with the wind from the coast making the telephone wires sing. Somehow, she felt the scent was a part of Jay, something which clung to him like old smoke. As she looked at him for a moment, he looked *gilded* somehow, as if lit from behind, filaments of brightness shooting from his hair, his clothes. Then the scent was gone, the light was gone, and there was nothing but the staleness of the unaired room and the dregs of the wine on the table in front of them. Kerry shook her head in disbelief. Her hands were trembling.

"I might just drive out to Le Pinot," she said at last. "Georges Clairmont tells me there was a production of *Clochemerle* filmed there recently. It might make a decent feature."

Jay smiled. "Good luck, Kerry."

———

When she had gone, he washed and put on a clean T-shirt and jeans. He considered for a moment what to do next. Even though he felt sure he'd done the right thing, he knew that in the real world—as opposed to in stories—that didn't always guarantee a happy ending.

Around him now the house was absolutely still. The buzz of energy which permeated the walls had vanished. No phantom scent of sugar and smoke remained. Even the cellar was quiet, where he'd stored some new bottles of wine he'd bought. Sauternes and Saint-Emilion and a dozen of young Anjou—still and silent. Waiting.

Sixty-Two

round noon Popotte brought a parcel and the news from the village. The film crew had never arrived, she reported excitedly. The English lady had interviewed no one. Georges and Lucien were furious. *"En tout cas,"* she said with a shrug. It was probably for the best. Everyone knew that their plans never came to anything. Georges was already talking about a new venture, some kind of development plan in Montauban.

———

The parcel was postmarked Kirby Monckton. Jay opened it alone, with care, unwrapping the stiff sheets of brown paper, untying the string. It was large, and heavy. As he removed

the packaging, an envelope fell out. He recognized Joe's writing. There was a single sheet of faded letter paper inside.

Pog Hill Lane, September 15th.
Dear Jay,
    Sorry about the rush. I never was any cop at goodbyes. I
meant to stay on a bit longer, but you know what things are
like. Bloody doctors won't tell you anything till the last minute.
They think that because you're old you've got no idea. I'm send-
ing you my collection—I reckon you'll know what to do with it.
You should have learned something by the time you get this.
Make sure you get the soil right.
Affectionate regards,
Joseph Cox.

Jay read the letter again. He touched the words on the
page, written in black ink in that careful, shapeless hand. He
even lifted the paper to his face to see if anything of Joe
remained—a whiff of smoke, maybe, or the faint scent of ripe
blackberries. But there was nothing. If there had been magic,
it was elsewhere. Then he looked inside the package.

Everything was there. The contents of the seed chest, hundreds of tiny envelopes and twists of newspaper, dried bulbs,
grains, corms, seed fluff no more substantial than a puff of
dead dust, every one marked and numbered. Everything alight
with the scent of exotic places, *Tuberosa rubra maritima*, *Tuberosa diabolica*, *Tuberosa panax odarata*, thousands of seeds
for potatoes, squash, peppers, carrots—Joe's entire collection.
And, of course, the Specials. *Tuberosa rosifea* in all its glory,
the true jackapple, the rediscovered original.

Jay looked at them for a long time. Later he would sort
through them all, placing each packet in the correct drawer
of the old spice chest. Later there would be time for labeling

and numbering and cataloguing, until at last every one was in place again.

But first there was one more thing he had to do. Someone to see. And something to find. Something in the cellar.

———

Though there were many bottles in the cellar, there was only one possible choice. He wiped off the dust from the glass with a cloth, hoping time had not soured the contents. A bottle for a special occasion, he thought, the very last of his Specials, *Blackberry '75*. He wrapped the bottle in tissue paper and put it in his jacket pocket. A peace offering.

———

She was sitting in the kitchen when he arrived, shelling peas. She was wearing a white shirt over her jeans, and the sunlight was red on her autumn hair. Outside he could hear Rosa calling to Clopette.

"I brought you this," he told her. "I've been saving it for a special occasion. I thought maybe you and I could drink it together."

She stared at him for a long time, her face unreadable. Her eyes were cool, verdigris, appraising. Finally she took the outstretched bottle and looked at the label.

"Blackberry '75?" she said, and smiled. "My favorite."

Postscript

Taken from the *Lansquenet-gratuit*:

Obituaries
Mireille Annabelle Faizande (née Foudouin), suddenly after a short illness. Leaves a nephew, Pierre-Emile, daughter-in-law Marise and granddaughter Rosa.

Property Sales
To Mme. Marise d'Api, four hectares of cultivated and non-cultivated agricultural land between Rue des Marauds, Boulevard St-Espoir and the Tannes, including a farmhouse and outbuildings, from Pierre-Emile Foudouin, Rue Geneviève, Toulouse.

From the *Courrier d'Agen:*

A local landowner has become the first known person since the seventeenth century to produce the *Tuberosa rosifea*, otherwise known as Demoiselle des Landes potato. This ancient species, thought to have been brought out of South America in 1643, is a large, sweet-scented pink tuber which thrives in our marshy, lime-rich soil. M. Jay Mackintosh, a former writer who emigrated from England eighteen months ago, plans to cultivate these and other rare species of vegetable at Château Cox in Lansquenet-sous-Tannes.

"I intend to reintroduce many of these old varieties for general consumption," he told our reporter recently. "It's only through luck that some of these species have not been lost forever." When questioned on the origins of these precious seeds, M. Mackintosh remains evasive. "I'm just a collector," he explains modestly. "I have collected a large number of different seeds on my travels around the world."

M. Mackintosh's unconventional products have already spread beyond his own small farm. Local farmers have recently joined him in setting aside part of their land to cultivate these old varieties. M. André Narcisse, M. Philippe Briançon and Mme. Marise d'Api have also decided to test the new seeds. And with *Tuberosa rosifea* retailing at a hundred francs or more per kilo, the future looks rosy once again for the farmers of Lansquenet-sous-Tannes.

WMWilliam Morrow

NEW IN HARDCOVER FROM JOANNE HARRIS:

FIVE QUARTERS OF THE ORANGE

It has taken me fifty-five years to begin . . . .
  The war is vividly remembered in Les Laveuses. There are people here who still don't speak to each other. My mother is an evil legend here.
  There are so many things for you to understand. Why my mother did what she did. Why we hid the truth for so long. And why I'm telling my story now . . . .

In this haunting novel, Joanne Harris weaves a powerful tale of tragedy, secrets, and the relationship between a daughter and her mother. As a child, Framboise Dartigen and her family were driven from their small Loire village because of a tragedy that took place during the German occupation – an event that still haunts the town. Now the adult Framboise will find the terrible truth of that long-ago time hidden among the newspaper clippings, herbal cures, and cherished recipes that fill the pages of the scrapbook her mother bequeathed to her.

ISBN 0-06-019813-3

Available wherever books are sold, or call 1-800-331-3761 to order.

WMWilliam Morrow

NEW IN HARDCOVER FROM JOANNE HARRIS:

FIVE QUARTERS OF THE ORANGE

It has taken me fifty-five years to begin . . . .
The war is vividly remembered in Les Laveuses. There are people here who still don't speak to each other. My mother is an evil legend here.
There are so many things for you to understand. Why my mother did what she did. Why we hid the truth for so long. And why I'm telling my story now . . . .

In this haunting novel, Joanne Harris weaves a powerful tale of tragedy, secrets, and the relationship between a daughter and her mother. As a child, Framboise Dartigen and her family were driven from their small Loire village because of a tragedy that took place during the German occupation – an event that still haunts the town. Now the adult Framboise will find the terrible truth of that long-ago time hidden among the newspaper clippings, herbal cures, and cherished recipes that fill the pages of the scrapbook her mother bequeathed to her.

ISBN 0-06-019813-3